**Lisa Kleypas** graduated from Wellesley College with a political science degree. She is a RITA® Award-winning author of both historical romance and contemporary women's fiction. Her novels are published in fourteen different languages and are bestsellers all over the world. She lives in Washington State with her husband, Gregory, and their two children.

Visit Lisa Kleypas online:

www.lisakleypas.com
Facebook & Twitter: @LisaKleypas

*Praise for Lisa Kleypas*:

'A funny and charming story that will delight readers from the first page to the last'
*Kirkus Reviews*

'Flawlessly written . . . pure reading magic'
*Booklist*

'Magical'
*RT Book Reviews*

# By Lisa Kleypas

# LISA KLEYPAS

# Chasing Cassandra

The Ravenels

piatkus

PIATKUS

First published in the United States in 2020 by Avon Books,
an imprint of HarperCollins publishers
First published in Great Britain in 2020 by Piatkus

1 3 5 7 9 10 8 6 4 2

A CIP catalogue record for this book is available from the British Library.

ISBN 978-0-349-40770-8

Printed and bound in Great Britain by Clays Ltd, Elcograf S.p.A.

Papers used by Piatkus are from well-managed forests
and other responsible sources.

MIX
Paper from
responsible sources
FSC® C104740

Piatkus
An imprint of
Little, Brown Book Group
Carmelite House
50 Victoria Embankment
London EC4Y 0DZ

An Hachette UK Company
www.hachette.co.uk

www.littlebrown.co.uk

To Carrie Feron,
my editor, my inspiration,
and my safe place in the storm.
Love always,
L. K.

# Chasing Cassandra

# Chapter 1

*Hampshire, England*
*June 1876*

IT HAD BEEN A mistake to invite himself to the wedding.

Not that Tom Severin gave a damn about politeness or etiquette. He liked barging into places where he hadn't been invited, knowing he was too rich for anyone to dare throw him out. But he should have anticipated the Ravenel wedding would be an utter bore, as weddings always were. Nothing but romantic drivel, lukewarm food, and far, *far* too many flowers. At the ceremony this morning, the tiny estate chapel of Eversby Priory had been stuffed to the rafters, as if the entire Covent Garden Flower Market had disgorged its contents there. The air had been so thick with perfume that it had given Tom a mild headache.

He wandered through the ancient Jacobean manor house, looking for a quiet place to sit and close his eyes. Outside, guests congregated at the front entrance to cheer for the newly married couple as they departed for their honeymoon.

With the exception of a few guests such as Rhys Winterborne, a Welsh department store owner, this was an aristocratic crowd. That meant the conversation consisted of subjects Tom couldn't give a rat's arse about. Foxhunting. Music. Distinguished ancestors. No one at these gatherings ever discussed business, politics, or anything else Tom might have found interesting.

The ancient Jacobean house had the typical dilapidated-but-luxurious look of an ancestral country manor. Tom didn't like old things, the smell of mustiness and the accumulated dust of centuries, the worn carpets, the ripples and distortions of antique window glass panes. Nor did the beauty of the surrounding countryside hold any enchantment for him. Most people would have agreed that Hampshire, with its green hills, lush woodland, and sparkling chalk streams, was one of the most naturally beautiful places on earth. In general, however, the only thing Tom liked to do with nature was cover it with roads, bridges, and railway tracks.

The sounds of distant cheers and laughter funneled into the house's quiet interior. No doubt the newlyweds were making their escape amid a shower of uncooked rice. Everyone here seemed genuinely happy, which Tom found both annoying and somewhat mystifying. It was as if they all knew some secret that had been kept from him.

After having made a fortune in railways and construction, Tom had never expected to feel the bite of envy again. But here it was, gnawing at him like woodworm in old timber. It made no sense. He was happier than most of these people, or at least richer, which was more or less the same thing. But why didn't he *feel* happy? It had been months since he'd felt much of anything at all. He'd been overtaken by a gradual, creeping awareness that all his usual appetites had been blunted. Things that usually gave him pleasure now bored him. Nothing, not even spending a night in the arms of a beautiful woman, had been satisfying. He'd never been like this before. He was at a loss to know what to do about it.

He'd thought it might do him some good to spend some time with Devon and West Ravenel, whom he'd known for at least a decade. The three of them, along with the rest of their disreputable crowd, had often caroused and brawled their way across London. But things had changed. Two years ago, Devon had unexpectedly inherited an earldom and had assumed the role of responsible family patriarch. And West, the formerly carefree drunkard, now managed the estate and tenants, and talked incessantly about the weather. *The weather,* for God's sake. The Ravenel brothers, formerly so entertaining, had become as tedious as everyone else.

Entering an empty music room, Tom found a large upholstered chair occupying a shadowy nook. After turning the chair to face away from the door, he sat and closed his eyes. The room was as silent as a sepulcher, except for the delicate ticking of a clock somewhere. An unfamiliar weariness settled over him as gently as mist, and he let out a sigh. People had always joked about his vitality and his fast-paced life, and how no one could keep up with him. Now it seemed he couldn't keep up with himself.

He needed to do something to jolt himself out of this spell.

Maybe he should marry. At the age of thirty-one, it was high time to take a wife and sire children. There were dozens of eligible young women here, all blue-blooded and well-bred. Marrying one of them would help to advance him socially. He considered the Ravenel sisters. The oldest, Helen, had married Rhys Winterborne, and Lady Pandora had married Lord St. Vincent this morning. But there was one sister left . . . Pandora's twin, Cassandra.

Tom had yet to meet her, but he'd caught a glimpse of her at dinner last night, through multiple bowers of greenery and forests of silver candelabra. From what he'd been able to tell, she was young, blond, and quiet. Which wasn't necessarily *all* he wanted in a wife, but it was a good start.

The sound of someone entering the room broke through his thoughts. *Damn.* Of the dozens of un-occupied rooms on this floor of the house, it would have to be this one. Tom was about to stand and make his presence known when the sounds of a female sob caused him to shrink deeper into the chair. *Oh, no.* A crying woman.

"I'm sorry," the unfamiliar feminine voice quavered. "I don't know why I'm so emotional."

For a moment Tom thought she might have been talking to him, but then a man replied.

"I imagine it's not easy to be separated from a sister who's always been your closest companion. A twin, no less." The speaker was West Ravenel, his tone far warmer and more tender than any Tom had ever heard him use before.

"It's only because I know I'll miss her. But I'm happy she's found true love. So very happy—" Her voice broke.

"So I see," West said dryly. "Here, take this handkerchief and let's wipe away those tears of joy."

"Thank you."

"It would hardly be unnatural," West commented kindly, "for you to feel a touch of jealousy. It's no secret that you've wanted to find a match, whereas Pandora has always been determined never to marry at all."

"I'm not jealous, I'm worried." The woman blew her nose with a soft little snort. "I've gone to all the dinners and dances, and I've met *everyone*. Some of the eligible gentlemen have been very pleasant, but even when there's nothing terribly wrong with one of them, there's nothing terribly right either. I've given up looking for love, I'm only searching for someone I could come to love over time, and I can't even find that. There's something wrong with me. I'm going to end up an old maid."

"There's no such thing as an old maid."

"Wh-what would you call a middle-aged lady who's never married?"

"A woman with standards?" West suggested.

"*You* might call it that, but everyone else says 'old maid.'" A glum pause. "Also, I'm too plump. All my dresses are tight."

"You look the same as always."

"My dress had to be altered last night. It wouldn't button up the back."

Twisting stealthily in the chair, Tom peeked around the edge. His breath caught as he stared at her in wonder.

For the first time in his life, Tom Severin was smitten. Smitten and slain.

She was beautiful the way fire and sunlight were beautiful, warm and glowing and golden. The sight of her dealt him a famished, hollow feeling. She was everything he'd missed in his disadvantaged youth, every lost hope and opportunity.

"Sweetheart," West murmured kindly, "listen to me. There's no need to worry. You'll either meet someone new, or you'll reconsider someone you didn't appreciate at first. Some men are an acquired taste. Like oysters, or Gorgonzola cheese."

She let out a shuddering sigh. "Cousin West, if I haven't married by the time I'm twenty-five . . . and you're still a bachelor . . . would you be my oyster?"

West looked at her blankly.

"Let's agree to marry each other someday," she continued, "if no one else wants us. I would be a good wife. All I've ever dreamed of is having my own little family, and a happy home where everyone feels safe and welcome. You know I never nag or slam doors or sulk in corners. I just need someone to take care of. I want to matter to someone. Before you refuse—"

"Lady Cassandra Ravenel," West interrupted, "that is the most idiotic idea anyone's come up with since Napoleon decided to invade Russia."

Her gaze turned reproachful. "Why?"

"Among a dizzying array of reasons, you're too young for me."

"You're no older than Lord St. Vincent, and he just married my twin."

"I'm older than him on the inside, by decades. My soul is a raisin. Take my word for it, you don't want to be my wife."

"It would be better than being lonely."

"What rubbish. 'Alone' and 'lonely' are entirely different things." West reached out to smooth back a dangling golden curl that had stuck against a drying tear track on her cheek. "Now, go bathe your face in cool water, and—"

"I'll be your oyster," Tom broke in. He stood from the chair and approached the pair, who stared at him in openmouthed astonishment.

Tom was more than a little surprised himself. If there was anything he was good at, it was negotiating business deals, and this was *not* the way to start off. In just a few words, he'd managed to put himself in the weakest possible position.

But he wanted her so badly, he couldn't help himself.

The closer he drew to her, the harder it became to think straight. His heart worked in a fast and broken rhythm he could feel against his ribs.

Cassandra moved close to West as if for protection, and stared at him as if he were a lunatic. Tom could hardly blame her. In fact, he already regretted this entire approach, but it was too late to hold back now.

West was scowling. "Severin, what the devil are you doing in here?"

"I was resting in the chair. After you started talking, I couldn't find a good moment to interrupt." Tom couldn't take his gaze from Cassandra. Her wide, wondering eyes were like soft blue midnight, star-glittered with forgotten tears. The curves of her body looked firm and sweet, no hard angles or straight lines anywhere . . . nothing but inviting, sensual softness. If she were his . . . he might finally have the sense of ease other men had. No more spending every minute of the day striving and hungering and never feeling sated.

"I'll marry you," Tom told her. "Any time. Any terms."

West gently nudged Cassandra toward the door. "Go, darling, while I talk with the insane man."

She gave her cousin a flustered nod and obeyed.

After she'd crossed the threshold, Tom said urgently, without thinking, "My lady?"

Slowly she reappeared, peeking at him from behind the doorjamb.

Tom wasn't sure what to say, only that he couldn't let her leave thinking she was anything less than perfect, exactly as she was.

"You're not too plump," he said gruffly. "The more of you there is in the world, the better."

As far as compliments went, it wasn't exactly eloquent, or even appropriate. But amusement sparkled in the one blue eye that was visible before Cassandra vanished.

Every muscle in his body tensed with the instinct to follow her like a hound on the scent.

West turned to face Tom, his expression puzzled and annoyed.

Before his friend could say a word, Tom asked urgently, "Can I have her?"

"No."

"I have to have her, let me have her—"

"*No.*"

Tom turned businesslike. "You want her for yourself. Perfectly understandable. We'll negotiate."

"You just overheard me refusing to marry her," West pointed out irritably.

Which Tom hadn't believed for a moment. How could West, or any man with working parts, not want her with this all-consuming intensity? "Obviously a strategy to reel her in later," he said. "But I'll give you a quarter of a railway company for her. Also shares in an excavation company. I'll throw in some hard cash. Name the amount."

"Are you mad? Lady Cassandra isn't a possession I can hand over like an umbrella. In fact, I wouldn't even give you an umbrella."

"You could talk her into it. It's obvious she trusts you."

"And you think I would use that against her?"

Tom was perplexed and impatient. "What's the point of having someone's trust if you won't use it against them?"

"Lady Cassandra is never going to marry you, Severin," West said in exasperation.

"But she's what I've always wanted."

"How do you know? So far all you've seen is a pretty young woman with blond hair and blue eyes. Does it occur to you to wonder what's on the inside?"

"No. I don't care. She can be whatever she wants on the inside, as long as she lets me have the outside." As Tom saw West's expression, he said with a touch of defensiveness, "You know I've never been one of those sentimental fellows."

"You mean the ones with actual human emotions?" West asked acidly.

"I have emotions." Tom paused. "When I want to."

"I'm having an emotion right now. And before it obliges me to wedge my boot up your arse, I'm going to put some distance between us." West skewered him with a lethal glance. "Stay away from her, Tom. Find some other innocent girl to corrupt. I already have enough excuses to murder you as it is."

Tom's brows lifted. "Are you still sour about that contract negotiation?" he asked with a touch of surprise.

"I will always be sour about that," West informed him. "You tried to cheat us out of the mineral rights to our own estate, when you knew we were at the verge of bankruptcy."

"That was business," Tom protested.

"What about friendship?"

"Friendship and business are two separate things."

"Are you trying to claim you wouldn't mind if a friend tried to fleece you, especially if you wanted the money?"

"I always want the money. That's why I have so much of it. And no, I wouldn't mind if a friend tried to fleece me; I would respect the effort."

"You probably would." West sounded far from admiring. "You may be a soulless bastard with the mindless appetite of a bull shark, but you've always been honest."

"You've always been fair. That's why I'm asking you to tell Lady Cassandra about my good qualities as well as the bad ones."

"*What* good qualities?" West inquired sharply.

Tom had to think for a moment. "How rich I am?" he suggested.

West groaned and shook his head. "I might feel sorry for you, Tom, if you weren't such a selfish arse. I've seen you like this before, and I already know where it will lead. This is why you own more houses than you can live in, more horses than you can ride and more paintings than you have walls. For you, disappointment is inevitable. As soon as you obtain the object of your desire, it loses its power to enchant you. Knowing that, do you think Devon or I would ever allow you to court Cassandra?"

"I wouldn't lose interest in my own wife."

"How could it be otherwise?" West asked softly. "All that matters to you is the chase."

# Chapter 2

AFTER LEAVING THE MUSIC ROOM, Cassandra had hurried upstairs to her room to wash her face. A cool, wet compress on her eyes had helped to soothe the redness. There was no remedy, however, for the dull ache that had started as soon as she'd watched Pandora's carriage pull away from the house. Her twin, her other half, had begun a new life with her husband, Lord St. Vincent. And Cassandra was alone.

Fighting the urge to cry again, Cassandra slowly descended one side of the grand double staircase in the great entrance hall. She would have to mingle with guests in the formal gardens where an informal buffet had been set out. Guests came and went as they pleased, filling their gold-banded plates with hot breads, poached eggs on toast, smoked quail, fruit salad, and slices of charlotte russe made with sponge cake and Bavarian cream. Footmen crossed through the entrance hall as they headed outside with trays of coffee, tea, and iced champagne.

Ordinarily this was the kind of event Cassandra would have enjoyed to no end. She loved a nice breakfast, especially when there was a little something sweet to finish it off, and charlotte russe was one of her favorite desserts. However, she was in no mood to make small talk with anyone. Besides, she'd eaten far too many sweets lately . . . the extra jam tart at tea-time yesterday, and all the fruit ices between dinner courses last night, and that entire éclair, stuffed with rich almond cream and roofed with a crisp layer of ic-ing. And one of the little decorative marzipan flowers from a platter of puddings.

Halfway down the stairs, Cassandra had to pause and gasp for air. She put a hand to her lower ribs, where her corset had been cinched more firmly than usual. As a rule, everyday corsets were close-fitting to support the back and promote good posture, but they weren't punishingly tight. She only tight-laced for special occasions such as this. With the extra weight she had recently gained, Cassandra felt miserably bound up and breathless and hot. The stays seemed to trap all the air near the top of her lungs. Red-faced, she sat at the side of the staircase and leaned against the balusters. The corners of her eyes were stinging again.

*Oh, this has to stop.* Vexed with herself, Cassandra took a handkerchief from the concealed pocket of her dress and pressed it hard over a new trickle of tears. After a minute or two had passed, she became aware of someone ascending the stairs in a measured tread.

Embarrassed to be caught crying on the steps like a lost child, Cassandra struggled to rise.

A low voice stopped her. "No . . . please. I only wanted to give you this."

Through a blur, she saw the dark form of Tom Severin, who had come to stand a step below her, with two glasses of iced champagne in his hands. He extended one to her.

Cassandra began to reach for it, but hesitated. "I'm not supposed to have champagne unless it's mixed with punch."

One corner of his wide mouth tipped upward. "I won't tell."

Cassandra took the glass gratefully, and drank. The cold fizz was wonderful, easing the dry tightness of her throat.

"Thank you," she murmured.

He gave her a brief nod and turned to leave.

"Wait," Cassandra said, although she wasn't sure whether she wanted him to stay or leave.

Mr. Severin turned back to her with a questioning glance.

During their brief encounter in the music room, Cassandra had been too flustered to notice much about him. He'd been so very odd, jumping out like that and offering to marry a complete stranger. Also, she'd been absolutely mortified for him to have overheard her tearful disclosure to West, especially the part about having her dress altered.

But now it was impossible not to notice how very good-looking he was, tall and elegantly lean, with dark hair, a clear, fair complexion, and thick brows set at a slightly diabolical slant. If she were to judge his features individually—the long nose, the wide mouth,

the narrow eyes, the sharply angled cheeks and jaw—
she wouldn't have expected him to be this attractive.
But somehow when it was all put together, his looks
were striking and interesting in a way she'd remember
far longer than conventional handsomeness.

"You're welcome to join me," Cassandra found
herself saying.

Severin hesitated. "Is that what you want?" he surprised her by asking.

Cassandra had to consider the question. "I'm not
sure," she admitted. "I don't want to be alone . . . but I
don't especially want to be with anyone either."

"I'm the perfect solution, then." He lowered to the
place beside her. "You can say whatever you like to
me. I make no moral judgments."

Cassandra was slow to reply, momentarily distracted
by his eyes. They were blue with dapples of brilliant
green around the pupils, but one eye had far more green
than the other.

"Everyone makes judgments," she said in response
to his statement.

"I don't. My sense of right and wrong is different
from most people's. You could say I'm a moral nihilist."

"What's that?"

"Someone who believes nothing is innately right or
wrong."

"Oh, that's dreadful," she exclaimed.

"I know," he said, looking apologetic.

Perhaps some gently bred young women would
have been shocked, but Cassandra was accustomed to

unconventional people. She'd grown up with Pandora, whose twisty-turny, hippity-hoppity brain had enlivened an unbearably secluded life. In fact, Mr. Severin possessed a kind of contained energy that reminded her a little of Pandora. One could see it in the eyes, the quicksilver workings of a mind that ran at a faster speed than those of other people.

After another sip of champagne, Cassandra was relieved to discover the urge to cry had passed, and she could breathe normally again.

"You're supposed to be a genius, aren't you?" she asked, recalling a discussion between Devon, West, and Mr. Winterborne, all friends with Severin. They'd agreed the railway magnate possessed the most brilliant business mind of anyone they knew. "Sometimes intelligent people can make something simple into something very complicated. Perhaps that's why you have difficulty with right and wrong."

That elicited a brief grin. "I'm not a genius."

"You're being modest," she said.

"I'm never modest." Mr. Severin drained the rest of his champagne, set down the glass, and turned to face her more fully. "I have an above-average intellect and a photographic memory. But that's not genius."

"How interesting," Cassandra said uneasily, thinking, *Oh, dear . . . more oddness.* "You take photographs with your mind?"

His lips twitched, as if he could read her thoughts. "Not like that. I retain information more easily than images. Some things—charts or schedules, pages from a book—I can recall in perfect detail, as if I'm looking at a picture. I remember the furniture arrangements and the art on the walls of nearly every house I've ever visited. Every word of every contract I've signed and business deal I've negotiated are in here." He tapped his temple with a long finger.

"Are you joking?" Cassandra asked in amazement.

"Unfortunately, no."

"Why on earth is it unfortunate to be intelligent?"

"Well, that's the problem: Recalling vast amounts of information doesn't mean you're intelligent. It's what you do with the information." His expression turned wry. "Remembering too many things makes the brain inefficient. There's a certain amount of information we're supposed to forget because we don't need it, or because it hinders us. But I remember all the failed attempts as well as the successes. All the mistakes and negative outcomes. Sometimes it's like being caught in a dust storm—there's too much debris flying about for me to see clearly."

"It sounds quite fatiguing to have a photographic memory. Still, you've made the most of it. One can't really pity you."

He grinned at that, and hung his head. "I suppose not."

Cassandra finished the last drops of champagne before setting aside her glass. "Mr. Severin, may I ask something personal?"

"Of course."

"Why did you offer to be my oyster?" A hot blush climbed her face. "Is it because I'm pretty?"

His head lifted. "Partly," he admitted without a hint of shame. "But I also liked what you said—that you never nag or slam doors, and you're not looking for love. I'm not either." He paused, his vibrant gaze holding hers. "I think we would be a good match."

"I didn't mean I don't *want* love," Cassandra protested. "I only meant I'd be willing to let love grow in time. To be clear, I want a husband who could also love me back."

Mr. Severin took his time about replying. "What if you had a husband who, although not handsome, was not altogether bad-looking and happened to be very rich? What if he were kind and considerate, and gave you whatever you asked for—mansions, jewels, trips abroad, your own private yacht and luxury railway carriage? What if he were exceptionally good at . . ." He paused, appearing to think better of what he'd been about to say. "What if he were your protector and friend? Would it really matter so much if he couldn't love you?"

"Why couldn't he?" Cassandra asked, intrigued and perturbed. "Is he missing a heart altogether?"

"No, he has one, but it's never worked that way. It's . . . frozen."

"Since when?"

He thought for a moment. "Birth?" he offered.

"Hearts don't start out frozen," Cassandra said wisely. "Something happened to you."

Mr. Severin gave her a slightly mocking glance. "How do you know so much about the heart?"

"I've read novels—" Cassandra began earnestly, and was disgruntled to hear his quiet laugh. "*Many* of them. You don't think a person can learn things from reading novels?"

"Nothing that actually applies to life." But the blue-green eyes contained a friendly sparkle, as if he found her charming.

"But life is what novels are about. A novel can contain more truth than a thousand newspaper articles or scientific papers. It can make you imagine, just for a little while, that you're someone else—and then you understand more about people who are different from you."

The way he listened to her was so very flattering, so careful and interested, as if he were collecting her words like flowers to be pressed in a book. "I stand corrected," he said. "I see I'll have to read one. Do you have any suggestions?"

"I wouldn't dare. I don't know your taste."

"I like trains, ships, machines, and tall buildings. I like the idea of traveling to new places, although I never seem to have the time to go anywhere. I don't like sentiment or romance. History puts me to sleep. I don't believe in miracles, angels, or ghosts." He gave her an expectant glance, as if he'd just laid down a challenge.

"Hmm." Cassandra puzzled over what kind of novel might appeal to him. "I'll have to give this some thought. I want to recommend something you'll be sure to enjoy."

Mr. Severin smiled, tiny constellations of reflected chandelier lights glinting in his eyes. "Since I've told you about my tastes . . . what are yours?"

Cassandra looked down at her folded hands in her lap. "I like trivial things, mostly," she said with a self-deprecating laugh. "Handiwork, such as embroidery, knitting, and needlepoint. I sketch and paint a little. I like naps and teatime, and taking a lazy stroll on a sunny day, and reading books on a rainy afternoon. I have no special talents or grand ambitions. But I would like to have my own family someday, and . . . I want to help other people far more than I'm able to now. I take baskets of food and medicine to tenants and acquaintances in the village, but that's not enough. I want to provide *real* help to people who need it." She sighed shortly. "I suppose that's not very interesting. Pandora's the exciting, amusing twin, the one people remember. I've always been . . . well, the one who's not Pandora." In the silence that followed, she looked up from her lap with chagrin. "I don't know why I just told you all that. It must have been the champagne. Could you please forget I said it?"

"Not even if I wanted to," he said gently. "Which I don't."

"Bother." Frowning, Cassandra retrieved her empty glass and stood, tugging her skirts into place.

Mr. Severin picked up his own glass and rose to his feet. "But you don't have to worry," he said. "You can say whatever you like to me. I'm your oyster."

Before she could restrain herself, an appalled giggle escaped her. "Please don't say that. You're no such thing."

"You can choose another word, if you like." Mr. Severin extended his arm to escort her downstairs. "But the fact is, if you ever need anything—any favor, any service, large or small—I'm the one to send for. No questions asked, no obligations attached. Will you remember that?"

Cassandra hesitated before taking his arm. "I'll remember." As they proceeded to the first floor, she asked in bewilderment, "But why would you make such a promise?"

"Haven't you ever liked someone or something right away, without knowing exactly why, but feeling sure you would discover the reasons later?"

She couldn't help smiling at that, thinking, *Yes, as a matter of fact. Just now.* But it would be too forward to say so, and besides, it would be wrong to encourage him. "I would be glad to call you a friend, Mr. Severin. But I'm afraid marriage will never be a possibility. We don't suit. I could please you only in the most superficial ways."

"I would be happy with that," he said. "Superficial relationships are my favorite kind."

A regretful smile lingered at her lips. "Mr. Severin, you couldn't give me the life I've always dreamed of."

"I hope your dream comes true, my lady. But if it doesn't, I could offer you some very satisfying substitutes."

"Not if your heart is frozen," Cassandra said.

Mr. Severin grinned at that, and made no reply. But as they neared the last step, she heard his reflective, almost puzzled murmur.

"Actually . . . I think it just thawed a little."

# Chapter 3

ALTHOUGH CASSANDRA MAINTAINED A circumspect distance from Mr. Severin during the informal buffet breakfast, she couldn't help stealing covert glances as he mingled with other guests. His manner was relaxed and quiet, and he made no effort to draw attention to himself. But even if Cassandra hadn't known who he was, she would have thought there was something extraordinary about him. He had a shrewdly confident look, the alertness of a predator. It was the look of a powerful man, she reflected, as she saw him talking with Mr. Winterborne, who also had it. They were very different from the men of her class, who had been raised from birth in ancient traditions and codes of behavior.

Men like Severin and Winterborne were common born but had made their own fortunes. Unfortunately, nothing was so mocked and disliked in upper-class circles as the brazen pursuit of profit. A man had to acquire wealth discreetly, pretending it had come through indirect means.

Not for the first time, Cassandra found herself wishing "unequal matches," as they were called, weren't so deplored by high society. During her first Season, she had met nearly every eligible gentleman of her class in London, and after counting out the confirmed bachelors as well as those who were too elderly or infirm to marry, there were no more than two dozen worth considering. By the end of the Season, she had received five proposals, none of which she had accepted. That had dismayed her patroness, Lady Berwick, who had warned she could end up like her sister Helen.

"She could have married anyone," Lady Berwick had said dourly. "But before the Season had even begun, she squandered all her potential by marrying a Welsh grocer's son."

Which was a bit unfair, since Mr. Winterborne was a splendid man, who loved Helen body and soul. He also happened to be extravagantly wealthy, having built his father's grocery shop into the world's largest department store. However, Lady Berwick had been right about society's reaction. It was said in private parlors that Helen had been degraded by the marriage. In the most elevated circles, the Winterbornes would never be completely accepted. Fortunately, Helen was too radiantly happy to care.

*I wouldn't mind marrying down, if I were in love*, Cassandra thought. Not at all. But unfortunately, true love never seemed to happen to someone who was looking for it. Love was a prankster, preferring to sneak up on people who were busy doing other things.

Lady Berwick appeared at her side. "Cassandra." The older woman was tall and majestic, like a four-masted sailing ship. She wasn't what anyone would describe as a cheerful woman. Usually she wore the expression of someone who'd just found crumbs in the jam. However, there was much about her to admire. She was a pragmatist, never fighting against what couldn't be helped, but achieving her goals through sheer will and persistence.

"Why are you not sitting at one of the tables with the guests?" Lady Berwick demanded.

Cassandra shrugged and replied sheepishly, "I had a little spell of melancholy after Pandora left."

The older woman's keen eyes softened. "Your turn is next, my dear. And I intend for you to make an even more brilliant match than your sister." She flicked a deliberate glance at a distant table where Lord Foxhall sat with companions. "As Lord Westcliff's heir, Foxhall will someday inherit the oldest and most distinguished title in the peerage. He will outrank everyone, even St. Vincent. Marry him, and you will someday have precedence over your sister, and walk in front of her when going in to dinner."

"Pandora would love that," Cassandra said, smiling at the thought of her mischievous twin. "It would give her the chance to whisper insults behind me, while I couldn't turn around to respond."

Lady Berwick didn't appear to share her amusement. "Pandora has always been resistant to my guidance," she observed crisply. "Nevertheless, she has somehow managed to marry well, and so shall you. Come, we will converse with Lord Foxhall and his brother Mr. Marsden, who is also a fine marital prospect."

Cassandra cringed inwardly at the thought of making stilted small talk with the two brothers under Lady Berwick's watchful eye. "Ma'am," she said reluctantly, "I've already met both gentlemen, and found them quite courteous. But I don't think either of them would suit me, nor I them."

"Whyever not?"

"Oh . . . they're both so . . . athletic. They like hunting, riding, fishing, outside games, and manly sorts of contests . . ." Her voice trailed away, and she made a comical little grimace.

"There's a wild streak in the Marsden brood," Lady Berwick said with a hint of disapproval, "which undoubtedly comes from the mother. American, you know. However, they've all been respectably raised and educated, and Westcliff's fortune is beyond calculation."

Cassandra decided to be blunt. "I'm certain I could never fall in love with Lord Foxhall or his brother."

"As I've told you before, that is irrelevant."

"Not to me."

"A love match has no more substance than one of those silly floating island desserts you're so fond of—a bit of sugar-foam one chases all around the plate with a spoon until it collapses."

"But ma'am, surely you're not against marrying for love if the gentleman is suitable in all other ways?"

"Indeed, I am against it. When the marital union begins with love, it inevitably descends into disappointment. But a union of interests, aided by *liking*, will result in a stable and productive marriage."

"That's not a very romantic view," Cassandra dared to say.

"Too many young women are romantic nowadays, and they are much the worse for it. Romance clouds the judgment and loosens the corset strings."

Cassandra sighed ruefully. "I wish I could loosen mine." She could hardly wait to rush upstairs after this interminable buffet and change into a regular corset and a comfortable day gown.

Lady Berwick gave her a fond but reproving glance. "Not so many biscuits at teatime, Cassandra. You could do with some slimming before the Season begins."

Cassandra nodded, coloring in shame.

"This is a dangerous time for you, my dear," Lady Berwick continued quietly. "Your first social Season was a triumph. You were acknowledged a great beauty, which excited much admiration and jealousy. However, turning down all those proposals could garner accusations of pride and vanity, and create the impression that you like to play with men's hearts. Obviously, nothing could be farther from the truth— but the truth hardly matters to London society. Gossip feeds on lies. You would do well to accept some appropriate gentleman's offer this next Season—the sooner, the better."

# Chapter 4

"I'M AFRAID THE ANSWER is no," Devon, Lord Trenear, said, disgruntled to find himself having a brandy in his private study with Severin instead of lounging in bed with his wife.

"But you gave Helen to Winterborne," Severin protested. "I can't be a worse prospect than he was."

Now that the wedding breakfast had concluded, the day had become relaxed and formless, the atmosphere easing like a pair of shoes that had been untied. Guests had dispersed in groups, some going out for walks or carriage drives, some enjoying lawn tennis or bowling, while others chose to rest in their rooms. Devon's petite, red-haired wife, Kathleen, had whispered provocatively in his ear that he should come join her upstairs for a nap, an idea he'd agreed to with great enthusiasm.

On the way upstairs, however, Tom Severin had cornered him with a request to speak privately. Devon wasn't at all surprised to learn what his friend wanted. He'd always suspected this would happen as soon as Severin, an avid collector of beautiful things, met Cassandra.

"I didn't *give* Helen to Winterborne," Devon said. "They both wanted to marry, and—" He broke off and sighed shortly. "No, that's not entirely true." Scowling, he wandered to the bank of glittering multipaned windows set in a deep wainscoted recess.

Two years ago, when Devon had unexpectedly inherited the earldom, he'd also become guardian to the three Ravenel sisters. His first thought had been to marry the sisters off as quickly as possible, ideally to wealthy men who would pay generously for the privilege. But as Devon had become acquainted with Helen, Pandora, and Cassandra, it had begun to sink in that they depended on him, and it was his job to look out for their interests.

"Severin," he said carefully, "two years ago, I had the incredible arrogance to offer Helen's hand in marriage to Rhys Winterborne as if she were an hors d'oeuvre on a tray."

"Yes, I know. May I have one too?"

Devon ignored the question. "The point is, I shouldn't have." His mouth twisted in self-mockery. "It's been impressed on me since then that women are actually thinking, feeling beings with hopes and dreams."

"I can afford Cassandra's hopes and dreams," Severin said promptly. "All of them. I can afford hopes and dreams she hasn't even thought of yet."

Devon shook his head. "There's much you don't understand about Cassandra and her sisters. Their upbringing was . . . unusual."

Severin looked at him alertly. "From what I've heard, they lived a sheltered existence in the country."

"'Sheltered' is one word for it. More accurately, they were neglected. Confined to a rural country estate and virtually forgotten. What attention their parents did spare from pursuing their selfish pleasures was given exclusively to their only son, Theo. And even after he inherited the title, he didn't bother to give any of the girls a Season."

Pushing away from the desk, Devon went to an open cabinet built into a niche on the other side of the study. A few ornamental objects had been arranged on the display shelves: an antique jeweled snuffbox, a collection of framed miniature portraits, a marquetry cigar case . . . and a trio of tiny taxidermied goldcrests perched on a branch, encased in the airless isolation of a glass dome.

"There's no object in the house," Devon commented, regarding the glass dome, "that I hate as much as this one. According to the housekeeper, the earl always kept it in his study. Either he was amused by the symbolism, or he didn't recognize it: I can't decide which is more damning."

Severin's incisive gaze went from the decoration to Devon's face. "Not everyone is as sentimental as you, Trenear," he said dryly.

"I made a promise to myself: When Cassandra is happily married, I'm going to smash this."

"Your wish is about to come true."

"I said *happily* married." Devon turned to set a shoulder against the cabinet, his arms folded across his chest. "After years of being rejected by the people who were supposed to love her, Cassandra needs closeness and attention. She needs *affection*, Tom."

"I can do affection," Severin protested.

Devon shook his head in exasperation. "You would eventually find her smothering—inconvenient—you'd grow cold to her, and then I'd have to kill you. And then I'd be obliged to revive you so West could have the satisfaction of killing you." Devon paused, at a loss for how to convey how utterly wrong the pairing would be. "You know a score of beautiful women who would marry you on the spot if you asked. Any one of them would serve your purposes. Forget this one. Cassandra wants to marry for love."

"What does love guarantee?" Severin scoffed. "How many cruelties have been committed in the name of love? For centuries, women have been abused and betrayed by the men who profess to love them. If you ask me, a woman would benefit far more from a diversified investment portfolio than love."

Devon's eyes narrowed. "I warn you, if you start talking circles around me, it's going to end with a hard right cross to your chin. My wife expects me to join her upstairs for a nap."

"How could a grown man sleep in the middle of the day? Why would you even want to?"

"I wasn't planning to sleep," Devon said curtly.

"Oh. Well, I would like to have my own wife to nap with. In fact, I'd like some good, hard napping on a regular basis."

"Why don't you take a mistress?"

"A mistress is a temporary solution to a long-term problem. A wife is more economical and convenient, and produces legitimate children, not bastards. Moreover, Cassandra would be the kind of wife I would actually want to sleep with." As Severin read the refusal in Devon's expression, he added quickly, "All I'm asking for is the chance to become acquainted. If she's willing. Let me call on the family once or twice when you're back in London. If it turns out she'd rather not see me, I'll keep my distance."

"Cassandra is free to exercise her own judgment. But I'll advise her to the best of my ability—and my opinion isn't going to change. This match would be a mistake for both of you."

Severin regarded him with a faint frown of concern. "Does this have something to do with the lease agreement? Is that something I should apologize for?"

Devon was torn between laughing and delivering the aforementioned right cross. "Only you would have to ask that."

He would never forget the hell of negotiating with Severin two years ago, over a lease deal that would allow Severin to build railway tracks over a corner of the estate land. Severin could think ten times faster than most people, and he remembered bloody *everything*. He loved to jab, duck, and dodge, all for the pure fun of keeping his opponent off balance. The mental exercise had exhausted and infuriated everyone, including the lawyers, and the most maddening part was the realization that Severin had been enjoying himself immensely.

Through sheer mulish stubbornness, Devon had managed to maintain his position and end up with a satisfactory deal. Only later had he discovered how perilously close he'd come to losing a fortune in mineral rights from his own property.

Not for the first time, Devon wondered how Severin could be so perceptive about people and yet understand so damned little about them. "It wasn't one of your finer moments," he said sardonically.

Looking troubled, Severin stood and began to pace. "I don't always think the way other people do," he muttered. "Negotiations are a game to me."

"I know," Devon said. "You were no more likely to tip your hand during those negotiations than you would have during a round of poker. You always play to win—it's why you're so good at what you do. But it was far from a game to me. Two hundred tenant families live on this estate. We needed the income from that quarry to help ensure their survival. Without it, we might have gone into bankruptcy."

Severin stopped at the fireplace mantel and reached up to rub the close-cropped hair at the nape of his neck. "I should have considered that the contract might mean something different to you than it did to me."

Devon shrugged. "It's not your place to worry about my tenants. They're my responsibility."

"It's also not my place to harm the interests of a good friend." Severin looked at him steadily. "I apologize for the way I acted that day."

It was at moments like this that Devon realized how seldom Severin held his gaze, or anyone's, for longer than a second. He seemed to ration his moments of connection as if they were somehow dangerous to him.

"Already forgiven," Devon said simply.

But Severin seemed determined to continue. "I would have reverted the mineral rights back to you as soon as I realized it was endangering your estate. I'm not saying that because of my interest in Cassandra. I mean it."

In the ten years of their acquaintance, Severin hadn't apologized to Devon more than a half-dozen times. As Severin's fortune and power had soared, his willingness to humble himself had declined proportionately.

Devon thought back to the night they'd met at an obscure London tavern. Earlier that day, West had appeared at the doorstep of Devon's terrace apartment with the news that he'd just been expelled from Oxford for setting fire to his room. Simultaneously furious and worried, Devon had hauled his younger brother to the darkest corner of the tavern, where they had talked and argued over pitchers of ale.

Unexpectedly, a stranger had broken into the private conversation. "You should be congratulating him," came a cool, assured voice from a nearby table, "not raking him over the coals."

Devon had glanced over to a dark-haired fellow sitting at a table of jug-bitten buffoons who were all crooning a popular drinking song. The young man had been lanky and broomstick-thin, with high cheekbones and piercing eyes.

"Congratulating him for what?" Devon had snapped. "Two years of wasted tuition?"

"Better than four years of wasted tuition." Deciding to abandon his companions, the man had dragged his chair to the Ravenels' table without asking to be invited. "Here's the truth no one wants to admit: At least eighty percent of what they teach at university is thoroughly useless. The remaining twenty percent is helpful if you're studying a particular scientific or technological discipline. However, since your brother will obviously never be a doctor or mathematician, he's just saved himself a great deal of time and money."

West had stared at the stranger owlishly. "Either you have two different colored eyes," he'd commented, "or I'm drunker than I thought."

"Oh, you're as drunk as a fiddler," the man assured him pleasantly. "But yes, they're two different colors: I have heterochromia."

"Is it catching?" West had asked.

The stranger had grinned. "No, it was from a sock in the eye when I was twelve."

The man had been Tom Severin, of course, who had voluntarily left the University of Cambridge out of disdain for having to take courses he had decided were irrelevant. He only cared to learn things that would help him make money. No one—least of all Tom—had doubted that he would someday become an extraordinarily successful businessman.

Whether he was successful as a human being, however, was still open to question.

There was something different about Severin today, Devon thought. A look of being stranded in some foreign place without a map. "How are you, Tom?" he asked with a touch of concern. "Why are you really here?"

Severin's usual response would have been something flippant and amusing. Instead, he said distractedly, "I don't know."

"Is there a problem with one of your businesses?"

"No, no," Severin said with a touch of impatience. "All that's fine."

"Your health, then?"

"No. It's only that lately . . . I seem to want something I don't have. But I don't know what it is. And that's impossible. I have *everything*."

Devon bit back a wry smile. The conversation always became somewhat tortured whenever Severin, who was habitually detached from his emotions, tried to identify one of them. "Do you think it could be loneliness?" he suggested.

"No, it's not that." Severin looked pensive. "What do you call it when everything seems boring and pointless, and even the people you know well are like strangers?"

"Loneliness," Devon said flatly.

"*Damn it*. That makes six."

"Six what?" Devon asked in bewilderment.

"Feelings. I've never had more than five feelings, and they're hard enough to manage as it is. I'll be damned if I'll add another."

Shaking his head, Devon went to retrieve his glass of brandy. "I don't want to know what your five feelings are," he said. "I'm sure the answer would worry me."

The conversation was interrupted by a discreet knock at the partially open study door.

"What is it?" Devon asked.

The estate's elderly butler, Sims, came to stand just inside the threshold. His expression was as imperturbable as ever, but he was blinking at a faster rate than usual, and his elbows were pulled in tightly at his sides. Since Sims wouldn't turn a hair even if a Viking horde were battering down the front door, these subtle signs indicated nothing less than catastrophe.

"I beg your pardon, my lord, but I find it necessary to inquire whether you might know Mr. Ravenel's whereabouts."

"He said something about plowing stubble on the turnip fields," Devon said. "But I don't know if he meant at the home farms or at a tenant leasehold."

"With your permission, my lord, I shall dispatch a footman to find him. We need his counsel regarding a predicament in the kitchen."

"What kind of predicament?"

"According to Cook, the kitchen boiler began to make a fearful clanging and knocking, approximately one hour ago. A metal part burst through the air as if it had been shot from a cannon."

Devon's eyes widened, and he let out a curse.

"Indeed, my lord," Sims said.

Problems with a kitchen boiler were nothing to take lightly. Fatal explosions resulting from faulty installation or mishandling were routinely reported in the newspapers.

"Was anyone hurt?" Devon asked.

"Fortunately not, sir. The range fire has been put out, and the pipe valve has been closed. Regrettably, the master plumber is on holiday, and the nearest one is in Alton. Shall I send a footman to—"

"Wait," Severin interrupted brusquely. "*Which* valve? The one to the cold water supply pipe or the one to the water-back?"

"I'm afraid I don't know, sir."

Devon looked at Severin sharply.

Severin's mouth curved with grim amusement. "If something were going to blow up," he said in answer to the unvoiced question, "it would have by now. But you'd better let me take a look at it."

Grateful that his friend was an expert in steam engine mechanics and could probably build a boiler while blindfolded, Devon led the way downstairs.

The kitchen was a ferment of activity, with servants rushing to and fro with baskets from the gardens, and crates from the icehouse and cellar.

"We'll make German potato salad," the grim-faced cook was saying to the housekeeper, who took notes.

"We'll serve it with cuts of beef, ham, tongue, and galantine of veal. On the side, relish trays with caviar, radishes, olives, and celery on ice—" Catching sight of Devon, the cook turned and curtsied. "My lord," she exclaimed, visibly fighting back tears, "it's a disaster. Of all times to lose the cooking range! We'll have to change the dinner menu to a cold buffet."

"As the weather has been so warm," Devon replied, "the guests would probably prefer that. Do your best, Mrs. Bixby. I'm sure the results will be excellent."

The housekeeper, Mrs. Church, looked harried as she spoke to him. "Lord Trenear, the kitchen boiler supplies hot water to some of the first- and second-floor bathrooms. Soon the guests will want to bathe and change before dinner. We've set up pots to boil on the old kitchen hearth, and the servants will carry up cans of hot water, but with such a large crowd and so many extra chores, they'll be pushed to their limit."

Severin had already gone to inspect the boiler, which still radiated heat even though the fire had been put out. The cylindrical copper tank was set on a stand beside the range and connected by copper pipes.

"The part that shot through the air was the safety valve," Severin said over his shoulder. "It did exactly what it was supposed to do: relieve built-up pressure before the boiler ruptured." Picking up a rag from the long kitchen worktable, he used it to open a range door, and lowered to his haunches to look inside. "I see two issues. First, the water tank inside the range is producing too much heat for a boiler this size to handle. It's straining the copper shell. You'll need to install a larger boiler—eighty gallons or more. Until then, you'll have to keep the oven fire lower than usual." He examined a pipe connected to the boiler. "This is the more serious problem—the supply pipe leading into the boiler is too narrow. If hot water is drawn out of the boiler faster than it's refilled, steam will build until it eventually causes a rip-roaring explosion. I can replace the pipe right away if you have the supplies."

"I'm sure we do," Devon replied ruefully. "Plumbing work never ends in this house."

Severin rose to his feet and took off his coat. "Mrs. Bixby," he said to the cook, "would you and your staff be able to stay clear of this area while I do the repairs?"

"Will your work be dangerous?" she asked apprehensively.

"Not at all, but I'll need room to measure and saw pipes, and spread out the tools. I wouldn't want to trip anyone."

The cook looked at him as if he were her guardian angel. "We'll keep to the other side of the kitchen and use the scullery sink."

Severin grinned at her. "Give me five or six hours, and I'll have everything back in working order."

Devon felt more than a little apologetic about putting him to work when all the rest of the guests were relaxing. "Tom," he began, "you don't have to—"

"Finally," Severin interrupted cheerfully, unbuttoning his shirt cuffs, "there's something interesting to do at your house."

# Chapter 5

ALTHOUGH CASSANDRA WAS TIRED after the excitement and bustle of Pandora's wedding, she couldn't seem to relax sufficiently to take a nap. Her thoughts were restless, her mind running in place. By now, Pandora and Lord St. Vincent had probably reached the Isle of Wight, where they would spend their honeymoon at a fine old hotel. Tonight, Pandora would lie in the arms of her husband and experience the intimacies of the marital relationship.

The thought caused a twinge of something that felt like jealousy. Although Cassandra was glad Pandora had married the man she loved, she wanted her own forever to begin. It didn't seem entirely fair that Pandora, who'd never wanted to marry, now had a husband, whereas Cassandra was facing the prospect of yet another London Season. The thought of meeting the same people, dancing the same dances, all that lemonade and stale conversation . . . God, how dismal. She couldn't fathom how the outcome would be any different the next time around.

Hearing the laughter and shouts of the younger guests playing lawn tennis and croquet, Cassandra considered going outside to join them. No. The effort of pretending to be cheerful was more than she could manage.

After changing into a yellow day dress with airy pagoda sleeves that ended at the elbow, she went to the family's private upstairs parlor. The family dogs, a pair of small black spaniels named Napoleon and Josephine, saw her in the hallway and trotted after her. The parlor was comfortably cluttered with heaps of colorful cushions on the furniture, a battered piano in the corner, and piles of books everywhere.

She sat cross-legged on the carpet with the dogs, smiling as they bounded in and out of her lap excitedly. "We don't need Prince Charming, do we?" she asked them aloud. "No, we do not. There's a patch of sun on the carpet and books nearby—that's all we need to be happy."

The spaniels stretched out in a bright yellow rectangle, wriggling and sighing in contentment.

After petting and scratching the dogs for a while, Cassandra reached out to a stack of books on a low table, and sorted through them idly. *Double Wedding . . . The Secret Duke . . . My Dashing Suitor,* and other romantic novels she had read and reread. Much lower in the pile, there were books such as *History of the Thirty Years' Peace* and *Life of Nelson*, the kind one read in case one was called upon to make insightful comments at dinner.

She came across a novel with a familiar title stamped in gilt on green leather: *Around the World in Eighty Days*, by Jules Verne. She and Pandora had especially liked the novel's hero, a wealthy and adventurous Englishman named Phileas Fogg, who was something of an odd duck.

As a matter of fact . . . this would be the perfect recommendation for Mr. Severin. She would make a gift of it to him. Lady Berwick would say it wasn't appropriate, but Cassandra was intensely curious about what he would make of it. If, of course, he bothered to read it at all.

Leaving the dogs to nap in the parlor, she headed to the grand double staircase that led to the main floor. She kept to the side of the hallway as one of the footmen, Peter, approached from the opposite direction with two large brass hot-water cans.

"Pardon, milady," the footman said, setting down the sloshing cans to flex his aching hands and arms.

"Peter," Cassandra said in concern, "why are you carrying all that water? Problems with the plumbing again?"

As soon as Devon had inherited Eversby Priory, he'd insisted on having the manor fully plumbed. The process was still ongoing, since much of the ancient flooring they had pulled up had been in a state of decay, and many of the walls had to be rebuilt and freshly plastered. The family had become accustomed to the fact that at any given time, something in the ancient house was being repaired.

"Kitchen boiler's broken," Peter said.

"Oh, no. I hope they can find someone to repair it soon."

"They already have."

"Thank goodness. Peter, do you happen to know which room Mr. Severin is occupying?"

"He's not staying at the manor, milady. He brought his private railway carriage to the estate quarry halt."

Cassandra frowned thoughtfully. "I'm not sure how to deliver this book to him. I suppose I'll ask Sims."

"He's in the kitchen. Not Sims . . . I mean Mr. Severin. He's the one working on the boiler."

Dumbfounded, Cassandra asked, "You're referring to Mr. Severin the railway magnate?"

"Yes, milady. Never seen a gentleman so handy with a wrench and saw. Took apart the boiler pipe system like a child's toy."

She tried to picture the urbane and impeccably dressed Tom Severin with a wrench in his hand, but even her lively imagination wasn't up to the task.

This had to be investigated.

Cassandra went downstairs, stopping briefly at the parlor on the main floor. After pouring a glass of chilled water from a silver refreshment tray, she continued to the basement, where the kitchen, scullery, pantry and larder, and servants' hall were located.

The cavernous kitchen was filled with quiet, frantic activity. Cook instructed a row of kitchen maids as they peeled and chopped vegetables at the long worktable, while the assistant cook stood at a solid marble bowl, grinding herbs with a pestle. A gardener came through the back door with a basket of greens and set it near the scullery sink.

It appeared as if an invisible line had been drawn through the kitchen. One side was teeming with servants, while the other side was empty except for a lone man in front of the cooking range.

A bemused smile crossed Cassandra's face as she saw Tom Severin kneeling on the floor with his thighs spread for balance, a steel pipe cutter in one hand. In contrast to his earlier polished elegance, he was in shirtsleeves with the cuffs rolled up over his forearms and the collar unfastened. A well-formed man, wide-shouldered and long in the bone. He was steaming in the residual heat from the range, the cropped hair at the back of his neck damp with sweat, the fine linen of his shirt clinging to a hard-muscled back.

Well. This was an eye-opener, in more ways than one.

Deftly he clamped a copper pipe into the cutter blades and trimmed it with a few controlled rotations. After inserting a wooden turnpin into one end, he reached for a nearby mallet and flipped it in the air to catch it by the handle. Every movement was skilled and precise as he hammered the cone-shaped turnpin into the pipe to create a flared edge.

As Cassandra approached, Mr. Severin paused and looked up, his eyes a jolt of intense blue-green. A peculiar feeling went through her, as if an electrical circuit had just been completed, and steady voltage were humming between them. A quizzical smile touched his lips. He seemed as surprised to see her in the kitchen as she was to find him there. Setting aside the tools, he made to stand, but she stopped him with a quick gesture.

"Are you thirsty?" she asked, handing him the glass of chilled water. He took it with a murmur of thanks. In just a few long gulps, he had drained it.

After blotting his perspiring face on a shirtsleeve, Mr. Severin said ruefully, "You've caught me at a disadvantage, my lady."

Cassandra was inwardly amused by his discomfort at being less than perfectly attired and groomed in front of her. But she actually preferred him like this, all disheveled and unguarded. "You're a hero, Mr. Severin. Without you, we would all be doomed to cold baths, and no tea for breakfast."

He handed back the empty glass. "Well, we can't have that."

"I'll leave you to your work, but first . . ." Cassandra gave the book to him. "I brought this for you. A gift." His thick lashes lowered as he studied the cover. She couldn't help noticing how beautiful his hair was, the black locks cut in well-shaped layers that almost begged to be played with. Her fingers actually twitched with the urge to touch him, and she curled them tightly against her palm. "It's a novel by Jules Verne," she continued. "He writes for young readers, but adults enjoy his work as well."

"What's it about?"

"An Englishman who accepts a wager to go around the world in eighty days. He travels by train, ships, horse, elephant, and even a wind-powered sledge."

Mr. Severin's perplexed gaze met hers. "Why read an entire novel about that when you could obtain the itinerary from a travel office?"

She smiled at that. "The novel isn't about the itinerary. What's important is what he learns along the way."

"Which is?"

"Read it," she challenged, "and find out."

"I will." Carefully he set the book beside a canvas plumber's bag. "Thank you."

Cassandra hesitated before leaving. "May I stay for a few minutes?" she asked impulsively. "Would that bother you?"

"No, but it's as hot as blue blazes in here, and it's a fine day outside. Shouldn't you spend time with the other guests?"

"I don't know most of them."

"You don't know me either."

"Then let's become acquainted," Cassandra said lightly, lowering herself to a cross-legged position. "We can talk while you work. Or do you need silence to concentrate?"

A small but noticeable stir ran through the kitchen staff as they saw one of the ladies of the house sitting on the floor.

"I don't need silence," Mr. Severin said. "But if you end up in trouble for this, I want it known I had nothing to do with it."

Cassandra grinned. "The only person who would scold is Lady Berwick, and she never sets foot in the kitchen." With a self-satisfied air, she gathered the excess fabric of her skirts and tucked it beneath her. "How do you know so much about all of this?"

Mr. Severin picked up a shave hook with a wickedly sharp blade and began to carve burrs from the pipe's copper edge. "As a boy, I apprenticed at a tramway construction company. I built steam engines during the day and took courses in mechanical engineering at night."

"What is that, exactly?" she asked. "The only thing I know about engineers is there's always one on the train." Seeing the beginnings of a smile on his lips, she rushed on before he could reply. "How stupid I must sound. Never mind—"

"No," he said swiftly. "There's nothing wrong about not knowing something. The stupid people are the ones who think they know everything."

Cassandra smiled and relaxed. "What does a mechanical engineer do?"

Mr. Severin continued to carve the inside of the copper pipe as he replied, "He designs, builds, and operates machines."

"Any kind of machine?"

"Yes. The engineer on the train is responsible for the operation of the locomotive and all its moving parts." He picked up a round brush and began to scrub the inside of the pipe.

"May I do that?" Cassandra asked.

Mr. Severin paused, giving her a skeptical glance.

"Let me," she coaxed, leaning closer to take the brush and pipe from him. His breath caught audibly, and he suddenly had the kind of dazed, unfocused expression men sometimes wore when they found her especially pretty. Patiently she eased the objects from his lax hands.

After a moment, Mr. Severin seemed to collect his wits. "Helping with plumbing repairs doesn't seem like something you should be doing," he commented, his gaze flickering to the gauzy sleeves of her dress.

"It isn't," Cassandra admitted, scrubbing the pipe. "But I don't always behave properly. It's difficult for someone who was raised with hardly any rules to learn a great many at once."

"I'm not fond of rules myself." Mr. Severin bent to inspect a copper fitting protruding from the boiler, and polished it with emery cloth. "They're usually for other people's benefit, not mine."

"You must have some personal rules, though."

"Three."

Cassandra lifted her brows. "Only three?"

Although his face was partially averted, she saw the flash of his grin. "Three good ones."

"What are they?"

Mr. Severin rummaged through the plumber's bag as he replied, "Never lie. Always do favors for people whenever possible. Remember everything they promise in the main part of the contract can be taken back in the fine print."

"Those sound like good rules," Cassandra said. "I wish I had only three, but I have to follow hundreds."

He opened a tin of paste labeled flux and used a forefinger to apply it to the pipe and fitting. "Tell me some."

Cassandra obliged readily. "When introduced to a gentleman, never look higher than his collar button. Don't accept costly gifts; it will put you under obligation. It's not nice to wear a tall hat while attending a play. And—this is an important one—never let the dogs stay in the room when you're working with feathers and glue. Also—"

"Wait," Mr. Severin said, sitting up and wiping his hands with a rag. "Why can't you look higher than a man's collar button when you meet him?"

"Because if I look at his face," Cassandra said primly, "he'll think I'm too bold."

"He may think you need an eye examination."

A chuckle escaped before she could restrain it. "Make fun if you like, but it's a rule one can't break."

"You looked directly at me when we first met," Mr. Severin pointed out.

Cassandra sent him a gently admonishing glance. "That wasn't really an introduction. Leaping out like that during a private conversation . . ."

He didn't even try to look contrite. "I couldn't help it. I had to offer you an alternative to marrying West Ravenel."

Hot color flooded over her face and body. The conversation had abruptly become far too personal. "That was a silly impulse on my part. I was anxious—

because sometimes it seems as if I'll never—but I wouldn't. Marry West, I mean."

His gaze searched her face intently. "You don't have feelings for him, then?" His voice had lowered a note or two, in a way that made the question seem even more intimate than it was.

"No, he's like an uncle."

"An uncle you proposed to."

"In a moment of desperation," she protested. "You've had one of those, surely."

He shook his head. "Desperation isn't one of my emotions."

"You've never felt desperate? About anything?"

"No, long ago I identified the feelings that were helpful to me. I decided to keep those and not bother with the rest."

"Is it possible to dispense with feelings you don't want?" she asked doubtfully.

"It is for me."

The hushed conversation was interrupted as Cook called out from the other side of the room, "How goes it with the boiler, Mr. Severin?"

"The end is in sight," he assured her.

"Lady Cassandra," the cook persisted, "mind you don't distract the gentleman while he's working."

"I won't," Cassandra replied dutifully. At Mr. Severin's quick look askance, she explained sotto voce, "Cook has known me since I was a little girl. She used to let me sit on a stool at the worktable and play with scraps of dough."

"What were you like as a little girl?" he asked. "Prim and proper, with your hair in curls?"

"No, I was a ragamuffin, with scraped knees and twigs in my hair. What were you like? Wild and playful, I suppose, as most boys are."

"Not especially," Mr. Severin said, his expression becoming shuttered. "My childhood was . . . short."

She tilted her head and regarded him curiously. "Why?"

As the silence spun out, she realized Mr. Severin was debating whether to explain. A slight frown appeared between his dark brows. "One day when I was ten," he eventually said, "my father took me with him to Kings Cross station. He was looking for work, and they were advertising for baggage men. But when we reached the station, he told me to go to the general office and ask for a job. He had to go away for a while, he said. I would have to take care of my mother and sisters until he came back. Then he went to buy a ticket for himself."

"Did he ever return?" she asked gently.

His reply was brusque. "It was a one-way ticket."

*Poor boy*, Cassandra thought, but she didn't say it, sensing he would resent anything that sounded like pity. She understood, though, about what it was like to be abandoned by a father. Even though hers had never left for good, he'd often spent weeks or even months away from Eversby Priory.

"Did they give you a job at the station?" she asked.

A brief nod. "I was hired as a train boy, to sell newspapers and food. One of the station agents advanced me enough money to make a decent start. I've supported my mother and sisters ever since."

Cassandra was quiet as she absorbed this new information about the man she'd heard described in such contradictory terms. Callous, generous, honest, crafty, dangerous . . . sometimes a friend, sometimes an adversary, always an opportunist.

But regardless of Severin's complexities, there was much to admire about him. He'd become acquainted with life's rougher edges at a tender age, and had assumed a man's responsibilities. And not only had he survived, he'd flourished.

Cassandra watched as he applied more of the flux paste along the pipe and joint seam. His hands were elegantly long-fingered, but also strong and capable. A few small scars were scattered over his well-muscled forearms, just barely visible beneath a dusting of dark hair.

"What are those?" she asked.

Severin followed her gaze down to his arms. "The scars? Spark burns. It happens during forging and welding. Little bits of flaming steel sear through gloves and clothing."

Cassandra winced at the thought. "I can't imagine how painful that must be."

"They're not so bad on the arms: They tend to bounce off sweaty skin." A reminiscent grin crossed his lips. "It's the occasional spark that burns through your trouser leg or boot—and sticks—that hurts like the devil." He struck a Lucifer match against the nearby range and bent to light an alcohol blow-lamp fitted with a perforated nozzle. Gently he adjusted a knob until the nozzle emitted a hissing spear of continuous flame. Gripping the lamp in one hand, he directed the flame against the flux-coated seam until the paste had melted and bubbled. "Now for the fun part," he said, giving her a bright sidelong glance, the corner of his mouth curling upward. "Would you like to help?"

"Yes," Cassandra said without hesitation.

"There's a thin stick of metal solder on the floor near the—yes, that's it. Hold it by one end. You're going to run a bead around the seam to seal it."

"Run a bead?"

"That means make a line with the tip. Start on the opposite side from where I'm holding the flame."

While Severin held the flame against the pipe, Cassandra guided the tip of the solder around the joining. The metal liquefied and flowed instantly. Oh, this *was* fun—there was something viscerally satisfying about watching the solder run around the seam to form a neat seal.

"That was perfect," Mr. Severin said.

"Is there something else that needs soldering?" she asked, and he laughed at her eagerness.

"The other end of the pipe."

Together they soldered the copper pipe to the joint coming from the wall, both of them intent on the task. They were kneeling a little too close for propriety, but Mr. Severin was being a gentleman. Far more respectful and polite, as a matter of fact, than most of the privileged lords she'd met during the London Season.

"How curious," Cassandra said, watching the melted solder run up the seam when it should have dripped downward. "It's defying gravity. It reminds me of how water runs up the hairs of a paintbrush when I dip it in."

"How sharp you are." There was a smile in his voice. "The cause is the same in both cases. Capillary action, it's called. In a very narrow space, like the seam of this pipe and fitting, the molecules of the solder are so strongly attracted to the copper, they climb up the surface."

Cassandra glowed at the praise. "No one ever calls me sharp. People always say Pandora's the sharp one."

"What do they say about you?"

She gave a self-deprecating little laugh. "Usually it's something about my looks."

Mr. Severin was silent for a moment. "There's much more to you than that," he said gruffly.

Shy pleasure suffused her until she turned pink from head to toe. She forced herself to concentrate on the soldering, grateful that her hands kept steady even though her heart was charging and halting like an unbroken horse.

After the pipe had been soldered, Mr. Severin extinguished the flame and took the metal stick from her. It seemed to cost him something to meet her gaze. "The way I proposed to you earlier . . . I'm sorry. It was . . . disrespectful. Stupid. Since then I've discovered at least a dozen reasons for proposing to you, and beauty is the least of them."

Cassandra stared at him in wonder. "Thank you," she whispered.

The humid air was scented of him . . . the pine-tar tang of rosin soap . . . the acrid bite of shirt starch softening from body heat . . . and the fresh sweat on his skin, salty and intimate, and oddly compelling. She wanted to lean even closer and take a deep breath of him. His face was over hers, a slant of light from a casement window catching the extra green in one eye. She was utterly fascinated by the cool, disciplined façade overlying something withheld . . . deeply remote . . . tantalizing.

What a pity his heart was frozen. What a pity she could never be happy living in his fast-paced, hard-edged world. Because Tom Severin was turning out to be the most attractive and compelling man she'd ever met.

The clatter of a bowl on the kitchen worktable recalled her to herself. She blinked and looked away, searching for a way to ease the tension between them. "We're returning to London soon," she said. "If you call on the family, I'll see that you're invited to dinner, and we can discuss the book."

"What if we argue?"

Cassandra laughed. "Never argue with a Ravenel," she advised. "We never know when to stop."

"I was already aware of that." A hint of friendly mockery entered his tone. "Would you like me better if I agreed with everything you said?"

"No," she said easily, "I like you just as you are."

Mr. Severin's expression turned inscrutable, as if she'd spoken in a foreign language he was trying to interpret.

She'd been too forward, saying such a thing. It had just slipped out. Had she embarrassed him?

To her relief, the tension was broken as Devon strode briskly into the kitchen, saying, "I arranged for a new boiler. Winterborne doesn't carry an eighty-gallon model in his store, but he knows a manufacturer who—" He stopped in his tracks, looking aghast as he beheld the two of them. "Cassandra, what the devil are you doing here with Tom Severin? Why don't you have a chaperone?"

"There are at least a dozen people working only a few yards away," Cassandra pointed out.

"That's not the same as a chaperone. Why are you on the floor?"

"I helped Mr. Severin solder a pipe," she said brightly.

Devon's outraged gaze shot to Mr. Severin. "You had her working with an open flame and molten metal?"

"We were being careful," Cassandra said defensively.

Mr. Severin seemed too preoccupied to explain anything. He bent to gather some of the tools and slid them back into the plumber's bag. One of his hands went to the center of his chest and rubbed surreptitiously.

Devon reached down to pull Cassandra up. "If Lady Berwick finds out about this, she'll come down on us like the wrath of Zeus." He glanced over her and groaned. "Look at you."

Cassandra grinned up at him, well aware that she was perspiring and bedraggled, with soot marks on her yellow dress. "You probably thought Pandora was the cause of all our misadventures. But as you see, I'm capable of getting into trouble all on my own."

"Pandora would be so proud," Devon said dryly, amusement flickering in his eyes. "Go change your dress before anyone sees you. We'll have afternoon tea soon, and I'm sure Kathleen will want you to help pour and entertain."

Mr. Severin stood as well, and executed a short bow. His face was expressionless. "My lady. Thank you for your assistance."

"I'll see you at tea, then?" Cassandra asked.

Mr. Severin shook his head. "I'm leaving for London right away. I have a business meeting early tomorrow morning."

"Oh," she said, crestfallen. "I'm sorry to hear that. I . . . I've so enjoyed your company."

"As I've enjoyed yours," Mr. Severin replied. But the blue-green eyes now held a chill of wariness. Why had he suddenly become guarded?

Annoyed and a bit hurt, Cassandra curtsied to him. "Well . . . good-bye."

An abbreviated nod was the only reply.

"I'll walk you to the servants' stairs," Devon told Cassandra, and she went with him willingly.

As soon as they had left the kitchen, Cassandra asked in a low voice, "Is Mr. Severin always so mercurial? He was perfectly charming, and then his mood turned sour for no reason."

Devon stopped in the hallway and turned her to face him. "Don't try to understand Tom Severin. You'll never come up with the right answer, because there isn't one."

"Yes, but . . . we were getting on so well, and . . . I liked him so much."

"Only because he wanted you to. He's a master at manipulation."

"I see." Her shoulders slumped as disappointment settled over her. "That must be why he told me the story about his father."

"What story?"

"About the day his father left, when he was a boy." As she saw Devon's eyes widen, she asked, "He hasn't told you that one?"

Looking perturbed, Devon shook his head. "He never speaks of his father. I assumed he'd passed away."

"No, he—" Cassandra stopped. "I don't think I should repeat a personal confidence."

Now Devon wore a troubled frown. "Sweetheart . . . Severin isn't like any other man you'll ever meet. He's brilliant, unprincipled, and ruthless by nature. I can't think of a single man in England, not even Winterborne, who's positioned so exactly at the center of forces that are changing life as we know it. Someday he may be mentioned in history books. But the give-and-take of marriage . . . the awareness of another person's needs . . . those things aren't in his capacity. Men who make history rarely make good husbands." He paused before asking gently, "Do you understand?"

Cassandra nodded, feeling a rush of affection for him. From the moment Devon had arrived at Eversby Priory, he had been kind and caring, the way she and Pandora had always wished their brother, Theo, would have been. "I understand," she said. "And I trust your judgment."

He smiled at her. "Thank you. Now, hurry upstairs before you're caught . . . and put Tom Severin out of your mind."

LATER THAT NIGHT, after the cold buffet supper, and music and games in the parlor, Cassandra retired to her room. She was sitting at her dressing table when her lady's maid, Meg, came in to help take down her hair and brush it out.

Meg set something down on the dresser. "This was found in the kitchen," she said matter-of-factly. "Mrs. Church told me to bring it up to you."

Cassandra blinked in surprise as she beheld the green leather cover of *Around the World in Eighty Days*. Realizing Mr. Severin had left it behind, she felt the cold weight of disappointment pressing down on her. It had been no accident, this rejection of her gift. He would not call on the family in London. There would be no discussions of books, or anything else.

He'd proposed marriage in the morning, and abandoned her by evening. What a frustrating, fickle man.

Slowly Cassandra opened the book and paged through it while the lady's maid pulled the pins from her hair. Her gaze happened to fall upon a passage in which Phileas Fogg's faithful valet, Passepartout, was reflecting on his master.

*Phileas Fogg, though brave and gallant, must be . . . quite heartless.*

# Chapter 6

$\mathscr{A}$FTER THREE MONTHS OF hard work and as many distractions as he'd been able to devise for himself, Tom still hadn't been able to put Lady Cassandra Ravenel out of his mind. Memories of her kept catching at the edge of his consciousness, sparkling like a tenacious strand of Christmas tinsel stuck in the carpet.

He wouldn't have guessed in a million years that Cassandra would have come down to the kitchen to visit him. Nor would he have wanted her to. He'd have chosen far different circumstances, somewhere with flowers and candlelight, or out on a garden terrace. And yet as they'd crouched together on a dirty floor, soldering boiler pipes in a room full of kitchen maids, Tom had been conscious of an unfolding sense of delight. She had been so clever and curious, with a sunny energy that had transfixed him.

Then had come that moment, when she'd said so artlessly, *"I like you just as you are,"* and he'd been shaken by his reaction.

From one moment to the next, Cassandra had gone from being an object of desire to a liability he couldn't allow. She posed a danger to him, something new and strange, and he wanted none of it. No one could ever have that kind of power over him.

He was determined to forget her.

If only that were possible.

It didn't help that he was friends with Rhys Winterborne, who was married to Cassandra's sister Helen. Tom often met Winterborne for a quick lunch at one of the cook shops or chop houses between their respective offices. It was on one of these occasions that Winterborne revealed West Ravenel had just become engaged to marry Phoebe, Lady Clare, a young widow with two small sons, Justin and Stephen.

"I suspected he would," Tom said, pleased by the revelation. "I went to Jenner's Club with him the night before last, and she was all he wanted to talk about."

"I heard about that," Winterborne commented. "It seems you and Ravenel encountered a bit of trouble."

Tom rolled his eyes. "Lady Clare's former suitor came to the table with a pistol in hand. It wasn't nearly as interesting as it sounds. He was soon disarmed and hauled off by a night porter." He leaned back in his seat as the barmaid set plates of chilled crab salad and celery in front of them. "But before that happened, Ravenel was rambling on about Lady Clare, and how he wasn't good enough for her because of his disreputable past, and how he was worried about setting a bad example for her children."

Winterborne's black eyes were keen with interest. "What did you say?"

Tom shrugged. "The match is to his advantage, and what else matters? Lady Clare is wealthy, beautiful, and the daughter of a duke. As for her sons . . . no matter what example you set, children insist on turning out how they will." Tom took a swallow of ale before continuing. "Scruples always complicate a decision unnecessarily. They're like those extra body parts none of us need."

Winterborne paused in the act of lifting a forkful of dressed crab to his lips. "What extra body parts?"

"Things like the appendix. Male nipples. The external ears."

"I need my ears."

"Only the inner parts. The outer ear structure is superfluous in humans."

Winterborne looked sardonic. "I need them to hold up my hat."

Tom grinned and shrugged, conceding the point. "In any case, Ravenel has managed to win the hand of a fine woman. Good for him."

They lifted their glasses and clinked them in a toast.

"Has a date been set for the wedding?" Tom asked.

"Not yet, but soon. They'll have the ceremony in Essex, at the Clare estate. A small affair, with only close friends and relations." Winterborne picked up a celery stalk and sprinkled it with a pinch of salt as he added, "Ravenel means to invite you."

Tom's fingers clenched reflexively on a lemon wedge. A drop of juice hit his cheek. He dropped the crushed rind and wiped his face with a napkin. "I can't fathom why," he muttered. "He's never put my name on a guest list before. I'd be surprised if he even knew how to spell it. In any case, I hope he won't waste paper and ink on an invitation for me, since I won't be going."

Winterborne gave him a skeptical glance. "You'd miss his wedding? You've been friends for at least ten years."

"He'll manage without my presence," Tom assured him testily.

"Does it have something to do with Cassandra?" Winterborne asked.

Tom's eyes narrowed. "Trenear told you," he said rather than asked.

"He mentioned you'd met Cassandra and taken a fancy to her."

"Of course I did," Tom said coolly. "You know my fondness for pretty objects. But nothing will come of it. Trenear thought it was a bad idea, and I couldn't agree more."

In a neutral tone, Winterborne said, "The interest wasn't only on your side."

The statement sent a quick, sharp thrill down to the pit of Tom's stomach. Abruptly losing interest in food, he used the tines of his fork to nudge a sprig of parsley across his plate. "How do you know?"

"Cassandra had tea with Helen last week. From what she said, it seems you made a strong impression on her."

Tom laughed shortly. "I make a strong impression on everyone. But Cassandra told me herself I could never give her the life she's always dreamed of—which includes a husband who could love her."

"And you couldn't?"

"Of course not. It doesn't exist."

Tilting his head, Winterborne stared at him quizzically. "Love doesn't exist?"

"No more than money."

Now Winterborne looked baffled. "Money doesn't exist?"

For answer, Tom reached inside a coat pocket, rummaged for a moment, and pulled out a bank note. "Tell me how much this is worth."

"Five pounds."

"No, the actual piece of paper."

"A ha'penny," Winterborne guessed.

"Yes. But this ha'penny slip of paper is worth five pounds because we've all agreed to pretend it is. Now, take marriage—"

"*Yr Duw*," Winterborne muttered, realizing where the argument was headed.

"Marriage is an economic arrangement," Tom continued. "Can people marry without love? Of course. Are we able to produce offspring without it? Obviously. But we pretend to believe in this mythical, floaty thing no one can hear, see, or touch, when the truth is, love's nothing but an artificial value we assign to a relationship."

"What about children?" Winterborne countered. "Is love an artificial value to them?"

Tom tucked the five-pound note back into his pocket as he replied, "What children feel as love is a survival instinct. It's a way of encouraging their parents to care for them until they can do it themselves."

Winterborne's expression was dumbfounded. "My God, Tom." He took a bite of the dressed crab, chewing methodically, taking his time before replying. "Love's real, it is," he said eventually. "If you've ever experienced it—"

"I know, I know," Tom said wearily. "Whenever I make the mistake of having this conversation, it's what everyone says. But even if love were real, why would I want it? People make irrational decisions for the sake of love. Some even die for it. I'm far happier without it."

"Are you?" Winterborne asked dubiously, and fell silent as the barmaid came with the pitcher of ale. After she had refilled their mugs and left, Winterborne said, "My mother used to tell me, *'Troubled are they who want the world, troubled are they who have it.'* I knew she had to be wrong—how could a man who'd gained the world be anything but happy? But after I made my fortune, I finally understood what she meant. The things that help us climb to the top are the same things that keep us from enjoying it once we're there."

Tom was about to protest he *was* enjoying himself. But Winterborne, damn him, was absolutely right. He'd been miserable for months. Holy hell. Was this what the rest of his life was going to be like? "There's no hope for me, then," he said grimly. "I can't believe in something without evidence. I don't take leaps of faith."

"More than once, I've seen you talk yourself into the wrong decision by thinking too much. But if you could manage to climb out of that labyrinth of a brain long enough to discover what you want . . . not what you *decide* you should want, but what your instinct tells you . . . you might find what your soul is calling for."

"I don't have a soul. There's no such thing."

Looking exasperated and amused, Winterborne asked, "Then what keeps your brain working and your heart beating?"

"Electrical impulses. An Italian scientist by the name of Galvani proved it a hundred years ago, with a frog."

Firmly, Winterborne said, "I can't speak for the frog, but you have a soul. And I'd say it's high time you paid attention to it."

AFTER LUNCH, TOM walked back to his offices on Hanover Street. It was a cool autumn day with sharp, sudden gusts coming from every possible direction—a "flanny" day, as Winterborne had put it. Stray gloves, cigar stubs, newspapers, and rags torn from clothes-lines went skittering along the street and pavement.

Tom paused in front of the building that housed the main offices of his five companies. A short distance away, a young boy diligently collected used cigar stubs from the gutter. Later the tobacco would be pulled out and made into cheap cigars to be sold at tuppence apiece.

The imposing entrance was twenty feet in height, surmounted by a massive pedimented arch. White Portland stone covered the first five stories, while the top two were faced with red brick and elaborate white stone carvings. Inside, a wide staircase occupied a light well that stretched up to a glass-paneled skylight on the roof.

It looked like a place where important people went to do important work. For years, Tom had felt a thrill of satisfaction every time he'd approached this building.

Now, nothing satisfied him.

Except . . . absurd as it was . . . he'd experienced some of that old sense of purpose and fulfillment while repairing the boiler at Eversby Priory. Working with his hands, relying on the skills he'd acquired as a twelve-year-old apprentice, with all of it still ahead of him.

He'd been happy back then. His boyish ambitions had been praised and nurtured by his old mentor, Chambers Paxton, who'd become the father figure he'd needed. In those days, it had seemed possible to find the answers to any question or problem. Even Tom's limitations had been an advantage: When a man didn't have to bother with love, honor, or other such rot, it left him free to make a lot of money. He'd enjoyed the hell out of that.

But recently, some of his limitations had started to feel like limitations. Happiness—at least the way he used to experience it—was gone.

The wind danced and pushed at him from every point of the compass. A particularly sharp gust whipped the black wool felt hat from his head. It went tumbling along the pavement before it was snatched up by the little cigar stub hunter. Clutching the hat, the boy looked at him warily. Assessing the distance between them, Tom concluded it was pointless to give chase. The child would elude him easily, disappearing into the maze of alleys and mews behind the main street. *Let him have it*, Tom thought, and headed into the building. If the hat were resold at even a fraction of its original price, it would mean a small fortune for the boy.

He went up to his suite of executive rooms on the fifth floor. His personal secretary and assistant, Christopher Barnaby, came immediately to take his black wool overcoat.

Barnaby looked askance at Tom's lack of a hat.

"Wind," Tom said brusquely, heading to his large bronze-topped desk.

"Shall I go out and search for it, sir?"

"No, it's long gone by now." He sat at his desk, piled with ledgers and stacks of correspondence. "Coffee."

Barnaby rushed away with an agility that belied his stocky form.

Three years ago, Tom had chosen the junior accountant to act as his secretary and personal assistant until he could find someone appropriate for the position. Ordinarily he would never have considered someone like Barnaby, who was perpetually rumpled and anxious, with a nimbus of wild brown curls that danced and quivered around his head. In fact, even after Tom had sent Barnaby to his tailor on Savile Row and footed the bill for some elegant shirts, three silk neckties, and two bespoke suits, one woolen and one broadcloth, the lad still managed to look as if he'd dressed from the nearest laundry hamper. A personal assistant's appearance was supposed to reflect on his employer. But Barnaby had quickly proved his worth, demonstrating such exceptional abilities to prioritize and attend to details that Tom didn't give a damn what he looked like.

After bringing coffee with sugar and boiled cream, Barnaby stood in front of his desk with a little notebook. "Sir, the Japanese delegation has confirmed their arrival in two months to purchase steam excavators and drilling equipment. They also want to consult about engineering issues of building the Nakasendo line through mountainous regions."

"I'll need copies of their topographical maps and geological surveys as soon as possible."

"Yes, Mr. Severin."

"Also, hire a Japanese tutor."

Barnaby blinked. "Do you mean a translator, sir?"

"No, a tutor. I'd rather understand what they're saying without an intermediary."

"But sir," the assistant said, nonplussed, "surely you're not proposing to become fluent in Japanese in two months . . . ?"

"Barnaby, don't be absurd."

The assistant began to smile sheepishly. "Of course, sir, it just sounded like—"

"It will take a month and a half at most." With his exceptional memory, Tom was able to learn foreign languages easily—although admittedly his accent usually left something to be desired. "Arrange for daily lessons starting Monday."

"Yes, Mr. Severin." Barnaby scribbled notes in his little book. "The next item is quite exciting, sir. The University of Cambridge has decided to bestow the Alexandrian prize on you for your hydrodynamics equations. You're the first non-Cambridge graduate to receive it." Barnaby beamed at him. "Congratulations!"

Tom frowned and rubbed the corners of his eyes. "Do I have to give a speech?"

"Yes, there'll be a grand presentation at Peterhouse."

"Could I have the prize without the speech?"

Barnaby shook his head.

"Decline the award, then."

Barnaby shook his head again.

"You're telling me no?" Tom asked in mild surprise.

"You can't decline," Barnaby insisted. "There's a chance you may someday earn a knighthood for those equations, but not if you turn down the Alexandrian award. And you want a knighthood! You've said so before!"

"I don't care about it now," Tom muttered. "It doesn't matter."

His assistant turned stubborn. "I'm putting it on the schedule. I'll write a speech about how humbled you are to be honored as one of the many intellects furthering the glory of Her Majesty's empire—"

"For God's sake, Barnaby. I have only five emotions, and 'humbled' isn't one of them. Furthermore, I would never refer to myself as 'one of the many.' Have you ever met anyone like me? No, because there's only one." Tom sighed shortly. "I'll write the speech myself."

"As you wish, sir." The assistant wore a small but distinctly satisfied smile. "Those are the only items for now. Is there anything you'd like me to do before I return to my desk?"

Tom nodded and stared down at his empty coffee cup, rubbing his thumb along the fine porcelain edge. "Yes. Go to the bookshop and buy a copy of *Around the World in Eighty Days.*"

"By Jules Verne," Barnaby said, his face lighting up. "You've read it?"

"Yes, it's a ripping good story."

"What lesson does Phileas Fogg learn?" Seeing the blank look on his assistant's face, Tom added impatiently, "During all the traveling. What does he discover along the way?"

"I couldn't spoil it for you," the young man said earnestly.

"You won't spoil it. I just need to know the conclusion a normal person would come to."

"It's quite obvious, sir," Barnaby assured him. "You'll find out for yourself when you read it."

After leaving Tom's office, Barnaby returned only a minute or two later. To Tom's surprise, his assistant was holding the lost hat. "The doorman brought this up," Barnaby said. "A street urchin returned it. Didn't ask for a reward." Regarding the felt brim critically, he added, "I'll make sure it's cleaned and brushed before the end of day, sir."

Pensively Tom stood and went to the window. The boy had returned to the gutter to resume his search for discarded cigar ends. "I'm going out for a minute," he said.

"Is there something you'd like me to do?"

"No, I'll handle it."

"Your overcoat—" Barnaby began, but Tom brushed by him.

He went out to the footpath, narrowing his eyes against a gust laden with grit. The boy paused in his labors but remained in a squat beside the gutter, looking up warily as Tom approached. He was skinny and ropy, with a young-old look of malnourishment that made it difficult to assess his age, but he couldn't have been more than eleven years old. Maybe ten. His brown eyes were rheumy and his complexion had the rough texture of a plucked hen. The long straggles of his black hair hadn't been brushed in days.

"Why didn't you keep it?" Tom asked without preamble.

"Ain't a thief," the boy said, harvesting another cigar end. His small hands were scaled with grime and dust.

Tom took a shilling from his pocket and extended it to him.

The boy didn't reach for it. "Don't need charity."

"It's not charity," Tom said, both amused and irritated by the show of pride from a child who could ill afford it. "It's a tip for service rendered."

The boy shrugged and took the coin. He dropped it into the same pouch as the harvested tobacco bits.

"What's your name?" Tom asked.

"Young Bazzle."

"And your first name?"

The boy shrugged. "Young Bazzle's wot I always been. Me farver was Old Bazzle."

Tom's better judgment advised him to leave the matter as it was. There was nothing special about this boy. While helping an individual child might satisfy a benevolent impulse, it did nothing for thousands who lived in filth and poverty. Tom had already donated large sums—as ostentatiously as possible—to a host of London charitable groups. That was enough.

But something nagged at him, probably because of Winterborne's lecture. His instincts were telling him to do something for this urchin—which was a good example of why he usually tried to ignore them.

"Bazzle, I need someone to do sweeping and cleaning in my offices. Do you want the job?"

The child looked at him suspiciously. "Ye hoaxing me, guvnah?"

"I don't hoax people. Call me 'Mr. Severin,' or 'sir.'" Tom gave him another coin. "Go buy yourself a little broom, and come to my building tomorrow morning. I'll tell the doorman to expect you."

"Wot o'clock do ye want I should come, sir?"

"Nine sharp." As Tom walked away, he muttered ruefully, "If he robs me blind, Winterborne, I'm sending you the blasted bill."

# Chapter 7

ONE MONTH LATER, TOM took the train to the Saffron Walden station in Essex, and then a hired coach to the Clare estate. It was quite a change from the comfort and insulation of his private railway carriage. He preferred to visit people without being at their mercy, maintaining his ability to come and go as he wished, eat whatever and whenever he liked, wash with his favorite soap, sleep without being disturbed by other people's noise.

On the occasion of West Ravenel's wedding, however, Tom was going to try something new. He would be part of the gathering. He would stay in a room where housemaids would come in at some ungodly hour of the morning to stir the grate. He would go downstairs to eat breakfast with other guests, and dutifully join them on walks to admire views of hills, trees, and ponds. The house would be infested with children, whom he would ignore or tolerate. In the evenings there would be parlor games and amateur entertainments, which he would pretend to enjoy.

The decision to subject himself to the coming ordeal had been a direct result of Rhys Winterborne's advice to follow his instinct. So far it hadn't turned out well. But Tom was so tired of months of numb, empty nothingness that even this panoply of discomforts seemed like an improvement.

In the distance, a classic Georgian manor with white columns occupied a gentle hill dressed with evergreens and low ivy-covered walls. Curls of smoke rose from a neat row of chimney stacks, dissolving continuously into the November sky. The nearby timbered groves had lost their foliage, leaving only stark branches swathed in a lace of black twigs. A heavy evening mist had started to sulk over bare harvested fields in the distance.

The hired carriage stopped before the front portico. A trio of footmen surrounded it, opening the lacquered door, setting out the step, and unloading luggage. Tom descended to the gravel drive and drew in a deep breath scented of wet leaves and frost. The air smelled better in the country than the city, he'd give them that.

Rows of sash windows afforded glimpses of an ample crowd milling in the front rooms. Abundant music and laughter were punctuated by the happy shrieks of children. Many children, from the sound of it.

"Small family affair, my arse," Tom muttered as he ascended the front steps. He reached the entrance hall, where a butler took his hat, coat, and gloves.

The interior of Clare Manor was spacious and airy, painted in serene shades of white, pale blue, and light green. Wisely, someone had chosen to decorate the house in keeping with its clean neoclassical façade, rather than filling the rooms with an avalanche of china figurines and embroidered cushions.

In a minute or two, West Ravenel and Phoebe, Lady Clare, came to welcome him. They were a handsome pair, the tall and perpetually sun-browned West, and the slender red-haired widow. A mysterious invisible connection seemed to link them, a quality of togetherness that had nothing to do with proximity or even marriage. Puzzled and interested, Tom realized his friend was no longer a completely independent being, but half of some new entity.

Phoebe sank into a graceful curtsy. "Welcome, Mr. Severin."

The woman had undergone a remarkable transformation since Tom had last seen her at Pandora's wedding. He'd thought her a beautiful woman at the time, but there had been something brittle about her composure, something frail and melancholy. Now she was relaxed and glowing.

West reached out to exchange a hearty handshake with Tom. "We're glad you've come," he said simply.

"I almost didn't," Tom replied. "It takes all the fun out of going somewhere when I've been invited."

West grinned. "Sorry, but I had to include you on the guest list. I'm still in your debt for what you did past summer."

"Fixing the boiler?"

"No, the other thing." Seeing Tom's perplexed expression, West clarified, "Helping to smuggle my friend out of London."

"Oh, that bit of business. That was nothing."

"You took a great risk, helping us with Ransom," West said. "Had the authorities discovered your involvement, there would have been hell to pay."

Tom smiled idly. "The risk was small, Ravenel."

"You could have lost your government contracts, and possibly ended up in jail."

"Not with all the politicians in my pocket," Tom said with a touch of smugness. At West's raised brows, he explained, "I've had to grease more palms in the Lords and Commons than you have hairs on your chin. So-called parliamentary expenses are part of every railway developer's budget. Bribery's the only way to push a private bill through the committee process and obtain the necessary permits."

"You still took a risk," West insisted. "And I'm in your debt more than you realize. I couldn't tell you before, but Ethan Ransom has close ties to the Ravenel family."

Tom glanced at him alertly. "What kind of ties?"

"As it turns out, he's the chance-born son of the old earl—which makes him Cassandra and Pandora's half brother. If he were legitimate, the title and estate would rightfully be his instead of my brother's."

"Interesting," Tom murmured. "And yet you don't view him as a threat?"

West looked sardonic. "No, Severin, Ransom has no interest in the estate whatsoever. In fact, he's so discreet about his connection to the Ravenels, I had to cajole and bully him into attending a family event.

He's here only because his wife wanted to come." He paused. "You'll recall Dr. Gibson, I'm sure."

"Dr. Garrett Gibson?" Tom asked. "She married him?"

West grinned at his surprise. "Who do you think took care of Ransom while he was recuperating at the estate?"

Noticing Tom's perturbed expression, Phoebe asked gently, "Did you have an interest in Dr. Gibson, Mr. Severin?"

"No, but . . ." Tom paused. Garrett Gibson was an extraordinary woman who had become the first licensed female physician in England after earning a degree at the Sorbonne. Despite her youth, she was a highly skilled surgeon, having been trained in antiseptic techniques by her mentor, Sir Joseph Lister. Since she was friends with the Winterbornes, and had established a medical clinic next to his store on Cork Street for the benefit of his employees, Tom had met her on a few occasions, and liked her immensely.

"Dr. Gibson is a refreshingly practical woman," Tom said. "Ransom is fortunate in having a wife who keeps both feet on the ground and doesn't care about romantic nonsense."

West grinned and shook his head. "I'm sorry to ruin your illusions, Severin, but Dr. Gibson is quite besotted with her husband, and adores his romantic nonsense."

West would have said more, but he was interrupted as a little boy came charging up to Phoebe and collided with her. Reflexively West reached out to steady them both.

"Mama," the child exclaimed, breathless and agitated.

Phoebe looked down at him in concern. "Justin, what is it?"

"Galoshes brought me a dead mouse. She dropped it on the floor right in front of me!"

"Oh, dear." Tenderly Phoebe smoothed his dark, ruffled hair. "I'm afraid that's what cats do. She thought it was a fine gift."

"Nanny won't touch it, and the housemaid screamed, and I had a fight with Ivo."

Although Phoebe's younger brother Ivo was technically Justin's uncle, the boys were close enough in age to play together and quarrel.

"About the mouse?" Phoebe asked sympathetically.

"No, before the mouse. Ivo said there's going to be a honeymoon and I can't go because it's for grown-ups." The boy tilted his head back to look up at her, his lower lip quivering. "You wouldn't go to the honeymoon without me, would you, Mama?"

"Darling, we've made no plans to travel yet. There's too much to be done here, and we all need time to settle in. Perhaps in the spring—"

"Dad wouldn't want to leave me behind. I know he wouldn't!"

In the electrified silence that followed, Tom shot a glance at West, who looked blank and startled.

Slowly Phoebe lowered to the ground until her face was level with her son's. "Do you mean Uncle West?" she asked gently. "Is that what you're calling him now?"

Justin nodded. "I don't want him to be my uncle—I already have too many of those. And if I don't have a dad, I'll never learn how to tie my shoes."

Phoebe began to smile. "Why not call him Papa?" she suggested.

"If I did, you'd never know which one I was talking about," Justin said reasonably, "the one in heaven or the one down here."

Phoebe let out a breath of amusement. "You're right, my clever boy."

Justin looked up at the tall man beside him with a flicker of uncertainty. "I can call you Dad . . . can't I? Do you like that name?"

A change came over West's face, his color deepening, small muscles contorting with some powerful emotion. He snatched Justin up, one of his large hands clasping the small head as he kissed his cheek. "I love that name," West said unsteadily. "I love it." The boy's arms went around his neck.

Tom, who hated sentimental scenes, felt incredibly uncomfortable. He glanced around the entrance hall, wondering if he could slink away and find his room later.

"Can we go to Africa for our honeymoon, Dad?" he heard Justin ask.

"Yes," came West's muffled voice.

"Can I have a pet crocodile, Dad?"

"Yes."

Phoebe produced a handkerchief from seemingly out of nowhere and tucked it discreetly into one of

West's hands. "I'll take care of Mr. Severin," she whispered, "if you'll do something about the dead mouse."

West nodded with a gruff sound, while Justin protested that he was being squashed.

Phoebe turned to Tom with an incandescent smile. "Come with me," she invited.

Relieved to escape the poignant scene, Tom fell into step beside her.

"Please excuse my son's timing," Phoebe said ruefully as they crossed the entrance hall. "To children, there's no such thing as an inconvenient moment."

"No apology necessary," Tom replied. "As this is a wedding, I expected some drama and weeping. I just didn't think it would all be coming from the bridegroom."

Phoebe smiled. "My poor fiancé has been flung headlong into fatherhood with no preparation. He's doing splendidly, however. My boys adore him."

"It's not a side of him I'm used to seeing," Tom admitted, and paused reflectively. "I never realized he wanted a family. He's always insisted he would never marry."

"'I'll never marry' is the song of every libertine and the refrain of every rake. However, most of them eventually succumb to the inevitable." Phoebe sent him an impish sidelong glance. "Perhaps it will be your turn next."

"I've never been a libertine or rake," Tom said dryly. "Those are words for blue-blooded men with trust funds. But I'm open to the possibility of marriage."

"How refreshing. Any candidates in mind?"

Tom glanced at her sharply, wondering if she were mocking him. Surely West had told her about his former interest in Cassandra. But there was no glint of malice in her light gray eyes, only friendly curiosity.

"Not at the moment," he replied. "I don't suppose you could recommend someone?"

"I have a sister, Seraphina, but I fear she might be too young for you. What kind of woman would suit you?"

A female voice interrupted. "Mr. Severin wants an independent and practical wife. Pleasant but not demonstrative . . . intelligent but not chatty. She'll go away when he wants, appear when he wishes, and never complain when he doesn't come home for dinner. Isn't that right, Mr. Severin?"

Tom stopped in his tracks as he saw Cassandra approaching from the opposite end of the hallway. She was unspeakably pretty in a pink velvet dress with pulled-back skirts that followed the shape of her waist and hips. The front hem kicked up in a froth of white silk ruffles with every footstep. His mouth went dry with excitement. His heart writhed and struggled like some live thing he'd just trapped inside a dresser drawer.

"Not really," he replied, staying very still while she came toward him. "I'm hardly looking to marry an automaton."

"But it would be convenient, wouldn't it?" Cassandra mused, coming to stand just a foot or two away from him. "A mechanical wife would never annoy or inconvenience you," she continued. "No love required on either side. And even with the expense of minor repairs and maintenance, she would be quite cost-effective."

Her tone held the delicate snap of icicles. Obviously, she was still displeased about the abrupt way he'd taken his leave at Eversby Priory.

Only a small part of Tom's brain functioned normally. The rest of it was busy gathering details: the whiff of perfumed dusting powder, the intense blueness of her eyes. He'd never seen a complexion like hers, fresh and faintly opalescent, like milk glass with pink light shining through it. Was her skin like that all over? He thought of the limbs and curves beneath the ruffles of her dress, and he was suffused with a sensation that recalled the way icy water could sometimes feel hot, or a burn could feel like a chill.

"That sounds like something from a Jules Verne novel," he managed to say. "I read the one you recommended, by the way."

Cassandra had crossed her arms, a gesture of annoyance that bolstered the sumptuous curves of her breasts just a bit higher and made him weak in the knees. "How is that possible when you left it at Eversby Priory?"

"I had my assistant purchase a copy."

"Why didn't you take the copy I gave you?"

"Why do you assume I left it deliberately?" Tom parried. "I might have forgotten it."

"No, you never forget anything." She wasn't about to let him off the hook. "Why didn't you take it?"

Although Tom could have easily come up with an evasive answer, he decided to tell her the truth. After all, it wasn't as if he'd been subtle about his interest in her so far.

"I didn't want to think about you," he said curtly.

Phoebe, who'd been looking back and forth between them, took a sudden interest in a flower arrangement on a console table, much farther down the hallway. She went to fuss with the greenery, pulling out a fern and sticking it into the other side of the display.

Something in Cassandra's expression eased, and the firm set of her mouth softened. "Why did you read it?"

"I was curious."

"Did you enjoy it?"

"Not enough to justify four hours of reading. One page would have been sufficient to explain the point of the novel."

Cassandra tilted her head slightly, her gaze encouraging. "Which is?"

"As Phileas Fogg journeys eastward, he gains four minutes every time he crosses a geographical longitude. By the time he returns to his starting point, he's a full day early, which allows him to win the bet. Clearly, the lesson is that when one travels in the direction of the earth's rotation in prograde motion, the hands of the clock must be pushed back accordingly—and therefore time is delayed."

*So there*, he thought smugly.

But Tom was confounded as Cassandra shook her head and began to smile. "That's the plot twist," she said, "but it's not the point of the novel. It has nothing to do with what Phileas Fogg comes to understand about himself."

"He set a goal and he achieved it," Tom said, nettled by her reaction. "What's there to understand beyond that?"

"Something important," Cassandra exclaimed, her amusement bubbling over.

Unaccustomed to being wrong, about anything, Tom said coolly, "You're laughing at me."

"No, I'm laughing *with* you, but in a slightly superior way."

Her gaze was teasing. As if she were flirting with him. As if he were some callow young suitor instead of a worldly man who knew every tactic of the game she was trying to play. But Tom was accustomed to experienced partners whose strategies were precise and identifiable. He couldn't tell what her objective was.

"Tell me the answer," he commanded.

Cassandra crinkled her nose adorably. "I don't think so. I'll let you discover it for yourself."

Tom kept his face expressionless, while inside he was dissolving in a feeling he'd never known before. It was similar to drinking champagne—one of his favorite things—while balancing on the steel framework of an elevated railway bridge—one of his least favorite things.

"You're not as sweet as everyone thinks you are," he said darkly.

"I know." Cassandra grinned and looked back over her shoulder at Phoebe, who had rearranged at least half the flowers by then. "I won't delay you any longer, Phoebe. Are you showing Mr. Severin to the guest cottage?"

"Yes, we're lodging a few of the unattached gentlemen there."

"Will I be seated near Mr. Severin at dinner?" Cassandra asked.

"I was instructed to keep the two of you as far apart as possible," Phoebe said dryly. "Now I'm beginning to understand why."

"Piffle," Cassandra scoffed. "Mr. Severin and I would be perfectly amicable. In fact . . ." She glanced up at Tom with an inviting half smile as she continued, ". . . I think we should be friends. Would you like that, Mr. Severin?"

"No," he said sincerely.

Cassandra blinked in surprise, her expression cooling. "That makes things easy, then."

As she walked away, Tom stared after her, mesmerized by her supple walk and the swish of intricately draped skirts.

When he finally thought to look in Phoebe's direction, he found her speculative gaze on him.

"My lady," Tom began warily, "if I could ask you not to mention—"

"Not a word," Phoebe promised. Seeming deep in thought, she set a slow pace along the hallway. "Shall I alter the seating arrangements," she asked abruptly, "and put you next to Cassandra?"

"God, no. Why would you suggest that?"

Phoebe looked wry and a bit sheepish. "Not long ago, I felt a sudden attraction for a man who couldn't have been more unsuitable. It was like one of those summer lightning storms that strike without warning. I decided to avoid him, but then we were seated next to each other at dinner, and it turned out to be one of the luckiest things ever to happen to me. Just now, seeing you with Cassandra, I thought perhaps—"

"No," he said tersely. "We're incompatible."

"I see." After a long pause, Phoebe said, "Something might change. One never knows. There's a very fine book I could recommend, titled *Persuasion*—"

"Another novel?" Tom asked, giving her a long-suffering glance.

"What's wrong with novels?"

"Nothing, as long as one doesn't mistake them for advice manuals."

"If it's good advice," Phoebe countered, "why does it matter where it came from?"

"My lady, there's nothing I want to learn from fictional people."

They exited the main block of the house and went outside to the paved garden path that led to a redbrick guest cottage.

"Indulge me in a game of pretend," Phoebe said. "Just for a moment." She waited for Tom's reluctant nod before continuing. "Recently a good friend of mine, Jane Austen, relayed to me that her neighbor Anne Elliot just wed a gentleman by the name of Captain Frederick Wentworth. They were betrothed seven years ago, but Anne was persuaded by her family to break it off."

"Why?"

"The young man lacked fortune and connections."

"Weak-minded girl," Tom scoffed.

"It was a mistake," Phoebe allowed, "but Anne has always been an obedient daughter. After years passed, they met again, when Captain Wentworth had made a success of himself. He realized he still loved her, but unfortunately at that point Anne was being courted by another man."

"What did Wentworth do?" Tom asked, interested despite himself.

"He chose to keep silent and wait for her. Eventually, when the time was right, he wrote a letter to express his feelings, and left it for her to find."

Tom sent her a dark glance. "I'm not impressed by anyone in this story."

"What should Captain Wentworth have done instead?"

"Pursue her," he said emphatically. "Or decide he was well rid of her. Anything but wait in silence."

"Doesn't pursuit sometimes require patience?" Phoebe asked.

"When it comes to business, yes. But I've never wanted any woman enough to wait for her. There are always more women."

Phoebe looked amused. "Oh, you are a difficult case, aren't you? I think you should read *Persuasion* to find out what you might have in common with Captain Wentworth."

"Probably not much," Tom said, "since I exist and he doesn't."

"Read it anyway," Phoebe urged. "It may help you to understand what Cassandra meant about Phileas Fogg."

Tom frowned in bewilderment. "He's in that book too?"

"No, but—" Phoebe broke off with a laugh. "My goodness, do you take everything so literally?"

"I'm an engineer," he said defensively, following her out to the guest cottage.

# Chapter 8

"WHY ARE YOU WALKING like that?" Pandora asked as she and her husband, Gabriel, accompanied Cassandra downstairs to dinner.

"What way?" Cassandra asked.

"The way we used to when we were little and had ballerina fights."

That drew a grin from Gabriel. "What's a ballerina fight?"

"A game to see who can stay on her toes the longest," Pandora explained, "without sinking back down to her heels or toppling over. Cassandra was always the winner."

"I don't feel like a winner at the moment," Cassandra said ruefully. She stopped by the side of the hallway, leaned back against the wall, and hiked the front hem of her dress up to the ankles. "I'm walking this way because of my new shoes."

Pandora crouched down to investigate, the skirts of her lavender silk evening dress billowing and collapsing like a gigantic petunia.

The blue satin shoes were narrow, pointed at the toes, and studded with pearls and beads. Unfortunately, no matter how often Cassandra had worn them around the house to break them in, the stiff leather lining wouldn't soften.

"Oh, how pretty," Pandora exclaimed.

"Yes, aren't they?" Cassandra said with a little bounce of excitement, followed by a wince of discomfort. The night hadn't even begun, and blisters had already started on her toes and the backs of her heels.

"The heels are so tall," Pandora observed, her forehead crinkling.

"Louis Quinze style," Cassandra told her. "We ordered them from Paris, so I have to wear them."

"Even if they're uncomfortable?" Gabriel asked, reaching down to help Pandora to her feet.

"These shoes are too expensive to be uncomfortable," Cassandra said glumly. "Besides . . . the dressmaker said tall heels would make me appear more slender."

"Why are you still worrying about that?" Pandora demanded.

"Because all my dresses are too tight, and it would take a great deal of time and money to have everything altered." She heaved a sigh. "Also . . . I've overheard the way men gossip at dances or parties. They point out all a girl's physical flaws and debate whether she's too tall or short, or if her complexion is smooth enough, or whether her bosom is adequate."

Pandora scowled. "Why don't *they* have to be perfect?"

"Because they're men."

Pandora looked disgusted. "That's the London Season for you: Casting girls before swine." Turning to her husband, she asked, "Do men really talk about women that way?"

"Men, no," Gabriel said. "Arsewits, yes."

THREE HOURS LATER, Cassandra limped into the quiet, empty conservatory. Soft ripples of light reflected from the indoor stream and jostled against shadows cast by ferns and palm fronds. It looked like the room of some underwater palace.

Painfully she made her way to the steps of a small stone bridge and sat in a billow of blue silk organza skirts. Tiny crystal beads had been scattered among the multiple layers of delicate fabric, casting glints across the floor. She sat with a groan of relief and reached down to work a shoe off her throbbing left foot.

Dinner had been lovely, actually, the atmosphere infused with wit and good cheer. Everyone had been genuinely happy for West and Phoebe, who had both seemed to be in a daze of bliss. The food itself had been spectacular, starting with rich circlets of foie gras laid out on slabs of ice arranged down the center of the mile-long table. An endless procession of courses had struck perfect chords of salt, butter, smokiness, and richness.

But all through the extravagant meal, Cassandra had been increasingly miserable as the chisellike edges of her shoes had cut into the backs of her heels and shredded her stockings. She'd finally resorted to slipping the shoes off beneath the table, and letting the air circulate over her pulsing, burning feet.

Thankfully she had been seated next to Lord Foxhall, whose engaging company had helped to take her mind off the discomfort. He was remarkably suitable and eligible, and so very nice . . . but he didn't stir her interest any more than she stirred his.

, Whereas Tom Severin and all his complexities seemed to have caught and stuck, burrlike, to her awareness. He'd been seated near the other end of the table, beside Lady Grace, one of Lord and Lady Westcliff's dashingly pretty daughters. She had glossy black hair and a wide smile with very white teeth. She had seemed rather taken with Severin, laughing frequently, taking obvious interest in their conversation.

Severin had looked superb in formal evening attire. A man like a blade . . . sleek and hard, his gaze sharp with intelligence. Even in a room full of accomplished and powerful men, he stood out. He hadn't once glanced in Cassandra's direction, but she'd had the feeling he was aware of her and was deliberately ignoring her.

Every time Cassandra had glanced at the pair, the food in her mouth had turned bitter, and she'd had difficulty swallowing. Her mood, not especially elevated to begin with, had deflated like a cooling soufflé.

The crowning indignity had occurred when dinner had finally, *finally* ended and Cassandra had tried to slip her feet back into the detested shoes. One of them was missing. She had slid an inch or two down in her chair and hunted for the shoe as inconspicuously as possible, but the blasted thing had disappeared.

Briefly she'd considered asking Lord Foxhall to

help. But he probably wouldn't have been able to resist the temptation of telling someone about it later—who could blame him?—and she couldn't bear the thought of being laughed at.

As she'd considered her dilemma, however, she'd realized it was unavoidable; she *would* be laughed at. If she left the dining hall without the shoe, a servant would find it and tell the other servants, who would tell their masters and mistresses, and then *everyone* would know.

Her toes had searched the floor frantically.

"Lady Cassandra," Lord Foxhall had asked quietly, "is something troubling you?"

She'd looked into his friendly dark eyes and forced her lips into the shape of a smile. "I'm afraid I'm not one for these long dinners with no opportunity to move about." Which hadn't been true, of course, but she could hardly tell him the problem.

"Neither am I," Foxhall had said promptly. "Shall we go for a stroll to stretch our legs?"

Cassandra had maintained her smile, her brain sorting through various responses. "How kind of you to ask—but the ladies will be gathering for tea, and I wouldn't want my absence to cause comment."

"Of course." Foxhall had gallantly accepted her excuse and stood to help her from her chair.

With one shoe on and the other missing, Cassandra's only recourse had been to proceed on her toes, ballerinalike, hoping her voluminous skirts would conceal that she was missing a shoe. Gliding toward the doorway, she'd tried to look composed while breaking out in a sweat of anxiety.

As she'd winced and cringed amid the chattering crowd of guests all making their way from the room, she'd felt a subtle touch on her bare elbow. Turning, she found herself looking up into Tom Severin's face.

"What is it?" he'd asked in a low undertone. Ice-cool and steady, a man who could fix things.

Feeling hot and foolish and off balance, she'd whispered, "I lost one of my shoes under the table."

Severin had registered that without even blinking. "I'll meet you in the winter garden."

And now she sat here, waiting.

Gingerly she pulled at the silk stocking where it stuck to the back of her heel. It smarted and stung, and came away with a little spot of blood. Grimacing, she rummaged beneath her skirts, unfastened her garters, and removed the ruined stockings. She compressed them into a wad and tucked them in a concealed pocket of her gown.

With a sigh, she picked up the discarded shoe and scowled at it. The pearls and intricate beading glittered in a slant of moonlight. So beautiful, and yet so incompetent at being a shoe. "I had such high hopes for you," she said dourly, and threw it, not with any real force, but with enough strength to hit a potted palm and send beads scattering.

Tom Severin's dry voice cut through the silence. "People in glass houses really shouldn't throw shoes."

# Chapter 9

CASSANDRA GLANCED UP WITH chagrin as Tom Severin entered the conservatory. "How did you know something was wrong?" she asked. "Was I that obvious?"

Mr. Severin came to a stop a few feet away from her. "No, you hid it well. But you winced as you stood from your chair, and you walked more slowly than usual."

Some part of her brain registered surprise that he'd noticed such details, but she was too preoccupied to follow the thought. "Did you find my missing shoe?" she asked apprehensively.

For answer, he reached to an inside pocket of his coat and pulled out the shoe.

Relief radiated through her. "Oh, *thank you*. How did you manage to retrieve it?"

"I told one of the footmen I wanted a look underneath the table, as one of the leaves wasn't quite level."

Her brows lifted. "You lied for my sake?"

"No, I noticed at dinner that the liquids in the wine and water glasses were slightly tilted. The leaf wasn't set in properly, so I adjusted it while I was down there."

Cassandra smiled and extended her hand for the shoe. "You've done two good deeds, then."

But Mr. Severin paused before giving it to her. "Are you going to throw this one as well?"

"I might," she said.

"I think I'd better keep it until I'm sure you can be trusted with it."

Cassandra drew her hand back slowly, staring into his glinting eyes. As she and Mr. Severin stood there with moonlight and shadows playing around them, it seemed as if they'd stepped out of time. As if they were the only two people in the world, free to do or say whatever they pleased.

"Will you sit beside me?" she dared to ask.

Mr. Severin hesitated for an unaccountably long moment, glancing at their surroundings as if he'd found himself in the middle of a minefield. He gave a single nod and moved toward her.

She gathered in her skirts to make room on the step, but some of the glittering blue silk spilled over his thigh as he sat. The scent of him was fresh with soap and starch, and a wonderful hint of dry resinous sweetness.

"How are your feet?" he asked.

"Sore," Cassandra replied with a grimace.

Mr. Severin examined the shoe critically, turning it this way and that. "Not surprising. This design is an engineering debacle. The heel is tall enough to displace your center of gravity."

"My what?"

"Furthermore," he continued, "no human foot is shaped like this. Why is it pointed where the toes should go?"

"Because it's stylish."

Mr. Severin looked sincerely perplexed. "Shouldn't the shoe be made for the foot, and not the foot for the shoe?"

"I suppose it should, but one must be fashionable. Especially now that the Season has started."

"This early?"

"Not officially," Cassandra admitted, "but Parliament is in session again, so there'll be private balls and entertainments, and I can't afford to miss any of them."

Mr. Severin set down the shoe with undue care and turned to face her more fully. "Why can't you afford to miss any?"

"It's my second Season. I have to find a husband this year. If I go for a third Season, people will think there's something wrong with me."

His expression turned inscrutable. "Marry Lord Foxhall, then. You won't find a better prospect, this year or any other."

Even though he was right, the suggestion nettled her. She felt as if she'd just been rejected and dismissed. "He and I don't suit," Cassandra said shortly.

"The two of you chatted all through dinner—you seemed to get on well enough."

"So did you and Lady Grace."

He considered that. "She's an amusing dinner companion."

Inwardly rankled, Cassandra said, "Perhaps you should court her."

"And have Lord Westcliff as a father-in-law?" he asked sardonically. "I wouldn't enjoy living under his thumb."

Now feeling restless and glum, Cassandra heard the lush music of a chamber orchestra as it filtered through a wire mesh window screen. "Bother," she muttered. "I wish I could go back to dance."

"Change into another pair of shoes," he suggested.

"Not with these blisters. I'll have to bandage my feet and go to bed." She frowned down at her bare toes peeking from beneath the hems of her skirts. "You should find Lady Grace and ask her for a waltz."

She heard his smothered laugh. "Are you jealous?"

"How silly," she said stiffly, drawing her feet back. "No, not at all; I have no claim on your attention. In fact, I'm glad you've become friends with her."

"You are?"

She forced herself to reply honestly. "Well, not *especially* glad, but I don't mind if you like her. It's only . . ."

Severin gave her a questioning glance.

"Why won't you be friends with *me*?" To Cassandra's chagrin, the question came out plaintive, almost childish. She looked down and rearranged the folds of her skirts, fidgeting with the crystal beads.

"My lady," he murmured, but she refused to look at him. One of his hands came to the side of her face to angle it upward.

It was the first time he'd ever touched her.

His fingers were strong but gentle, slightly cool against her hot cheek, and it felt so amazingly good that she trembled. She couldn't move or speak, only stared up into his lean, slightly wolfish face. A trick of moonlight had turned his blue-green eyes iridescent.

"That you'd even ask . . ." His thumb brushed over her skin in a slow stroke, and her breath stopped and started too fast, sounding like a tiny hiccup. There was no mistaking the experience in his touch, sending pleasure-chills down the back of her neck and all along her spine. "Do you really want to be friends?" His voice had softened into dark velvet.

"Yes," she managed to say.

"No, you don't." In the electric silence, he drew closer, his face right over hers, and her heart thundered as she felt the warm waft of his breath against her chin. His other hand came to the back of her neck in a light clasp. He was going to kiss her, she thought, her stomach tightening with excitement, her hands fluttering between their bodies like panicked moths.

Cassandra had been kissed before, during stolen moments at dances or soirées. Surreptitious and hasty kisses, each lasting no longer than a heartbeat. But no erstwhile suitor had ever touched her like this, his fingertips gently exploring the curve of her cheek and jaw. She began to feel unsteady, unfamiliar sensations coursing through her bloodstream, and she welcomed the support of his arm sliding around her. His lips looked firm and smooth as they hovered close to hers.

To her dismay, however, the expected kiss didn't happen.

"Cassandra," he murmured, "in the past I've made more than a few women unhappy. Never intentionally. But for some reason I'm not eager to dwell on, I don't want to do that to you."

"One kiss wouldn't change anything," she protested, and flushed as she realized how brazen that sounded.

Mr. Severin drew back enough to look down at her, his fingertips toying with the fine wisps of hair at the nape of her neck. A shiver chased through her at the delicate caress.

"If you drift off course by only one navigational degree," he said, "then by the time you've gone a hundred yards, you'd be off by about five feet. In a mile, you'd have strayed approximately ninety-two feet away from your original trajectory. If you'd set out from London to Aberdeen, you'd probably find yourself in the middle of the North Sea." Seeing her frown of incomprehension, he explained, "According to basic geometry, one kiss could change your life."

Twisting away from him, Cassandra said irritably, "You may not know this, but talking about mathematics eliminates any possibility of being kissed in the first place."

Mr. Severin grinned. "Yes, I know." Rising to his feet, he extended a hand down to her. "Would you settle for a dance?" His tone was calm and friendly, conveying how unaffected he was by moonlight and romantic moments and impulsive young women.

Cassandra was sorely tempted to refuse him, to demonstrate how little she cared about anything he might offer. But a Strauss waltz was playing in the background, the melody buoyant and yearning, and it so perfectly echoed her own emotions that she felt it down to the marrow of her bones. Oh, how she wanted to dance with him. Even if she were willing to sacrifice her pride, though, there was still the matter of her ruinous shoes. She couldn't put them on again.

"I can't," she said. "I'm barefoot."

"Why should that stop you?" A deliberate pause. "Ahh. I see. All those rules you like to follow—you'd be breaking too many of them at once. Alone with a man, no chaperone, no shoes—"

"It's not that I *like* to follow the rules, but I have no choice. Besides, the temporary enjoyment wouldn't be worth the risk."

"How do you know, when you've never danced with me?"

An agitated laugh broke from her. "No one's *that* good a dancer."

He stared at her, his hand still extended. "Try me."

The laughter dissolved in her throat.

Her insides were in a tumult, like birds darting and crisscrossing in flight. She reached out with a tremor in her fingers, and he pulled her up firmly. He caught her in a waltz hold, his right hand pressed to the center of her back. Automatically her left hand settled on his shoulder, her arm resting gently along his. He held her more closely than she was accustomed, their hips slightly offset, so his first forward step would slide precisely between her feet.

As he moved forward, the pressure at her back eased, and he steered her into the first turn. He was *very* good at this, his body a perfectly supportive frame, his signals so explicit she could follow without effort. It also helped that the shoulders of his coat weren't padded, as so many gentlemen's were, so she could feel the flex of muscle at the beginning of each rotation.

It was exciting and slightly embarrassing to feel the floor with her naked toes as he swept her into one luxurious full turn after another. Of course, the sensation of dancing with bare feet wasn't entirely new: She'd waltzed alone in her bedroom more than once, imagining herself in the arms of some unknown suitor. But it felt very different when her partner was a flesh-and-blood man. She relaxed and abandoned herself, following his guidance without effort or thought.

Although they'd started slowly, Mr. Severin had quickened their tempo to match the music. The waltz was flowing and swift, each turn making her skirts whirl in eddies of silk and glitter. It was like flying. Her stomach turned light, as if she were on a garden swing, soaring a little too high and coming down in a giddy arc. She hadn't felt so free since she'd been a young girl, running recklessly across the Hampshire Downs with her twin. The world was nothing but moonlight and music as the two of them swept through the empty conservatory with the ease of mist carried on a sea breeze.

She had no idea how much time had passed before she was panting from exertion, her muscles stinging with the need for respite. Mr. Severin began to slow their pace.

She protested, clinging to him, reluctant for the spell to break. "No, don't."

"You're tiring," he pointed out, sounding amused.

"I want to keep dancing," she insisted, even as she staggered.

Mr. Severin caught her with a low laugh, holding her securely. Unlike her, he was barely affected by the exercise. "Let's wait until you catch your breath."

"Don't stop," Cassandra commanded, tugging at the front of his coat.

"No one gives me orders," he murmured, but his tone was teasing, and his touch was gentle as he smoothed back a disheveled curl that dangled over one of her eyes.

Laughing breathlessly, she managed to tell him, "You're supposed to say, 'Your wish is my command.'"

"What is your command?"

"Dance with me, and never stop."

Mr. Severin made no reply, his gaze riveted on her flushed face. He was still holding her, fast and close, in what had undeniably become an embrace. Even with the clouds of silk and chiffon skirts between them, she felt the hard strength of him all along her, the steely support of his arm. This was something she had never known but had always craved . . . to be enfolded, anchored, wanted . . . exactly like this. The sense of lightness left her, her limbs feeling loose and pleasantly weighted.

As Mr. Severin felt the yielding pliancy of her body, he took an unsettled breath. His intent gaze slid to her mouth. A new tension invaded the muscles of his arms and chest, as if he were struggling with an impulse too powerful to resist.

Cassandra saw the moment he broke, when he wanted her too much for anything else to matter. His head lowered, his mouth finding hers, and she closed her eyes at the careful, enticing pressure. Gently his hand came up to cradle the back of her head, his mouth moving over hers with erotic lightness . . . moment after moment . . . breath after breath. Embered warmth spread inside her, as if her bloodstream had been filled with sparks.

A faint moan escaped her as his lips broke from hers, straying down to her throat. The shaven bristle of his cheek was an electrifying abrasion as he nuzzled into the soft skin. He worked his way down her neck, seeking the frantic throb of her pulse. His broad, hard palms slid up and down her bare arms, soothing gooseflesh, while his teeth closed gently against the tender muscle of her shoulder. The tip of his tongue touched her lightly, as if he were tasting something sweet.

Disoriented, robbed of equilibrium, she sank against him, her head tipping back against his supportive arm. His mouth returned to hers with full, warm pressure, coaxing her to open for him. She gasped at the stroke of his tongue, silky and intimate as he searched slowly, until a knot of pleasure formed at the pit of her belly.

He gripped her hard against him for a few searing seconds. "This is why we can't be friends," came his rough whisper. "I want this every time I see you. The taste of you . . . the feel of you in my arms. I can't look at you without thinking of you as mine. The first time I saw you—" He broke off, his jaw hardening. "My God, I don't want this. If I could, I'd crush it like a cinder beneath my boot."

"What are you talking about?" Cassandra asked unsteadily.

"This . . . *feeling*." He uttered the word as if it were a profanity. "I don't know what it is. But you're a weakness I can't afford."

Her lips felt too sensitive, a little swollen, as if from a light burn. "Mr. Severin, I—"

"Call me by my first name," he interrupted, as if he couldn't help himself. "Just once." After a long hesitation, he added in a softer tone, "Please."

They were both motionless except for the matched rhythms of their breathing.

"Is it . . . short for Thomas?" Cassandra asked hesitantly.

He shook his head, his gaze not moving from hers. "Just Tom."

"Tom." She dared to reach up and gently touch his lean cheek. A wistful smile fluttered at her lips. "I suppose we'll never dance together again, will we?"

"No."

She didn't want to stop touching him. "It was lovely. Although I . . . I think you may have ruined waltzing for me."

His face, brooding and saturnine in the shadows, could have belonged to some lesser god in a realm far below Olympus. Powerful, secretive, enigmatic. He turned his head until his lips nudged her palm with a tenderness she knew somehow was reserved for her alone.

After assuring himself of her balance, he let go and went to retrieve the shoe she'd thrown earlier.

Feeling as if she were waking from a dream, Cassandra fumbled to set herself to rights, smoothing her skirts and pinning back a lock of hair that had escaped her coiffure.

Tom came to her with both shoes, and she reached out to take them. They stood like that, linked by a mutual clasp on a few scraps of satin, leather, wood, and beading.

"You're returning to your room barefoot?" Tom asked.

"I have no choice."

"Is there something I can do to help?"

Cassandra shook her head. "I can sneak upstairs by myself." She let out a quick little laugh. "Like Cinderella *sans* pumpkin."

He tilted his head in that inquiring way he had. "Did she have a pumpkin?"

"Yes, haven't you ever read the story?"

"My childhood was short on fairy tales."

"The pumpkin becomes her carriage," Cassandra explained.

"I'd have recommended a vehicle with a longer date of expiration."

She knew better than to try explaining fairy-tale magic to such a pragmatic man. "Cinderella didn't have a choice of transportation," she said. "Or footwear, the poor girl. I'm sure those glass slippers were a misery."

"One must be fashionable," he reminded her.

Cassandra smiled up at him. "I've changed my mind about uncomfortable shoes. Why limp when I could dance?"

But he didn't smile back, only gave her a brooding glance and shook his head slightly.

"What?" she whispered.

His reply was halting and gruff. "Perfection is impossible. Most mathematical truths can't be proved. The vast majority of mathematical relations can't be known. But you . . . standing here in your bare feet in that dress . . . you're perfect."

He bent over her, kissing her with pure molten longing. A shock of pleasure went through her, the sound of distant melody drowning in the heavy drum of her pulse. The shoes dropped from her nerveless fingers. She sank against him, grateful for the support of his hard arms as they wrapped around her, locking her close and tight.

When at last his mouth lifted, setting her free, Cassandra let her forehead drop to his shoulder. The smooth silk and wool fabric of his evening coat absorbed the fine sheen of perspiration from her skin as she listened to the undisciplined force of his breathing.

"I'll never be able to forget this," she heard Tom say eventually. He sounded far from pleased by the fact. "I'll have to go a lifetime with you lurking in my head."

Cassandra wanted to offer reassurance, but trying to think was like wading through a pool of honey. "You'll find someone else," she finally said, her voice not quite her own.

"Yes," he said vehemently. "But it won't be you."

It sounded like an accusation.

He let go of her while he was still able, and left her in the winter garden with the discarded evening shoes at her feet.

# Chapter 10

$\mathcal{B}$Y ANY STANDARDS, TOM was an ass for most of the autumn. He knew that. But patience and tolerance required too much effort. He was brusque and short-tempered with Barnaby, his assorted private secretaries, accountants, lawyers, and the heads of his executive departments. Work was everything. He spared no time for friends, and turned down social invitations unless they pertained to business. There were political breakfasts and luncheons with financiers who'd agreed to supply capital for a continuation of his underground line.

Near the middle of October, Tom had arranged to purchase an estate north of London, which comprised two hundred and fifty acres. The seller was Lord Beaumont, a viscount drowning in debt, like so much of the landowning nobility these days. Since few people could afford to buy large tracts of land, Tom had bought the estate at a bargain price, with the intention of developing it with shops and accommodations for approximately thirty thousand residents. He'd always wanted his own town. It would be satisfying to see that it was planned and laid out properly.

Of course, the viscount's family despised Tom for having bought their ancestral land. Their disdain hadn't stopped them, however, from introducing him to one of their younger daughters, Miss Adelia Howard, in the hopes he would marry her and replenish the family coffers.

Amused by their obvious struggle to hold their noses at the prospect of him as a son-in-law, Tom had accepted an invitation to dinner. The meal had been long, stilted, and formal . . . but the well-bred Adelia had impressed him. She seemed to share his understanding of marriage as a businesslike partnership, in which each party's roles were separate and defined. He would make money and pay the bills. She would have the children and manage the household. After a sufficient number of offspring had been produced, they would pursue their separate pleasures and pretend to look the other way. No romantic foolishness about cozy cottages and walking hand in hand through country meadows. No poetry, no treacle.

No moonlight waltzes.

"I'm the best prospect you'll ever have," Adelia had said with an admirable lack of melodrama, when they'd talked privately at her family's home. "Most families like mine wouldn't dream of mixing good blood with common stock."

"But you wouldn't mind?" Tom asked skeptically.

"I would mind it far less than marrying a poor man and living in a pokey little house with only two or three servants." Adelia had glanced over him coolly.

"You're rich and well-dressed, and you look as though you'll keep your hair. That sets you above most of my potential suitors."

Tom had realized that, like a peach, the soft bloom of her exterior concealed a hard, tough core—which made him like her all the better. They would have done well together.

It was an opportunity that wouldn't come again for a long time, if at all.

But he hadn't been able to bring himself to offer for her yet, because he couldn't stop longing for Lady Cassandra Ravenel. Damn her.

Perhaps he'd ruined waltzing for her, but she'd ruined far more than that for him.

For the first time in his life, Tom had actually forgotten something: what it was like to kiss other women. There was only the memory of Cassandra's sweet, yielding mouth, the lush curves of her body molding perfectly to his. Like a melody that kept repeating itself throughout a symphony, she was his *idée fixe*, haunting him whether dreaming or awake.

Everything inside demanded that he chase Cassandra, do whatever was necessary to win her. But if he succeeded, he would destroy everything that made her worth having.

Unable to resolve the paradox on his own, Tom decided to consult the known authority on such matters: Jane Austen. He bought a copy of *Persuasion* as Phoebe had recommended, hoping to find an answer about how to deal with his personal dilemma.

As Tom read the novel, he discovered to his relief that Miss Austen's writing wasn't florid or syrupy. To the contrary, her tone was dry, ironic, and sensible. Unfortunately, he couldn't stand the story or any of the characters. He would have hated the plot if he'd been able to find one, but it was only chapter after chapter of people talking.

The so-called heroine, Anne Elliot, who'd been persuaded by her family to end her engagement to Captain Wentworth, was appallingly passive and restrained. Wentworth, for his part, was understandably aloof.

Tom had to admit, however, that he'd felt a few moments of kinship with Anne, who had such trouble identifying and expressing her feelings. He understood that all too well.

And then he reached the part where Wentworth poured out his emotions in a love letter: *You pierce my soul. I am half agony, half hope.* For some reason, Tom had felt a genuine sense of relief when Anne discovered the letter and realized Wentworth still loved her. But how could Tom experience a real feeling about someone who'd never existed, and events that had never happened? The question left him puzzled and fascinated.

The deeper meaning of the novel, however, had remained a mystery. As far as Tom could tell, the point of *Persuasion* was never to let relatives interfere with one's engagement.

Soon, however, Tom found himself returning to

the bookshop and asking the bookseller for recommendations. He returned home with *Don Quixote*, *Les Misérables*, and *A Tale of Two Cities*, although he wasn't sure why he was compelled to read them. Maybe it was the sense they all contained clues to an elusive secret. Maybe if he read enough novels about the problems of fictional people, he might find some clue about how to solve his own.

"BAZZLE," TOM SAID absently as he read contracts at his desk, "stop that infernal scratching."

"Yes, sir," came the dutiful reply. The boy continued sweeping around the edge of the office with a broom and dustpan.

There was much about Bazzle that Tom had come to appreciate during the past few weeks. It wasn't that the boy was particularly intelligent—he was uneducated and knew only enough math to count small currency. Nor was Bazzle a handsome lad, with his short jaw and slum-pallor complexion. But the boy's character was solid gold, which was miraculous for anyone who'd come from dangerous and disease-ridden slums.

Life hadn't been kind to Bazzle, but he took each day as it was and maintained a sort of dogged cheerfulness that Tom liked. The boy was never late, sick, or dishonest. He wouldn't take so much as a crust of bread if he thought it belonged to someone else. More than once, Tom's assistant Barnaby had dashed off harum-scarum on some errand, and left the remains of his lunch—a half sandwich, or a hand pie, or a few scraps of bread and cheese—lying unwrapped on his desk. Tom found the habit supremely annoying, since uneaten food tended to attract vermin. He'd hated insects and rodents ever since his days working as a train boy, when the only room he'd been able to afford had been a freight yard shack crawling with pests.

"Have Barnaby's leftover lunch," Tom had told Bazzle, whose spindly frame needed some bolstering. "There's no use wasting it."

"Ain't a thief," the boy had replied, after a quick, hollow-eyed glance at the discarded food.

"It's not stealing if I tell you to take it."

"But it's Mr. Barnaby's."

"Barnaby's well aware that any food he leaves behind will be disposed of before he returns. He'd be the first to tell you to have it." At the boy's continuing hesitation, Tom had said curtly, "Either it goes into the rubbish bin or your innards, Bazzle. You decide."

The boy had proceeded to devour the hand pie so fast that Tom had feared it might come up again.

On another occasion, Tom had tried and failed to give Bazzle a cake of paper-wrapped soap from the cabinet of supplies near one of the building lavatories.

Bazzle had eyed the soap as if it were a dangerous substance. "Don't need it, sir."

"Emphatically, child, you do." As Tom saw the boy sniff beneath his arm, he added impatiently, "No one can detect their own odor, Bazzle. You can only take my word for it that with my eyes closed, I could easily mistake you for a dockside ass-cart."

The boy had still declined to touch it. "If I wash today, I'd be dirty again ter-morrer."

Tom had regarded him with a frown. "Do you *never* wash, Bazzle?"

The boy had shrugged. "I runs under the pump at a stable, or splashes meself from a trough."

"When was the last time?" After watching the boy struggle to come up with an answer, Tom had glanced heavenward. "Don't think so hard, you're about to sprain something."

After that, since Tom had been occupied with several projects, it had been easy to ignore the issue of Bazzle's hygiene.

This morning, however, after hearing another burst of furtive, furious scratching, Tom lifted his head and asked, "Bazzle, do you have a problem?"

"No, sir," the boy said reassuringly. "Just a few chats."

Tom froze, a hideous, creepy-crawly dread racing over him. "For God's sake, don't move."

Bazzle stood obligingly still, broom in hand, giving him a questioning stare.

After coming out from behind the desk, Tom went to inspect the child. "There's no such thing as 'a few chats,'" he said, gingerly nudging the boy's head this way and that, observing the small red bumps scattered over the skinny neck and hairline. As he expected, a wealth of telltale nits littered the woolly tangle of hair.

"Holy hell. If lice were people, your head would host the population of Southwark."

Befuddled, the boy repeated, "If lice was people . . . ?"

"Analogy," Tom said curtly. "A way of making a subject clearer by comparing one thing to another."

"Noffing's clear when ye say lice is people."

"Never mind. Set the broom against the wall and come with me." Tom passed a reception desk in the foyer and went to his assistant's office. "Barnaby, stop whatever it is you're doing. I have a task for you."

His assistant, who was in the middle of polishing his glasses with a handkerchief, peered owlishly around a tower of books, folios, maps, and plans. "Sir?"

"This boy is crawling with lice," Tom said. "I want you to take him to a public bath house and have him washed."

Looking aghast, Barnaby reflexively scratched his own luxuriant mass of lively brown curls. "They won't let him bathe if he has lice."

"Ain't going to no baff house," Bazzle said indignantly. "I'll take one of them soaps to a stable and wash meself there."

"No stable would allow you in," the assistant informed him. "Do you think they'd want their horses afflicted?"

"Find somewhere to have him washed," Tom told his assistant flatly.

Barnaby stood, jerked his waistcoat down over his stocky midsection, and squared his shoulders. "Mr. Severin," he said resolutely, "as you know, I've done many things that aren't listed among my job requirements, but this—"

"Your job requirements are whatever I say they are."

"Yes, but—" Barnaby paused to pick up a pleated file folder and shoo Bazzle away. "Boy, would you mind standing a bit farther away from my desk?"

"It's just a few chats," Bazzle protested. "Everybody 'as chats."

"I don't," Barnaby said, "and I'd like to keep it that way." His gaze returned to Tom. "Mr. Severin, I neglected to mention this earlier, but . . . I have to leave the office earlier than usual today. Now, as a matter of fact."

"Really," Tom said, his eyes narrowing. "Why?"

"It's my . . . grandmother. She has a fever. The ague. I have to go home to take care of her."

"Why can't your mother do it?" Tom asked.

Barnaby thought for a moment. "She has the ague too."

"Did she get it from a baff?" Bazzle asked suspiciously.

Tom sent his assistant a scathing glance. "Barnaby, do you know what lying has in common with bullfighting?"

"No, sir."

"If you can't do it well, it's better not to do it at all."

His assistant looked sheepish. "The truth is, Mr. Severin, I'm terrified of lice. Just hearing about them makes me itch all over. One time I had dandruff and thought it was lice, and I was so distraught, my mother had to mix me a sedative. I think my problem started when—"

"Barnaby," Tom interrupted curtly, "you're talking about your feelings. It's me, remember?"

"Oh, yes. Pardon, Mr. Severin."

"I'll deal with the boy. Meanwhile, arrange to have every room on this floor thoroughly cleaned, and every inch of carpeting sponged with benzene."

"Right away, sir."

Tom glanced at Bazzle. "Come," he said, and left the office.

"I won't bathe," the boy declared anxiously as he followed. "I quit!"

"I'm afraid anyone who works for me is required to give a fortnight's notice—in writing—before they're allowed to quit." Which was pushing the margins of his strict honesty policy, but Tom would make an exception for a boy who was being eaten alive by parasites.

"I'm illegitimate," the boy protested.

"What has that to do with it?"

"Means I can't write no notice."

"The word is 'illiterate,'" Tom said. "In which case, Bazzle, it appears you'll be working for me indefinitely."

THE BOY COMPLAINED and argued every step of the way as Tom took him to Cork Street. Most of the avenue was occupied by Winterborne's department store, with its marble façade and huge plate-glass windows filled with lavish displays. The store's famed central rotunda, with its dazzling stained-glass dome, glowed richly against the gray November sky.

They went to a much smaller and more inconspicuous building at the far end of the street. It was a medical clinic and surgery, established for the benefit of the thousand or so employees of Winterborne's.

Two years ago, Rhys Winterborne had hired Dr. Garrett Gibson to serve on the clinic's medical staff, despite people's suspicions that a woman wasn't suited for such a demanding profession. Garrett had dedicated herself to proving them wrong, and in a short time had distinguished herself as an unusually skilled and talented surgeon as well as physician. She was still regarded as something of a novelty, of course, but her reputation and practice had grown steadily.

As they approached the front doors of the clinic, the boy stopped and dug in his heels. "What's this?"

"A medical clinic."

"Don't need no sawbones," Bazzle said in alarm.

"Yes, I know. We're only here to use the facilities. Specifically, a shower bath." The clinic was the only place Tom could think of to take him. There would be tiled rooms, hot water, medicine, and disinfectants. Better yet, Garrett wouldn't dare turn them away in the light of the favor Tom had done for her husband.

"Wots a shower baff?" Bazzle asked.

"It's a small room with a curtain all around. Water comes down like rain from an overhead fixture."

"Rain won't scare off me chats," the boy informed him.

"A good scrubbing with borax soap will." Tom pushed open the doors and ushered the child inside. He kept a hand on Bazzle's shoulder, half suspecting the boy might bolt. Upon being approached by the waiting area receptionist, a brisk and businesslike matron, Tom said, "We need an appointment with Dr. Gibson."

"I'm afraid Dr. Gibson's schedule is full today. However, Dr. Havelock may have an opening, if you wish to wait."

"I'm too busy to wait," Tom said. "Tell Dr. Gibson I'm here, please."

"Your name, sir?"

"Tom Severin."

The receptionist's frown vanished, her eyes widening in something like awe. "Oh, *Mr. Severin*, welcome to the clinic! I very much enjoyed the market fair and fireworks display you put on for the public when your underground railway was opened."

Tom smiled at her. "I'm so glad." As he had intended, paying for the city-wide celebrations had not only enhanced his image, but had also dazzled people into overlooking the multitude of aggravations the railway construction project had caused.

"You've done so much for London," the woman continued. "What a public benefactor you are, Mr. Severin."

"You're too kind, Miss . . ."

"Mrs. Brown," she supplied, beaming. "Pardon, sir, I'll fetch Dr. Gibson right away."

As the woman hurried away, Bazzle looked up at Tom speculatively. "Are ye the most important man in London, sir?" he asked, scratching his head.

"No, that would be the editor-in-chief of *The Economist*. I'm lower down on the list, somewhere between the police commissioner and the prime minister."

"How do ye know who's above and below?"

"When two creatures meet in the jungle, they both have to decide which one of them would kill the other in a fight. The winner is the more important one."

"Analogy," Bazzle said.

That surprised a grin out of Tom. "Yes." The boy might be sharper than he'd originally thought.

Before another minute had passed, Garrett Gibson came to the waiting area. Her dark dress was topped with an impeccably white surgeon's smock, her chestnut-brown hair pulled back tightly in a neat braided coiffure. She was fresh-faced and smiling as she reached out to shake his hand as a man would. "Mr. Severin."

He grinned at her and returned the shake in a firm grip. "Dr. Garrett Gibson," he said, "this young fellow, Bazzle, is one of my employees. He's in need of your professional attention."

"Master Bazzle," Garrett murmured, inclining her head in a brief bow.

The boy regarded her in bewilderment, scratching the side of his head and neck.

"Bazzle," Tom said, "bow to the lady . . . like this."

The child obeyed halfheartedly, still staring at Garrett. "*She's* the sawbones?" he asked Tom skeptically.

"As of now, the only licensed female physician in England," Tom said.

Garrett smiled, her incisive gaze traveling over Bazzle as he scratched. "The reason for your visit has quickly become apparent." She glanced at Tom. "I'll have a nurse give you the necessary items and explain how to delouse him at home—"

"It has to be here," Tom interrupted. "He lives in a rookery, so it can't be done there."

"Why not at your house?" Garrett suggested.

"Good God, woman, I'm not bringing him past my front door."

"It's just a few chats," Bazzle protested. He smacked his palm on his forearm, adding, "Maybe a couple o' biddies too."

"Biddies?" Tom repeated, recoiling and brushing at his own sleeves reflexively. "You have fleas?"

Garrett looked sardonic. "Very well, I'll have a nurse see to him here. We have a tiled room with a shower bath and a sink, where he can be thoroughly—"

"No, I want you to do it, so I know it's been done properly."

"Me?" Her fine brows lowered. "I'm about to have lunch with my sister-in-law."

"This is an emergency," Tom told her. "The boy is suffering. *I'm* suffering." He paused. "What if I make a large donation to the charitable institution of your choice? Name the place, and I'll write a check before I leave."

"Mr. Severin," she said crisply, "you seem to think your money is a panacea for every problem."

"Not a panacea, a balm. A wonderful soothing balm, especially when applied in a heavy layer."

Before Garrett could reply, a new voice joined the conversation, coming from behind Tom.

"We can delay our lunch, Garrett, or have it another time. This is more important."

Gooseflesh rose all over Tom's body. With disbelief, he turned to find Lady Cassandra Ravenel standing behind him. She had just entered the clinic and approached the reception area, while a Ravenel footman waited beside the doorway.

Over the past few weeks, Tom had tried to convince himself that his memory of her had become embellished over time. Even his brain, accurate as it was, was capable of subtly altering his perception of the facts.

But Cassandra was even more breathtaking than he remembered. Her golden sunstruck beauty illuminated the sterile environment of the clinic. She was wonderfully dressed in a green velvet walking dress and a matching hooded cloak trimmed with white fur. Her hair, so shiny it looked molten, had been pinned up in a complex mass of coils and topped with a flirtatious little excuse for a hat. He felt her presence like a shock, every nerve tingling.

"My lady," Tom managed to say, grimly aware that he'd been caught at a disadvantage. He was embarrassed to have her see him there with a raggedy, scratching child in the middle of a workday, when he should have been busy with something dignified and businesslike. "I wasn't aware that you—I wouldn't deprive you of your lunch—" He broke off, cursing himself silently for sounding like a blithering idiot.

But there was no mockery or disapproval in Cassandra's gaze as she approached. She was smiling as if she were glad to see him. She gave him her slim gloved hand, a gesture of closeness and familiarity.

The day instantly became the best one he'd had in weeks. His heart thumped joyfully at her nearness. The shape of her hand fit his as if every joint and fine muscle and soft ligament had been designed for perfect alignment. It had been like this when they'd waltzed, their bodies fitting together, moving together, with magical coordination.

"How are you?" he asked, holding her hand a few extra seconds before letting go.

"Quite well, thank you." Her sparkling gaze fell to Bazzle. "Will you introduce me to your companion?"

"Lady Cassandra, this is—" Tom paused as the boy retreated behind him. "Bazzle, come around and bow to the lady."

The boy didn't budge.

Tom could well understand. He remembered how overwhelmed he'd been by his first glimpse of Cassandra's rich and luminous beauty. She was probably like nothing human Bazzle had ever seen before.

"Just as well," Tom said to Cassandra. "You should keep your distance from him."

"I 'as chats," came Bazzle's muffled voice from behind him.

"How very trying," Cassandra said sympathetically. "It could happen to anyone."

No response.

Cassandra continued speaking to Tom, although the words were clearly meant for the boy. "You've brought him to the right place, obviously. Dr. Gibson is a very nice lady, and knows just what to do about chats."

Bazzle leaned cautiously around Tom's side. "I been itchin' somefing awful," he said.

"Poor boy." Cassandra crouched to bring her face level with his, and smiled. "You'll feel much better soon." She tugged off her glove and extended her hand. "I'm Lady Cassandra. Will you shake hands, Bazzle?" Her gentle fingers closed around a small, grubby paw. "There . . . now we're friends."

Tom, who was terrified she was going to catch something from the walking plague that was Bazzle, turned to Garrett. "Should she be touching him?" he asked curtly. At the same time, his gaze pleaded and commanded *Do something.*

Garrett sighed and asked Cassandra, "Would you mind if we rescheduled lunch? I must attend to this boy, and I expect it will take a while."

"I'll stay and help," Cassandra offered, standing and continuing to smile down at the boy.

*"No,"* Tom said, inwardly appalled by the idea.

"That would be most appreciated," Garrett told Cassandra. "I'll start treating Bazzle, if you'll pop over to Winterborne's with Mr. Severin and help him select some ready-made boy's clothing. We'll have to dispose of the ones he's wearing."

"I don't need help," Tom said.

"Lady Cassandra is familiar with the layout of Winterborne's," Garrett told him, "and she'll know exactly what Bazzle needs. If you go alone, heaven knows how long you'll take."

Cassandra ran an assessing gaze over Bazzle's small form. "Children's sizing is labeled by age. I think seven to nine years would suffice."

"But I'm fourteen," Bazzle said sadly. When all three adults' gazes flew to his face, he gave them a gap-toothed grin, indicating it had been a joke. It was the first time Tom had ever seen him smile. The effect was endearing, although it revealed the urgent need for an application of tooth powder and a good brushing.

Garrett laughed. "Come, young rascal, let's dispose of your uninvited guests."

"THERE'S NO NEED for you to accompany me," Tom muttered as he and Cassandra went through the ready-made clothing department at Winterborne's. "I'm perfectly capable of asking a sales clerk to find clothes for Bazzle."

Tom knew he was being a surly ass, when he should have been making the most of the opportunity by trying to charm her. But this situation was *not* something he wanted Cassandra to associate him with.

The last time they had been together, they'd waltzed in a winter garden. Now, they were de-lousing a pestilent street urchin.

It wasn't exactly progress.

Moreover, it would make Tom look even worse in comparison to the well-bred gentlemen who were undoubtedly pursuing her.

Not that he was competing for her. But a man had pride.

"I'm delighted to help," Cassandra assured him with annoying cheerfulness. She stopped at a table with goods displayed for browsing, sorting through stacks of little folded things. "May I ask how you came to meet Bazzle?"

"He was collecting cigar stubs from the gutter outside my building. The wind blew my hat from my head, and he brought it to me instead of running off with it. I hired him to sweep and dust my offices."

"And now you're taking care of him," she exclaimed, beaming.

"Don't make too much of it," Tom muttered.

"You took valuable time out of your workday to bring him to the doctor yourself," she pointed out.

"Only because my assistant refused to do it. I'm merely trying to minimize the amount of vermin in my workplace."

"No matter what you say, you're helping a child who needs it, and I think it's splendid."

As Tom followed her through the clothing department, he had to admit Cassandra knew what she was doing. She went briskly past counters and shelves, addressed store clerks by name, and located what she wanted without hesitation.

"You shop very efficiently," he said begrudgingly.

"Practice," came her airy reply.

She selected a pair of trousers, a cotton shirt, a gray wool broadcloth jacket, thick knit stockings, a wool cap and a muffler. A pair of sturdy leather shoes was added to the pile, after Cassandra estimated the size and decided to err on the side of larger rather than smaller.

"Miss Clark, would you wrap these immediately, please?" she asked a sales clerk. "We're rather pressed for time."

"Right away, Lady Cassandra!" the young woman replied.

While the sales clerk listed the items on a sales slip and totaled them, Cassandra glanced regretfully at the entrance to the stairwell. "The toy department is right beneath us," she told Tom. "I wish we had time to buy a toy for him."

"He doesn't need toys," Tom said.

"Every child needs toys."

"Bazzle lives in a St. Giles rookery. Any toy you gave him would be stolen immediately."

Cassandra's good cheer deflated like a cooling soufflé. "He has no family to look after his belongings?"

"He's an orphan. He lives with a gang of children and a man they call Uncle Batty."

"You're aware of this, and yet you allow him to go back?"

"He's better off there than in a workhouse or orphanage."

She nodded, looking perturbed.

Tom decided to change the subject. "How has your Season gone so far?"

Cassandra smoothed her expression, following his lead. "I miss the sun," she said lightly. "I've been keeping the hours of a hedgehog. Dinners never start before nine o'clock in the evening, receptions never before ten, and dances routinely begin at eleven. Then I go home at dawn, sleep for most of the day and wake up all muddled."

"Have you set your sights on anyone?"

Her smile didn't reach her eyes. "They're all the same. Just like last year."

Tom tried to feel badly about that. But he couldn't help feeling a primal pang of relief, his heartbeat settling into a satisfied rhythm . . . *Still mine . . . still mine.*

They returned to the clinic with the parcel from Winterborne's. A nurse showed him into a white tiled room with a shower bath, a steel-clad bathtub and sink, steel tables and supply cabinets, and a drain in the floor. The acrid bite of disinfectant hung in the air, along with the unmistakable scents of borax and carbolic soap. Bazzle was leaning over a sink in the corner, while Garrett rinsed his head with a spray nozzle and rubber hose attached to the faucet.

"I've doused Bazzle's scalp with a chemical solution," Garrett said, blotting the child's head with a towel. "I'll need help cutting his hair: I'm afraid it's not one of my skills."

"I can do it," Cassandra volunteered.

Garrett nodded toward a supply cabinet. "Smocks, aprons and rubber gloves are over there. Use any of the scissors from the tray, but be careful: they're all extremely sharp."

"How short do you want the hair?"

"About an inch in length should do."

Bazzle's plaintive voice came from the towel. "I don't want noffin' cut orf."

"I know this isn't a pleasant process," Garrett told the boy apologetically, "but you've been very well-behaved, and that helps things go much faster." She lifted Bazzle onto a metal stool, while Cassandra donned a long white apron.

As Cassandra approached Bazzle and saw his features scrunched in worry, she smiled and reached out to gently push some matted locks back from his forehead. "I'll be very careful," she promised. "Would you like to hear a song while I cut your hair? There's one my sister Pandora and I wrote, called *Pig in the House*."

Looking intrigued, Bazzle nodded.

Cassandra launched into a sublimely ridiculous song about the antics of two sisters trying to hide their pet pig from the farmer, the butcher, the cook, and a local squire who was especially fond of bacon. While she sang, she moved around Bazzle's head, snipping off long locks and dropping them into a pail Garrett held for her.

Bazzle listened as if spellbound, occasionally chortling at the silly lyrics. As soon as the song was finished, he demanded another, and sat still while Cassandra continued with *My Dog Thinks He's a Chicken,* followed by *Why Frogs are Slimy and Toads are Dry.*

Had Tom been capable of falling in love, he would have right there and then, as he watched Lady Cassandra Ravenel serenade a ragamuffin while cutting his hair. She was so capable and clever and adorable, it made his chest ache with a hot pressure that threatened to fracture something.

"She has a marvelous way with children," Garrett murmured to him at one point, clearly delighted by the situation.

She had a way with everyone. Especially him. He'd never been besotted like this.

It was intolerable.

After Cassandra had finished combing and trimming Bazzle's hair, she stood back to view the results critically. "What do you think?" she asked.

"Perfect," Garrett exclaimed.

"Good God," Tom said. "There was a boy beneath all that wool."

The mass of snarled, straggly locks had been cropped

to reveal a nicely shaped head, a skinny neck, and a pair of small ears. Bazzle's eyes looked twice as large now that they weren't peering out through thick wads of hair.

Bazzle heaved a world-weary sigh. "Wots next?" he asked.

"The shower-bath," Garrett replied. "I'll help you wash."

"*Wot?*" The boy looked outraged by the suggestion. "Ye can't 'elp me."

"Why not?"

"Yer a girl!" He shot an indignant glance at Tom. "I'd never let a girl see me tallywag."

"I'm a doctor, Bazzle," Garrett said gently, "not a girl."

"She 'as bubbies," Bazzle told Tom, with the impatience of someone having to explain an obvious fact. "That makes 'er a girl."

Tom struggled to hold back a grin as he saw Garrett's expression. "I'll help him," he said, and stripped off his coat.

"I'll start the water," Garrett said, and went to the other side of the room.

After removing his waistcoat, Tom looked for a place to set his clothes.

"Give them to me," Cassandra said, coming forward.

"Thank you." He handed the garments to her, and began to unknot his necktie. "Wait—take this too."

Cassandra's eyes widened as he began on his shirt cuffs. "How much more clothing do you plan to remove?" she asked uneasily.

Tom grinned, not missing the quick, interested flick of her gaze over him. "I'm only rolling up my sleeves." He paused, his hands going to the top button of his collar. "Although if you insist—"

"No," she said quickly, blushing at his teasing. "That's quite enough."

A warm mist had started to spread through the room, sweating the white tiles. Cassandra's skin was turning luminous from the humid air. Little wisps of hair at her forehead had drawn up into delicate curls he longed to play with.

Instead, he turned his attention to Bazzle, who wore the expression of a prisoner confronting the gallows. "Go undress behind that curtain, Bazzle."

Reluctantly the boy went to stand just inside the rubber-lined curtain, and began to remove his clothing piece by piece. Following Garrett's instructions, Tom took each ragged garment and dropped it into a lidded pail partially filled with carbolic solution.

Bazzle's pale, spindly body was startling in its frailty. Tom registered the sight with a stab of some unfamiliar feeling . . . guilt? . . . concern? . . . As the boy stepped into the falling water, Tom pulled the circular curtain completely closed.

The boy's exclamation echoed in the tiled room. "Blarm me, it *is* like rain!"

Tom took a bath brush from Garrett, rubbed the bristles into a cake of soap, and handed it through the curtain opening. "Start scrubbing your little carcass with this. I'll do the places you can't reach."

After a moment, Bazzle's worried voice came from behind the curtain. "Me skin's comin' orf."

"It's not skin," Tom said. "Keep washing."

Not ten seconds had passed before Bazzle said, "I'm done now."

"You've barely begun," Tom replied in exasperation. As Bazzle tried to climb out of the shower bath, he herded him back inside and took up the brush. "You're filthy, Bazzle. You need to be scrubbed, if not descaled."

"I'll be dirty again ter-morrer," the boy protested, spluttering and staring up at him miserably.

"Yes, you've said that before. But a man keeps himself clean, Bazzle." Tom clamped his hand on a slippery, bony shoulder and scrubbed the child's back in gentle but steady circles. "First, because it's good for your health. Second, it's a mercy to those who have to be in your proximity. Third, ladies don't like it when you look and smell like last year's corpse. I know you don't care about that now, but someday—confound it, Bazzle, hold still." Exasperated, Tom called through the curtain, "Cassandra, do you know a washing song?"

Instantly she began one called *Some Ducks Don't Like Puddles*. To Tom's relief, Bazzle subsided.

After scrubbing and rinsing the child three times, Tom washed his hair with borax shampoo paste until the dark locks were squeaky clean. By the time they were done, Tom's entire front was wet, and his own hair was dripping. He wrapped Bazzle's now pink and white body in a length of dry toweling, picked him up, and carried him to the stool.

"I feel as if I've just wrestled a barrel of monkeys," Tom said, breathing with exertion.

Garrett laughed as she used a towel to dry Bazzle's hair. "Well done, Mr. Severin."

"What about me?" Bazzle protested. "I was the monkey!"

"Well done, you," Garrett told him. "Now, you must be patient just a bit longer, while I run a nit comb through your hair."

"I will donate an extra thousand pounds to the charitable cause of your choice," Tom told Garrett, "if you'll brush his teeth as well."

"Done."

Tom turned away and ran his hands through his hair, and shook his head like a wet dog.

"Wait," he heard Cassandra say, amusement shimmering in her voice. She hurried over to him with some fresh dry toweling.

"Thank you." Tom took a towel and rubbed it roughly over his hair.

"My goodness, you're nearly as wet as Bazzle." Cassandra used another towel to dab at his face and throat. Smiling, she reached up to smooth the damp chaos of his hair with her fingers.

Tom stood still while she fussed over him. Part of him wanted to bask in the little attentions, which felt almost . . . wifely. But the ache in his chest had worsened, and his body was steaming in the wet clothes, and he began to feel not altogether civilized.

He glanced over her head at Garrett, who faced away from them, meticulously combing Bazzle's hair.

His gaze returned to Cassandra's face, which would haunt him to the last minute of life. He had collected every smile of hers, every kiss, to hoard like a treasure chest of jewels. These few seconds with her were all he had, or would ever have.

Swiftly he bent and pressed his mouth to hers, gentle but urgent. There was no time for patience.

Her breath caught. Her lips parted tentatively.

He kissed her for all the midnights and mornings they would never share. He kissed her with a tenderness he would never be able to express in words, and felt her response in his blood, as if her sweetness had sunk into his marrow. His mouth pulled softly at hers, taking one last fervent taste . . . then slid away.

The skin of her cheeks was damp and sweet, as if she'd just come in from the rain. He brushed her closed eyelids with his lips, the surfaces fragile and silky, the sweeps of her eyelashes like feather dusters.

Blindly he let go of her and turned away, pacing aimlessly until he saw his coat and waistcoat draped over a steel table. He dressed without a word, and struggled to regain his self-discipline.

As the passionate longing cooled, it hardened into bitterness.

He'd been taken apart by her and reassembled differently. Outwardly, everything seemed to work well enough, but he wasn't the same inside. Only time would tell the ways in which she'd changed him. But he was fairly certain he wasn't the better for it.

He forced his mind back to what it should be focusing on: Business. Recalling he had a meeting to attend that afternoon—and would first have to go home to change into dry clothes—he glanced at his pocket watch and frowned. "My time is short," he told Garrett brusquely. "Can you comb any faster?"

"Ask me that again," Garrett replied equably, "and this comb will soon be lodged in a place it wasn't meant to go."

Bazzle snickered, evidently gathering her meaning.

Shoving his hands in his pockets, Tom wandered around the room. He didn't spare a glance at Cassandra.

"I suppose I should be going now," he heard her say uncertainly.

"You've been an angel," Garrett told her. "Shall we try again for lunch tomorrow?"

"Yes, let's." Cassandra went to Bazzle, who was still perched on the stool. She smiled into his face, which was nearly level with hers. "It was a pleasure to meet you, Bazzle. You're a good boy, and a handsome one, too."

"Good-bye," Bazzle whispered, staring at her with huge, dark eyes.

"I'll see you out," Tom said gruffly.

Cassandra was quiet until they had left the tiled room and closed the door. "Tom," she ventured as they headed to the reception area, "what are you going to do about Bazzle?"

"I'm going to send him home to St. Giles," Tom replied in a matter-of-fact tone.

"If you send him back, he'll soon become as infested as before."

"What do you want me to do?" he asked curtly.

"Take him in as a ward, perhaps."

"There are thousands of children out there, in his situation or worse. How many bloody orphans do you think I should take in?"

"Just one. Just Bazzle."

"Why don't you take him?"

"I'm in no position to do so. I don't yet have my own household, nor will I have access to my dowry until I marry. You have the means and ability to help him, and you and he are—" Cassandra broke off, evidently thinking better of what she'd been about to say.

But Tom knew. And he became more offended with each passing moment. He stopped with her in the hallway, just before they reached the front waiting area. "Would you make the same suggestion to one of your upper-class suitors?" he asked brusquely.

Cassandra appeared bewildered. "Would I . . . you mean . . . to take in a child as a ward? Yes, I—"

"No, not *a* child. *This* child. This skinny, flea-bitten, illiterate child with a cockney accent. Would you ask Lord Foxhall to take him in and raise him?"

Taken aback by the question, and the signs of his temper, she blinked rapidly. "What does Lord Foxhall have to do with this?"

"Answer the question."

"I don't know."

"The answer is no," Tom said tautly, "you wouldn't. But you suggested it to me. Why?"

"You and Bazzle have similar backgrounds." She stared at him in confusion. "You're in a position to understand and help him more than anyone else could. I thought you would have sympathy for him."

"Sympathy's not one of my feelings," Tom snapped. "And I have a name, damn it. It's not a noble name, but I'm not a bastard, and I was never filthy. Regardless of what you think, Bazzle and I aren't cut from the same cloth."

Cassandra digested that in the pause that followed, and her brows rushed down as she seemed to reach a conclusion. "You do have some things in common with Bazzle," she said quietly. "I think he must remind you of things you'd rather not think about, and it makes you uncomfortable. But none of that has anything to do with me. *Don't* try to make me out to be some kind of snob. I've never said you weren't good enough for me—Heaven knows I've never thought it! The circumstances of your birth, or mine, are not the problem. *This* is the problem." Glaring at him, she smacked her hand on the center of his chest and kept it there. "Your heart is frozen because you want it to be. It's safer for you that way, never to let anyone in. So be it." She drew her hand away. "I intend to find someone I can be happy with. As for poor little Bazzle . . . he needs more than your occasional off-hand kindness. He needs a home. Since I can't give him one, I'll have to leave his fate to your conscience."

She strode away from him, toward the footman waiting near the doorway.

And later that day, Tom—who had no conscience— sent the boy back to St. Giles.

*Chapter 11*

ALTHOUGH THE AUTUMN SOCIAL calendar didn't offer events of the same magnitude as the Season proper, there was still a lively array of dinners and parties attended by gentlemen about town. Lady Berwick had set out a strategy of starting early, so Cassandra was able to meet the most promising new bachelors while many of the other girls were still at their families' estates during autumn shooting.

The Season seemed very different this year, now that Pandora was no longer taking part. Without her twin's companionship and impish humor, the constant rounds of dinners, soirees and balls had already begun to feel like drudgery to Cassandra. When she said as much to Devon and Kathleen, they had been understanding and sympathetic.

"This process of husband hunting seems unnatural to me," Devon had commented. "You're thrown into proximity with a limited selection of men, and chaperoned too closely to allow for any genuine interactions. Then after a fixed period of time, you're expected to choose one of them as a partner for life."

Kathleen had poured more tea with undue concentration. "The process has its pitfalls," she had agreed, her expression pensive.

Cassandra had known exactly what Kathleen was thinking about.

It seemed a lifetime ago that Kathleen had married Cassandra's brother, Theo, following a whirlwind courtship. Tragically, Theo had died in a riding accident a few days after the wedding. In that short amount of time, however, Kathleen had discovered there was another side to the charming young man who'd courted her so gallantly during the Season. A volatile and abusive side.

Devon had leaned over to press a nuzzling kiss among the soft red curls of his wife's coiffure. "No one in this family will ever be left to the mercy of someone who doesn't treat them well," he said quietly. "I'd fight to the death for every last one of you."

Kathleen had turned her face to smile at him tenderly, her fingers coming up to stroke his lean cheek. "I know you would, darling."

Privately Cassandra had wondered if she would ever find a man who'd be willing to sacrifice himself for her. Not that she would ever want him to, of course. But something in her longed to be loved and needed that intensely.

The problem was, she had started to feel a tiny bit desperate. And desperation might eventually cause her to chase after love as if she were participating in the greased pig race at the county fair.

*"There's only one sure way to catch a greased pig,"* West had once commented. *"Give him a reason to come to you."*

If she wanted love, therefore, she would have to be patient, calm, and kind. She would have to let it find her in its own way and time.

Since *Love is a greased pig* wasn't a particularly dignified motto, she decided the Latin translation was more elegant: *Amor est uncta porcus.*

"WHAT ABOUT MR. SEDGWICK?" Cassandra asked Lady Berwick sotto voce, at the last dance in October. The lavish and crowded event, given to mark the coming out of the Duke of Queensberry's niece, Miss Percy, was held at a grand house in Mayfair.

"I'm afraid his credentials are lacking," the older woman replied. "It would not do to encourage his attentions."

"But at least he's dancing," Cassandra protested in a whisper. "Hardly any of the other eligible men are."

"It's a disgrace," Lady Berwick said grimly. "I intend to speak to the other London hostesses about these scoundrels, and ensure they are denied invitations from now on."

Lately it had become the habit of fashionable bachelors to loiter in the doorways and corners, putting on superior airs and declining to dance. Instead, they headed for the supper room as soon as the doors were opened, indulged themselves with fine food and wine, then proceeded to another ball or soirée and did the same thing over again. Meanwhile, there were rows of girls who had no one to dance with other than married gentlemen or boys.

"Arrogant peacocks," Cassandra said wryly, her gaze traveling over the clusters of privileged young males. A particularly handsome specimen, slim and golden-haired, lounged near an arrangement of potted palms. He had an air of swaggering even while standing still. As he glanced at a group of disconsolate wallflowers in the corner, his lips quirked with amused disdain.

Lady Berwick recaptured her attention. "I was told Mr. Huntingdon will attend tonight. When he arrives, you must ingratiate yourself further with him. He's due to inherit an earldom from his uncle, who is gravely ill and will not last the year."

Cassandra frowned. She'd met Mr. Huntington on two previous occasions, and he'd struck her as pleasant but slow-witted. "I'm afraid he won't do for me, ma'am."

"Won't do? The earldom was created by Queen Mary in 1565. One would be hard-pressed to find a more ancient dignity. Do you object to being the mistress of a glorious country estate? To belonging in the very best social circles?"

"No, my lady."

"Then what is the problem?"

"He's stodgy and dull. It's no fun talking to him—"

"One has friends for conversations, not husbands."

"—and that chinstrap beard is dreadful. A man should either shave or grow a proper beard. Anything in between looks accidental."

Lady Berwick looked stern. "A girl in her second Season cannot afford to be particular, Cassandra."

Cassandra sighed and nodded, wondering when the supper room would be opened.

Following her gaze, Lady Berwick said quietly, "No dashing off to fill your plate when they ring the bell. I can see the beginnings of a bulge on your upper back, at the top of your corset. You may indulge your appetite after you are wed, but not before."

Shamed, Cassandra wanted to protest that she was hardly a glutton. It was just that Pandora was no longer there to keep her busy, and it was difficult to shed pounds while attending endless rounds of dinners and soirées, and having to sleep all day. If only she'd looked at her back view before leaving the house that night. Was there really a bulge?

Her mind went blank as she saw a tall, dark form enter the ballroom. It was Tom Severin, escorting a slender dark-haired woman, whose arm was firmly tucked in his. Cassandra had a sinking, sick feeling in her stomach. She'd never seen Tom at one of these events before, and she could only assume he was courting the woman.

"Oh, there's Mr. Severin," she said casually, while poisonous jealousy flooded her. "Who is he with?"

Lady Berwick glanced at the couple. "Miss Adelia Howard. One of Lord Beaumont's daughters. The family's financial difficulties must be dire indeed, if they're willing to sacrifice her to a social nobody."

Cassandra stopped breathing for a moment. "Are they engaged to marry?" she managed to ask.

"Not yet, as far as I'm aware. No announcements have been made, nor banns posted. If he's escorting her publicly, however, it won't be long in coming."

Trying to calm herself, Cassandra nodded. "Mr. Severin's not a nobody," she dared to say. "He's a very important man."

"Among his kind," Lady Berwick allowed. Her eyes narrowed as she assessed the couple, who had joined a group of guests in conversation. "Socially ill-matched though he and Miss Howard are, one can't deny they're a striking pair."

They were, Cassandra thought miserably. Both tall, slim and dark-haired, wearing identical expressions of cool reserve.

Tom flexed his shoulders, as if against a sudden tightness, and glanced around the room. He caught sight of Cassandra and stared at her, seemingly riveted, until she looked away. She clenched her trembling hands in her lap, and tried to think of an excuse to leave the dance early. It had been a week since she'd encountered him at Garrett Gibson's clinic, and she'd been melancholy and frustrated ever since. No, she couldn't leave—that would be cowardly, and it might make the evening easier for him, which she wasn't about to do. She would stay and ignore him, and give every appearance of having a wonderful time.

Across the room, the young golden-haired man was fiddling with his left cuff. It appeared to have come loose beneath his jacket sleeve, and he couldn't fasten it. The cuff link was either broken or missing. She watched him discreetly, her attention diverted by his small dilemma.

On impulse, she decided to do something about it. "Ma'am," she whispered to Lady Berwick, "I have to visit the necessary."

"I will accompany you—" the older woman began, but paused at the approach of a pair of longtime friends. "Oh, here are Mrs. Hayes and Lady Falmouth."

"I'll be quick," Cassandra assured her, and slipped away before Lady Berwick could reply.

She left through one of the open arches and went along a side hallway, before stealing back into the ballroom behind the screen of potted palms. Reaching into the concealed pocket of her dress, she took out a tiny wooden needle case. She'd carried it ever since a dance last year, when a nearsighted old gentleman had stepped on the hem of her skirts and torn a ruffle.

After extracting a safety pin, she screwed on the top of the needle case and returned it to her pocket. Drawing close behind the golden-haired bachelor, she said quietly, "Don't turn around. Put your left hand behind your back."

The man went very still.

Cassandra waited with great interest to see what he would do. A smile crossed her face as he obeyed slowly. Brushing aside a few palm fronds, she grasped the edges of the loose cuff and lined up the empty cuff link holes.

The man turned his head to the side to murmur, "What are you doing?"

"I'm pinning your cuff so it doesn't flap around your wrist. Not that you deserve my help. Hold still." Deftly she opened the safety pin and speared it through a pinch of fabric.

"Why do you say I don't deserve help?" she heard him ask.

Cassandra replied in a dry tone. "It may have something to do with the way you and the other bachelors stand about preening. Why attend a ball if you're not going to dance with anyone?"

"I was waiting to find someone worth asking."

Annoyed, she informed him, "Every girl in this room is worth asking. You and the other young men weren't invited to please yourselves, you're here to serve as dance partners."

"Will you?"

"Will I what?"

"Dance with me."

Cassandra let out a nonplussed laugh. "With a man who thinks so highly of himself? No, thank you." She closed the safety pin and tugged his coat sleeve down to conceal it.

"Who are you?" he asked. When she didn't reply, he begged, "*Please* dance with me."

She took a moment to consider it. "First, dance with some of those girls in the corner. Then you may ask me."

"But they're wallflowers."

"It's not nice to call them that."

"But that's what they are."

"Very well," Cassandra said briskly. "Good-bye."

"No, *wait.*" A long pause. "How many of them must I dance with?"

"I'll let you know when it's been enough. Also, don't be condescending when you ask them. Be charming, if at all possible."

"I am charming," he protested. "You have the wrong impression of me."

"We'll see." Cassandra began to draw back, but he turned to catch her by the wrist.

He nudged a palm leaf to the side, his breath catching as they came face-to-face.

At this close distance, she saw that he was no older than she was. He had hazel eyes and a complexion as smooth as biscuit porcelain, except for a few speckles of recently healed acne on his forehead. The handsome face beneath the perfectly trimmed waves of blond hair was that of someone who had yet to experience hardship or loss. Someone with the assurance that all his mistakes would be smoothed over before he ever had to face the consequences.

"God," he breathed. "You're beautiful."

Cassandra gave him a reproving glance. "Unhand me, please," she said mildly.

He let go of her immediately. "I saw you across the room earlier—I was planning to introduce myself."

"Thank goodness," she said. "I was on tenterhooks, wondering if you would."

As he heard the delicate note of sarcasm in her voice, a dumbfounded expression crossed his face. "Don't you know who I am?"

It took all Cassandra's force of will to hold back a laugh. "I'm afraid not. But everyone else here thinks you're a man who talks to potted plants." She turned and strode away.

As soon as she reached Lady Berwick's side, she was promptly approached by Mr. Huntingdon, who had secured the next place on her dance card. Fixing a cheerful smile on her face, Cassandra accompanied him to the main floor. They danced to a Chopin waltz, and then she was claimed by the next gentleman on her dance card, and the next. She went from one pair of arms to another, laughing and flirting.

It was nothing short of grueling.

She was aware of Tom's presence the entire time. And all the while, she was painfully aware that none of this was remotely comparable to that evening in the Clare winter garden, when Tom had waltzed her through shadows and moonlight as if on midnight wings. She'd never experienced that kind of ease, almost a rapture of movement, before or since. Her body still remembered the touch of his hands, so capable and gentle, guiding her without push or pull. So effortless.

She was trying so hard to feel something, *anything*, for any of these nice, eligible men. But she couldn't.

It was all his fault.

When she finally reached a blank space on her dance card, Cassandra turned down further invitations, pleading temporary fatigue. She returned to Lady Berwick's side for a moment's respite. As she fanned her hot face and neck, she saw that her chaperone's attention was focused on someone in the midst of the crowd.

"Who are you looking at, ma'am?" she asked.

"I've been observing Lord Lambert," Lady Berwick replied. "One of the bachelors I complained about earlier."

"Which one is he?"

"The fair-haired gentleman who just finished a waltz with shy little Miss Conran. I wonder what inspired him to ask her."

"I can't imagine."

The older woman sent her a sardonic glance. "Could it be something you said to him while standing behind the palms?"

Cassandra's eyes widened, and a guilty blush swept over her face.

Lady Berwick looked slightly smug. "I may be old, child, but I'm not blind. You went in the opposite direction of the privy."

"I only offered to pin the loose cuff on his sleeve," Cassandra explained hastily. "His cuff link was missing."

"Far too bold," her chaperone pronounced. One steel-colored brow arched. "What did you say to him?"

Cassandra related the conversation, and to her relief, Lady Berwick seemed amused rather than disapproving.

"He's coming this way now," the older woman said. "I will overlook your little fishing expedition, as it seems to have done the trick."

Cassandra ducked her head to hide a grin. "It wasn't a fishing expedition. I was merely curious about him," she admitted.

"As the heir to the Marquis of Ripon, Lord Lambert is highly eligible. The family is well-connected and respectable, and their ancestral estate boasts one of the best grouse moors in England. They're under pressure of debt, as everyone in good society is these days, and therefore the marquis would be gratified for his son to marry a girl with a dowry such as yours."

"Lord Lambert is younger than I would prefer," Cassandra said.

"That isn't necessarily a detraction. For women in our position, the only important choice in life we're allowed to make is what man will govern us. It's easier to maintain the upper hand with a young husband than one who is already set in his ways."

"Ma'am, forgive me, but that's a dreadful way of putting it."

Lady Berwick smiled with a touch of grim amusement. "The truth usually is dreadful." She seemed to want to say more, but at that moment Lambert reached them and introduced himself with a smart bow.

"Roland, Lord Lambert, at your service."

Roland. It suited him perfectly, a name for a fairy-tale prince or an intrepid knight on a quest. He was a few inches taller than she, his build slim and taut. Despite the practiced bow and the confidence of his posture, there was something a bit puppyish about the way he looked at her, an expectation of reward after having successfully performed a trick.

After Lady Berwick had introduced Cassandra, and pleasantries were exchanged, Lambert asked, "May I have the pleasure of the next dance?"

Cassandra hesitated before responding.

The appalling truth was, she didn't especially care whether she danced with him or not. Why was it so difficult to work up any interest in this young man and his fresh-from-a-bandbox handsomeness? Maybe it was the air of entitlement that clung to him like strong cologne. Maybe it was the sense that it didn't matter whether she ended up with Lambert, or Huntingdon and his chinstrap beard, or any of the other bachelors here. None of them stirred her. Certainly none of them struck her as someone she would like to be governed by.

But the flash of uncertainty in Lambert's hazel eyes caused her to soften. *Be fair to him,* she told herself. *Be kind and give him a chance.*

Smiling with as much warmth as she could manufacture, she placed a light hand on his arm. "I would love to," she said, and let him lead her toward the center of the room.

"I did my penance," Lord Lambert remarked. "In

fact, I chose the plainest girls in the row to dance with."

"How nice for them," Cassandra replied, and winced inwardly as she heard how waspish that sounded. "I'm sorry," she said before he could reply. "I'm not usually so sharp-tongued."

"It's all right," Lambert assured her immediately. "I would expect it of a woman who looks like you."

She blinked in surprise. "What?"

"I meant that as a compliment," he said in a rush. "That is . . . when a woman is as beautiful as you . . . there's no need for you to be . . ."

"Pleasant? Polite?"

His lips parted in dismay, a flush rising in his fair complexion.

Cassandra shook her head and laughed suddenly. "Are we going to dance, my lord, or simply stand here insulting each other?"

Lambert looked relieved. "We should dance," he said, and drew her into a waltz.

"Look at that," one of the gentlemen in Tom's group marveled. "A golden couple." Tom followed his gaze to the center of the ballroom, where Cassandra waltzed with an exceptionally handsome blond man. Even without knowing who the man was, Tom had no doubt he was of noble birth. He looked like the result of generations of selective breeding, producing more refinement and quality until finally the ideal specimen had been achieved.

"Lambert and Lady Cassandra," someone else in the group, Mr. George Russell, commented. Dryly he added, "The pairing is too perfect. They ought never to be separated."

Tom looked at him alertly, recognizing the name. Lambert's father was the Marquis of Ripon, one of the more corrupt dealmakers in the House of Lords, with heavy investments in the railway business.

"The lady is selective, however," Russell continued. "Five proposals last season, as I heard, and she turned them all down flat. Lambert may have no better luck."

"A belle like that may be as selective as she pleases," someone else said.

Adelia spoke then, her voice like musical notes flagged with razors. "She's what you all want," she laughingly accused the gentlemen in the group. "Men may profess their yearning to find a modest and sensible girl to marry. But none of you can resist chasing after a golden-haired flirt with a well-endowed figure, all dimples and giggles—without giving a passing thought to how empty-headed she might be."

"Guilty as charged," one of the men admitted, and they all chuckled.

"She's not empty-headed," Tom said, unable to keep silent.

Adelia gave him a piercing glance, her smile firmly fixed. "I forgot—you're acquainted with the family. Don't say Lady Cassandra is a secret intellectual? An unacknowledged genius of our modern times?"

Another round of chuckles, this time more subdued.

"She's highly intelligent," Tom replied coolly, "and quick-witted. She's also extraordinarily kind. I've never heard her speak ill of anyone."

Adelia flushed at the subtle rebuke. "Perhaps you should court her," she said lightly. "If you think she'd have you."

"Let's give her credit for more discernment than that," Tom said, and the group laughed.

He danced with Adelia after that, and dutifully acted as her escort until the end of the evening, and they both pretended the exchange hadn't happened. But beneath the surface, they were both aware that any possibility of courtship had been sliced to ribbons with a few sharp words.

FOR THE REST of that evening and over the course of the next month, Lambert nearly drowned Cassandra in the deluge of his attentions. He was present at every social event she attended, and called frequently at Ravenel House, and sent extravagant flower arrangements and sweets in gilded tins. People began to remark on the increasing familiarity between them, and made small jokes about what a pretty pair they were. Cassandra went along with all of it because there seemed to be no good reason not to.

Roland, Lord Lambert, was everything she should want, or very nearly so. She didn't have any significant objection to him, only a number of small ones that would have sounded rather petty if she'd expressed them out loud. The way he had referred to himself as a member of the "ruling class," for example, and said he expected to turn his attentions to diplomacy someday—even though he didn't have any qualifications for managing international relations.

To be fair, there were many things to like about Lord Lambert: He was educated and well-spoken, and had entertaining stories to tell about his experiences on his Grand Tour of last year. He was also capable of warmth and affection, as he'd demonstrated while telling her about his mother passing away three years ago. She liked how tenderly he spoke of his mother, and how fond he seemed of his two sisters. He described his father, the Marquis of Ripon, as stern but not unkind, a father who had always wanted the best for him.

Lambert belonged to what was called "high-toned" society, in which gentlemen had the bluest blood, the whitest waistcoats, and the most upturned noses. The intricate rules of the upper class were as natural to him as breathing. If she married him, they would stay in town for the Season, and spend the rest of the year at the estate in Northumberland, with all that beautiful unspoiled moorland bordering Scotland. It would be terribly far from her family, but there was the train, which would shorten the travel time considerably. There would be busy mornings and quiet evenings. The familiar rhythms of country life—plowing, planting, the seasonal harvests—would shape her days.

There would be marital intimacy, of course. She wasn't sure how she felt about that. When she'd let Lord Lambert steal a kiss after a carriage drive one afternoon, the pressure of his lips had been so enthusiastic—forceful, even—that there had been no room left for her to respond. But no matter how that part of their relationship turned out, there would be compensations. Children, in particular.

"Marriage first and love afterward," she had told Pandora during a private conversation. "Many people do it in that order. I suppose I'll be one of them."

Looking troubled, Pandora had asked, "Do you feel *any* attraction to Lord Lambert? Butterflies swirling inside?"

"No, but . . . I do like his looks . . ."

"It doesn't matter if he's handsome," her sister had said with authority.

Cassandra had smiled wryly. "Pandora, it's not as if you married a bridge troll."

With a shrug and a sheepish grin, her sister had replied, "I know, but even if Gabriel weren't handsome, I'd still want to share a bed with him."

Cassandra had nodded with a gathering frown. "Pandora, I've felt that with someone before. The nerves and excitement and the butterflies. But . . . it wasn't Lord Lambert."

Her sister's eyes turned very round. "Who was it?"

"It doesn't matter. He's not available."

Pandora's voice lowered to a dramatic whisper. "Is he *married*?"

"My goodness, no. He's . . . well, it's Mr. Severin." Sighing, Cassandra waited for her sister to say something comical or teasing.

Blinking, Pandora took a moment to absorb the information. She surprised Cassandra by saying thoughtfully, "I can see why you would like him."

"You can?"

"Yes, he's very good-looking, and his personality has interesting corners and edges. And he's a man, not a boy."

How like Pandora to accurately identify the reasons Cassandra found Tom Severin so compelling, and Lord Lambert so . . . not.

Lambert had been born to privilege, and his character was still unformed in many ways. He'd never had to make his own way in life, and likely never would. Tom Severin, by contrast, had started with nothing except his wits and will, and had become powerful by anyone's standards. Lord Lambert enjoyed a life of languid ease, while Tom blazed through his days with relentless energy. Even the side of Tom that was cool and calculating was exciting. Stimulating. There was hardly any doubt in Cassandra's mind that Lambert would be easier to live with . . . but as to the one she would rather share a bed with . . .

"Why isn't he available?" Pandora asked.

"His heart is frozen."

"Poor man," Pandora said. "It must be solid ice if he can't fall in love with you."

Cassandra smiled and reached out to hug her.

"Do you remember when we were little," she heard Pandora ask over her shoulder, "and you would bruise your shin or stub your toe, and I would pretend I'd hurt myself in exactly the same place?"

"Yes. I must say it was a bit annoying to watch you limp around when I was the one with the injury."

Pandora chuckled and drew back. "If you felt pain, I wanted to share it with you. That's what sisters do."

"There's no need for anyone to feel badly," Cassandra said with determined cheerfulness. "I intend to have a very happy life. Really, it's not important whether I desire Lord Lambert or not: They say attraction fades in time anyway."

"It fades in some marriages, but not all of them. I don't think it's gone away for Gabriel's parents. And even if it does fade eventually, wouldn't you at least like to start out that way?" Seeing the indecision on Cassandra's face, Pandora answered her own question firmly. "Yes, you would. It would be revolting to sleep with a man you don't desire."

Cassandra rubbed her temples distractedly. "Is it possible to make my feelings do what I want them to do? Can I talk myself into wanting someone?"

"I don't know," Pandora said. "But if I were you, I'd find out before I made a decision about the rest of my life."

# Chapter 12

AFTER A GREAT DEAL of pondering, Cassandra decided even though she wasn't sure what she might feel for Lord Lambert, she didn't *not* desire him. She owed it to him, and herself, to find out if there was even a flicker of compatibility between them.

The opportunity came quite soon, when a charity banquet called the event of the month was held at the Belgravia home of Lord Delaval.

The evening included a private art exhibition and auction to benefit the Artists' Benevolent Fund. Recently a talented but only moderately successful landscape painter named Erskin Gladwine had passed away, leaving behind a wife and six children with no means to support themselves. The proceeds of the art sale would go into a fund for the Gladwines and other families of deceased artists.

Since Lady Berwick had taken a well-earned night off from chaperoning, Cassandra attended the charity benefit with Devon and Kathleen.

"We'll try to do a proper job of watching over you," Kathleen had said with mock concern, "but I fear we won't be strict enough, as we undoubtedly need a chaperone ourselves."

"We're Ravenels," Devon had pointed out. "There's only so much good behavior people will find believable."

Soon after their arrival, Cassandra was disconcerted to discover Lord Lambert's father, the Marquis of Ripon, was also attending. Although she had known she would meet him sooner or later, she didn't feel prepared. At the very least, she would have worn a more flattering dress than this one, a moiré silk that was her least favorite. The extra weight she'd gained had made it necessary to let out the waist, but the square-cut yoke of the bodice couldn't be altered without ruining it, so the top curves of her breasts plumped over the edge of the neckline. And the wavy "watered" fabric, in a shade of golden brown, gave it the unfortunate appearance of wood grain.

Lambert introduced her to his father, the marquis, who was younger in appearance than she'd expected. He was dark where his son was fair, his hair a mixture of cinder black and silver, his eyes the shade of bitter chocolate. The lines of his face were handsome but hard, textured like weathered marble. As Cassandra curtsied and rose, she was mildly startled to catch his gaze flicking upward from her breasts.

"My lady," he said, "the accounts of your beauty were by no means exaggerated."

Cassandra smiled in thanks. "An honor to make your acquaintance, my lord."

The marquis studied her with a calculating gaze. "Are you here as an art lover, Lady Cassandra?"

"I know little about art, but hope to learn more. Will you bid on a painting tonight, my lord?"

"No, I intend to make a donation, but the painter's work is no more than mediocre. I wouldn't have it hanging in my scullery."

Although Cassandra was disconcerted by the jab at the late Mr. Gladwine's work—at a charity benefit for his widow and children, no less—she tried to show no reaction.

Seeming to realize how unkind the marquis had sounded, Lambert interceded hastily. "My father is very knowledgeable about art, particularly landscapes."

"From what I've seen so far," Cassandra said, "I admire Mr. Gladwine's skill at conveying light—a moonlit scene, for example, or the glow of a fire."

"Visual tricks aren't the same as artistic merit," the marquis said dismissively.

She smiled and shrugged. "I like his work nonetheless. Perhaps someday you might do me the kindness of explaining what makes a painting worthy, and then I'll know better what to look for."

The marquis stared at her appraisingly. "You have pretty ways, my dear. It's to your credit that you wish to heed a man's opinions and enter into his views." His lips curved slightly as he remarked, "A pity I didn't meet you before my son did. As it happens, I'm also searching for a wife."

Although that seemed intended as a compliment,

Cassandra thought it a rather odd thing to say, especially in front of Lord Lambert. Perturbed, she ransacked her brain for a suitable reply. "I'm sure any woman would be honored by your attentions, my lord."

"So far I've found no one worthy of them." His gaze traveled over her. "You, however, will be a charming addition to my household."

"As *my* bride," Lambert said, chuckling. "Not yours, Father."

Cassandra kept silent. With a flare of testiness and worry, she realized both men regarded the marriage as a *fait accompli*, as if courtship and consent weren't even required.

The way the marquis looked at her was disturbing. Something in those flinty eyes made her feel blowsy and trivial at the same time.

Lord Lambert presented his arm to her. "Lady Cassandra, shall we view the rest of the paintings?"

She curtsied to the marquis once more and went with Lambert.

Slowly they wandered through the circuit of public rooms on the main floor of the house, where artwork had been hung up for display. They stopped before a painting of Vesuvius erupting in red and yellow fury.

"Don't mind my father's forwardness," Lord Lambert said casually. "He doesn't mince words when it comes to expressing his opinions. What's important is that he approves of you."

"My lord," Cassandra said quietly, conscious of people passing behind them, "somehow we seem to have come to a misunderstanding . . . an assumption . . . that an engagement is a foregone conclusion."

"It isn't?" he asked, looking amused.

"*No.*" Hearing the edge in her own voice, she moderated it before continuing more calmly, "We haven't had a formal courtship. The Season proper hasn't even started. I won't be ready to consent to anything before we become far more familiar with each other."

"I see."

"Do you?"

"I understand what you want."

Cassandra relaxed, relieved that he didn't seem to have taken offense. They progressed along the row of paintings . . . a view of castle ruins at night . . . the burning of the old Drury Lane theater . . . a moonlit river estuary. She was unable to focus on the artwork, however. Her mind buzzed with the uneasy awareness that the more often she saw Lord Lambert, the less she was coming to like him. The possibility that she might have her own thoughts and dreams didn't seem to have occurred to him. He expected—as his father had put it—for her to enter into *his* views. How could he ever love her if he had no interest in who she really was?

But dear God, if she rejected this man, this scion of the aristocracy, who was universally regarded as perfect . . .

People would say she was mad. They would say there was no pleasing her. That the fault lay not with him, but with her.

Maybe they would be right.

Abruptly, Lord Lambert tugged her out of the main circuit of rooms and into a hallway.

Stumbling a little, Cassandra let out a surprised laugh. "What are you doing?"

"You'll see." He pulled her into a private room, the kind of small, cozy retreat often referred to as a snuggery, and closed the door.

Disoriented by the sudden darkness, Cassandra reached out blindly to steady herself. Her breath stopped as Lord Lambert's arms went around her.

"Now," came his self-satisfied purr, "I'll give you what you asked for."

Both irritated and amused, Cassandra pointed out, "I didn't ask to be dragged into a dark room and manhandled."

"You wanted to become more familiar with me."

"I didn't mean *this*—" she protested, but his mouth came to hers, too hard, his lips wriggling against hers with swiftly increasing pressure.

For heaven's sake, didn't he understand that she'd wanted to spend time talking with him to discover their mutual likes and dislikes? Did he have *any* interest in her as a person?

The force of his kiss was bruising, almost belligerent, and she reached her hands up to his cheeks, stroking lightly in the hopes of soothing him. When that didn't work, she twisted her face away and gasped, "My lord . . . Roland . . . not so hard. Be gentle."

"I will. Darling . . . darling . . ." His mouth found hers again, the pressure only slightly mitigated.

Cassandra steeled herself to hold still, enduring his kisses rather than enjoying them. She tried to will herself to feel some kind of pleasure, anything except this creeping sense of distaste. His arms were crushing bands around her. In his excitement, the surface of his chest pumped like fireplace bellows.

It was becoming farcical, actually, a scene depicting an impassioned buffoon imposing himself on an outraged virgin. Worthy of Molière. Wasn't there a scene like this in *The Love-Tiff*? Or maybe it was *Tartuffe* . . .

The fact that she was thinking about a seventeenth-century playwright at this moment was not a good sign.

*Concentrate*, she commanded herself. His mouth wasn't unpleasant in itself. Why did it feel so different to kiss one man as opposed to another? She wanted so much to like this, but it wasn't at all similar to that night in the winter garden . . . the cool night air scented of shadows and green fern . . . standing on her bare toes as she sought the delicious pressure of Tom Severin's mouth . . . sensitive but urgent . . . and tendrils of warmth began to uncurl inside.

But then Lord Lambert forced her lips apart, and the wet spear of his tongue filled her mouth.

Spluttering a little, Cassandra jerked her head back. "No . . . wait . . . *no*." She tried to shove him away, but he was holding her too tightly for her to wedge her hands between them. "My family will be looking for me."

"They won't draw attention to your absence."

"Let go. I don't like this."

They grappled briefly, and he pinned her against the wall. "Another minute or two," he said, panting with excitement. "I deserve it after the flowers and gifts I sent."

*Deserve?*

"Did you think you were buying me with those?" she asked in disbelief.

"You want this, no matter what you pretend. With a body like yours . . . everyone knows it, just by looking at you."

A nasty shock went through her.

He was groping at her breasts now, tugging hard at her neckline and shoving his hand inside her bodice. She felt a rude, rough squeeze over her breast.

"Don't, that hurts!"

"We're going to marry. What does it matter if I have a taste of it now?" There was a pinch at one of her nipples, sharp enough to bruise the tender flesh.

"*Stop.*" Fear and outrage jolted through her. Reflexively she grabbed his fingers and bent them back hard. He let go of her with a grunt of pain.

Their sharp breathing cut the darkness into rags. After jerking up her bodice, Cassandra lunged for the door, but froze as she heard his composed voice.

"Before you flounce off, give a thought to your reputation. A scandal, even one not of your making, would ruin you."

Which was horridly unfair. But true. Incredibly, her entire future depended on leaving this room calmly, with him, and giving no hint about what had just happened.

Her outstretched hand curled into a fist and lowered to her side. She forced herself to wait, dimly able to perceive that he was straightening his clothes, doing something with the front of his trousers. Her lips were dry and sore. The tip of her breast throbbed painfully. She felt shamed and sweaty and utterly miserable.

Lord Lambert spoke in a light, casual tone. It chilled her that he'd switched moods like the flip of a coin. "There's something you should learn, darling. When you tease a man into a state and leave him frustrated, we don't take it well."

The accusation bewildered her. "What have I done to tease you?"

"You smile and flirt, and sway your hips when you walk—"

"I do not!"

"—and you wear those tight dresses with your breasts pushed up beneath your chin. You advertise your assets, and then complain when I give you what you were asking for."

Unable to bear any more, Cassandra fumbled for the doorknob. The door swung open gently, and she took a deep, desperate gasp of air as she left the room.

Lord Lambert fell into step beside her. Out of the periphery of her vision, she saw that he'd offered his arm. She didn't take it. The thought of touching him made her ill.

As they headed back to the public rooms, she spoke without looking at him, her voice trembling only slightly. "You're mad if you think I'd want anything to do with you after this."

By the time they reappeared, Kathleen was discreetly searching for them. At first she looked relieved to see Cassandra. As they drew closer, however, she saw the signs of strain in Cassandra's expression, and her face turned carefully blank. "Dear," Kathleen said lightly, "there's a sunrise landscape I'm thinking of bidding on—I must have your opinion." Kathleen glanced at Lord Lambert as she added, "My lord, I'm afraid I have to reclaim my charge, or people will say my chaperoning skills are woefully lax."

He smiled. "I yield her to your care."

Kathleen linked arms with Cassandra as they walked away. "What happened?" she asked softly. "Did you have a quarrel?"

"Yes," Cassandra replied with difficulty. "I want to leave early. Not early enough to cause gossip, but as soon as possible."

"I'll come up with an excuse."

"And . . . don't let him come near me."

Kathleen's voice was excessively calm, while her hand came to press tightly over Cassandra's. "He won't."

They made their way to Lady Delaval, the evening's hostess, and Kathleen relayed regretfully they would have to leave early, as the baby had colic and she wanted to go home to him.

Cassandra was only distantly aware of the mur-mured conversation around her. She felt dazed, a little off balance, the way she did when she'd gotten out of bed before she'd quite awakened. Her mind combed ceaselessly through everything Lord Lambert had said and done.

*. . . everyone knows what you want . . . you advertise your assets . . .*

Those words had made her feel even worse than the groping, if that were possible. Did other men look at her that way? Was that what they thought? She wanted to shrink and hide somewhere. Her temples throbbed as if there were too much blood in her head. Her breast ached in the places he'd gripped and pinched.

Now Kathleen was talking to Devon, asking him to send for the carriage.

He didn't bother with a pleasant social mask. His face went taut, his blue eyes narrowing. "Is there something I should know right now?" he asked softly, looking from his wife's face to Cassandra's.

Cassandra responded with a quick little shake of her head. Above all, she couldn't risk making a scene. If Devon knew how Lord Lambert had insulted her . . . and Lambert was in the vicinity . . . the results might be disastrous.

Devon gave her a hard stare, obviously not happy about departing without knowing exactly what had happened. To her relief, however, he relented. "You'll tell me on the way home?"

"Yes, Cousin Devon."

Once they were bundled in the carriage and headed back to Ravenel House, Cassandra was able to breathe more easily. Kathleen sat beside her, holding her hand.

Devon, who occupied the seat opposite them, regarded Cassandra with a frown. "Let's have it," he said brusquely.

Cassandra told them everything that had happened, including how Lambert had groped her. Although it was humiliating to recount the details, she felt they needed to understand exactly how offensive and insulting he'd been. As they listened carefully, Devon's expression went from thunderstruck to furious, while Kathleen's face turned white and set.

"It was my fault for not objecting more strongly at the beginning," Cassandra said miserably. "And this dress—it's too tight  not ladylike enough, and—"

"God help me." Although Devon's voice was quiet, it had the intensity of a shout. "You caused *none* of what he did. Nothing you said or did, nothing you wore."

"Do you think I would let you go out wearing something inappropriate?" Kathleen asked curtly. "You happen to be well-endowed—which is a blessing, not a crime. I'd like to go back and horsewhip that bastard for suggesting this was somehow your fault."

Unused to hearing such language from Kathleen, Cassandra stared at her in round-eyed amazement.

"Make no mistake," Kathleen continued heatedly, "this is a taste of how he would treat you after the wedding. Except it would be a thousand times worse, because as his wife, you would be at his mercy. Men like that never take responsibility—they lash out, and then say someone else provoked them into doing it. 'See what you made me do.' But the choice is always theirs. They hurt and frighten others to make themselves feel powerful."

Kathleen might have continued, but Devon leaned forward to settle his hand gently on her knee. Not to check or interrupt her, but because he seemed to feel the need to touch her. His eyes were warm, dark blue as he stared at his wife. An entire conversation transpired in their shared gaze.

Cassandra knew they were both thinking about her brother, Theo . . . Kathleen's first husband . . . who'd had a violent temper, and had often lashed out verbally and physically at the people around him.

"I was subjected to the Ravenel temper often during childhood," Cassandra said quietly. "My father and brother even seemed proud of it at times . . . the way it made people nervous. I think they wanted to be thought of as powerful."

Devon looked sardonic. "Powerful men don't lose their tempers. They stay calm while others are shouting and blowing up." He sat back in his seat, inhaled deeply, and let out a long breath. "Thanks to my wife's influence, I've learned not to yield to my temper quite so easily as I did in the past."

Kathleen regarded him tenderly. "The effort and the credit for self-improvement are all yours, my lord.

But even at your worst, you'd never have dreamed of treating a woman the way Lord Lambert did tonight."

Cassandra lifted her gaze to Devon's. "Cousin, what's to be done now?"

"I'd like to start by beating him to a pulp," Devon said darkly.

"Oh, please don't—" she began.

"Don't worry, sweetheart. It's what I'd like to do, not what I'm going to do. I'll corner him tomorrow and make it clear that from now on, he's to avoid you at all cost. No visits to the house, no flowers, no interaction of any kind. Lambert won't dare bother you again."

Cassandra grimaced and laid her head on Kathleen's shoulder. "The Season's not even under way and it's going to be ghastly. I can tell."

Kathleen's small hand came up to smooth her hair. "It's better to have learned about Lord Lambert's true character now rather than later," she murmured. "But I'm so very sorry it turned out this way."

"Lady Berwick will be devastated," Cassandra said with a wan chuckle. "She had such high hopes for the match."

"But not you?" came the soft question.

Cassandra shook her head slightly. "Whenever I tried to imagine a future with Lord Lambert, I felt nothing. Nothing at all. I can't even work up the will to hate him now. I think he's horrid, but . . . he's not important enough to hate."

# Chapter 13

"SIR," BARNABY SAID OMINOUSLY, having come to the threshold of Tom's office unannounced, "they're back."

Tom's gaze didn't stray from the pages of masonry and bridging estimates in front of him. "Who's back?" he asked absently.

"The chats."

Blinking, Tom lifted his head. "What?"

"Bazzle's chats," Barnaby clarified, looking grim.

"Is Bazzle here with them, or did they decide to drop by on their own?"

His assistant was too distraught to find humor in the situation. "I told Bazzle he couldn't come in. He's waiting outside."

Tom let out an exasperated sigh and stood. "I'll handle it, Barnaby."

"If I may point out, sir," Barnaby dared to say, "the only way to be rid of the chats is to get rid of Bazzle."

Tom shot him a sharp glance. "Any child, rich or poor, can be afflicted with lice."

"Yes, but . . . do we have to have one in the office?"

Tom ignored the question and went downstairs with irritation needling all through him.

This had to stop. He couldn't stand interruptions, vermin, or children, and Bazzle was all three combined. At this moment, other men of his position were attending to their business, as he should be doing. He would give the boy a few coins and tell him not to come back. Bazzle wasn't his concern. The boy would be no better or worse off than thousands of other little ruffians who roamed the streets.

As Tom passed through the marble entrance foyer, he saw a workman on a tall ladder, festooning ledges and window sashes with swags of greenery tied up in red bows.

"What's that for?" Tom demanded.

The workman glanced down at him with a smile. "Good morning, Mr. Severin. I'm putting up Christmas decorations."

"Who told you to do that?"

"The building manager, sir."

"It's still bloody November," Tom protested.

"Winterborne's just unveiled their holiday window displays."

"I see," Tom muttered. Rhys Winterborne, with his unflagging appetite for profit, was singlehandedly starting the Christmas shopping season earlier than ever before. Which meant Tom would have to endure a full month of holiday festivities, with no possible escape. Every house and building would be choking

with evergreens and silver gilt decorations, every doorway hung with a mistletoe kissing-bunch. There would
be stacks of Christmas cards in the post, and pages of
Christmas advertisements cluttering the newspapers, and
endless performances of *Messiah*. Packs of carolers
would roam the streets and assault innocent pedestrians
with off-tune warbling in exchange for spare pennies.

It wasn't that Tom hated Christmas. Usually he tol-
erated it with good grace . . . but this year he couldn't
have felt less like celebrating.

"Should I stop hanging the evergreens, Mr. Severin?"
the workman asked.

Tom pasted a shallow smile on his face. "No, Meagles.
Go about your work."

"You remembered my name," the workman exclaimed, pleased.

Tom was tempted to reply, *You're not special: I remember everyone's name*, but he managed to restrain
himself.

The bitter wind cut down to the bone as he stepped
outside. It was the kind of cold that shortened the
space between each breath, and made the lungs feel
brittle enough to shatter.

He saw Bazzle's small, knobbly form huddled on
the side of the stone steps, with a broom laid across his
knee. The boy was clad in garments that could have
been pulled straight from the ragman's bin, his head
topped with a threadbare cap. As he sat facing away
from Tom, he reached up to scratch the back of his
neck and head in an all-too-familiar gesture.

What a small, inconsequential wisp of humanity, clinging to the very edge of survival. If Bazzle suddenly vanished from the face of the earth, few people would care or even notice. Tom was damned if he knew why the fate of this boy should matter to him.

But it did.

*Damn it.*

Slowly he made his way to Bazzle's side and sat on the steps beside him.

The boy started and turned to glance at him. There was something different about Bazzle's gaze today, the pupils like the dark centers of broken windows. As the wind whipped across the stairs, he vibrated with chills.

"Where are your new clothes?" Tom asked.

"Uncle Batty said they was too lardy-dardy for me."

"He sold them," Tom said flatly.

"Yes, sir," the child said through chattering teeth.

Before Tom could air his opinion of the thieving bastard, a frozen gust caused the boy to steel himself against a wracking shudder.

Reluctantly Tom took off his suit coat, made of superfine black wool and lined with silk, delivered just last week from his tailor at Strickland and Sons. It was cut in the latest style, single-breasted with no seam at the waist, and deep fixed cuffs on the sleeves. Naturally, he would have worn this new coat today instead of an older one. Suppressing a sigh, he settled the luxurious garment over the boy's dirty frame.

Bazzle made a little sound of surprise as the

warm cocoon of wool and silk surrounded him. He clutched the coat around himself and drew his knees up inside it.

"Bazzle," Tom said, feeling as if every word were being pried out of him with steel tweezers, "would you like to come work for me?"

"Already do, sir."

"At my house. As a hall boy, or apprentice footman. Or they might need you at the stables or gardens. The point is, you would live there."

"With you?"

"I wouldn't say *with* me. But yes, in my house."

The boy thought it over. "Who would sweep your office?"

"I suppose you could come here with me in the mornings, if you like. In fact, it will annoy Barnaby so much, I'll have to insist on it." At the boy's silence, he prompted, "Well?"

Bazzle was unaccountably slow to respond.

"I didn't expect you to jump for joy, Bazzle, but you could at least try to look pleased."

The child gave him a profoundly troubled glance. "Uncle Batty won't like it."

"Take me to him," Tom said readily. "I'll talk to him." As a matter of fact, he was damned eager for the chance to tear a few strips out of Uncle Batty's hide.

"Oh, no, Mr. Severin . . . a toff like ye . . . they'd cut yer liver an' lights out."

A bemused smile touched Tom's lips. He'd spent most of his childhood in slums and train yards, fending for himself, constantly exposed to every manner of vice and filth humanity was capable of. Fighting to defend himself, fighting for food, for work . . . for everything. Long before Tom had been able to grow a proper beard, he'd been as seasoned and hard-bitten as any adult man in London. But of course, this boy had no way of knowing any of that.

"Bazzle," he said, looking down at him steadily, "there's no need to worry on that account. I know how to handle myself in worse places than St. Giles. I can protect you as well."

The boy continued to frown, and gnawed distractedly on the lapel of the wool coat. "No need asking Batty noffing about noffing. 'E's not me uncle."

"What kind of arrangement do you have with him? He takes your earnings in exchange for room and board? Well, you can work exclusively for me now. The accommodations are better, you'll have enough to eat, and you can keep the money you make. What do you say to that?"

Bazzle's rheumy eyes narrowed suspiciously. "You ain't after breeching me? I ain't a sod."

"My tastes don't run to children," Tom said acidly. "Of either gender. I prefer women." One in particular.

"No buggerin'?" the boy persisted, just to be sure.

"No, Bazzle, you're in no danger of being buggered. I have no interest in buggering you, now or in the future. The amount of buggery at my house will be zero. Have I managed to make that clear?"

There was a flicker of amusement in the boy's eyes,

and he began to look more like his usual self. "Yes, sir."

"Good," Tom said briskly, standing and dusting off the back of his trousers. "I'll fetch my overcoat, and we'll call on Dr. Gibson. I'm sure she'll be overjoyed by yet another surprise visit from us.'"

Bazzle's face fell. "Another shower baff?" he asked in dread. "Like before?"

Tom grinned. "You'd better accustom yourself to soap and water, Bazzle. There's going to be a great deal of it in your future."

AFTER BAZZLE HAD been washed, deloused, and outfitted in new clothes and shoes . . . again . . . Tom took the boy to his house at Hyde Park Square. He'd bought the white stucco-fronted mansion four years earlier, with most of the furnishings intact. It was four stories in height, with a dormered mansard roof, and private gardens he rarely visited. He'd kept on most of the staff, who had reluctantly adjusted to serving a common-born master. To Tom's amusement, his servants seemed to feel they'd experienced a comedown in the world, as their previous master had been a baron from North Yorkshire.

The housekeeper, Mrs. Dankworth, was cold-natured, efficient, and remarkably impersonal, which had made her Tom's favorite of all the servants. Mrs. Dankworth rarely bothered him, and she never seemed taken aback by anything, even when Tom invited guests without forewarning. She hadn't even turned a hair on the occasion when one of his acquaintances from an industrial science laboratory had conducted a chemical experiment in the parlor and ruined the carpet.

For the first time in four years, however, Mrs. Dankworth seemed flustered—no, dumbfounded—when Tom presented her with Bazzle and requested that she "do something with him."

"He'll need a job here for the afternoons," Tom had told her. "He'll also need a place to sleep and someone to explain his duties and the house rules. And teach him how to brush his teeth properly."

The short, stocky woman stared at Bazzle as if she'd never seen a boy before. "Mr. Severin," she'd said to Tom, "there's no one here to look after a child."

"He doesn't need looking after," Tom had assured her. "Bazzle is self-sufficient. Just make sure he's fed and watered regularly."

"How long will he be staying?" the housekeeper asked apprehensively.

"Indefinitely." Tom had departed without ceremony, and returned to his office for a late-day meeting with two members of the Metropolitan Board of Works. After the meeting, he ignored the urge to go back home and see how Bazzle was faring. Instead, he decided to have dinner at his club.

At Jenner's, something interesting was always happening. The atmosphere of the legendary club was opulent but soothing, never too noisy, never too quiet. Every detail, from the expensive liquor served in cut-crystal glasses, to the plush Chesterfield chairs and sofas, had been chosen to make the club members feel indulged and privileged. To gain membership, a man was required to submit character references from existing members, provide financial records and credit balances, and put his name on a waiting list for years. An opening occurred only when a member died, and anyone fortunate enough to be offered the next place in line knew better than to quibble about the exorbitant annual fee.

Before going to the supper buffet, Tom went into one of the club rooms for a drink. Most of the chairs were occupied, as they always were this time of night. As he walked through the circuit of connected rooms, various friends and acquaintances gestured for him to join them. He was about to signal a porter to bring an extra chair when he noticed a minor disturbance a few tables away. Three men were having a quiet but intense discussion, tension clouding the air like smoke.

Tom glanced at the small group and recognized Gabriel, Lord St. Vincent, in their midst. It was hardly a surprise to find St. Vincent here, since his family owned the club, and his maternal grandfather had been Ivo Jenner himself. In recent years, St. Vincent had taken over the management of the club from his father. By all accounts, he was doing an excellent job of it, with his customary cool and relaxed aplomb.

At the moment, however, there was nothing relaxed about St. Vincent. He pushed his chair back and stood, and dropped a newspaper to the table as if it had just caught fire. Although he made a visible effort to compose himself, his jaw flexed repeatedly as he ground his teeth.

"My lord," Tom said easily, drawing closer. "How are you?"

St. Vincent turned toward him, instantly assuming a polite mask. "Severin. Good evening." He reached out to shake Tom's hand, and proceeded to introduce him to the two men at the table, who had both risen to their feet. "Lord Milner, Mr. Chadwick, it's my pleasure to introduce Mr. Severin, our newest member."

They both bowed and offered congratulations.

"Severin," St. Vincent murmured, "ordinarily I'd invite you to have a brandy with me, but I'm afraid I have to leave at once. I beg your pardon."

"Not bad news, I hope?"

Looking distracted, St. Vincent responded with a faint, grim smile. "Yes, it's bad. God knows what I can do about it. Probably not much."

"Can I be of service?" Tom asked without hesitation.

St. Vincent focused on him then, his winter-blue eyes warming at the offer. "Thank you, Severin," he said sincerely. "I'm not sure what's needed yet. But I may prevail on you later if necessary."

"If you could give me an idea of the problem, I might have some suggestions."

St. Vincent contemplated him for a moment. "Walk with me."

Tom responded with a single nod, his curiosity growing by leaps and bounds.

After retrieving the discarded newspaper, St. Vincent murmured to his friends, "Thank you for the information, gentlemen. Your drinks and dinners are on the house tonight."

They reacted with smiles and appreciative murmurs.

As St. Vincent left with Tom, his pleasant expression vanished. "You'll hear about this soon enough," he said. "The problem has to do with my wife's sister. Lady Cassandra."

Tom drew in a sharp breath. "What happened? Has she been hurt?" From the quick glance the other man sent him, he realized his reaction had been too forceful.

"Not physically." St. Vincent led the way to a spacious vestibule off the entrance hall. The room, fitted with nickel rods and mahogany shelves, had been crammed with overcoats and sundry articles.

A porter approached them immediately. "My lord?"

"My hat and coat, Niall." While the porter disappeared into the vestibule, St. Vincent spoke quietly to Tom. "Lady Cassandra has been slandered by a rejected suitor. The rumors started circulating two or three days ago. The man described her to his friends as a heartless and promiscuous flirt—and he made sure to do it at his club, within hearing of as many people as possible. He claims she freely allowed him sexual liberties and then rejected him callously when he tried to redeem her honor with an offer of marriage."

Tom had always known rage as a scalding emotion. But this went beyond that . . . this feeling was colder than ice.

There was only one thing he needed to know. "Who is it?"

"Roland, Lord Lambert."

Tom went to the threshold of the vestibule. "I want my coat too," he said brusquely in the porter's direction.

"Right away, Mr. Severin," came the muffled reply.

"Where are you going?" St. Vincent asked as Tom turned back to him.

"I'm going to find Lambert," Tom growled, "and shove a damned pole up his arse. Then I'm going to drag him to the front courtyard of the Guildhall and prop him up until he publicly retracts every lie about Lady Cassandra."

St. Vincent regarded him with forced patience. "The last thing the Ravenels need is for you to go out half-cocked and do something impulsive. Besides, you don't know the whole of the story yet. It gets worse."

Tom blanched. "Sweet Christ, how could it be worse?" In the eyes of society, a woman's reputation was everything. *Everything.* If there was any smudge on Cassandra's honor, she would be ostracized, and the disgrace would fall on her family as well. Her chances of marrying any man of her class would be smashed. Her former friends would have nothing to do with her. Her future children would be snubbed by their peers. Lambert's actions had been the height of cruelty: He had known full well his petty vengeance would ruin Cassandra's life.

St. Vincent handed Tom the newspaper he'd tucked under his arm. "This is the evening edition of the *London Chronicle*," he said tersely. "Read the top column on the society page."

Tom looked at him sharply before lowering his gaze to the column, which, he noted with contempt, had been written by someone willing to identify himself only as "Anonymous."

> *It is time for us now to reflect on a species well known to London: the Heartless Flirt. Many such creatures have recently descended on society to renew the pleasures of the Season, but one in particular serves as the most notorious example of her kind.*
>
> *Collecting broken hearts like so many trophies is a game to this certain lady, to whom we shall refer as "Lady C." She has received more proposals than a well-bred young woman should, and there's no mystery as to why. She plays at lovemaking, having perfected the sidelong glance, the teasing whisper, and other incitements to the male ardor. It is her habit to lure a man to some quiet corner, inflame him with furtive kisses and wanton explorations, then accuse the poor fellow of taking advantage.*
>
> *Lady C will, of course, protest her innocence and claim her little experimentations are harmless. She will toss her golden curls and go on her*

*merry way, leading more men to make fools of themselves for her private amusement. Now that her impropriety has been exposed, it is up to those in good society to decide what price, if any, she will pay for her shameless ways. Let their judgment be a warning to other young temptresses that it is wicked—nay, fiendish—to toy with the affections of honorable young men, and degrade herself in the process.*

*In short, let Lady C serve as an example.*

Tom was dumbstruck by the sheer malice of the column. It was character assassination. He'd never seen nor heard of such a public attack on an innocent girl. If it was retaliation by Lord Lambert for having been rejected, it was so wildly disproportionate a response, one had to question his sanity. And now that the rumor had entered the public domain, it would be taken up by women in society, who weren't generally known for showing mercy to their own kind.

Before the week was out, Cassandra would be a pariah.

"Why would the editor agree to publish this?" Tom demanded, shoving the paper back at him. "It's bloody libel."

"No doubt he's banking on the fact that Cassandra's family won't want to put her through the ordeal of a lawsuit. Furthermore, it's possible this 'Anonymous' has some kind of leverage against him or the paper's owner."

"I'll find out who wrote the column," Tom said.

"No," St. Vincent said instantly. "Don't take the matter into your own hands. I'll convey your offer of assistance to the Ravenels. I'm sure they'll appreciate it. But it's for the family to decide how to handle the situation."

The porter came with St. Vincent's coat and helped him into it, while Tom stood there brooding.

He couldn't stand by and do nothing. Something inside him had been let out of its cage, and it wouldn't go back in until he'd made the world pay for hurting Cassandra.

When he thought of what she might be feeling, how frightened and furious and wounded she must be . . . a strange and terrible emotion twisted all through him. He wanted Cassandra in his arms. He wanted to shield her from all this damned ugliness.

Except he had no right to do anything where Cassandra was concerned.

"I won't interfere," Tom said gruffly. "But I want your word you'll notify me if there's something I can do. Even some small service."

"I will."

"You're going to them now?"

"Yes, I'm going to collect my wife and take her to Ravenel House. She'll want to be with Cassandra." St. Vincent looked simultaneously angry and world-weary. "That poor girl. It's never been a secret that what Cassandra wants most is a conventional life. But with a few malicious words, Lambert has all but ruined her chances of having it."

"Not when the rumor he started is exposed as a blatant lie."

St. Vincent smiled cynically. "You can't kill a rumor that way, Severin. The more facts you throw at a lie, the more people insist on believing it."

# Chapter 14

$\mathcal{P}$UBLIC SHAME, CASSANDRA REFLECTED dully, was drowning in deep water. Once you disappeared beneath the surface, you kept sinking.

It had been twenty-four hours since Pandora and Gabriel had called at Ravenel House. Ordinarily, the unexpected visit would have been a delightful surprise, but from the moment Cassandra had seen Pandora's bone-white face, she'd understood something was very wrong. Life-altering wrong.

They had all gathered in the family parlor, with Kathleen and Devon seated on either side of Cassandra. Pandora had been too agitated to sit, pacing around the room and occasionally breaking in with loud exclamations, while Gabriel had carefully explained the situation.

As the realization of what Lord Lambert had done to her sank in, Cassandra had turned cold with shock and fright. Devon had brought her a brandy and insisted that she drink it, his large hands closing over hers to keep the glass steady as she raised it to her lips. "You have a family," he'd said firmly. "You have many people to love and defend you. We're going to fight this together."

"We'll start by killing Lord Lambert!" Pandora had cried, storming back and forth. "In the longest, most painful way possible. We'll take him apart bit by bit. I'm going to murder him with *tweezers*."

While her twin had continued to rant, Cassandra had gone into Kathleen's arms and whispered, "It will be like battling smoke. There's no way to win."

"Lady Berwick will be able to help us more than anyone," Kathleen had said calmly. "She'll enlist the sympathy and support of her friends—all influential society matrons—and advise us on how best to weather this storm."

But like most storms, it would leave wreckage in its wake.

"You'll have the support of my family," Gabriel had assured her. "They won't tolerate any slight against you. Whatever you require, they'll provide."

Cassandra had thanked him woodenly, forbearing to point out that the duke and duchess, powerful as they were, wouldn't be able to force people to risk ruin by mixing their reputations with hers.

She'd sipped the brandy until she'd finished all of it, while the rest of the group discussed what to do. They'd agreed that Devon would enlist Ethan Ransom to find Lord Lambert, who had probably run to ground after the havoc he'd caused. St. Vincent would go to the offices of the *London Chronicle* in the morning and pressure the editor into revealing the identity of the anonymous columnist. Kathleen would send for Lady Berwick, who would devise a strategy to counteract the damaging rumors.

Although Cassandra had tried to pay attention, a gloom of exhaustion had settled over her, and she sat with her head and shoulders drooping.

"Cassandra's feeling floppulous," Pandora had announced. "She needs to rest."

Kathleen and Pandora had accompanied her upstairs, while Devon and Gabriel had continued to talk in the parlor.

"I don't mean to sound self-pitying," Cassandra had said numbly, sitting at the vanity table while Kathleen brushed her hair, "but I can't think what I did to deserve this."

"You don't deserve it," Kathleen had said, meeting her gaze in the looking glass. "As you know, life is unfair. You had the bad luck to attract Lord Lambert, and you had no way of knowing what he would do."

Pandora had come to kneel beside her chair. "Shall I stay here with you tonight? I don't want to be far away from you."

That had brought the trace of a smile to Cassandra's dry lips. "No, the brandy's made me sleepy. All I want is to rest. But I'll need to see you tomorrow."

"I'll come back first thing in the morning."

"You'll have work to do," Cassandra had objected. Pandora had started her own board game company and was in the process of fitting up a small factory space and visiting suppliers. "Come back later in the day, when you've taken care of your responsibilities."

"I'll be here by teatime." Looking up at Cassandra more closely, Pandora commented, "You're not behaving the way I expected. I've done all the crying and screaming, and you've been so quiet."

"I'm sure I'll cry eventually. Right now, though, I only feel rather ill and gray."

"Should I be quiet too?" Pandora had asked.

Cassandra had shaken her head. "No, not at all. It feels as if you're crying and screaming for me when I can't."

Pandora had pressed her cheek against Cassandra's arm. "That's what sisters do."

The atmosphere in the house this morning was ominously quiet. Devon had left, and Kathleen was busy writing a blizzard of notes and letters, enlisting friends' support in the brewing scandal. The servants were unusually subdued, Napoleon and Josephine were listless, and even the usual noises of street traffic from outside were absent. It felt as if someone had died.

In a way, someone had. Cassandra had awakened into a new life with a different future. She had yet to find out all the ways it had changed, and what the extent of her humiliation would be. But regardless of how people treated her, she had to admit her own responsibility in this mess. She was at least partly to blame. *This* was the reason for all Lady Berwick's rules.

All the minor flirtations and stolen kisses Cassandra had enjoyed in the past had now been cast in a different light. It had seemed like innocent fun at the time, but she'd been playing with fire. Had she stayed safely next to her chaperone or relations and behaved with decorum, Lord Lambert would have never been able to pull her aside and accost her the way he had.

The only benefit to being ruined, Cassandra thought morosely as she dressed with the help of her lady's maid, was that she'd lost her appetite. Perhaps she would finally lose the extra pounds that had plagued her ever since the beginning of summer.

When teatime approached, Cassandra descended the stairs eagerly, knowing Pandora would arrive soon. Late-afternoon tea was a sacred ritual for the Ravenels, whether they were in Hampshire or in London. Here at Ravenel House, tea was served in the double library, a spacious long rectangle of a room, lined with acres of mahogany bookshelves and filled with cozy groupings of deep upholstered furniture.

Cassandra's steps slowed as she approached the library and heard Lady Berwick's familiar crisp tones mingling with Kathleen's subdued ones. Oh, God . . . facing Lady Berwick would be the worst part of this entire debacle. The older woman would be stern and disapproving, and so very disappointed.

Cassandra's face burned with shame as she went to the threshold and peeked around the jamb.

". . . in my day, there would have been a duel," Lady Berwick was saying. "Were I a man, I would have called him out already."

"Please don't say that in my husband's hearing,"

Kathleen said dryly. "He needs no encouragement. His surface is civilized, but it only goes so deep."

Hesitantly Cassandra entered the room and curtsied. "Ma'am," she managed to choke out. "I'm so very sorry, I—" Her throat closed, and she couldn't speak.

Lady Berwick patted the place beside her on the settee. Obeying the summons, Cassandra went to her. She sat and forced herself to meet the older woman's gaze, expecting reproof and condemnation. But to her surprise, the steel-gray eyes were kind.

"We've been dealt a wretched hand, my dear," Lady Berwick said calmly. "You're not to blame. Your conduct has been no worse than that of any other girl in your position. Better than most, as a matter of fact, and I include my own two daughters in that estimation."

Cassandra could have let herself weep then, except it would have made the older woman, who prized self-control, exceedingly uncomfortable. "I brought this on myself," she said humbly. "I shouldn't have flouted any of your rules, for even a second."

"Nor should Lord Lambert have abandoned *all* semblance of gentlemanly conduct," Lady Berwick exclaimed with icy indignation. "His behavior has been dastardly. My friends and confidantes in society all agree. Furthermore, they know what position I expect them to take regarding Lambert." After a brittle pause, she added, "That won't be enough, however."

"You mean to save my reputation?" Cassandra managed to ask.

Lady Berwick nodded. "Let us make no bones

about it—you're in trouble, my dear. Something must be done."

"Perhaps," Kathleen suggested cautiously, "it's worth considering a trip abroad? We could send Cassandra to America. We have connections in New York through Lord St. Vincent's family. I'm sure they would let her stay for as long as necessary."

"It would cool the heat of scandal," Lady Berwick allowed, "but Cassandra would be a nonentity upon her return. No, there's no escape from this. She must have the protection of a husband with a respectable name." She pursed her lips thoughtfully. "If St. Vincent is willing to approach his friend Lord Foxhall delicately, and prevail on his sense of chivalry . . . I believe there was some earlier interest in Cassandra—"

"Please, no," Cassandra groaned, a wave of humiliation rolling over her.

"—and if Foxhall won't have her," Lady Berwick continued inexorably, "his younger brother might."

"I can't bear the idea of begging someone to marry me out of pity," Cassandra said.

The older woman gave her an implacable look. "No matter how emphatically we proclaim your innocence and denounce Lambert as a cad, your position is precarious. According to my sources, you were seen slipping out of the ballroom with Lambert. I'm trying to save you from being ostracized from good society altogether. My girl, if you do not marry immediately, you'll cause untold difficulty for your family and friends.

Wherever you go, there will be cuts and snubs. You'll venture out less and less, to spare yourself hurt and embarrassment, until you become a prisoner in your own home."

Cassandra fell silent, letting the discussion continue without her. She was relieved when Helen and Winterborne arrived, both of them consoling and sympathetic, and then Devon came in with Pandora and St. Vincent. She took comfort in being surrounded by her family, who all wanted what was best for her, and would do whatever they could to help.

Unfortunately, there was little encouraging news. Devon reported that Ethan Ransom was in the process of tracking down Lord Lambert, who so far hadn't been found.

"What will Ethan do when he finds Lord Lambert?" Cassandra asked.

"There's not much he can do," Devon admitted, "but at the very least, Ransom will scare the wits out of him."

"If that's possible," Cassandra said, finding it difficult to envision the arrogant Lambert being frightened of anything.

Winterborne spoke up then, having had longer acquaintance with Ethan than any of them. "When Ransom was a government agent," he said quietly, "he was the one they sent to terrify the terrorists."

That made Cassandra feel a little better.

Devon turned his attention to Lord St. Vincent.

"How did it go at the *London Chronicle*? Did you find out who wrote the column?"

"Not yet," St. Vincent admitted. "I tried bribery as well as threats of legal action and bodily harm, but the chief editor kept waving 'liberty of the press' in front of me like a little parade flag. I'll exert pressure in various ways until he gives in, but it will take some time."

"As if 'liberty of the press' gives someone the right to commit libel," Helen exclaimed indignantly.

"Libel is difficult to prove," Winterborne said, holding his wife's hand and playing lightly with her fingers. "If a published opinion isn't based on a deliberate misstatement of fact, it's not libelous. Whoever wrote the column was careful in the wording of it."

"Obviously Lord Lambert wrote it," Pandora said.

"I wouldn't be so sure," Helen commented thoughtfully. "It doesn't have the tone of a young person. The manner is scolding . . . lecturing . . . not unlike a disapproving parent."

"Or chaperone," Pandora added, grinning at Lady Berwick, who gave her an admonishing glance.

"But who would be motivated to single out Cassandra as a scapegoat?" Kathleen asked.

Lady Berwick shook her head. "It is unfathomable. She hasn't a single enemy that I know of."

The tea was brought in, along with plates of refreshments: lemon tea cakes with fluted edges, currant scones, plates of tiny sandwiches, and toasted muffins with jam. Cassandra briefly considered nibbling on a tea cake, but she was afraid she might not be able to swallow it without choking.

Midway through the tea, the butler came to the doorway and announced a visitor. "My lord . . . the Marquis of Ripon."

The room fell abruptly silent.

Cassandra felt the cup and saucer rattle in her hands.

Lady Berwick instantly took them from her. "Breathe, and remain calm," she murmured near Cassandra's ear. "You need say nothing to him."

Devon stood to greet the marquis, who came in with his hat and gloves to indicate he would not stay long if his presence wasn't wanted. "Ripon," he said darkly, "this is unexpected."

"Forgive me, Trenear. I don't mean to intrude. In light of recent events, however, I felt it necessary to speak to you as soon as possible."

The marquis sounded very grave, his voice stripped of its former sneering edge. Cassandra risked a glance at him. He had a certain hawklike handsomeness, his form slim and smartly dressed, his black hair threaded with silver. "I came to tell you how thoroughly I condemn my son's actions," he said. "It grieved and angered me to learn of his conduct. Nothing in his up-bringing would explain or excuse it. Nor can I fathom why he would speak so recklessly about it afterward."

"I can answer that," Pandora broke in heatedly. "He started the rumor out of spite, because my sister didn't want him."

Ripon looked directly at Cassandra. "I apologize most humbly on his behalf."

She nodded slightly, comprehending that he wasn't a man who was often given to humbling himself for any reason.

Lady Berwick spoke frostily. "One would wish, Ripon," she said, "that your son had come to tender the apology on his own behalf."

"Yes." A rueful note colored his reply. "Unfortunately, I have no knowledge of his whereabouts. I'm sure he dreads my reaction to what he's done."

"What of the column in the *Chronicle*, Ripon?" St. Vincent asked, staring at him intently. "Who do you think wrote it?"

"I know nothing about that," Ripon said, "other than it was reprehensible." His attention returned to Devon. "For me, the issue of paramount importance is how best to help Lady Cassandra. Her reputation has been harmed . . . but perhaps the damage is not irreversible." The marquis lifted his hands as if anticipating a volley of arrows. "I beg you to allow me to explain." He paused. "Lady Cassandra, if I were to bring my son before you, penitent and profoundly apologetic—"

"No," Cassandra said, her voice bowstring-taut. "I have no interest in him. I never want to see him again."

"As I thought. In that case, there's another candidate I would like to put forth for your consideration: myself." Seeing her astonishment, Ripon continued carefully. "I am a widower. For some time, I've searched for someone with whom I could share the kind of contentment I enjoyed with my late wife. I find you ideal in every regard. Marriage to me would restore your reputation and lift you to a high place in society. You would be the mother to my future children, and the mistress of a great estate. I would be a generous husband. My wife was a very happy woman—anyone who knew her would attest to that."

"How could I possibly become Lord Lambert's stepmother?" Cassandra asked, revolted.

"You would never have to see him. I'll banish him from the estate altogether if you wish. Your happiness and comfort would take precedence over all else."

"My lord, I couldn't—"

"Please," Ripon interrupted gently, "don't give me an immediate answer. I beg you to do me the honor of taking some time to consider the idea."

"She will consider it," Lady Berwick said flatly.

Cassandra glanced at her in mute protest, but managed to hold her tongue. She owed it to Lady Berwick not to contradict her in company. But she knew exactly what the other woman was thinking. This offer, from this caliber of man, wasn't something to turn down summarily.

"I've been lonely for a long time, Lady Cassandra," Ripon said quietly. "I've missed having someone to care for. You would bring much joy into my life. I'm sure the difference in our ages gives you pause. However, there are advantages to having a mature husband. If you were mine, every obstacle, every thorn and rough patch, would be cleared from your path."

Cassandra glanced at Lady Berwick, whose brows lifted an infinitesimal but significant distance, as if to say, *You see? He's not so terrible after all.*

"You will have many questions and concerns, of course," the marquis said. "Whenever you would like to talk with me, I'll come at once. In the meantime, I'll do everything I can to publicly defend your honor."

A new voice entered the conversation. "Well. That would be a refreshing change."

Cassandra felt her heart jolt painfully as her gaze went to the doorway, where Tom Severin stood.

## Chapter 15

THE BUTLER, WHO HAD been waiting for an opportune moment to announce the new arrival, was clearly disgruntled at having being preempted before he could perform his duty correctly. "My lord," he said to Devon, "Mr. Severin."

Unlike the marquis, Tom had already dispensed with his hat and gloves, as if he intended to stay for a while.

Devon went to him, deftly blocking his way. "Severin . . . not now. We're dealing with a family matter. I'll meet with you later and explain—"

"Oh, you want me to be here," Tom assured him nonchalantly, and walked around him to enter the library. "Good afternoon, all. Or evening, I should say. Are we having tea? Splendid, I could do with a cup."

Devon turned to watch him with a perplexed frown, wondering what his friend was up to.

Tom looked relaxed and supremely confident, a man who was thinking five steps ahead of everyone else. The tantalizing sense of something dangerous held in reserve, a hidden volatility beneath the coolness, was still there.

Weak with longing, Cassandra stared at him, but his gaze didn't meet hers.

"Mr. Severin," Kathleen asked pleasantly, reaching for a fresh cup and saucer from the tea tray, "how do you prefer your tea?"

"Milk, no sugar."

Devon began to make introductions. "Lord Ripon, I'd like to present—"

"No need," Tom said casually. "We're already acquainted. Ripon happens to sit on a select committee that awards contracts to railway developers. Oddly enough, the most lucrative contracts tend to go to a railway company in which he's heavily invested."

Ripon stared at him with cold disdain. "You dare to impugn my integrity?"

Tom reacted with mock surprise. "No, did I sound critical? I meant to sound admiring. Private graft pairs so beautifully with public service. Like Bordeaux with aged beef. I'm sure I couldn't resist the temptation any more than you."

Lady Berwick, bristling with indignation, addressed Tom directly. "Young man, not only are you an unwelcome distraction, you have the manners of a goat."

That drew a flashing grin from Tom. "I beg your pardon, madam, and ask your indulgence for a minute or two. I have a good reason for being here."

Lady Berwick huffed and regarded him suspiciously.

After taking the teacup from Kathleen and declining the saucer, Tom went to brace his shoulder against the fireplace mantel. The firelight played over the gleaming short layers of his hair as he glanced around the room.

"I suppose the subject of the missing Lord Lambert has already been brought up," he remarked. "Has there been any sign of him?"

"Not yet," Winterborne replied. "Ransom has dispatched men to find him."

Cassandra suspected Tom knew something no one else did. He seemed to be playing some kind of cat-and-mouse game. "Do you have information regarding his whereabouts, Mr. Severin?" she asked unsteadily.

Tom looked directly at her then, the nonchalant mask temporarily falling away. His intense, searching gaze somehow burned through the numbness of the past twenty-four hours. "No, sweetheart," he said gently, as if there were no one else in the room. The deliberate endearment caused a few breaths to catch audibly, including hers.

"I'm sorry for what Lambert did to you," Tom continued. "There's nothing more repellent than a man who forces his attentions on women. The fact that he went on to malign you publicly proves he's a liar as well as a bully. I can't think of two more damning qualities in a man."

Ripon's face darkened. "He's your better, in every way," he snapped. "My son had a lapse in judgment, but he's still the cream of the crop."

Tom's mouth twisted. "I'd say the cream of the crop has gone sour."

Ripon turned to Devon. "Will you allow him to stand there crowing like a cock on his own dung hill?"

Devon shot Tom a vaguely exasperated glance. "Severin, could we go to the point?"

Obligingly, Tom drained his tea in two swallows and continued. "After reading that slanderous rubbish in the *Chronicle*, I found myself puzzled. Lord Lambert had already done enough damage with his rumormongering . . . why butter the bacon by writing a society column on top of it? There was no need. But if he didn't write it, who did?" He set the empty teacup on the mantel and wandered insouciantly around the library as he spoke. "I came up with a theory: After discovering his son had hopelessly botched any chance of winning your hand, Lord Ripon decided to take advantage of the situation. He's made no secret of his desire to marry again, and Lady Cassandra is an ideal candidate. But to obtain her, he first had to destroy her reputation so thoroughly that it left her with few practical alternatives. After having brought her sufficiently low, he would step forth and present himself as the best solution."

Silence descended over the room. Everyone looked at the marquis, whose complexion had turned purple. "You're mad," he snapped. "Your theory is absolute rot, as well as an insult to my honor. You'll never be able to prove it."

Tom looked at St. Vincent. "I assume the editor at the *Chronicle* refused to divulge the writer's identity?"

St. Vincent looked rueful. "Categorically. I'll have

to find a way to pry it out of him without bringing the entire British press to his defense."

"Yes," Tom mused, tapping his lower lip with a fingertip, "they tend to be so touchy about protecting their sources."

"Trenear," Lord Ripon said through gritted teeth, "will you kindly throw him out?"

"I'll see myself out," Tom said casually. He turned as if to leave, and paused as if something had just occurred to him. "Although . . . as your friend, Trenear, I find it disappointing that you haven't asked about my day. It makes me feel as if you don't care."

Before Devon could respond, Pandora jumped in. "I will," she volunteered eagerly. "How was your day, Mr. Severin?"

Tom sent her a brief grin. "Busy. After six tedious hours of business negotiations, I paid a call to the chief editor of the *London Chronicle*."

St. Vincent lifted his brows. "After I'd already met with him?"

Trying to look repentant, Tom replied, "I know you said not to. But I had a bit of leverage you didn't."

"Oh?"

"I told him the paper's owner would dismiss him and toss him out on the pavement if he didn't name the anonymous writer."

St. Vincent stared at him quizzically. "You bluffed?"

"No, that is what the business negotiations were about. I'm the new owner. And while the chief editor happens to be a staunch advocate for freedom of the press, he's also a staunch supporter of not losing his job."

"You just bought the *London Chronicle*," Devon said slowly, to make certain he hadn't misheard. "Today."

"No one could do that in less than a day," Ripon sneered.

Winterborne smiled slightly. "He could," he said, with a nod toward Tom.

"I did," Tom confirmed, picking idly at a bit of lint on his cuff. "All it took was a preliminary purchase agreement and some earnest money. It will come as no surprise to you, Ripon, that the editor named you as the anonymous author."

"I deny it! I denounce him, and you!"

Tom pulled a piece of folded parchment from an inside coat pocket and regarded it reflectively. "The most dangerous substance on earth is wood pulp flattened into thin sheets. I'd rather face a steel blade than certain pieces of paper." He tilted his head slightly, his steady stare fixed on the marquis. "The original column," he said with a flutter of the parchment. "In your hand."

In the suffocated silence that followed, Tom glanced over the page in his hand. "I have so many interesting plans for my newspaper," he mused. "Tomorrow, for example, we're running a special feature about how an unprincipled nobleman conspired with his spoiled whelp of a son to ruin an innocent young woman's name, all for the sake of greed and lechery. I've already set my editor to work on it." He sent the marquis a taunting glance. "At least now the mudslinging will be reciprocal."

"I'll sue you for libel," Lord Ripon cried, his facial nerves twitching, and stormed out of the library.

The group sat in stunned silence for a full half minute.

After exhaling slowly, Devon approached Tom to shake his hand heartily. "Thank you, Severin."

"It won't reverse all the damage that's been done," Tom said soberly.

"It will help, by God."

"Publicity of any kind is distasteful," Lady Berwick said severely, glowering at Tom. "It would be better to hold your silence and refrain from printing any kind of story about Cassandra."

Helen spoke up quietly. "Forgive me, ma'am, but I should think we want the truth to be spread as widely as the falsehoods were."

"It will only stoke the controversy," Lady Berwick argued.

Tom looked at Cassandra. Something in his eyes caused a twinge of heat deep at the pit of her stomach. "I'll do whatever you say," he said.

She could hardly think. It was difficult to wrap her mind around the fact that he was there, bigger than life, that he hadn't forgotten about her, that he'd done all this to defend her. What did it mean? What did he want? "Publish it, please," she faltered. "You . . ."

"Yes?" Tom prompted softly as she hesitated.

"You bought an entire newspaper business . . . for my sake?"

Tom thought for a long moment before answering. Now his voice was different than she'd ever heard it, quiet and even a little shaken. "There are no limits to what I would do for you."

Cassandra was speechless.

As she sat there in helpless silence, she realized that for once, no one else in the family was certain what to do either. They were all dumbfounded by Tom's statement, as well as the dawning understanding of why he was there.

As Tom beheld the row of blank faces before him, a crooked, self-mocking smile emerged. He shoved his hands in his pockets and paced a little. "I wonder," he ventured after a pause, "if it might be possible for Lady Cassandra and I to—"

"Absolutely not," Lady Berwick said firmly. "No more unchaperoned conversations with . . . gentlemen." A deliberate pause before the last word implied her doubt as to whether it applied to him.

"Severin," Devon said, his expression implacable, "Cassandra has endured enough for one day. Whatever you wish to say to her can wait."

"No," Cassandra said anxiously. She was well aware of Devon's opinions about Tom, that although he was worthy as a friend, he would be an unacceptable husband. But after what Tom had just done for her, she couldn't let her family send him away so abruptly—it would be rude and ungrateful. And although she still remembered Devon's assessment of Tom's character, she didn't agree with it now.

Not entirely, at any rate.

Trying to sound dignified, she said, "At least allow me to thank Mr. Severin for his kindness." She slid a pleading glance to Kathleen behind Lady Berwick's back.

"Perhaps," Kathleen suggested diplomatically, "Cassandra and Mr. Severin could talk at the other end of the library while we remain here?"

Lady Berwick relented with a reluctant bob of her head.

Devon let out a quiet sigh. "No objections," he muttered.

Cassandra rose on weak legs and shook out the folds from her skirts. She went with Tom to the other half of the library, where rows of tall, multipaned windows bracketed a glass door that opened to a side entrance of the house.

Tom drew her to a corner, where a slant of weak light from the pebble-colored sky came through the windows. Lightly his fingers came to her arm, just above the elbow, a careful pressure she barely felt through the sleeve.

"How are you?" he asked gently.

Had he started any other way, she might have been able to maintain her composure. But that simple question, and the wealth of concern and tenderness in his gaze, caused the blank, sick feeling to melt away, far too fast. Cassandra tried to answer, but no sound emerged: She could only breathe in quick, shallow pulls. In the next moment, she shocked both of them, and undoubtedly everyone else in the library, by bursting into tears. Mortified, she put her hands over her face.

In the next moment, she felt him pulling her into a deep embrace. His voice was low and soothing in her ear. "No . . . no . . . it's all right . . . easy, now. My sweet darling. Poor buttercup."

She choked on a sob, and her nose trickled. "H-handkerchief," she wheezed.

Somehow Tom deciphered the muffled word. He eased her away just far enough to reach into his coat, and produced a folded square of white linen. She took it and swabbed her eyes, and blew her nose. To her relief, Tom pulled her close again. "Do I really need to have an audience for this?" she heard him ask irritably over her head. After a moment, he said, "Thank you," although he didn't sound all that grateful.

Gathering that her family was leaving the library, Cassandra rested against him.

"You're shaking," Tom exclaimed softly. "Sweetheart . . . you've been through hell, haven't you?"

"It's been h-horrid," she sniffled. "So humiliating. I've already been uninvited to a dinner and a ball. I can't believe Lord Lambert would behave so ab-bominably and spread lies about me, and people would believe him so easily!"

"Shall I kill him for you?" Tom asked, sounding alarmingly sincere.

"I'd rather you didn't," she said in a watery voice, and blew her nose again. "It's not nice to murder people, even if they deserve it, and it wouldn't make me feel better."

"What would make you feel better?" Tom's tone was gentle and interested, his hands comforting as they moved over her.

"Just this," she said with a shuddering sigh. "Just hold me."

"For as long as you want. I'll do anything for you. Anything at all. I'm here, and I'll take care of you. I won't let anyone hurt you."

Sometimes there were words a woman needed to hear, even if she didn't believe them.

"Thank you for coming to me," she whispered.

"Always."

The warmth of his lips strayed across her face, absorbing the taste of her tears. Blindly she lifted her mouth, wanting more of the soft, tantalizing pressure. He gave it to her slowly, gently parting her lips. Breathing in unsettled sighs, she reached around his neck. His kiss shaped and stroked and teased, settling deeper into her response.

Her fingers laced into the clean, satiny locks of his hair, urging his head down over hers, wanting more pressure, more intimacy. He gave it to her, in a kiss so full and famished, it made her weak, heat pulsing in every limb and collecting at the tips of her fingers and toes. It felt like something she could die from.

A tremor went through Tom's frame. He crushed

his lips amid the disheveled locks of her hair, his breath rushing down to her scalp like bursts of steam. She twisted, trying to recapture his mouth, but he resisted. "I've wanted you for so long," he said gruffly. "There hasn't been anyone for me, Cassandra. Ever since—No, wait. Before I say anything else—You owe me nothing, do you understand? I would have leaped at any chance to expose Lord Ripon as a lying fraud, even if you hadn't been involved."

"I'm still grateful," Cassandra managed to say.

"God help me, don't be grateful." Tom took an unsteady breath. "I'll hold you 'til the end of time, if that's all you want from me. But there's so much more I could do for you. I would treasure you. I would—" He broke off, leaning so close she felt as if she were drowning in the tropical azure and ocean green of his eyes. "Marry me, Cassandra—and we'll tell them all to go to hell."

# Chapter 16

As TOM WAITED FOR her answer, he gently framed Cassandra's face between his hands. His thumbs stroked the fine-grained skin of her cheeks, delicately mottled with pink in the aftermath of tears. Her lashes were long, wet spikes, like the rays of stars.

"Tell who to go to hell?" she asked in confusion.

"The world." It occurred to Tom that as far as marriage proposals went, his might have been expressed a bit better. "Let me reword that—" he began, but she had already pulled away from him. He swore quietly.

Cassandra went to a nearby bookcase and stared fixedly at a row of leather-bound volumes. "We've already come to an understanding of why marriage wouldn't work for us," she said unsteadily.

Tom knew she wasn't in the best condition to have this discussion. Not by half. For that matter, he wasn't either. But he was fairly certain waiting would gain him nothing, nor would it help her.

His brain instantly began collating a list of arguments. "I've decided it would work for us after all. Circumstances have changed."

"Not mine," Cassandra countered. "No matter what's happened, or what anyone says, marriage isn't my only choice."

"You were discussing it with Ripon," Tom said, annoyed.

Turning to face him, Cassandra rubbed her forehead in a brief, weary gesture. "I don't want to quarrel with you. One might as well try to face down an oncoming locomotive."

Realizing his demeanor was too combative, Tom softened his voice and let his arms relax to his sides. "It wouldn't be a quarrel," he said innocently, reasonably. "I just want the same chance to make my case that you gave to Lord Ripon."

A corner of Cassandra's mouth curled with reluctant amusement. "You're trying to appear as harmless as a lamb. But we both know you're not."

"I have lamblike moments," Tom said. At her dubious glance, he insisted, "I'm having one right now. I'm one hundred percent lamb."

Cassandra shook her head. "I'm truly grateful for your offer, but I have no interest in a hectic, fast-paced life in the middle of the world's largest city, with a husband who can never love me."

"That's not what I'm offering," Tom said swiftly. "At least, it's not *all* I'm offering. You should at least find out more about what you'd be turning down." Catching sight of the abandoned chairs and place settings on the other side of the library, he exclaimed, "Tea. Let's have tea, while I mention a few points for you to consider."

Cassandra continued to look skeptical.

"All you have to do is listen," Tom coaxed. "Only for as long as it takes to drink one cup of tea. You can do that for me, can't you? Please?"

"Yes," Cassandra said reluctantly.

Tom didn't let his expression change, but he felt a stab of satisfaction. During bargaining talks, he always tried to maneuver the other side into saying yes as early and as often as possible. It made them far more likely to agree to concessions later on.

They went to the settee and low table. Tom remained standing, while Cassandra took some items from the tea cart and arranged a new place setting. She gestured to the place on the settee where she wanted him to sit, and he obeyed immediately.

Cassandra sat beside him and arranged her skirts, and reached for the teapot. With deft, ladylike grace, she poured tea through a tiny silver strainer and stirred milk into the cups with a silver spoon. When the ritual was done, she lifted her own cup to her lips and glanced at him expectantly over the gilded porcelain rim. The sight of her wet eyes launched his heart into chaos. He was nothing but raw nerves and longing. She was everything he'd ever wanted, and against all odds, he had half a chance of winning her if he could just find the right words, the right argument . . .

"You once told me it was your dream to help people," he said. "As lady of the manor, you'd be limited to knitting stockings and caps for the poor, and taking baskets of food to local families, which is all fine and proper. But as my wife, you could feed and educate thousands. Tens of thousands. You could help people on a scale you've never dared to imagine. I know you don't care about my money, but you definitely care about what it can do. If you marry me, you might not be part of the select circles of the upper class, but your political and financial power would go far beyond theirs."

Tom paused, covertly assessing Cassandra's reaction. She seemed more perplexed than enthusiastic, trying to envision the kind of life he was describing. "Also . . ." he added meaningfully, ". . . unlimited shoes."

Cassandra nodded distractedly, reaching for a cake, but then drew her hand back.

"You'd have freedom as well," Tom continued. "If you won't bother me about my comings and goings, I won't bother you about yours. Write your own rules. Arrange your own schedule. Raise the children however you like. The house will be your territory to run any way you choose." He paused to glance at her expectantly.

No reaction.

"Furthermore," Tom said, "I'd give you all the benefits of companionship with none of the difficulties of love. No ups and downs, no turmoil, no thwarted expectations. You'll never have to worry about your husband falling out of love with you, or falling in love with someone else."

"But I want to be loved," Cassandra said, frowning down at her lap.

"Love is the worst thing that can happen to people in novels," Tom protested. "What good did Heathcliff and all his passionate foaming at the mouth do for Cathy? Look at Sydney Carton—if he'd loved Lucie just a little less, he would have waited until her husband was guillotined, married her himself, and carried on with his successful law practice. But no, he did the noble thing, because love made him stupid. And then there's Jane Eyre, an otherwise sensible woman so dazzled by lovemaking, she didn't happen to notice the scurrying of an arsonous madwoman overhead. There would be far more happy endings in literature if people would just stop falling in love."

Cassandra's jaw had gone slack with astonishment. "You've been reading novels?"

"Yes. The point is, if you could just overlook this one small issue of my inability to form emotional attachments to other human beings, we'd be very happy together."

She was still focused on novels. "How many have you read?"

Tom went through them in his head. "Sixteen. No, seventeen."

"Which author is your favorite?"

He considered the question, weaving his fingers together and flexing them a few times. "So far, either Charles Dickens or Jules Verne, although Gaskell is quite tolerable. Austen's marriage plots are tedious, Tolstoy is preoccupied with suffering, and nothing by anyone named Brontë bears even a passing resemblance to real life."

"Oh, but Jane Eyre and Mr. Rochester," Cassandra exclaimed, as if the couple were the epitome of romance.

"Rochester is an irrational arse," Tom said flatly. "He could have simply told Jane the truth and installed his wife in a decent Swiss clinic."

Cassandra's lips twitched. "Your version of the plot may be more sensible, but it's not nearly as interesting. Have you tried any American novelists?"

"They write books?" Tom asked, and was gratified when Cassandra chuckled. Noticing he had now earned her full attention, he asked slowly, "Why does my novel reading interest you?"

"I'm not exactly sure. I suppose it makes you seem a bit more human. With all your talk of business and contracts, it's hard to—"

"Contracts," he exclaimed with a snap of his fingers.

Cassandra, who had been reaching for a tea cake again, jumped a little and snatched her hand back. She gave him a questioning glance.

"We'll negotiate a contract, you and I," Tom said. "A mutually agreed-upon set of marital expectations to use as a reference and amend as we go along."

"You mean . . . a document drawn up by lawyers . . . ?"

"No, none of it would be legally enforceable. It would just be for our private use. Most of what we put down would be too personal for anyone else's eyes." He had her full attention now. "It will give us both a better idea of what the future will look like," he continued. "It may help to ease some of your worries. We'll start designing our life together before it even starts."

"Design," she repeated with a faint laugh, regarding him as if he were a lunatic. "As if it were a building or a machine?"

"Exactly. Our own unique arrangement."

"What if one of us doesn't uphold the contract?"

"We'll have to trust each other. That's the marriage part." Seeing her steal another glance at the tea cakes, Tom picked up the plate and set it in front of her. "Here, would you like one?"

"Thank you, but no. That is, I would like one, but I can't."

"Why not?"

"I'm trying to reduce."

"Reduce what?"

Cassandra blushed and looked annoyed, as if he were being deliberately obtuse. "My weight."

Tom's gaze slid over her opulent and spectacularly curved form. Mystified, he shook his head. "Why?"

Cassandra's color deepened as she admitted, "I've gained nearly a stone since Pandora's wedding."

"Why does that matter?" Tom asked, increasingly baffled. "Every inch of you is gorgeous."

"Not to everyone," she said wryly. "My proportions have expanded past the ideal. And you know how people gossip when one is less than perfect."

"Why don't you try not giving a damn?"

"Easy for you to say, when you're so lean."

"Cassandra," he said sardonically, "I have two different colored eyes. I know all about the things people say when one is less than perfect."

"That's different. No one thinks of eye color as a lack of self-discipline."

"Your body isn't an ornament designed for other people's pleasure. It belongs to you alone. You're magnificent just as you are. Whether you lose weight or gain more, you'll still be magnificent. Have a cake if you want one."

Cassandra looked patently disbelieving. "You're saying if I gained another stone, or even two stones, on top of this, you'd still find me desirable?"

"God, yes," he said without hesitation. "Whatever size you are, I'll have a place for every curve."

She gave him an arrested stare, as if he'd spoken in a foreign language and she was trying to translate.

"Now," Tom continued briskly, "about the contract—"

He was caught off guard as Cassandra launched herself at him with enough momentum to knock him off balance and back into the corner of the settee. Her soft mouth fastened to his, her body molding to his. It felt so paralyzingly good that his hands remained suspended in mid-air for one, two, three seconds, before his arms closed around her. Bewildered, he shaped his mouth to hers, and felt the supple flick of her little tongue against his, venturing past his teeth, touching his inner cheek. He went instantly hard, dying with the need to devour, stroke, squeeze, kiss, feel her everywhere. She fit her body into the space between his thighs with an instinctive little wiggle, and he couldn't stifle a groan as a wave of pleasure nearly unmanned him.

Thank God they were lying down: He couldn't have stood after that. A white-hot glow had filled his groin, radiating outward in rings of sensation: It would be a miracle if this didn't end with him disgracing himself. Struggling for a measure of control, he lifted his right leg onto the settee and braced his left foot on the floor for balance. He slid his hands over her body, feeling the delicious shape of her through rustling layers of taffeta and velvet.

The rich ivory swell of her bosom plumped against the neckline of her bodice. Carefully his palms slid up to clasp the vault of her rib cage, and he hitched her a few inches higher on his chest. He pressed his lips to skin as smooth as glass, but soft and warm. His mouth traversed the lavish curve of her breast until he reached her cleavage. Very lightly, he let the tip of his tongue delve into the deep shadow, and savored the reflexive shiver that ran through her.

Hooking two fingers into her bodice, he eased one side down. Her flesh was revealed by millimeters, a beautiful rose-pink nipple budding in the cool air. She was so exquisite, so luscious. All the desire he'd ever known was nothing compared to this, a need that tore ragged edges along every breath. He put his mouth on her, sucking the tender peak past his lips, letting her feel the edges of his teeth, the velvety flat of his tongue. Soon he found a rhythm, tugging and lap-ping. He couldn't help undulating his pelvis upward in lewd, subtle nudges, rubbing the swollen length of his shaft up against the sweet weight of her. She was too voluptuous and wonderful for him to be able to lie completely still.

Soon, however, he approached the brink and was forced to stop moving. He released her breast with a growl of frustration, panting heavily.

Cassandra whimpered in protest. "No, please . . . Tom . . . I feel . . ."

"Desperate?" he asked. "Feverish? Knotted up inside?"

She nodded and swallowed convulsively, and dropped her forehead to his shoulder.

Tom turned his head and rubbed his lips against her temple. She smelled like crushed flowers and salt and damp talc. Bewitched and aroused, he breathed deeply of her. "There are two ways to make it better," he murmured. "One is to wait."

In a moment, he heard her muffled voice. "What's the other way?"

Despite the surfeit of aching, throbbing desire, a faint smile touched his lips. He lowered her to the settee until she was on her side facing him, with his arm fitted beneath her neck. Taking her mouth with his, he probed gently with his tongue, stroking and caressing the tender depths of her. He reached down to the heavy velvet swaths of her skirts and pulled up the front, until he found the shape of her hip covered in thin cambric.

Cassandra broke the kiss with a gasp.

Tom went still, his hand remaining clasped on her hip. He looked into her flushed face, assessing her mood, her quick-breathing excitement. God, he could hardly remember what it was like to be so innocent.

"I won't hurt you," he said.

"Yes, I'm . . . just so nervous . . ."

Tom leaned over her, his lips tracing the crest of her cheek and wandering lightly over her face. "Cassandra," he whispered, "everything I have, everything I am, is at your service. All you have to do is tell me what you want."

She turned a deeper shade of scarlet, if that were possible. "I want you to touch me," she brought herself to say timidly.

Carefully he smoothed the cambric over her hip with slow circles of his palm. Her bottom was full and firm, as delectable as a fresh peach. He wanted to bite her there, press his teeth gently into the cushiony surface. His wandering hand strayed to her front, where the stiff edge of her corset dug into her abdomen. Searching lower, he found the open seam at the crotch of her drawers, and lightly fingered the lace-trimmed edges. His knuckles slipped beneath the cambric, grazing a thatch of soft curls as if by accident. She jerked a little at the touch. He let his knuckles drag gently along each side of the soft furrow, up and down, until he heard a slight moan. Encouraged, he slid his hand farther into the garment, cupping the beautiful female shape of her. His fingertips delved gently into the intricate layers of softness, stroking back and forth between the labia, finding heat . . . tenderness . . . a slick of moisture.

He could hardly believe she was letting him touch her so intimately. Softly he played with her, sensitive to every twitch and pulse of the vulnerable flesh. Taking hold of the silky inner petals, he tugged softly at each in turn. Trembling, Cassandra turned her face against his shoulder, her knees pressing together.

"No, stay open for me," Tom urged, nuzzling into the little hollow beneath her ear.

Hesitantly her thighs parted, letting him tease and search until he found the melting heat of her entrance. He stroked across it gently, and she bit her lip with surprised dismay at the awareness of how wet she was. Tenderly he drew a damp fingertip upward, circling the half-hidden bud of her clitoris, awakening sensation but never quite touching where she most wanted.

Cassandra's eyes closed. A loose tendril of golden hair strayed across her cheek, fluttering with every deliciously uneasy breath. Tom built her pleasure slowly, relentlessly, stroking down the sweet cleft and massaging his way back up again. He concentrated on her responses, adoring the way she gasped and writhed and pushed herself at him. Leaning down, he drew the tip of her breast into his mouth and nibbled delicately. Her pelvis began a helpless rhythm, lifting and lifting. Very gently, he pressed the tip of his middle finger to the entrance of her body. Virginal muscles tightened against him, but he waited patiently, his fingertip wriggling deeper at the first hint of yielding. The first joint of his finger gently entered the silky channel. Deeper . . . to the knuckle . . . deeper. Her flesh pulled at him, grasping delicately as if to welcome the intrusion.

His mouth went to her other breast, kissing the turgid nipple, using his teeth and tongue. He searched inside her, tickling lightly, finding places that made her squirm. She crushed her parted lips against his throat, panting and kissing his skin feverishly.

Gradually he withdrew his finger, hot and wet from the elixir of her body, and caressed the little pearl in soft, even circles. Within seconds, she was gasping and writhing as she approached the pinnacle. His mouth found hers, absorbing her moans, sucking and licking at the sounds of her pleasure as if he were pulling honey from the comb.

An abrupt noise broke through the haze of lust—a decisive knock on the door—followed by the turn of the knob.

Cassandra squeaked in fright and stiffened in his arms. With a savage growl, Tom rolled her beneath him, concealing her naked breasts from view.

*"Don't . . . open . . . that . . . door,"* Tom snapped at the would-be intruder.

# Chapter 17

*T*HE DOOR CRACKED OPEN sufficiently to allow Devon's voice to come through. "We're all waiting in the parlor with nothing to do. You've had enough time to talk."

Despite Cassandra's blind panic, Tom kept his hand between her thighs, fondling and teasing her through one helpless spasm after another. Her climax had already begun, and he'd be damned if he'd let it be ruined. "Trenear," he said with lethal calm, "I have few enough friends as it is. I would hate to kill you. But if you don't leave us alone—"

"Lady Berwick is going to kill me if I don't bring Cassandra back to the parlor," Devon's muffled voice informed him. "Given the choice, I'd rather take my chances with you. Also, bear in mind that regardless of what the two of you may be trying to decide, *nothing* is going to happen unless I give my consent. Which is damned unlikely, given what I know about you after ten years' acquaintance."

It was close to impossible for the usually articulate Tom to form a reply with Cassandra quivering beneath him. She shook and arched, burying her face against his coat to keep silent. He slid his finger inside her, relishing the strong clamping of her muscles around him. A flash of heat went through him at the thought of being joined with her and feeling her flesh wringing and clenching on him—

"We haven't decided anything yet," he told Devon brusquely. "I may ask for your consent later, but right now, what I want is your absence."

"What does Cassandra want?" Devon asked.

Tom was about to reply for her, but Cassandra jerked her face back, bit her lip after a hard shudder, and spoke in an astonishingly composed voice. "Cousin Devon, if you could allow us five minutes more . . . ?"

A short silence passed. "Very well," Devon said. The door closed fully.

Cassandra dove her face against Tom's chest, gasping uncontrollably. His experienced fingers soothed her through the last few twitches and tremors, his thumb swirling over the little bud, his middle finger stroking deep inside her. Eventually he withdrew his finger and gently petted the silky-coarse curls.

"I'm sorry, buttercup," he murmured, cuddling her spent and trembling form against his. "You deserve time and privacy, and consideration. Not to be fondled in the library over the tea service."

Cassandra surprised him with an unsteady chuckle. "I asked for it," she reminded him. To his satisfaction, she was calm and glowing in the aftermath, the signs of strain gone from her face. She drew in a deep breath and let it out slowly. "Oh, my," she said faintly.

Tom couldn't stop himself from kissing her again. "You're the sweetest thing I've ever held in my arms," he whispered. "I want to be the one who pleasures you. The one you reach for in the night." He nuzzled and nipped at the velvety surface of her lips. "I want to fill the empty places inside you . . . give you whatever you need. My beautiful Cassandra . . . tell me what I have to do to be with you. I'll meet you on your terms. I've never said that to anyone in my life. I—" He stopped, painfully aware of the inadequacy of words. Nothing could convey the magnitude of his desire for her, the lengths to which he was willing to go.

Cassandra moved to sit up, slow and sluggish, as if she were under water. He watched regretfully as she pulled up her bodice, concealing the wondrous breasts from view. Her face was partially averted from his, her expression distant, as if she were deep in thought.

"Cousin Devon said negotiating with you was a nightmare," she commented after a long silence. "He said he was surprised it didn't end in murder."

With a leap of hope, Tom realized she was asking for reassurance.

"It wouldn't be like that for us," he replied instantly. "You and I would negotiate in good faith."

A frown knitted the space between her brows. "You wouldn't try to mislead me? You wouldn't add fine print to the contract?"

It occurred to Tom that her suspicious expression was very much like Bazzle's when he'd asked Tom about buggering.

"No fine print," he said immediately. "No tricks." When she didn't look convinced, he exclaimed, "Good God, woman, I would hardly expect to deceive my wife and live happily with the consequences. We'll have to trust each other."

"That's the marriage part," Cassandra said absently, echoing his words of a few minutes earlier. Her gaze lifted to his, her face turning pink and radiant as she seemed to come to a decision. "All right, then."

His heart stopped. "All right what?"

"I accept your proposal, contingent upon our negotiations, and subject to my family's approval."

A flush of mingled triumph and awe swept over Tom. For a moment, all he could do was stare at her. Despite what he'd wanted and hoped for and had thought might happen, the words came as a surprise after all. He was afraid to believe she actually meant it. He wanted it written down, engraved on something, so he could reassure himself later that she'd really said it. She'd said yes. Why had she said yes?

"Was it the shoes?" he asked.

That drew a quick laugh from her. "That part didn't hurt," she said. "But it was the idea of being met on my terms. And I want very much to help people in a large way." She paused, turning serious. "This won't be easy. Our life together will be a leap into the unknown, and I've never been comfortable with newness. I could have chosen a far lesser man than you and not felt nearly this afraid. You'll have to be patient with me, as I intend to be with you."

Tom nodded, his mind already assessing potential obstacles. Nothing could be allowed to stop this from happening. He had to be with her. "When you said our engagement is subject to your family's approval," he ventured, "I hope you don't expect it to be unanimous."

"I would like it to be. But it's not a requirement."

"Good," he said. "Because even if I manage to talk Trenear into it, debating with West will be like tilting at windmills."

She looked up at him alertly. "Was *Don Quixote* one of the books you read?"

"To my regret, yes."

"You didn't like it?"

Tom gave her a sardonic glance. "A story about a middle-aged lunatic who vandalizes private property? Hardly. Although I agree with Cervantes' point that chivalry is no different from insanity."

"That's not at all what he was saying." Cassandra regarded him ruefully. "I'm beginning to suspect you've missed the point of every novel you've read so far."

"Most of them are pointless. Like the one about the French bread thief who violated his parole—"

"*Les Misérables?*"

"Yes. It took Victor Hugo fourteen hundred pages to say, 'Never let your daughter marry a radical French law student.' Which everyone already knows."

Her brows lifted. "Is *that* the lesson you took from the novel?"

"No, of course not," he said promptly, reading her expression. "The lesson of *Les Misérables* is . . ." Tom paused cagily before taking his best guess. ". . . 'It's usually a mistake to forgive your enemies.'"

"Not even close." Amusement lurked at the corners of her mouth. "I have my work cut out for me, it seems."

"Yes," Tom said, encouraged by the remark. "Take me on. Influence me for the better. It will be a public service."

"Hush," Cassandra begged, touching his lips with her fingers, "before I change my mind."

"You can't," Tom said, knowing he was taking the words more seriously than she'd intended. But the very idea was like an ice pick to the heart. "That is, don't. Please. Because I . . ." He couldn't break their shared gaze. Her blue eyes, as dark as a cloudless midnight, seemed to stare right inside him, gently and inexorably prying out the truth. ". . . need you," he finally muttered.

Shame caused his face to sting as if from spark burns. He couldn't believe what he'd just said, how weak and unmanly it had sounded.

But the strange thing was . . . Cassandra didn't seem to think less of him for it. In fact, she was looking at him with more certainty now, nodding slightly, as if his mortifying admission had just cemented the bargain.

Not for the first time, Tom reflected there was no understanding women. It wasn't that they were illogical. Just the opposite. Their logic was of a higher order, too complex and advanced to submit to a complete proof calculus. Women assigned mysterious values to details a man would overlook, and were able to draw piercing conclusions about his innermost secrets. Tom suspected that Cassandra, after their handful of encounters, had already acquired a more thorough knowledge of him than his friends of more than a decade. More troubling still was the suspicion she understood things about him even he wasn't aware of.

"Let me talk to my family first," Cassandra said, reaching out to make little adjustments to his collar and necktie, smoothing his coat lapels. "I'll send for you tomorrow, or possibly the day after, and then you can make your case to them."

"I can't stay away from you that long," Tom said, affronted. "And I'll be damned if I let you handle this by yourself."

"You don't trust me?"

"It's not that! Letting you handle it without me has every appearance of cowardice."

"Tom," she said dryly, "your love of confrontation is a secret to no one. There's no danger of anyone accusing you of cowardice. However, nothing you say will make headway with the Ravenels until I convince them this is what *I* want."

"Is it?" Tom asked before he thought better of it, and cursed himself silently. Hang it all, now he was begging, doglike, for scraps of reassurance. He couldn't believe the power she had over him. This was what he'd been afraid of since the beginning.

Cassandra, alert to every subtle color of his mood, reached for him without hesitation. Grasping the coat lapels she'd just smoothed, she pulled him close and kissed him, soothing the rough edges of his anxiety. He kissed her deeply, taking as much as he could, while the sweet fervor of her response sent a fresh surge of arousal coursing through him. His flesh thickened, his lungs pumping with wild and uneven force. The self-control he'd always prided himself on had been reduced to smoldering rubble. He felt too much, all at the same time—it was all the colors mixed together. It was madness.

When at last their lips parted, their breath mingling in rapid gusts, Cassandra stared into his eyes and said firmly, "I want you. I won't change my mind. If we're to trust each other, Tom . . . let's start now."

# Chapter 18

"ALL WE CAN DO is advise you," Devon told Cassandra the next day. "The decision is ultimately yours."

"For God's sake," West said in exasperation, "don't tell her that."

Devon sent his younger brother a sarcastic glance. "It's not Cassandra's decision?"

"Not when she's obviously in no condition to make it for herself. Would you let her dance at the edge of a railway platform when she's drunk?"

"I haven't been drinking," Cassandra protested. "Nor would I ever be so silly as to dance at the edge of a railway platform."

"I didn't mean it literally," West retorted.

"It's still a mischaracterization. You're implying I don't know what I'm doing, when I happen to understand my own situation better than you do."

"I wouldn't necessarily agree—" West began, but quieted as Phoebe lightly dug her elbow in his ribs.

The five of them—Devon, Kathleen, West, Phoebe, and Cassandra—were out walking through Hyde Park, having felt the need to escape the confines of Ravenel House. With such a volatile topic of discussion, the large double library had seemed as pressure-filled as a kettle at full boil.

After having received a telegram from Devon the previous day, West and Phoebe had arrived on the first train from Essex this morning. To no one's surprise, West was in a temper, longing for vengeance against Ripon and his son for daring to slander a Ravenel.

The rest of the family would arrive later for dinner, but for now it was enough just to handle West and Devon, who were both strongly against the idea of her marrying Tom Severin. Kathleen seemed at least open to the idea, and Phoebe was maintaining a policy of strict neutrality.

"What have the others said?" West asked, in the manner of a general assessing troop strength. "I hope no one else supports this asinine idea."

"Mr. Winterborne and Lord St. Vincent have refrained from giving their opinions," Cassandra replied. "Helen said she wants whatever I want. Pandora likes Mr. Severin and thinks it's a splendid idea—"

"She would," West muttered.

"—and Lady Berwick said it's a disaster, and she won't have any part of it."

West looked glum. "This is the first time the old battle-ax and I have ever agreed on anything."

The group meandered across the broad natural landscape of Hyde Park. In spring and summer, the park teemed with carriages, riders, and pedestrians, but in the chill of winter, it was nearly deserted. Flowerbeds had gone dormant, tree limbs were bare, and the

trampled parade grounds had been left in peace to recover. A flock of rooks squabbled among a grove of
ancient oak, presenting such a perfect reflection of the
Ravenels' mood that Cassandra was amused despite
herself.

"Let's set aside the subject of Tom Severin for a
moment," West told Cassandra. "Phoebe and I have
come up with a plan."

"It's West's plan," Phoebe said.

"You'll recall she has a younger brother named Raph-
ael," West continued. "Tall, unmarried, nice teeth. He's
perfect."

"He's not at all perfect," Phoebe said. "And how do
you know he's tall and has nice teeth?"

"Your parents are obviously incapable of producing
a less than superior human being. We'll introduce him
to Cassandra, he'll want to marry her right away, and
everyone will be happy."

"What about Tom?" Cassandra asked.

"He'll be happy as soon as he finds some other
woman's life to ruin."

She gave him a reproachful glance. "I thought you
liked him."

"I do, absolutely. He occupies a high place on the
list of things I don't respect myself for liking, right
between street food and filthy drinking songs."

Cassandra was aware that it had always been West's
habit—as well as Devon's and Winterborne's—to
make sarcastic remarks about Tom Severin, in the

way of longstanding friends. But it rankled now in a way it never had before. "After all Mr. Severin has done for our family," she said quietly, "he deserves more respect than that."

They were all silent, darting surprised glances at her. Until that moment, Cassandra had never dared to utter one word of reproof to him.

To West's credit, he considered the point, and relented. "You're right," he said in a different tone. "I beg your pardon for being a facetious arse. But I know both of you well enough to be certain you don't belong together."

Cassandra met his gaze without blinking. "Is it possible that Mr. Severin and I might know each other in a different way than you know either of us?"

"Touché. Is it possible that you might think you know him far less than you actually do?"

"Touché," Cassandra replied reluctantly.

West's face softened. "Listen to me, Cassandra: If you spend enough time around Severin, you'll come to love him. It's your nature. Even knowing it's a bad idea under the circumstances, you'll end up doing it, the way I used to sing in the bath."

Phoebe slid her husband a surprised glance. "When was that?"

"When I lived alone. But I was obliged to stop after I moved to Eversby Priory, when Kathleen told me it was scaring the servants."

"It sounded nonhuman," Kathleen said. "We all thought someone was performing an exorcism."

Entertained by the revelation, Phoebe grinned and slipped her arm through West's.

West turned his attention back to Cassandra. "Sweetheart, none of us could bear seeing you in a one-sided marriage. Don't expect Severin to change. You can't love someone into loving you back."

"I understand," Cassandra said. "But even if Tom is never able to return my feelings, he has qualities that make up for it."

"What qualities?" Devon asked, plainly bewildered. "I've always thought I understood you well, but this . . . you and Severin . . . it makes no sense to me."

As Cassandra considered how to explain, she heard Phoebe point out with a touch of amusement, "It's not *that* improbable, is it? Mr. Severin is a very attractive man."

Both Ravenel brothers looked at her blankly.

"Oh, yes," Kathleen agreed. "Not to mention charming."

West rolled his eyes and gave Devon a resigned glance. "He's always had it," he said flatly. "That thing women like."

"What thing?" Devon asked.

"The secret, mysterious thing I've always wished someone would explain so we could pretend to have it too."

They approached a massive weeping beech tree, its silvery branches draping down to the ground to form an umbrella-shaped skeleton. In the summer, its rich, dark foliage turned the tree into a living cave, and inspired some to refer to it as "the upside-down tree." At this time of year, only a few pale brown leaves clung to the branches, shivering and crackling in the breeze.

Cassandra wandered slowly among the trailing branches and sprays of threadlike twigs as she tried to explain. "I've always found Tom very appealing," she said, and was grateful for the chill of December air against her hot cheeks. "Despite his eccentricities, and perhaps even because of them. I wasn't able to envision myself as the wife of such a man before, but yesterday he made some compelling arguments. And the moment he suggested the contract, I knew for certain I wanted to marry him."

"What bloody contract?" The word had instantly riled Devon. "Severin has no business mentioning contracts without someone there to protect your financial interests—"

"Not that kind of contract," Cassandra replied quickly. She went on to explain Tom's proposition to write an agreement together, about the things they valued and needed, the compromises they would be willing to make, the lines that had to be drawn.

"But it wouldn't be legal," Devon said.

"I think," Kathleen ventured, "the point is that it shows Cassandra's thoughts and feelings matter to Mr. Severin."

"It means he wants to listen to her," Phoebe added, "and take her opinions into consideration."

"Diabolical bastard," West muttered, although the corner of his mouth twitched with rueful amusement.

Cassandra paused to curl her gloved hand around a beech branch. A wondering smile broke out on her face as she regarded her family. "He's not like anyone else I've ever met. His brilliant mind won't let him view anything, even his wife, in a conventional way. He sees more potential in me than I've imagined for myself. I'll admit, I'm surprised by how much I like it."

"Has Severin told you he has only five feelings?" West asked sardonically.

"He told me. But recently he's been forced to add a few, which I find encouraging."

Devon approached Cassandra, gazing at her in the manner of a concerned older brother. He leaned down to kiss her cheek, and sighed. "From my own experience, I can say this with authority: There's no better way to become familiar with Tom Severin than negotiating a contract with him. If you're still speaking to him by the end of it . . . I'll consent to the match." At the periphery of his vision, he saw West begin to object, and added firmly, "You have my word."

"SIR, THIS WAS just delivered by a footman in full livery."

Barnaby approached Tom Severin's desk with a sealed letter, intensely curious about its contents. Although it wasn't unheard-of for correspondence to arrive at the office in such a manner—Severin had business dealings with people from all walks of life—it was somewhat more unusual for the address to have been written in a feminine hand. On top of that . . . the letter was lightly scented. The fragrance reminded Barnaby of a field full of tiny white flowers, so delicate and alluring that he ducked his head and sniffed it discreetly before handing it to Severin.

Severin seemed riveted by the sight of the letter. Barnaby could have sworn his employer's hand trembled slightly as he reached out to take it. There was something very off about Severin. It had started with that business over the *London Chronicle* yesterday, when Severin had impulsively decided to buy the newspaper. He'd gone about it with maniacal determination, bypassing his usual business protocols, and hounding lawyers, accountants, and bankers to have it accomplished immediately. Then this morning, Severin had been incredibly distracted and edgy, checking his pocket watch over and over, and jumping up every few minutes to stand at one of the windows and stare blankly down at the street.

Now seated at his desk, Severin broke the wax seal and hesitated unaccountably before unfolding the letter. His gaze moved swiftly over the written lines. One of his hands came up to rub his lower jaw slowly as he read it over again.

The black head lowered, as if Severin were overcome by illness . . . or emotion, which for Severin amounted to the same thing . . . and Barnaby was tempted to panic. Dear God, what was happening? What terrible news did the letter contain? But then Barnaby realized with a little shock that Severin had bent to press his lips to the scented parchment.

"Barnaby," came his employer's unsteady voice. "Clear my schedule for the rest of the week."

"The entire week? Starting tomorrow?"

"Starting right now. I have preparations to make."

Unable to stop himself, Barnaby asked hesitantly, "What has happened, sir?"

Severin grinned, a flush climbing in his fair complexion. His eyes were an intense blaze of blue-green. Such an apparent extremity of excitement was not at all normal for the man, and it made Barnaby nervous. "Nothing to worry about. I'll be occupied with negotiations."

"More to do with the *Chronicle*?"

Severin shook his head. "Another business entirely." A brief, wondering laugh escaped him. "The merger of a lifetime."

# Chapter 19

AT EIGHT O'CLOCK IN the morning, Tom arrived at Ravenel House, dressed in a beautiful dark suit of clothes with a royal-blue four-in-hand necktie. As he entered the breakfast room and bowed, he was so obviously pleased with the entire situation that even West was moved to reluctant amusement.

"I expected you to look like the cat who swallowed a canary," West said, standing to shake Tom's hand, "but you look more like a cat who swallowed another entire cat."

At Kathleen's invitation, Tom went to the sideboard and helped himself to coffee from a silver urn. He took the unoccupied chair between Cassandra and Phoebe. "Good morning," he murmured.

Cassandra could hardly meet his gaze. She felt ridiculously shy and giddy, and embarrassed by the memory of their intimacy . . . those deep, consuming kisses . . . the wicked exploration of his fingers . . .

"Good morning," she replied, and quickly took refuge in her tea. She was vaguely aware of the conversation taking place around her, a few pleasantries, and a tentative question from Phoebe about where he and Cassandra would take up residence after the wedding.

"The betrothal isn't official yet," Tom replied seriously. "Not until Cassandra is satisfied with the outcome of our negotiations."

"But assuming you'll reach an agreement . . . ?" Phoebe pressed.

"At the moment," Tom said, looking at Cassandra, "I live at Hyde Park Square. We could live in that one if you like it. But it would be an easy matter to move to one of the others, if you would prefer."

Cassandra blinked in confusion. "You have more than one house?"

"Four," Tom replied in a matter-of-fact tone. Seeing her expression, he appeared to realize how odd she found it, and continued more cautiously, "I also have a few undeveloped residential lots in Kensington and Hammersmith, and recently I acquired an estate in Edmonton. But it would be impractical to live that far from my offices. So . . . I thought I might turn that one into a town."

"You're going to start a town?" Kathleen asked blankly.

"For the love of God," West said, "don't name it after yourself."

A vaguely uneasy feeling crept over Cassandra. "Why do you have so many houses?" she asked Tom.

"Sometimes when a freehold property comes on the market at a decent price, I'll buy it as an investment."

"The London Ironstone railway isn't your only source of income, then," Cassandra said, trying to make sense of it. "You also deal in real estate."

"Yes, and I do some speculative building here and there."

"How many businesses do you have?" she asked.

Registering the keenly interested gazes focused on him, Tom asked uncomfortably, "Aren't we supposed to refrain from discussing this at the breakfast table?"

"You never follow the rules," Cassandra reminded him.

His reluctance was obvious. However, being Tom, he answered honestly. "I've grouped several companies with London Ironstone to form a conglomerate. Freight, steel and concrete production, factories that make hydraulic pumps, dredging and excavating equipment, an engineering and design firm, and so on. When I build a new railway line, I don't need to hire outside contractors, I use my own. I also have service companies for maintenance, communications and signaling, safety equipment—" He paused as he saw the color drain from her face. "What's the matter?"

"I just realized," Cassandra said in a suffocated voice, "you don't have a railway, you have an empire."

"That's not how I think of it," Tom said with a slight frown.

"No matter what word one uses . . . you must be nearly as rich as Mr. Winterborne."

Tom devoted a great deal of attention to buttering his toast.

Reading into his silence, Cassandra asked apprehensively, "Are you *richer* than Mr. Winterborne?"

"There are many different ways to calculate wealth," Tom said evasively, reaching for a pot of jam.

Her stomach sank. "Oh, God, how much richer?"

"Why must I be compared to Winterborne?" Tom parried. "He does well at his business, and so do I. Let's leave it at that."

Devon replied to Cassandra in a matter-of-fact tone. "The two aren't really comparable. Although Winterborne is a dominating force in commerce, Severin's business affects *everything*: transportation, trade, manufacturing, communications, and urban development. He's not only changing the way business is done, but how and where people live." Devon stared at Tom speculatively as he continued. "My guess is, Severin's fortune is half again as much as Winterborne's, and before long will be approximately double."

Tom gave him an oblique glance, but didn't deny it.

"I see," Cassandra said sickly, thinking of her quiet, cozy life in the country, with dogs and gardens and relaxed afternoon walks.

"You won't be burdened by my business affairs," Tom told her, his brows lowering. "All of that will be kept separate from my home life."

"The question is," Devon said quietly, "how much home life will there be? You're only one man, Tom, doing the work of at least ten—and the demands on you will only grow worse over time."

"That's for me to worry about."

West spoke then, making no effort to hide his concern. "I'd say it's for your future wife to worry about."

Tom's eyes narrowed. "Whatever my wife needs or desires of me," he said with cool arrogance, "she'll have it. I can arrange my schedule in any way I wish. I do as little or as much work as I want, go wherever I please, and stay or leave as it suits me. No one owns me or my time. That's the point of being me."

Ordinarily, Devon or West would have said something mocking in reply, but they were both silent. Something in Tom's face communicated that he'd been pushed far enough. For the first time, Cassandra had an inkling of how he must appear to other people: someone to be respected and even feared. A man who possessed vast power and authority, and was entirely comfortable wielding it. This was a side he rarely, if ever, revealed to the Ravenels. He'd always been willing to tolerate a few jabs and teasing from his friends with good grace . . . but he didn't have to.

In fact, there was very little Tom Severin had to tolerate.

He would be nearly impossible to manage, Cassandra thought apprehensively. One might as well try to harness a storm. But he'd brought himself to confess he needed her, which had been extraordinarily difficult for him. That wasn't a guarantee of anything . . . but it wasn't a bad start.

AT THE CONCLUSION of breakfast, Kathleen walked with Cassandra and Tom to the library, where a jug of water and glasses had been set out on the long table, along with a neat stack of parchment, pens, and an inkwell.

"Ring for the servants if there's something you require," Kathleen said. "I'm going to leave the door ajar, and I suspect someone might come to check on you now and then. But that someone won't be me."

"Thank you," Cassandra replied, smiling affectionately after the woman who'd been such a steady and loving presence in her life.

When they were alone, she turned to Tom. Before she could say a word, he reached around her, pulled her up against him, and kissed her. She responded helplessly, lifting her arms around his neck, pressing tightly against his solid form. He made a hungering sound and altered the angle of the kiss to make it deeper, more intimate.

All too soon, Tom broke the kiss, his eyes cinder-bright, the set of his mouth brooding. "You won't be getting half a husband," he said brusquely. "Just the opposite. You'll probably have more of me than you want."

"My family—" she began apologetically.

"Yes. I know why they're concerned." His hand smoothed over her back, up and down the length of her spine. "My work is important to me," he said. "I need the challenge, or I'd go mad from boredom. But it's not all-consuming. As soon as I'd achieved what

I'd set out to do, there was nothing left to prove. It all started to seem like more of the same. Nothing has been exciting or satisfying for years. With you, though, everything is new. All I want is to be with you."

"Even so," Cassandra said, "there will always be many voices clamoring for your attention."

He drew back enough to look at her. "Yours is the one I'll heed first. Always."

She smiled slightly. "Perhaps we should put that in the contract."

Taking the remark seriously, Tom reached inside his coat and extracted a pencil. He bent to the table, writing something on the sheet of parchment in front of them and finishing with a decisive period.

As he turned back to her, Cassandra stood on her toes to kiss him. He claimed his reward immediately, fitting his mouth to hers and taking a long, ardent taste. Her head swam, and she welcomed the exploration of his tongue. He savored and consumed her, with a kiss more aggressive than any he'd given her before. It made her knees weak and turned her bones fluid. Her body listed toward his and was instantly gathered into the hard urgency of his embrace. Desire curled through her in hot tendrils that insinuated themselves in deep, private places. Her throat caught on a whimper of protest as his mouth lifted from hers.

"We'd better start negotiating," he said raggedly. "The first issue is how much time you'll want to spend with me."

"All of it," Cassandra said, and sought his lips again.

Tom chuckled. "I would. I . . . oh, you're so sweet . . . no, I'm . . . *God*. It's time to stop. Really." He crushed his mouth against her hair to avoid her kisses. "You're about to be deflowered in the library."

"Didn't that already happen?" she asked, and felt the shape of his smile.

"No," he whispered, "you're still a virgin. Albeit slightly more experienced than two days ago." He brought his mouth closer to her ear. "Did you like what I did?"

She nodded, her face turning so hot that she could feel her cheeks throb. "I wanted more."

"I'd like to give you more. As soon as possible." Tom released her with a roughcast sigh. He seated her, and instead of taking the chair on the opposite side of the table, he occupied the one beside her. Picking up the metal propelling pencil, he used his thumb to push down the top, which clicked as it let out some of the graphite lead inside. "I'll record the points of agreement as we go along, if you'll write the final draft in ink."

Cassandra watched as he made a few notes on the page in small, neatly formed print. "What interesting penmanship."

"Drafting font," he said. "Engineers and draftsmen are taught to write like this, to make technical drawings and specifications easy to read."

"Who sent you to engineering classes?"

"My employer at the tramway company, Mr. Chambers Paxton."

"That was kind of him."

"His motives weren't selfless," Tom said dryly. "My skills were put to use designing and building engines for him. But he was a good man." He paused, his gaze turning distant. "He changed my life."

"When did you meet him?"

"I was twelve, working as a train boy. Every week, Mr. Paxton rode the eight twenty-five express from London to Manchester and back again. He hired me, and took me in to live with him and his family. Five daughters, no boys."

Cassandra listened carefully, sensing the wealth of important details tucked between the simple statements. "How long did you live with the family?"

"Seven years."

"Mr. Paxton must have seemed like a father to you."

Tom nodded, examining the mechanism of the metal pencil. *Click*. He pushed some of the lead back in.

"Will you invite him to the wedding?" Cassandra asked.

His opaque gaze angled up to hers. "He passed away two years ago. Disease of the kidneys, so I heard."

"You *heard* . . ." Cassandra repeated, perplexed.

*Click. Click*. "We fell out of communication," Tom said casually. "I'd worn out my welcome with the Paxton family."

"Tell me what happened," she invited gently.

"Not now. Later."

Something in his pleasant manner made Cassandra feel shut out. Pushed away. As he neatened the stack of writing paper, he looked so solitary that she instinctively reached out to rest her hand on his shoulder.

Tom stiffened at the unexpected touch. Cassandra began to draw her hand back, but he caught it swiftly. He drew her fingers to his lips and kissed them.

She realized he was doing his best to share his past with her, yielding his privacy and his secrets . . . but it would take time. He wasn't accustomed to making himself vulnerable to anyone, for any reason.

Not long ago, she'd seen a comedy at Drury Lane, featuring a character who had fitted the door of his house with a ridiculous variety of locks, latches, and bolts that went all the way from the top to the bottom. Any time someone new entered the scene, it necessitated a laborious process of searching through keys and painstakingly unfastening the entire row. The resulting frustrations of all the characters had put the audience in stitches.

What if Tom's heart wasn't frozen after all? What if it were merely guarded . . . so guarded that it had become a prison?

If so, it would take time and patience to help him find his way out. And love.

*Yes.* She would let herself love him . . . not as a martyr, but as an optimist.

# Chapter 20

"SO FAR, THIS HAS been much easier than I expected," Cassandra said, straightening an accumulating stack of pages with headings, sections, and subsections. "I'm beginning to think you weren't nearly as intolerable at the bargaining table as Cousin Devon said you were."

"No, I was," Tom said ruefully. "If I had it to do over, I would handle the situation far differently."

"You would? Why?"

Tom looked down at the page before him, using the pencil to scrawl absently in the margins. Cassandra had already noticed his habit of drawing shapes and scribbles while mulling something over: gears, wheels, arrows, railway tracks, tiny diagrams of mechanical objects with no discernible purpose. "I've always been competitive," he admitted. "Too focused on winning to care about collateral damage. It didn't occur to me that while I was treating it as a game, Trenear was fighting for his tenant families."

"No harm was done," Cassandra said prosaically. "You didn't succeed in taking the mineral rights."

"Not for lack of trying." The mechanical pencil connected a pair of curving parallel lines with little cross marks, turning them into railroad tracks. "I'm grateful Trenear chose not to hold it against me. He made me aware there are more important things than winning—which is a lesson I needed to learn."

Resting her chin on her hand, Cassandra reached out to touch one of the little drawings in the margin. "Why do you do that?" she asked.

Tom followed her gaze down to the page. His abashed grin was uncharacteristically boyish, and it gave her a pang of delight. "Sorry. It helps me to think."

"Don't apologize. I like your quirks."

"You won't like all of them," he warned. "Trust me on that."

11:00 *A.M.*

"*I* CAN'T ABIDE CLUTTER," TOM said. "That includes long dusty curtains, and china figurines, and those little tablemats with holes in them—"

"Doilies?"

"Yes, those. And fringe trimming. I *hate* fringe."

Cassandra blinked as she saw him write, *7D: No doilies or fringe.*

"Wait," she said. "No fringe *at all*? Not even on lampshades? Or pillows?"

"Especially not pillows."

Cassandra rested her crossed arms on the table and gave him a mildly exasperated glance. "Was there an accident involving fringe? Why do you hate it?"

"It's ugly and waggly. It dangles like caterpillar legs."

Her brows lowered. "I reserve the right to wear fringe trim on my hats or clothing. It happens to be fashionable this year."

"Can we exclude it from nightwear and robes? I'd rather not have it touching me." Faced with her baffled annoyance, Tom looked down at the paper somewhat sheepishly. "Some quirks can't be overcome."

11:30 A.M.

"BUT EVERYONE LIKES DOGS," Cassandra protested.

"I don't *dis*like dogs. I just don't want one in my house."

"Our house." She braced her elbows on the table and massaged her temples. "I've always had dogs. Pandora and I couldn't have survived our childhood without Napoleon and Josephine. If cleanliness is what worries you, I'll make certain the dog is bathed often, and accidents will be disposed of right away."

That drew a grimace from him. "I don't want there to be accidents in the first place. Besides, you'll have more than enough to keep you busy— you won't have time for a pet."

"I need a dog."

Tom held the propelling pencil between his first and second fingers, and flipped it back and forth to make the ends tap on the table. "Let's look at this logically—you don't really *need* a dog. You're not a shepherd or a rat catcher. Household dogs serve no useful purpose."

"They fetch things," Cassandra pointed out.

"You'll have an entire staff of servants to fetch anything you want."

"I want a companion who'll go on walks with me, and sit on my lap while I pet him."

"You'll have me for that."

Cassandra pointed to the contract. "Dog," she insisted. "I'm afraid it's nonnegotiable."

Tom's hand closed around the pencil. *Click. Click.* "What about fish?" he suggested. "They're soothing. They don't ruin carpets."

"One can't pet a fish."

A long silence passed. Tom scowled as he read the determination on her face. "This is a major concession on my part, Cassandra. If I give in on this point, I'll want a proportionately large something-or-other in return."

"I gave in on fringe," she protested.

"The dog will be your companion, not mine. I don't want to be bothered by it."

"You'll hardly know it's there."

Tom snorted in disbelief and adjusted the lead in the mechanical pencil. He touched the pencil to the paper and paused. "Damn it," he muttered.

Cassandra pretended not to hear.

"Wife will acquire no more than one domestic canine companion," Tom said grimly as he wrote. "A: Not to exceed twelve inches in height at the withers, chosen from a list of acceptable breeds to be determined later. B: Canine companion will sleep in designated areas at night, and C:"—his voice turned stern—"Will *under no circumstances* be allowed on beds or upholstered furniture."

"What about ottomans?"

The tip of the graphite pencil lead snapped and flew off the table with a *ping*.

Cassandra interpreted that as a no.

12:00 *P.M.*

"... *Y*OU'LL HAVE TO WAKE up early if you want to breakfast with me," Tom said. "Most of your kind stay awake half the night at balls and parties, and never arise before noon."

"My kind?" Cassandra repeated, her brows lifting.

"I arrive at the office no later than half past eight. Working London keeps different hours than aristocratic London."

"I'll awaken as early as necessary," Cassandra said.

"You may not find it worth the effort."

"Why? Are you grumpy in the morning?"

"No, but I wake up on the go. I don't like to linger over breakfast."

"You must not be doing it right. Lingering is *lovely*. I do it all the time." She stretched her arms and shoulders, and arched her sore upper back, her breasts lifting with the motion.

Tom stared at her, mesmerized. "I might stay just to watch you linger."

*1:00 P.M.*

"WHAT ABOUT SLEEPING ARRANGEMENTS?"

Cassandra felt her stomach flip, not unpleasantly, and her face began to warm. "Perhaps we should have our own rooms, and you could visit?"

"Certainly." Tom fiddled with the pencil. "I'll want to visit fairly often."

She glanced at the empty doorway before turning her attention back to him. "How often?"

Tom set down the pencil and drummed his fingers on the tabletop. "In the past, I've gone for long periods of time without . . . hang it, what's the polite word for it?"

"I don't think there is a polite one."

"During a drought, so to speak, I've always focused my energy on work. But when it's available . . . that is . . . when I've found the right woman . . . I tend to be . . ." Tom paused, mentally riffling through various words. ". . . demanding. Do you understand?"

"No."

That provoked a wry grin. Tom lowered his head briefly, then slanted a look up at her. A flicker of firelight caught in his green eye and made it gleam like a cat's. "What I'm trying to say is, I expect I'll be keeping you busy every night, for a while."

Cassandra nodded, coloring deeply. "It's the husband's right, after all."

"No," he said immediately. "As I said before, your body is your own. You've no obligation to lie with me, if you don't want. Not ever. That's why I agreed with the idea of separate rooms. But I would ask something of you . . ." He hesitated.

"Yes?"

A succession of emotions crossed his features . . . self-mockery . . . chagrin . . . uncertainty. "That whenever you're angry or annoyed with me . . . you won't use silence as a weapon. I can't abide it. I'd choose any other punishment."

"I would never do that," Cassandra said gravely.

"I didn't think so. But I'd like to put it in the contract, if I may."

Cassandra studied him for a moment. The hint of vulnerability she saw just now . . . this was something new. She liked it very much.

Silently she extended her hand for the propelling pencil, and Tom gave it to her. She wrote, *Wife will never give husband the cold shoulder*, and impulsively drew a little picture beside it.

Tom's thick lashes lowered as he looked at the page. "What's that?" he asked.

"My shoulder. There's my collarbone, and there's my neck."

"I thought it was a bird smashing into a building." He smiled at her pretend frown and retrieved the mechanical pencil. "Your shoulder isn't nearly so angular," he said, drawing a smooth curve. "The muscle at the top gives it a beautiful slope . . . like this. And the line of your collarbone is long and straight . . . tipping upward here . . . like the edge of a butterfly's wing."

Cassandra admired the drawing. With just a few expressive strokes, he had captured an accurate likeness of her shoulder and throat, and the soft line of her neck leading up to her jaw. "Are you an artist, on top of everything else?" she asked.

"No." His smiling eyes met hers. "But I've dreamed of you in that blue dress every night since we danced in the winter garden."

Moved, Cassandra leaned close to kiss him.

The pencil dropped to the table, rolled, and fell to the carpet.

Time ceased its spinning, the draft of minutes broken, the world itself forgotten. Tom pulled her into his lap, and she curled her arms around his neck the way she wanted to wrap her body around him. To her delight, he let her take the lead, leaning back as she experimented with kisses, dragging her lips across his, then fastening tight and ravening slowly. She loved the silky-wet warmth of his mouth . . . the way his body flexed and tightened beneath her . . . the quiet pleasure sounds he couldn't quite hold back. He took his hands from her and gripped the arms of the chair so tightly, it was a wonder the wood didn't crack.

"Cassandra," he muttered, panting. "I can't . . . do this anymore."

She lowered her forehead to his, her fingers sliding through the thick black layers of his hair. "One more kiss?"

Tom's face was flushed, his eyes dilated. "Not even one."

"*Ahem.*" The sound of someone clearing his throat at the doorway caused them both to start. West stood at the threshold, one shoulder braced against the doorjamb. His expression wasn't disapproving, only bemused and a bit wry. "I came to ask how the negotiations were going."

Tom gave a savage groan and turned his face against Cassandra's throat.

Although Cassandra was pink with embarrassment, she sent West a glance of suppressed mischief. "We're making progress," she told him.

West's brows lifted slightly. "Although I seem to have caught the two of you in a compromising position, my moral pedestal is, alas, too short to give me a clear view of who's doing what to whom. Therefore, I'll spare you the sanctimonious finger wagging."

"Thank you," Tom said in a muffled voice, uncomfortably adjusting Cassandra on his lap.

"Phoebe and I are departing for Essex within the hour," West continued. "I'll bid you farewell on her behalf as well as mine. And Tom—" He waited until

Tom turned his head with a glance of baleful inquiry. "I apologize," West continued simply. "It occurs to me I've been hypocritical: My past is far more tarnished than yours. God knows you never disgraced yourself in public as I did on a regular basis. You're a good friend, and you came here with an honorable proposition. I'm damned if I have the right to judge your fitness as a potential husband. If Cassandra decides she wants you, you'll both have my full support."

"Thank you," Tom said again, this time sounding as if he meant it.

"One more thing," West continued. "Ransom just sent word that Lord Lambert was found and detained in Northumberland."

Cassandra felt a new tension in Tom's body. He sat up straighter, his gaze focusing on West. "Is he still there?"

"I don't think so. Ransom went up to have a talk with him. In his usual cryptic fashion, Ransom writes that Lambert is now 'out of the country.'"

"What the devil does that mean?" Tom asked curtly.

"Who knows? It's Ransom. It could mean Lambert's fled to France, or he's been shanghaied, or . . . I'm afraid to speculate. I'll try to get more information out of Ransom, but that's like pulling teeth from a crocodile. The point is, Lambert won't be bothering anyone for a long while." West pushed away from the door frame. "I'll leave the two of you to your negotiating. If that's what we're calling it."

3:00 P.M.

"BUT YOU'LL HAVE TO spend time with the children," Cassandra insisted. "They'll need your influence."

"My influence is the last thing they'll need, unless you're planning to raise a pack of immoral little devils."

She took the pencil and began a subsection. "At the very least, you'll have to participate in family time in the parlor every night after dinner, outings on Sundays, and then there are birthdays, holiday festivities—"

"I don't mind older children, who can be threatened with Scottish boarding schools," Tom said. "It's the younger ones, who cry and scream and totter from one catastrophe to another. They're nerve-wracking and tedious at the same time."

"It's different when it's your own children."

"So I've heard." Tom settled back in his chair, looking vaguely surly. "I'll go along with whatever you think is appropriate, but don't call on me to discipline them. I'm not going to whip or thrash them, even if it's for their own good."

"I wouldn't ask you to do that," Cassandra said hastily. "There are other ways to teach right from wrong."

"Good. Life doles out enough inevitable pain for each of us—my children won't need extra helpings from me."

She smiled at him. "I think you'll make a fine father."

His mouth twisted. "The only part I'm looking forward to is their conception."

4:00 P.M.

"WHY THE DEVIL DO we have to put Bazzle in the contract?"

"I've worried about him ever since the day I met him at the clinic," Cassandra said. "I want to find him and take him out of the dangerous situation he's living in."

"You won't have to look far," Tom said sardonically, "since he's at my house."

"*What?*" she asked, both incredulous and relieved. "You took him in after all?"

"I sent him back that day," Tom admitted, "and as you predicted, there was a repeat infestation soon thereafter. I realized having him become part of the household was cheaper and more convenient than hauling him back to Dr. Gibson's clinic every week."

"How is he?" Cassandra asked eagerly. "What kind of schedule have you arranged for him? Have you found a tutor or school for him? I'm sure there hasn't been time to decorate his room yet, but I—"

"No. You misunderstand. I didn't take him in as a ward, he's one of the household staff."

Cassandra quieted, some of her excitement fading. "Who looks after him?"

"No one needs to look after him. As I understand it, the housekeeper won't let him come to the dinner table unless he's clean, so he'll soon learn to overcome his scruples about bathing. With decent food and regular sleep, I expect he'll be much healthier." Tom smiled briefly. "Problem solved. Now, on to the next issue."

"Are there other children for him to play with?"

"No, I don't usually hire children—I made an exception for Bazzle."

"What does he do all day?"

"So far, he's come to the office with me in the mornings to sweep and do odd jobs, and then I send him home in a cab."

*"By himself?"*

Tom looked at her sardonically. "He's navigated some of the most dangerous areas of London by himself for years."

Cassandra frowned. "What does he do for the rest of the day?"

"He's a hall boy. He does . . . hall boy things." Tom shrugged irritably. "I believe polishing shoes are among his tasks. He's better off than he was before. Don't make too much of this."

Cassandra nodded thoughtfully, shuttering her expression. For some reason, the issue of Bazzle was sensitive territory. She realized she would have to proceed with care when it came to making decisions about the child. But she was determined to have her way, even if it meant using the iron-hand-in-a-velvet-glove approach.

"Tom," she said, "it was wonderfully kind of you, and so very generous, to take Bazzle in as you have."

One corner of his mouth curled upward. "You're laying it on with a trowel," he said dryly. "But continue."

"I feel strongly that Bazzle must be taught to read.

It will benefit him for the rest of his life, and it will help you for as long as he continues to work for you, in the running of errands, and so forth. The cost of his education would be minimal, and it would allow him to be in the company of other children."

Tom considered the points, and nodded. "Very well."

"Thank you." Cassandra smiled brilliantly. "I'll make the arrangements, once I'm able to take stock of his situation." She hesitated before adding carefully, "There may be other adjustments I'll want to make, for the sake of his wellbeing. However you wish to write it in the contract . . . I'll require some leeway where he's concerned."

He picked up the pencil and looked down at the paper. "Leeway," he said darkly, "but not free rein. Because I'm fairly certain your concept of Bazzle's future doesn't match mine."

*5:00 P.M.*

"WHAT ABOUT BELGIUM?" TOM asked. "We could go from London to Brussels in approximately seven hours."

"I couldn't enjoy a honeymoon while feeling uncertain about where I'll live afterward."

"We've already agreed to live at Hyde Park Square."

"I want to spend some time there for a while, and become acquainted with the house and servants. I want to nest a little. Let's go on a proper honeymoon later in the spring or summer."

Tom shrugged out of his coat and loosened his necktie. The hearth fire had made the room too hot. He tossed the coat over the back of a chair and went to open a window. A welcome rush of ice-cold air cut through the stuffy atmosphere. "Cassandra, I can't marry you and go about business as usual the next day. Newlyweds need privacy."

He had a point. But he looked so disgruntled, Cassandra couldn't resist teasing. With a glance of wide-eyed innocence, she asked, "What for?"

Tom appeared increasingly flustered as he tried to come up with an explanation.

Cassandra waited, gnawing on the inside of her lips.

Tom's face changed as he saw the dance of laughter in her eyes. "I'll show you what for," he said, and lunged for her.

Cassandra fled with a shriek, skirting nimbly around the table, but he was as fast as a leopard. After snatching her up with ease, he deposited her on the settee, and pounced. She giggled and twisted as the amorous male weight of him lowered over her.

The scent of him was clean but salted with sweat, a touch of bay rum cologne sharpened with body warmth. His face was right above hers, a few locks of dark hair tumbling on his forehead. Grinning at her efforts to dislodge him, he braced his forearms on either side of her head.

She'd never played with a man like this, and it was incredibly entertaining and fun, and the tiniest bit scary in a way that excited her. Her giggles collapsed slowly, like champagne froth, and she wriggled as if to twist away from him even though she had no intention of doing so. He countered by settling more heavily into the cradle of her hips, pressing her into the cushions. Even through the mass of her skirts, she felt the unfamiliar pressure of his arousal. The thick ridge fit perfectly against the juncture of her thighs, aligning intimately with her in a way that was both embarrassing and stirring.

A stab of desire went through her as she realized this was how it would be . . . the anchoring weight of him, all hard muscle and heat . . . his eyes heavy-lidded and hot as he stared down at her.

Dazedly she reached up and pulled his head to hers. A whimper of pleasure escaped her as he kissed her thoroughly, wringing sensation from her softness, licking deep. Her body welcomed him instinctively, legs spreading wider beneath her skirts. The pit of her stomach clenched as she felt his hips adjust reflexively, the hard ridge finding the mound of her sex again, nudging and settling.

A series of rapid knocks at the doorjamb broke through the sensuous haze. Jarred by the interruption, Cassandra gasped and blinked as she looked toward the threshold.

It was Kathleen, wearing a profoundly apologetic expression, her gaze carefully averted. "Pardon. I'm so sorry. Cassandra, dear . . . the maids are coming to roll in the tea carts. You'll want to put yourself to rights, and . . . I'll give you a few minutes." She fled.

Cassandra could barely think. Her entire body throbbed with a frustration she'd never known. She clawed a little at the satiny back of Tom's sleeveless waistcoat, then let her arms flop weakly down to her sides.

"*This*," Tom said with a vehement glance at the doorway, "is why we need a honeymoon."

6:00 *P.M.*

"*I* DIDN'T SAY NEVER. I said it's unlikely." Tom stood with one hand braced on the hearth mantel, staring down into the lively blaze. "It's not really important, is it? You're going to share a life with me, not my family."

"Yes, but never to *meet* them?" Cassandra asked in bewilderment, pacing around the library.

"My mother has refused to see me for years—she'll have no interest in meeting my wife." He paused. "I could arrange to introduce you to my sisters at some point in the future."

"I don't even know their names."

"Dorothy, Emily, and Mary. I communicate with them rarely, and when I do, they don't tell my mother for fear of upsetting her. My youngest sister's husband is an accountant at my engineering firm—I speak with him now and then. He seems to be a decent fellow." After pushing away from the fireplace, Tom went to half sit, half lean against the table. "You're never to contact anyone in my family without my knowledge—I want that in the contract. I know your intentions would be good. But the terrain is sown with land mines."

"I understand. But won't you tell me what caused such a rift?" At his long hesitation, she said, "Whatever it is, I'll take your side."

"What if you don't? What if you decide I was in the wrong?"

"Then I'll forgive you."

"What if I did something unforgivable?"

"Tell me, and we'll find out."

Silence. Tom had gone to the window, bracing his hands on either side of the frame.

Just as Cassandra thought he really wasn't going to tell her, he spoke in a near monotone, without pause, as if the information needed to be delivered as efficiently as possible. "My father came to my offices five years ago. I hadn't seen or heard from him since the day he left me at the train station. He said he wanted to find my mother. I'd moved her to a new house, far from the rented rooms we'd once lived in. He said all the things one would expect—he was sorry for having abandoned the family, wanted another chance, and so on.

"There were crocodile tears, of course, and much wringing of hands. He begged me to give him another chance. I felt nothing except a crawling sensation at the back of my neck. I offered him a choice: He could have my mother's address, or I'd pay him a generous sum to disappear, and never approach her or my sisters."

"He chose the money," Cassandra guessed quietly.

"Yes. He didn't even stop to think about it. Later, I told my mother about it. I thought she'd agree we were well rid of him. Instead, she fell apart. She was like a madwoman. The doctor had to come and sedate her. Since then, she's regarded me as the source of all evil. My sisters were angry with me about what they saw as a betrayal, but they softened over time. Where my mother is concerned, however, there's no forgiveness. There never will be."

Cassandra went to him and touched his rigid back with a gentle hand. He wouldn't turn to face her. "She blamed you for offering the bribe, but not him for taking it?" she asked.

"She knew I could have arranged for him to go back to her. She knew I could have supported both of them."

"It wouldn't have made her happy. She would have always known deep down that he was only there to take advantage of her, and of you."

"She wanted him back regardless," Tom said flatly. "I could have made that happen, but I chose not to."

Cassandra slid her arms around his lean midriff and rested her head against his back. "You chose to protect her from someone who'd hurt her in the past, and would undoubtedly have hurt her again. I don't call that a betrayal." When he didn't react, she said even more softly, "You mustn't blame yourself for sending him away. Honoring one's parents doesn't mean you have to let them tear you apart over and over. You can honor them from a distance, by trying to be 'a light unto the world.'"

"I haven't done that either," she heard him say bitterly.

"Now you're being contrary," she chided. "You've done much good for other people so far, and there's more to do, and so you will."

He put a hand over hers, pressing it to the center of his chest, where his heart thumped powerfully. She felt some of the ferocious tension leave his muscles.

"Are the negotiations almost finished?" he asked in a husky voice. "Are there any important questions left? I've already spent too many days of my life without you, Cassandra."

"One last question." She pressed her cheek against the smooth, satiny back of his waistcoat. "What is your position on a Christmas wedding?"

Tom went very still, then inhaled deeply and let out a sigh of relief. Keeping possession of her hand, he reached into the front welt pocket of his vest. Her eyes widened as she felt him slide something on the ring finger of her left hand, a smooth, cool weight.

Tugging her hand free of his, Cassandra looked down at an astonishing multicolored gem set in a platinum filigree of tiny diamonds. She stared at it in wonder, tilting her hand in the light. The breathtaking stone contained flashes of every imaginable color, almost as if tiny flowers had been embedded beneath the surface. "I've never seen anything like this. Is it an opal?"

"It's a new variety, discovered in Australia last year. A black opal. If it's too unconventional for your taste, we can easily exchange it."

"No, I *love* it," she exclaimed, beaming at him. "You may proceed with the question."

"Should I kneel?" He looked chagrined. "Damn it, I'm doing this in the wrong order."

"No, don't kneel," Cassandra said, feeling a bit light-headed as she realized it was really happening; her entire life was about to change. "There's no wrong order. We make our own rules, remember?" The opal glowed with unearthly color as she lifted her hand to his jaw.

Tom closed his eyes for a moment, as if the gentle touch devastated him. "Please marry me, Cassandra," he said hoarsely. "I don't know what will happen to me if you won't."

"I will." A radiant smile spread across her face. "I will."

His mouth came to hers, and for a long time after that, there were no more words.

# Chapter 21

THEY MARRIED AT EVERSBY PRIORY, in a private family ceremony. As it turned out, the Christmas Day wedding suited Tom's tastes perfectly. Instead of masses of flowers thickening the air with heavy perfume, the house and chapel were decorated with fresh boughs of evergreen: balsam, holly, and Scotch pine. The entire household was in a cheerful mood, and there was an abundance of good food and drink. Outside, it was gray and damp, but the house was cozy and well lit, with fires crackling in every hearth.

Unfortunately, not long before the ten o'clock ceremony was to begin, a crack of thunder signaled an approaching storm. As the ancient chapel was detached from the house, the bridal party and family members would have to walk through the rain to reach it.

Winterborne, who'd agreed to act as Tom's best man, went out to have a look at the chapel and returned to the library, where Tom waited with Ethan Ransom, St. Vincent, and Devon. The women had gone upstairs to keep Cassandra company as she readied herself for the ceremony.

"It's about to rain forks and knives," Winterborne reported, water drops glittering on his hair and the shoulders of his coat. He reached for a glass of champagne from a silver tray on the table, and raised it in Tom's direction. "Good luck it is, for the wedding day."

"Why is that, exactly?" Tom asked, disgruntled.

"A wet knot is harder to untie," Winterborne said. "The marriage bond will be tight and long lasting."

Ethan Ransom volunteered, "Mam always said rain on a wedding day washed away the sadness of the past."

"Not only are superstitions irrational," Tom said, "they're inconvenient. If you believe in one, you have to believe them all, which necessitates a thousand pointless rituals."

Not being allowed to see the bride before the ceremony, for example. He hadn't had so much as a glimpse of Cassandra that morning, and he was chafing to find out how she was feeling, if she'd slept well, if there was something she needed.

West came into the room with his arms full of folded umbrellas. Justin, dressed in a little velveteen suit, was at his heels.

"Aren't you supposed to be upstairs in the nursery with your little brother?" St. Vincent asked his five-year-old nephew.

"Dad needed my help," Justin said self-importantly, bringing an umbrella to him.

"We're about to have a soaker," West said briskly. "We'll have to take everyone out to the chapel as soon as possible, before the ground turns to mud. Don't open one of these indoors: It's bad luck."

"I didn't think *you* were superstitious," Tom protested. "You believe in science."

West grinned at him. "I'm a farmer, Severin. When it comes to superstitions, farmers lead the pack. Incidentally, the locals say rain on the wedding day means fertility."

Devon commented dryly, "To a Hampshireman, nearly everything is a sign of fertility. It's a preoccupation around here."

"What's fertility?" Justin asked.

In the sudden silence, all gazes went to West, who asked defensively, "Why is everyone looking at me?"

"As Justin's new father," St. Vincent replied, making no effort to hide his enjoyment, "that question is in your province."

West looked down into Justin's expectant face. "Let's ask your mother later," he suggested.

The child looked mildly concerned. "Don't you know, Dad?"

Tom went to the nearby window, frowning as raindrops seemed to come down faster than the pull of gravity, as if they were being shot from rifles. Cassandra might be fretting about the storm. Her shoes and the hem of her wedding dress were going to be wet and muddy, which he didn't give a damn about, but it might distress her. He'd wanted the day to be perfect for her. Blast it, why hadn't the Ravenels built a covered walkway to the chapel?

Winterborne came to join him at the window. "'Tis throwing down, now," he said, watching the rain.

"If this is good luck," Tom said acidly, "I could do with a bit less." He gave a short sigh. "I don't believe in luck anyway."

"Neither do you believe in love," Winterborne reminded him with a touch of friendly mockery. "But here you stand with your heart in your fist."

The phrase was one of those Welshisms that sounded like a misstatement, but upon reflection made sense. A man who wore his heart on his sleeve was displaying his emotions . . . but a man with his heart in his fist was about to offer it to someone.

Not long ago, Tom would have responded with a mocking gibe of his own. Instead, he found himself replying with a raw humility he rarely permitted himself to show anyone. "Christ, Winterborne . . . I don't know what I believe anymore. I have feelings coming at me I don't even know the names for."

Winterborne's dark eyes twinkled warmly. "You'll sort it all out." He took an object from his coat pocket and handed it to Tom. "Here. A Welsh custom." It was the champagne cork, with a silver sixpence partially inserted into a slit at the top. "A memento of the day," he explained, "and a reminder that a good wife is a man's true wealth."

Tom smiled, reaching out to shake his hand firmly. "Thank you, Winterborne. If I believed in luck, I'd say I was damned lucky to have you as a friend."

Another belt of lightning whipped across the dark sky, setting loose a heavy mantling of rain.

"How is Cassandra going to reach the chapel without being drenched?" Tom asked with a groan. "I'm going to tell Trenear and Ravenel to—"

"Let them take care of her for now," Winterborne counseled. "Soon enough she'll belong to you." He paused before adding slyly, "And then you'll be lighting your fire on a new hearth."

Tom gave him a quizzical glance. "She'll be moving into my house."

Winterborne grinned and shook his head. "I meant your wedding night, you spoony half-wit."

AFTER CASSANDRA REACHED the vestibule of the chapel, there was a flurry of activity involving umbrellas, toweling, and what seemed to be a canvas tarp. Tom could see little from his vantage point at the front of the chapel, but West, after folding the tarp, caught his eye and gave him a short nod. Taking it to mean they'd somehow managed to spirit Cassandra to the chapel in good condition, Tom relaxed slightly.

Within two minutes, Winterborne came to the front of the chapel to stand next to Tom, and the music began. A quartet of local musicians had been recruited to play the wedding march using small gold handbells, with exquisite results. Having only heard Wagner's *Bridal Chorus* on the organ, Tom had always thought it a heavy-handed piece, but the bells gave it a delicate, almost playful lilt that was perfect for the occasion.

Pandora, as the matron of honor, proceeded demurely up the aisle, and sent Tom a quick grin before taking her place.

Then Cassandra came into view, walking toward him on Devon's arm. She wore a dress of white satin, elegant and unusual in its simplicity, with no fussy ruffles and frills to distract from the lovely shape of her figure. Instead of wearing the traditional veil, she had drawn the sides of her hair up to the crown of her head and let the rest cascade down her back in long golden coils. Her only ornamentation was a tiara of graduated diamond stars, which Tom had sent upstairs that morning as a Christmas present. The wealth of rose-cut gems glittered madly in the candlelight, but they couldn't eclipse her sparkling eyes and radiant face. She looked like a snow queen walking through a winter forest, too beautiful to be entirely human.

And there he stood, with his heart in his fist.

What was the name of this feeling? It was as if he'd fallen through the surface of his life into some strange new territory, a place that had always existed even though he hadn't been aware of it. All he knew was that the careful distance he'd put between himself and other people had finally been crossed by someone . . . and nothing would ever be the same.

AFTER A LENGTHY Christmas feast, the family went downstairs for the annual dance in the servants' hall, a tradition by which everyone in the household mingled freely, danced together, and drank wine and hot rum punch. Cassandra, who'd been careful to drink only a few sips of wine at dinner, indulged in a cup of the hot punch during the dance, and felt it go straight to her knees. She was happy but weary, drained from all the conversation and cheerful banter, her cheeks sore from smiling, Ironically, although it was their wedding day, she and Tom had spent practically no time together. She glanced around the servants' hall and saw him dancing with Mrs. Bixby, the cook. The stout older woman was pink-cheeked and giggling like a girl. Tom seemed as vigorous as he had been hours earlier, with a full supply of untiring energy. Ruefully Cassandra reflected that she would have a difficult time keeping up with him.

Tom saw her from across the room. Although he was smiling, there was an assessing quality in his gaze. Cassandra straightened her posture automatically, but he'd already seen the signs of her fatigue.

In a few minutes, he'd made his way over to her. "You look like a little sunbeam, standing here," he murmured, reaching out to lightly finger a long golden curl. "What do you say to the idea of leaving a bit sooner than we'd planned?"

She nodded immediately. "Yes, I would like that."

"Good. I'll whisk you out of here in short order. There's no need for drawn-out good-byes, since we'll only be gone for a week. By now, the train is stocked and ready to depart."

They were scheduled to leave for Weymouth in Tom's private railway carriage. Despite his assurances they would be comfortable, Cassandra wasn't looking forward to spending her wedding night on a train. No matter how one presented its merits, it was, after all, a moving vehicle. However, she hadn't objected to the plan, since they would be lodged in a nice hotel the next night. The honeymoon itself was a gift from Winterborne and Helen, who had arranged for them to travel by private yacht from Weymouth to Jersey Island, the southernmost of the Channel Islands.

"According to Winterborne," Tom had reported, "the climate is mild, and the views of St. Aubin's Bay from the hotel are very fine. As for the hotel itself—I know nothing about it. But we'll have to trust Winterborne."

"Because he's a good friend?" Cassandra had asked.

"No, because he knows I'd kill him immediately upon our return if the hotel is shabby."

Now, as Cassandra stood with Tom in the servants' hall, she said wistfully, "I wish we were already on the island." The thought of all they had yet to endure . . . a train ride and at least six hours on a ship . . . it made her shoulders droop.

Tom's gaze was caressing. "You'll be able to rest soon." He pressed his lips to her hair. "Your luggage was taken to the railway halt earlier, and your lady's maid laid out your traveling clothes upstairs. She's ready to help you change whenever you wish."

"How do you know that?"

"She told me when I danced with her a few minutes ago."

Cassandra smiled up at him. The boundless energy that had seemed so daunting before now seemed rather safe and comforting, something to be wrapped around her.

"Of course," Tom said softly, "you could leave in your wedding dress, and go with me straight to the railway carriage . . . where I could help you remove it."

A quicksilver shiver chased through her. "Would you prefer that?"

His palm smoothed over the satin of her upper sleeve, and then he rubbed an edge of the fabric gently between his thumb and forefinger. "As a man who likes to unwrap his own presents . . . yes."

# Chapter 22

$\mathcal{A}$s CASSANDRA MIGHT HAVE expected, the private luxury carriage went far beyond anything she could have imagined. It was two carriages, technically, connected by an accordion-shaped rubber hood that created enclosed walkways between the vehicles. An experimental design, Tom explained, that had the added benefit of making the ride smoother and quieter. One carriage contained a full-sized kitchen, with a pantry and chilled larder, and accommodations for the staff.

The main carriage was a mansion on wheels, with a double stateroom and attached dressing room, lavatories with hot and cold running water, a study, a parlor, and even a drawing room. It was handsomely appointed with wide windows, high ceilings covered in embossed leather, and thick Wilton carpeting on the floors.

In contrast to the current fashion of ornate embellishments and gilded trim, the carriage had been decorated with understated elegance and an emphasis on craftsmanship. The walnut paneling on the walls had not been varnished to a high gloss, but instead hand rubbed to a quiet, rich finish.

After touring the train and meeting the staff and the chef, Cassandra returned to the stateroom, while Tom consulted with the engineer. It was a beautiful room with a lofty ceiling, built-in cabinetry, a wide fixed bed of rosewood, and stained-glass transom windows that opened on hinges. Her lady's maid, Meg, was in the process of unpacking the valise that contained every-thing Cassandra would require until they boarded the ship tomorrow morning.

Meg had leaped at the chance to accompany Cas-sandra to a new situation, saying emphatically that she preferred town life to the country. She was an efficient and quick-witted girl, with an effervescent nature that made her a pleasant companion.

"Milady," Meg exclaimed, "have you ever seen such a train? There's a bathtub in the lavatory—*a bathtub*—the steward says as far as he knows, this is the only train in all the world that has one." As if fearing Cassandra might not have understood, she re-peated, "*In all the world.*" Busily Meg proceeded to lay out various items on the dresser: a traveling box of gloves and handkerchiefs, and a vanity case contain-ing a brush, comb, racks of pins, porcelain jars of face cream and powder, and a bottle of rose perfume. "The porter told me there's something about the train's de-sign that makes the ride as smooth as velvet. A special kind of axle . . . and who do you think invented it?"

"Mr. Severin?" Cassandra guessed.

"*Mr. Severin*," Meg confirmed emphatically. "The porter said Mr. Severin may be the cleverest man alive."

"Not about all things," Cassandra said with a small, private smile, "but about many things."

Meg set the valise beside the dresser. "I hung your clothes and dressing robe in the cabinet, and put your unmentionables in the dresser. Will you want to change out of your wedding dress now?"

"I think . . ." Cassandra hesitated, her face warming. "Mr. Severin will assist me."

The lady's maid blinked. Since it was a well-known fact that a man couldn't possibly manage the intricacies of fastening a woman's garments, any "assistance" Tom provided would be limited to the removal of clothing. And once Cassandra was undressed, there was little doubt about what would happen next.

"But . . ." Meg ventured, ". . . it's not even dinnertime."

"I know," Cassandra said uncomfortably.

"It's still light outside."

"*I know*, Meg."

"Do you think he'll really want to—" the lady's maid began, but broke off at Cassandra's exasperated glance. "I'll just go settle my things in my room, then," Meg said with artificial brightness. "It's in the next carriage. The steward said there's a fine parlor and dining room for the staff." She averted her gaze as she continued in a rush, "Also . . . after my older sister married . . . she told me it doesn't take too long. Gentlemen and their doings, I mean. Quick as a dog can trot a mile, she said."

Gathering that the words were meant to be reassuring, Cassandra nodded and murmured, "Thank you, Meg."

After her lady's maid had left, Cassandra unlocked her vanity case and lifted the lid, which was fitted with a mirror. She removed the pins from the side twists of her hair, and removed the diamond tiara from her head. As she set it on the dresser, a movement from the periphery of her vision caught her attention.

Tom had come to stand at the doorway, his warm gaze taking her in.

A nervous thrill went through her, and her fingers trembled a little as she combed them through her hair to search for any stray pins. Although they'd been alone before, relatively speaking, this was the first time they'd been alone as a married couple. No clock to declaim each passing minute, no admonishing knocks to rattle the door.

A decidedly handsome man, her husband, appearing taller than usual in the confines of the room. Dark, coolly confident, and as unpredictable as a force of nature. But she sensed a carefulness in his manner, a desire not to worry or frighten her, and that made her flush with pleasure.

"I haven't yet thanked you for the tiara," she said. "When I opened it this morning, I nearly fell off my chair. It's beautiful."

Tom came up behind her, his hands stroking her satin-covered arms, his lips gentle as they brushed the rim of her ear. "Would you like the rest of it?"

Her brows lifted in surprise as their gazes met in the little vanity mirror. "There's more?"

For answer, he went to the other dresser, picked up a flat mahogany box, and gave it to her.

Cassandra lifted the lid, her eyes widening as she saw more diamond stars and a chain of woven platinum mesh. "A necklace? And earrings? Oh, this is too extravagant. You're too generous."

"Let me show you how it works," Tom said, picking up the tiara. "The largest star can be detached, and either worn as a brooch or added to the necklace." Deftly he disconnected the star, manipulating the tiny catches and fasteners. How like him, Cassandra thought with a surge of affection, to have given her jewelry that could be taken apart and reconfigured, almost like a puzzle.

She tried on the star-shaped earrings, and shook her head a little to make them dance. "You've given me a constellation," she said with a grin, looking at her glittering reflection.

Tom turned her to face him, his hands moving lightly through her hair, letting the golden locks sift and spill through his fingers. "You're the brightest star in it."

Cassandra stood on her toes to kiss him, and Tom gathered her more securely against him. He seemed to luxuriate in the kiss, wanting every detail of her taste, texture, scent. Slowly his palm moved beneath the curtain of her hair and up her spine. As the delicate tugging weights of the earrings dangled from her earlobes, a few diamond points lightly touched her neck and sent a shiver through her.

Turning her mouth from his, Cassandra said breathlessly, "I have a gift for you."

"Do you?" His lips grazed the tender skin beneath her jaw.

"A small one," she said ruefully. "I'm afraid it can't compare to a suite of diamond jewelry."

"Marrying me was the gift of a lifetime," he said. "I don't need anything else."

"Nevertheless . . ." She went to the valise beside the dresser, and pulled out a parcel wrapped in tissue paper and tied with red ribbon. A little blue beadwork ornament dangled from the ribbon. "Happy Christmas," she said, handing it to him.

Tom untied the ribbon and held up the ornament to look at it closely. "Did you make this?"

"Yes, for our tree next year."

"It's beautiful," he said, admiring the tiny stitches that secured the beads. He proceeded to unwrap the gift, a book bound in red cloth with black and gilt lettering. "*Tom Sawyer*," he read aloud, "by Mark Twain."

"Proof that Americans write books," Cassandra said cheerfully. "It was published in England a few months ago, and is just now coming out in America. The author is a humorist, and the bookseller said the novel is a breath of fresh air."

"I'm sure I'll enjoy it." Tom set the book on the dresser and pulled her into his arms. "Thank you."

Cassandra melted against him, resting her head on his shoulder. A hint of bay rum cologne, with its distinctive notes of bay leaf, cloves, and citrus, drifted to her nostrils. It was a somewhat old-fashioned scent, very masculine and crisp. How unexpectedly traditional of him, she thought with a touch of private amusement.

One of his hands came up to smooth her hair. "You're tired, buttercup," he murmured. "You need to rest."

"I feel much better now that we're away from all the clamor at Eversby Priory." A hush gathered around them, easy and relaxed. She was not in the hands of an impatient boy, but an experienced man who was going to treat her very, very well. Anticipation filled the spaces between her heartbeats. "Will you help me change out of my clothes?" she dared to ask.

Tom hesitated for a long moment before he went to close the curtains. Her stomach suddenly felt light, as it did when a fast-moving carriage crossed a dip in the road. Pulling her hair over one shoulder, she waited for him to come up behind her. The dress laced up the back with a decorative satin cord that finished in a bow at the bottom. She considered explaining the placket of hidden buttons beneath the lacing, but suspected he would enjoy figuring it out for himself.

Gently Tom tugged at the bow. "You looked like a queen when you came into the chapel," he said. "You took my breath away." After he'd untied the satin cord, he stroked the placket that ran along her spine and felt the outline of tiny flat buttons. He searched for the miniature hooks that held the placket closed and unfastened them even more adeptly than a lady's maid. As each button was undone, the satin bodice loosened and began to slip downward from the weight of the skirts.

Cassandra pulled her arms from the sleeves and let the heavy garment drop to the floor. After stepping out of the shimmering pale heap, she picked up the garment and went to set it in the cabinet. She turned to find his gaze drinking her in, every detail, from the ruffle trimming the top of her chemise to her light blue shoes.

"A superstition," Cassandra said as she saw him staring at the shoes for an extra moment. "The bride is supposed to wear something old, something new, something borrowed, and something blue."

Tom scooped her up, set her on the bed, and bent for a closer look at the shoes, which had been embroidered with silver and gold thread and embellished with tiny crystals. "They're lovely," he said, removing them one at a time.

She flexed her stocking-clad toes, which ached a little after the long, busy day. "I'm so glad to be off my feet."

"I'm glad you're off them too," Tom said. "Although probably for different reasons." He reached around her to loosen her corset laces, and carefully lowered her to her back, to unhook her busk. "I smell roses," he said, inhaling appreciatively.

"Helen gave me a flask of perfumed oil this morning," Cassandra replied. "It contains the attar of seven kinds of roses. I sprinkled it in my bath." A quiver went through her as Tom bent to kiss her midriff through the crumpled linen chemise.

"Seven is my favorite number," he said.

"Why?"

He nuzzled gently at her stomach. "There are seven colors in a rainbow, seven days of the week, and . . ." His voice lowered seductively, ". . . seven is the lowest natural number that can't be represented as the sum of the squares of three integers."

"Mathematics," she exclaimed, laughing breathlessly. "How stirring."

Tom smiled and pushed away from her. He stood to remove his coat, waistcoat, and neck cloth, then took up one of Cassandra's feet and began to rub it. She squirmed in surprised pleasure as his strong thumbs stroked up her sensitive arches.

"*Ohh*," she said, lying back more heavily on the mattress as he gently kneaded up and down the sole of her foot, finding every sore, tender spot. She began to dissolve in bliss as he wiggled her toes and pulled at them, one by one, through the silk of her stockings. It felt nicer than she could have imagined, pleasure zinging up to all different parts of her body. "No one's ever rubbed my feet before. You're so good at it. Don't stop yet. You're not going to stop, are you?"

"No."

"And you'll do the other foot?"

He laughed quietly. "Yes."

As he found a particularly sensitive place, she writhed and purred, and stretched her arms over her head. When her eyes opened, she followed the direction of Tom's gaze, and realized the open crotch seams of her drawers were gaping apart. With a gasp, she quickly reached down to conceal the fluff of blond curls.

There was a flash of deviltry in his eyes. "Don't hide it," he said gently.

The suggestion shocked her. "You want me to lie here and expose my . . . my . . . fanny to you?"

Amusement deepened the faint creases at the outer corners of his eyes. "It would provide an excellent incentive for me to do the other foot."

"You were going to do it anyway," she protested.

"Think of it as my reward, then." He bent, and she felt his mouth touch the tip of her big toe, his breath filtering hotly through the silk of her stocking. "Let me have a peek," he coaxed. "It's such a pretty view."

"It's not at all a pretty view," she protested in an agony of shyness.

"It's the prettiest view in the world."

It would have been literally impossible for a human being to blush any harder than Cassandra was at the moment. While she dithered, Tom continued to rub her feet. His thumbs worked up her arch in a ladder of pressures that sent tingles from her soles all the way up to the top of her spine.

Closing her eyes, Cassandra recalled what Pandora had advised her yesterday.

*"You may as well toss your dignity overboard right away,"* Pandora had said. *"It's dreadfully awkward, your first time. He'll want to do things involving body parts that really shouldn't be keeping company. Just remind yourself the things you and he do in private are secrets only the two of you will share. There's nothing shameful about an act of love. And at some moments, it stops being about bodies or thoughts or words, it's only feeling . . . and it's beautiful."*

At some point during Cassandra's pondering, the train had started, and was now accelerating smoothly. Instead of the usual rattles and jolts, the railway carriage proceeded with liquid ease, as if it were suspended over the tracks instead of rolling along them. Her childhood home, her family, everything familiar, were slipping away. There was only this rosewood bed, and her dark-haired husband, and the train wheels conveying them somewhere she'd never been. This moment, and whatever else happened tonight, would become secrets between the two of them.

She bit her lip and surrendered her dignity, letting go of the open seam of her drawers.

Tom continued massaging her foot, his thumbs and fingers pressing exquisite little circles at the base of her toes. After a few minutes he moved to her other foot, and she relaxed with a little moan.

The rain-sifted light was weaker now, coming in

through the transom windows in pallid silver and dark rainbow dapples. Through heavy-lidded eyes, she watched the play of muted color and shadow across Tom's shirt. Eventually his long-boned, eloquent hands slid up over her knees and beneath the legs of her drawers. He untied her white lace garters and rolled her silk stockings down into neat circles. After dropping them to the floor, he unfastened his shirt and discarded it, taking his time, letting her look her fill.

His body was beautiful, built with the long, efficient lines of a rapier, every inch wrought with tough muscle. A light furring of hair covered his chest and narrowed down toward his midriff. Cassandra sat up on the mattress and touched the black fleece, her fingertips as shy and fleet as a hummingbird in flight.

Still standing by the side of the bed, Tom reached out to gather her against his chest.

Cassandra shivered at the feel of being surrounded by so much bare skin and body hair, so much hardness. "Did you ever imagine we would be doing this?" she said in a wondering tone.

"Sweet darling . . . I imagined it about ten seconds after we met, and I haven't stopped since."

A bashful grin tugged at her lips, and she dared to kiss his bare shoulder. "I hope I won't be a disappointment."

Gently Tom guided her to look up at him, his palm cradling her cheek and jaw. "There's nothing for you to worry about, Cassandra. All you have to do is relax." He drew her blush-heated face closer to his, and stroked the wild pulse in her throat with light finger-tips. His faint smile held a sensual edge that dismantled her thoughts completely. "We'll go slowly. I know how to make it good for you. You're going to leave this bed a happy woman."

*Chapter 23*

$\mathcal{J}$OM'S HEAD LOWERED, AND the light, erotic pressure of his mouth sent pleasure coursing through her. Every time she thought the kiss would end, he found a new angle, a deeper taste. Her body turned hot from the inside out, as if he were pouring sunlight into her. Dazed with pleasure, Cassandra slid her arms around his neck. Her fingers sank into the heavy, close-cut locks of his hair, as rich as black satin against her palms.

Without haste, he reached down to the hem of her chemise and gripped handfuls of fabric to pull it upward. She lifted her arms to help him, gasping at the feel of cool air on her naked breasts. He eased her back onto the bed and ran a gentle hand down her body before beginning on the fastenings of his trousers. Her heartbeat hammered violently as he removed his clothes. For the first time in her life, she beheld the sight of a naked man, aroused and splendidly healthy. She couldn't help staring at his robust erection, swollen to a prominent angle.

A brief grin crossed Tom's face as he saw her expression. He was entirely comfortable in his nakedness, whereas she was a collection of inhibitions all held together with a blush. Climbing into bed like a prowling cat, he lowered himself beside her, one hairy leg settling between hers.

She wasn't sure where to put her hands. One of her palms came to the taut row of muscles at his midriff, her fingertips resting at the edge of a rib.

Taking her hand in a light hold, Tom guided it down to his groin. "You can touch me," he encouraged, a new huskiness infusing his voice.

Hesitant but willing, she stroked the silky, rigid length of him, discovering unexpected pulses within drum-tight hardness. She blinked in surprise as she encountered a slick of moisture at the tip.

After taking a ragged breath, Tom explained, "That . . . happens when my body is ready for yours."

"So quickly?" she asked, abashed.

His mouth clamped into a firm line, as if he were struggling not to smile. "Men are generally much faster than women." Lazily he sifted a few locks of her hair through his fingers. "It takes a bit more time and effort to make you ready for me."

"I'm sorry."

"Not at all—that's the fun part."

"I feel as if I might be ready now," she ventured.

Tom lost the inner struggle, a grin breaking out. "You're not," he said, pulling the drawers down over her hips and legs.

"How will you know?"

For one heart-stopping moment, his fingertips swirled over her abdomen and down into the triangle of private curls. He smiled into her dilated eyes. "I'll know when you're wet here," he whispered. "I'll know when you're trembling and begging."

"I'm not going to beg," Cassandra protested.

His dark head bent over her breast, his breath like steam against the tender skin. After catching the budded peak with his lips, he raked his velvet tongue over it, and caught it gently with his teeth.

"Or if I do . . ." she added, squirming beneath him, "it will be very brief, and . . . it will be more like asking . . ."

"You don't *have* to beg," Tom murmured, gathering her breasts together and kissing the deep valley between them. "It was a suggestion, not a requirement."

He slid lower down her body, his mouth browsing in lazy paths, brushing, tugging, licking, tormenting.

The train's smooth *clickety-clack* raced through nightfall toward the last splinters of sunset. Her husband was like a dream figure in the darkness, his powerful form cast in silhouette as he moved over her. He pressed her thighs apart and settled between them. Every hair on her body lifted as she felt his warm breath on her stomach. His tongue touched the delicate rim of her navel, tracing it all the way around. Desire tightened her insides and coiled her muscles until she felt her knees drawing upward. She gasped as he licked inside her navel, a hot, silky wriggle. His tongue swirled and stabbed softly, and she couldn't help squirming.

A trace of amusement thickened his voice. "Be still, buttercup."

But as his tongue flickered again, her body twisted at the ticklish sensation.

His hands closed around her ankles, warm manacles to keep her in place, and the small, private muscles inside her throbbed and clenched in response. To her amazement, he moved even lower, tracing the verge of soft skin and fleecy curls . . . and she began to have an inkling of what her sister had meant about body parts that shouldn't be keeping company. His mouth and nose nudged through the curling hairs, inhaling the intimate scent.

"Tom . . ." she said, her voice plaintive.

"Mmm?"

"Should you . . . oh, God . . . should you be doing that?"

His reply was a muffled but emphatic affirmative.

"I only ask because . . . you see . . . I thought I knew what to expect, but . . ." She stiffened as she felt the wet upward stroke of his tongue, parting the lips of her sex. "No one mentioned anything about this . . ."

Tom didn't seem to be listening to her with anything close to his usual attentiveness. All his focus was centered on the soft place between her thighs, his restless tongue swirling through intricate folds and petals as if it couldn't decide where to settle. He nibbled lightly on the swollen edges of the outer lips, tugging softly.

She struggled to breathe, her hands fluttering down to his dark head as the delicate but insistent exploration continued. He found the entrance of her body with teasing wet strokes, the brush of his shaven beard prickly against the tender skin. As his tongue came to soothe the temporary irritation, a moan resonated in her throat. He was dismantling her self-control, seducing her into some mindless version of herself. The sinuous length of his tongue slipped inside her. Unimaginable. Irresistible. Each time it thrust in and out, a shot of pleasure went up her spine. Her inner muscles contracted in a helpless rhythm, as if trying to catch and hold the slick intrusion.

He built the tension slowly, relentlessly, while sensation washed over her until she was shaking. Helplessly she tried to angle her hips to bring his mouth where she most needed it. He made her wait, his tongue dancing and tormenting without mercy, never quite touching the little peak that ached to be caressed. She was so wet . . . was all of it from her, or was some from him too?

Sweat broke on the surface of her skin. Her breath came in broken cries. She felt his finger enter her . . . no, two fingers . . . She shrank away from the uncomfortable fullness, but he slid them deeper every time her flesh pulsed and relaxed. It began to hurt, especially when his knuckles gently stretched the entrance. He fastened his mouth over the stiff bud, his tongue flicking softly, quickly, and then there was only pleasure. She strained and panted, her hips riding upward on a flare of euphoric heat, her body clamping on the gently invading fingers, again and again, each contraction stronger than the last.

Relief flooded her, shuddered through her in waves, until she was limp and calm. His careful touch withdrew, leaving her flesh to pulse and close on emptiness. She made an inarticulate sound, reaching for him, and he gathered her against his chest, murmuring how lovely she was, how she pleased him, how much he desired her. The hair on his chest felt delicious against her bare breasts, a softly teasing abrasion.

"Stay relaxed," Tom whispered as he settled into the cradle of her thighs.

"I have no choice," Cassandra managed to say. "I feel as if I've been run through a washing mangle."

His husky laugh caressed her ears. Carefully his hand shaped over her vulva, stroking the quivery wetness. "Sweet little wife . . . will you let me inside you now?"

She nodded, entranced by his gentleness.

But he hesitated, laying the side of his face against the streaming locks of her hair. "I don't want to hurt you. I never want to hurt you."

She reached around his back, stroking the long plane of muscle. "That's why it's all right."

Tom's head lifted, and he stared down at her, his breath shaking a little. She felt pressure centering against the vulnerable opening of her body, hard and yet so slow, easing forward by millimeters. "Easy," he whispered. "Try to open for me."

The pressure filled her with a slow and ruthless ache. He reached down to spread her thighs farther apart, and pressed back the lips of her sex. Gently, repeatedly, his hips rocked forward, easing deeper into the tight clasp of untried muscles. Despite her discomfort, she relished the signs of his pleasure, the erotic tension on his face, the heat-blurred gaze that, for once, had lost its alertness. Eventually the careful progress halted, and he held still, half buried inside her. His mouth came to hers in a sweetly wanton kiss, until she began to feel not quite so lethargic, her nerves tingling with renewed excitement.

"Is that as far as you can go?" she asked hesitantly when their lips parted, wincing at the thick inner pressure where they were joined.

"It's as far as your body will let me in," he said, his fingertips stroking back the strands of hair that clung to her damp forehead and temples. "For the moment."

Cassandra couldn't hold back a little sigh of relief as the invading hardness retreated.

His hands coaxed her to lie on her side, facing away from him. He spoke slowly, as if it were difficult to form words. "My beautiful Cassandra . . . let's try this . . . if you'll . . . yes. Rest against me." He had pulled her back so their bodies fit like two spoons in a drawer. She felt him lift her top leg and ease it back to rest over his. He adjusted her position, his hands caressing her intimately. "I've wanted you for so many nights . . . God, I hope this is real. Don't be a dream."

The head of his sex slid along the tender cleft between her thighs, back and forth, before lodging in the sore opening again. He pressed forward only an inch and held, a hard presence inside her. As she lay cradled in his arms, he caressed her front, his clever hands finding new places of sensation, chasing quivers across her skin. By the time he reached the place where their bodies were joined, the full flush of desire had come over her again, and she strained and fidgeted against him. He played with the soft lips of her sex and every tender place within. Moaning with frustrated craving, Cassandra tried to press closer to those tantalizing fingers, following every light caress.

Tom wasn't breathing at all well, panting unevenly at her ear. Deep inside, she felt the hard, heavy weight of him, and she realized she'd writhed and pushed herself all the way down the length of his shaft. His fingers massaged the swollen nub with maddening skill, somehow knowing the exact rhythm she needed. Her body gripped him in rapturous spasms as she went over the edge, lost in the pulsing intensity of feeling. His breath caught, and then he made a sound low in his throat, a velvety growl, while the heat of his release spread inside her.

They relaxed together slowly in the aftermath, their joined flesh resonant with deep twitches and throbs of pleasure.

Cassandra sighed and purred as his hands coasted over her tired limbs. "I think I was begging," she admitted, "near the end."

Tom pressed a soft laugh against the side of her throat, and kissed her flushed skin. "No, sweet. I'm sure that was me."

DAYLIGHT CAME IN through the transom windows, slowly melting away the shadows inside the railway carriage stateroom. It was with mild surprise that Tom awakened to discover Cassandra sleeping next to him. *I have a wife*, he thought, propping himself up on an elbow. The situation was so agreeable and interesting that he found himself smiling down at her idiotically.

His wife looked vulnerable and lovely, like a nymph sleeping in a wood. The fantastical profusion of her hair was like something from a mythological painting, curling golden locks spreading everywhere in lavish disarray. At some point during the night, she had donned a nightgown. He hadn't even been aware of it—he, who always snapped awake at the slightest noise. But he supposed it was only natural to have slept heavily after the hectic pace of the wedding day, followed by an evening of the most mind-obliterating pleasure he'd ever experienced.

For Tom, discovering what pleased and excited a woman, what made her unique, was a challenge he had always relished. He'd never slept with a woman he hadn't genuinely liked, and he'd applied himself enthusiastically to satisfying his partners. But there had always been limits to the intimacy he had shared with them—he'd been able to lower his guard only so far. Some of his affairs had ended badly as a result, eroding into bitterness.

With Cassandra, however, he'd discarded many of his defenses before they had ever set foot in the bedroom. That hadn't been deliberate on his part; it had just . . . happened. And while he'd never had the slightest inhibition about physical nakedness, making love to her had brought him dangerously close to emotional nakedness, which had been more than a little terrifying. And at the same time, astonishingly erotic. He'd never known anything like it, every sensation magnified and reflected infinitely, like pleasure repeating itself in a hall of mirrors.

In the aftermath, he'd brought Cassandra a warm compress for between her thighs, and water to drink, and then he'd lain beside her while his mind had begun its usual process of sorting through the events of the day. To his surprise, he'd felt her inch closer until she was pressed all along his side. "Are you cold?" he had asked in concern.

"No," came her drowsy reply as she'd settled her head on his shoulder, "just cuddling."

Cuddling had never been part of Tom's bedroom repertoire. Bodily contact had always been the prelude to something else, never an end in itself. After a moment, he'd reached over with his free hand to pat her head awkwardly. He'd felt her cheek curve against his shoulder.

"You don't know how to cuddle," she said.

"No," Tom had admitted. "I'm not sure what it's for."

"It's not *for* anything," Cassandra had said with a yawn. "I just want to." She'd snuggled even closer, hooking a slender leg over one of his—and had promptly fallen asleep.

Tom had stayed very still, with the weight of her head on his shoulder, brooding over the realization of how much he had to lose. He was so damned happy to be with her. She was his worst liability, as he'd always known she would be.

Now as his wife lay there illuminated by morning, Tom's fascinated gaze moved along the long, lace-trimmed sleeve of her nightgown to her slender hand. The white crescents of her fingernails were smoothly filed, the surface buffed to a glassy sheen. He couldn't resist touching one of them.

Cassandra stirred and stretched, her deep blue eyes unfocused in her sleep-flushed face. Blinking, she took in her unfamiliar surroundings, and smiled slightly. "Good morning."

Tom leaned over her, brushed his lips across hers, and moved lower to rest his head on the upper slope of her chest. "I once told you I didn't believe in miracles," he said. "I take it back. Your body is definitely a miracle." He played with the intricate fine tucks and ruffles of the nightgown. "Why did you put this on?"

She stretched beneath him and yawned. "I couldn't sleep unclothed."

He adored her prim tone. "Why not?"

"I felt exposed."

"You should always be exposed. You're too beautiful for clothes." He would have expounded on the theme, but was distracted by the sound of her stomach growling.

Blushing, Cassandra said, "We didn't have dinner last night. I'm starving."

Tom smiled and sat up. "The chef on this train," he told her, "knows over two hundred ways to make eggs." He grinned at her expression. "You linger in bed. I'll take care of the rest."

As TOM HAD expected, the travel arrangements made by Rhys Winterborne were superb. After breakfasting on the train, Tom and Cassandra were conveyed to Weymouth Harbor, where they boarded a two-hundred-and-fifty-foot private steam yacht. The captain himself showed them to the owner's suite, which included a private glass observation room.

Their destination was Jersey, the largest and southernmost of the Channel Islands. The lush and prosperous bailiwick, only fourteen miles off the coast of France, was famed for its agriculture and breathtaking landscapes, but most of all for the Jersey cow, a breed that produced unusually rich milk.

Tom had been a bit skeptical when Winterborne had told him the honeymoon destination. "You're sending me to a place predominantly known for its cows?"

"You won't even notice your surroundings," Winterborne had pointed out laconically. "You'll be in bed most of the time."

After Tom had pressed him for more details, Winterborne had revealed that the hotel, La Sirène, was a seafront resort with every modern comfort and convenience imaginable. With its secluded gardens and individual balconies, it had been designed to ensure privacy for its guests. A superbly talented chef from Paris had already made a name for himself at the restaurant, creating exquisite dishes from the abundance of fresh produce on the island.

Thanks to the skill of the yacht's captain and crew, who were familiar with the strong currents and ridges of sunken rock around the archipelago, the crossing was relatively smooth. They arrived within five hours, first approaching the high, rocky headland, then rounding the southwest corner of the island. The terrain became increasingly lush and green-mantled as they came to the bay of St. Aubin, framed with immaculate white sand beaches. La Sirène presided serenely over the scene from a series of elevated garden terraces.

As Tom and Cassandra disembarked, the chief harbormaster welcomed them onto the pier with a great show of deference. He was accompanied by a coast guard officer, who became wildly flustered as soon as he was introduced to Cassandra. Looking a bit dazed, the young officer began to talk to her without pause, offering a wealth of information about the island, its weather, its history, and anything else he could think of to keep her attention.

"Give your tongue a holiday, lad," the harbormaster

said with a touch of amused resignation, "and let the poor lady have a moment's peace."

"Yes, Chief."

"Now, you may escort Lady Cassandra to the covered parapet over there, while Mr. Severin confirms that all luggage has been brought out of the ship."

Tom frowned, glancing at the crowded pier.

The white-haired harbormaster seemed to read his thoughts. "It's but a short distance, Mr. Severin. Your bride will be more comfortable there than standing here with cargo being unloaded and wharfmen running about."

Cassandra gave Tom a reassuring nod. "I'll wait for you at the parapet," she said, and took the young officer's arm.

The harbormaster smiled as he watched them leave. "I hope you'll pardon the lad for his jabbering, Mr. Severin. Great beauty such as your wife's can make a man nervous."

"I supposed I'd better become accustomed to it," Tom said ruefully. "She causes a stir every time we're out in public."

The elderly harbormaster smiled reminiscently. "When I came of age to take a wife," he said, "I set my heart on a girl in the village. A beauty who couldn't so much as boil a potato. But I was sore in love with her. My father warned me, *'He who weds a beauty courts trouble.'* But I put on a lofty air and told him I was too high-minded to hold her looks against her."

They both chuckled.

"Did you marry her?" Tom asked.

"I did," the harbormaster admitted with a grin. "And thirty years of that sweet smile has made up for many a burnt chop and dry potato."

After the steamer trunks and luggage had been accounted for, a trio of porters undertook to load it all on a coach from the hotel. Tom turned toward the covered area of the pier in search of Cassandra. An incredulous scowl crossed his face as he saw a gathering of dockworkers, porters, and cabmen near his wife. A navvy called out to her—"Gi' me a smile, ye sweet tidbit! One little smile! What's yer name?"

Cassandra tried to ignore the catcalls, while the coast guard officer stood by, doing nothing to shield her.

"Now, now, Mr. Severin—" the old harbormaster said, following as Tom headed toward Cassandra with swift, ground-eating strides.

Tom reached his wife, blocked her from view, and sent a chilling glance at the navvy. "My wife doesn't feel like smiling. Is there something you'd like to say to me?"

The catcalls faded, and the navvy met his gaze, taking his measure . . . deciding to back down. "Only that you're the luckiest bastard alive," the navvy said cheekily. The crowd broke up with a mixture of chuckles and guffaws.

"On your way now, lads," the harbormaster said, briskly dispersing the gathering. "Time to go about your business."

As Tom turned to Cassandra, he was relieved to see that she didn't seem upset. "Are you all right?" he asked.

She nodded immediately. "No harm done."

The officer looked sheepish. "I thought they would tire of their sport if we ignored them long enough."

"Ignoring doesn't work," Tom said curtly. "It's the same as permission. Next time, pick the ringleader and go for him."

"He was twice my size," the officer protested.

Tom shot him an exasperated glance. "The world expects a man to have a backbone. Especially when a woman is being harassed."

The younger man scowled. "Pardon, sir, but these are rough, dangerous men, and this is a side of life you wouldn't know about."

As the officer strode away, Tom shook his head in perplexed annoyance. "What the devil did he mean by that?"

Cassandra reached out a gloved hand to stroke his coat lapel, and looked up at him with laughing eyes. "I think, my dear Tom, you were just accused of being a gentleman."

# Chapter 24

"**I**THOUGHT YOU NEVER SLEPT late," Cassandra said the next morning, as she saw her husband stir in bed. She stood at the French doors that opened onto the private balcony, shivering slightly at the cool morning breeze.

Tom stretched lazily, like a big cat. He rubbed his face and sat up, his voice sleep-scratchy. "My wife kept me awake for most of the night."

Cassandra loved the way he looked with his eyes heavy-lidded and his hair tousled. "That wasn't my fault," she told him. "I had planned to go to sleep right away."

"You shouldn't have come to bed in a red nightgown, then."

Biting back a grin, Cassandra turned to gaze at the stunning view of St. Aubin's Bay, with its long stretches of clean white sand and intensely blue water. A rocky islet at the end of the bay featured the ruins of a Tudor castle, which the hotel concierge had said they could visit at low tide.

Last night she'd dared to put on a scandalous garment Helen had given her for the honeymoon. It couldn't really be called a nightgown—in fact, there was hardly enough of it to qualify even as a chemise. It was made of pomegranate-red silk and gauze, fastening in the front with a few coquettish ribbon ties. Helen had used a French word for it . . . *negligée* . . . and had assured her it was exactly the kind of thing husbands liked.

After one look at his wife dressed in nothing but a few scraps of silk and a blush, Tom had tossed aside the novel in his hands and pounced on her. He'd spent a long time caressing and fondling her over the thin fabric, licking her skin through the gauze. His mouth and hands had charted the sensitive terrain of her body, exploring by millimeters.

Gently, ruthlessly, he had teased her into a state of erotic frustration until she'd felt like an overwound watch. But he hadn't taken her fully, whispering that she was too sore, that they would have to wait until tomorrow.

She had moaned and pressed herself against him, struggling for the elusive pleasure, while he'd laughed softly at her impatience. He'd untied the little ribbon fastenings of the *negligée* with his teeth, and had worked his tongue down between her thighs. The delicate prodding and stroking had gone on until her over-stimulated nerves had ignited in a deep and wracking release. He'd caressed her for a long time afterward, his touch as light as eiderdown, until it had seemed as if the darkness itself had been moving over her, slipping tenderly between her thighs, feathering the tips of her breasts.

Now, recalling her own wanton enjoyment of the intimate acts they'd shared, Cassandra felt pleased but shy in the light of day. She adjusted the belt of her velvet robe and didn't quite meet his gaze as she suggested brightly, "Shall we ring for breakfast? And then go out to explore the island?"

He grinned at her studied casualness. "By all means."

A simple but well-prepared breakfast was brought up and arranged on a table near one of the wide plate-glass windows. There were poached eggs, broiled grapefruit halves, a rasher of bacon, and a basket of small oblong cakes that appeared to have been twisted and turned partially inside out before they had been deep-fried to golden brown.

"What are these?" Cassandra asked the waiter.

"Those are called Jersey Wonders, milady. They've been made on the island since before I was a boy."

After the waiter had finished setting out the food and left, Cassandra picked up one of the cakes and took a bite. The outside was lightly crisp, the inside soft and flavored with ginger and nutmeg. *"Mmm."*

Tom chuckled. He came to seat her at the table, and bent to kiss her temple. "A cake that's shaped like a shoe," he murmured. "How perfect for you."

"Have a taste," she urged, lifting it to his mouth.

He shook his head. "I'm not fond of sweets."

"Try it," she commanded.

Relenting, Tom took a small bite. Meeting her expectant gaze, he said a touch apologetically, "It's like a fried washing-up sponge."

"Bother," she exclaimed, laughing. "Is there any kind of sweet you like?"

His face was just over hers, his eyes smiling. "You," he said, and stole a quick kiss.

THEY WENT ON a walk along the esplanade, enjoying the sun and the snap of cool sea air. Next, they headed inland to the town of St. Helier, with its proliferation of shops and cafés. Cassandra bought a few gifts to bring back to England, among them some figurines carved of local pink and white granite, and a walking stick for Lady Berwick, made from the stem of a giant Jersey cabbage, which had been dried and varnished.

While the shop owner wrapped the items, which would be conveyed to La Sirène later in the afternoon, Tom browsed over some merchandise displayed on shelves and tables. He brought a small object to the counter, a wooden toy boat with a carved sailor figure holding an oar. "Will this float upright in the bath?" he asked.

"Yes, sir," the shopkeeper replied with a grin. "The local toymaker weights it to make sure. Can't have a boat from Jersey floating sideways!"

Tom handed it to him, to wrap up with the rest.

After they had left the shop, Cassandra asked, "Is that for Bazzle?"

"It might be."

Smiling, Cassandra paused in front of the next shop window, filled with displays of perfume and eau de cologne. She affected interest in the gold and filigree bottles. "Do you think I should try a new scent?" she asked idly. "Jasmine, or lily of the valley?"

"No." Tom stood behind her and spoke softly near her ear, as if imparting some highly confidential information. "There's nothing better in the world than the scent of roses on your skin."

Their shared reflection in the plate glass blurred as she leaned back against the hard support of his body. They stood together, breathed together, for a few hazy moments before continuing on.

At the corner of a narrow granite-paved street branching off Royal Square, Cassandra stopped at a handsome stone house. "A date stone," she exclaimed, staring at the lintel over the door, formed of chiseled granite blocks. "I read about these in the guidebook in our suite."

"What is it?"

"It's an ancient Jersey Island tradition that when a couple marries, they chisel their initials in granite, along with the date the household was established, and set it over the door. Sometimes they join their initials with a symbol, such as a pair of entwined hearts, or a Christian cross."

Together they scrutinized the stonework on the lintel.

### *J.M. 8 G.R.P.*
### *1760*

"I wonder why there's a number eight between their names?" Cassandra asked, puzzled.

Tom shrugged. "It must have had personal significance to them."

"They might have had eight children," she suggested.

"Or eight shillings left after they built the house."

Cassandra laughed. "Maybe they had eight Jersey Wonders for breakfast every morning."

Tom drew closer to the lintel, staring intently at the masonry work. After a moment, he commented, "Look at the pattern of the granite. Vein-cut, with horizontal stripes running across the surface. But on the center block with the number eight, the stripes are vertical, and the mortar is newer. Someone repaired it and put it back the wrong way."

"You're right," Cassandra said, examining the masonry. "But that would mean it was originally a sideways number eight. That makes no sense at all. Unless . . ." She paused as understanding dawned. "You think it was the symbol for infinity?"

"Yes, but not the usual one. A special variant. Do you see how one line doesn't fully connect in the middle? That's Euler's infinity symbol. *Absolutus infinitus.*"

"How is it different from the usual one?"

"Back in the eighteenth century, there were certain mathematical calculations no one could perform because they involved series of infinite numbers. The problem with infinity, of course, is that you can't come up with a final answer when the numbers keep increasing forever. But a mathematician named Leonhard Euler found a way to treat infinity as if it were a finite number—and that allowed him to do things in

mathematical analysis that had never been done before." Tom inclined his head toward the date stone.
"My guess is, whoever chiseled that symbol was a
mathematician or scientist."

"If it were my date stone," Cassandra said dryly,
"I'd prefer the entwined hearts. At least I would understand what it means."

"No, this is much better than hearts," Tom exclaimed,
his expression more earnest than any she'd seen from
him before. "Linking their names with Euler's infinity
symbol means . . ." He paused, considering how best
to explain it. "The two of them formed a complete
unit . . . a togetherness . . . that contained infinity.
Their marriage had a beginning and end, but every
day of it was filled with forever. It's a beautiful concept."
He paused before adding awkwardly, "Mathematically
speaking."

Cassandra was so moved and charmed and surprised, she couldn't speak. She only stood there holding Tom's hand tightly. She wasn't certain whether she
had reached for his hand, or he'd reached for hers.

How eloquent this man was on nearly any subject
except his own feelings. But there were moments such
as now, when he allowed her extraordinary glimpses
into his heart without even seeming to be aware of it.

"Kiss me," she said, her voice barely audible.

Tom tilted his head in that inquiring way she had
come to love, before he drew her to the side of the
house. They stopped behind a sheltering arbor of winter jasmine starred with tiny golden blooms. His head

bent, his mouth finding hers. Wanting more, she let the tip of her tongue play against the seam of his lips. He opened for her, and she kissed him more insistently, until their tongues had entwined and his arms had clamped around her.

She sensed rather than felt his body changing in response to her nearness. Her heart drummed with excitement at the thought of what was happening to him. She wanted to feel all his skin against hers, and take him deep inside herself.

Tom finished the kiss and lifted his head slowly, his heat-drowsed eyes staring into hers. "Now what?" he asked huskily.

"Take me back to La Sirène," she whispered. "I want a few minutes of infinity with you."

IN THE QUIET afternoon hush of their hotel suite, Cassandra undressed Tom slowly, pushing his hands aside when he began to reciprocate. She wanted to see him, explore him, without the distraction of her own nakedness. As the tailored garments came off one at a time, Tom was patient, submitting to the procedure with the faintest hint of a smile.

She flushed a little as she worked at the buttons of his trousers. He was so aroused that the waistband of the trousers caught on the jut of his erection. She reached out to unhook the fabric from the swollen tip, and carefully pushed the trousers down over his hips. His body was so elegantly made, the muscles cut clean and fine, the bones long and perfectly symmetrical, as if turned by lathe work. A light flush had started on his upper chest, rising over the fair skin of his throat and face.

Coming to stand in front of him, Cassandra traced the strong lines of his clavicle, and pressed her palms to the hard muscle of his chest. "You're mine," she said quietly.

"I am." There was a flicker of amusement in his voice.

"All of you."

"Yes."

Slowly Cassandra trailed her fingers downward through the hair on his chest, letting the tips of her nails scrape gently over the little points of his nipples. His breath altered, roughening, deepening. She stroked down to his straining erection, and took it gently in both hands. He was heavy, thick, pulsing with readiness.

"And this is mine," she said.

"Yes." No amusement now. His tone had thickened with arousal, his body rigid with the effort to hold himself in check.

Delicately, as if performing a ritual, she cupped the cool weight of him below, tenderly kneading the twin spheres and feeling the movements within. Her fingers inched up the rock-hard shaft. She let the soft pads of her thumbs ease across the silken tip, and glanced up as he made rough sounds, almost as if he were in pain.

The flush had spread over his face. His eyes had dilated and darkened.

Holding his gaze, she curled her fingers around the thick length of him, and stroked up and down.

She felt him pull a few strategic pins from her hair. His fingers slid into the loosened mass and gently rubbed her scalp, and nerves all over her body tingled with delight. Beneath the layers of her skirts, she pressed her thighs together against the throb of arousal. Following an impulse, she sank down to kneel in front of him, and gripped the upright shaft with her hands. She wasn't quite sure what she was doing, but she knew how the intimate kisses he'd given her had felt. She wanted to give him that same pleasure.

"May I?" she whispered, and he uttered with a few words that, although not terribly coherent, sounded like enthusiastic consent. Careful and intent, she lapped at the soft, dense weights below before running her tongue up the satiny length of him. The texture was silkier, smoother, than she'd ever thought skin could be, and brazier-hot.

A tremor shook Tom's fingers as they moved lightly in her hair. She continued to explore the hard shape of him, kissing and stroking with her tongue, then trying to fit her mouth around him.

"Cassandra . . . my God . . ." Panting, Tom pulled her up and fumbled with the fastenings at the back of her dress, the long placket of hidden buttons. He was impassioned to the point of clumsiness, tugging until a few of the buttons popped.

"Wait," she said, trembling and laughing. "Be patient, let me—" She tried to reach around to undo them herself. It was impossible. The dress had been designed only for women who had lady's maids and ample leisure time. Tom was in no mood to wait.

He picked her up and sat her on the edge of the bed, rummaging roughly beneath the mass of her skirts. With a few demanding tugs, he stripped off her drawers and stockings. Her legs were pushed apart and held wide as he made a space for himself. She shivered as she felt his hot breath against the tender skin of her thighs . . . the graze of his tongue against the little peak. A sigh stuck in her throat and melted like honey, and she collapsed slowly on her back. Every stroke of his tongue sent a delicious curl of sensation through her belly. He licked at the throbbing as it grew stronger, the weight of pleasure building inside her, searching for release. The muscles of his arms and hairy chest pressed against her bare legs, keeping her open, anchoring her.

He climbed over her, settling between her widespread thighs. "I can't wait," he said hoarsely.

She reached for him, moaning, hitching upward. There was the smooth, hard pressure she craved, the head of the shaft entering her, stretching the wet flesh. Shaking with excitement, she ran her hands over his naked body, loving the flexing strength of him over her, inside her, working deeper. His hips rocked and circled gently, the thickness caressing different places within her. He pushed deep in long strokes, using his weight to press down on her in exactly the right way. It felt maddeningly good, each impact creating more tension, more pleasure, until nothing existed except the steady thrusting between her thighs. She arched and spread herself wider, wanting more, and he gave it to her.

"Is this too hard?" he asked huskily.

"No . . . no . . . just like that . . ."

"I feel you tighten on me . . . every time I go in."

"More . . . please . . ." She bent her knees and lifted her feet, and whimpered as he went deeper.

"Too much?" he asked raggedly, but she couldn't answer, only gripped him between her thighs as the waves of release rolled over her, tumbling her, washing her senses with ecstasy. He went rigid, his heat pumping inside her, and that made the feeling go on and on, quivers echoing through her body.

Tom made a project of undressing her fully after that, rolling her to her stomach and working on the row of tiny, stubborn buttons. It took a long time, especially because he kept pausing to reach inside the openings of her dress, or beneath the crumpled skirts, caressing her with his mouth or fingers. She loved the sound of his voice, sated and deep, as if he spoke to her from drowsy distances. "You're so beautiful everywhere, Cassandra. Along your back, there's the faintest line of golden down, like a peach . . . and here's your magnificent bottom . . . so full and sweet . . . so firm in my hands. You drive me mad. Look at how your little toes are curling. They do that right before you come for me . . . they clench and turn pink, every time . . ."

After Tom had unfastened the last button, the dress was tossed unceremoniously to the floor. He kissed her everywhere, and made love to her with diabolical slowness. After coaxing her to her hands and knees, he took her from behind, his body a sturdy frame around hers. He slid his hands to her front, cupping the hanging weights of her breasts, pinching and tweaking her nipples softly, teasing them into hard points. All the while, he thrust straight into the core of her body, in deep, lustful plunges.

It felt primitive, being taken like this. It felt like something she shouldn't be enjoying this much. Her face was hot, her insides clenching with desire. He reached down to the wet triangle between her thighs and massaged lightly, steadily. At the same time, she felt his mouth at the top of her shoulder, his teeth clamping in a gentle love bite. She shuddered hard, her body squeezing powerfully around his, detonating his release. He pushed deep and held, while she buried her face in a pillow to stifle her sharp cries.

Eventually Tom eased them both to their sides, his body still clasped within hers. She sighed in contentment as his muscular forearms wrapped around her.

His lips brushed the soft skin behind her ear. "How's this for cuddling?" he asked.

"You're learning," she told him, and closed her eyes in contentment.

# Chapter 25

"IF YOU DON'T LIKE this house," Tom said as the carriage came to a halt at Hyde Park Square, "you can choose another one. Or we'll build one. Or we'll find something else on the market."

"I'm resolved on liking this one," Cassandra said, "rather than having to move an entire household somewhere else."

"You'll probably want to do some decorating."

"I may be quite pleased with what's already there." She paused. "Although I'm sure it's crying out for fringe."

He smiled and helped her from the carriage.

Hyde Park Square was an elegant and prosperous area that was coming to rival Belgravia. It occupied a district filled with private gardens, cream stucco terraces, and spacious brick and stone mansions.

Cassandra's gaze moved over the façade of the picturesque house. It was large and handsome, with bay windows overlooking the landscaped grounds. There was an adjoining coach house and fine modern stabling, and a glass conservatory attached to the main building.

"There are eight bedrooms on the first floor and five on the second floor," Tom murmured as he escorted her through the wide entrance vestibule framed with columns and ornamental brickwork. "After I bought the house, I added several bathrooms with hot and cold water supply."

They entered a square hall with a lofty ceiling and roof lights of stained glass. A row of servants had been lined up to greet them. As soon as they caught sight of Cassandra, there was a volley of whispers, and even a muffled squeal from some of the younger housemaids.

"They're always so excited to see me," Tom remarked blandly, his eyes glinting with amusement. A short, matronly housekeeper dressed in black bombazine approached them and curtsied. "Welcome home, master," she murmured.

"Lady Cassandra, this is Mrs. Dankworth, our remarkably efficient housekeeper—" Tom began.

"*Welcome*, my lady," the woman exclaimed, curtsying yet again, her square face beaming. "We're all so very pleased—overjoyed, in fact!—to have you here."

"Thank you, Mrs. Dankworth," Cassandra said warmly. "Mr. Severin has spoken so highly of you. He's praised your abilities to the heavens."

"You're too kind, my lady."

Tom's brows lifted as he looked at the housekeeper. "You're smiling, Mrs. Dankworth," he remarked in bemusement. "I didn't know you could do that."

"If you'll allow me to introduce the servants," the housekeeper said to Cassandra, "they would be most honored."

Cassandra went with her to the line of servants, meeting them in turn. As she exchanged a few words with each one, and tried to commit their names to memory, she was touched by their friendliness and eagerness to please.

Out of the periphery of her vision, she saw a small, swift shape hurtling past the line and colliding with Tom, who was standing off to the side.

"That would be Bazzle, the hall boy," Mrs. Dankworth said ruefully. "A good boy, but quite young, as you see, and sorely in need of supervision. We all do our best to look after him, but we have our daily chores to attend to."

Cassandra met the woman's gaze and nodded, understanding much of what was being left unsaid. "Perhaps later," she said, "you I and might discuss Bazzle's situation in private."

The housekeeper gave her a look of mingled gratitude and relief. "Thank you, my lady. That would be most helpful."

After Cassandra had met all the servants, and introduced her lady's maid, she went toward Tom, who had lowered to his haunches as he talked with Bazzle. She was struck by the obvious affection between the two, which she was certain Tom wasn't even aware of. The boy chattered without stopping, clearly thrilled to have his attention. Tom reached into his pocket and took out a cup and ball game with a handle, one of the presents he'd bought for Bazzle on the island.

"For bashin' someone on the noggin?" Bazzle asked, inspecting the ball that was attached by a string.

Tom chuckled. "No, it's not a weapon, it's a toy. Swing the ball and try to make it drop into the cup."

The boy struggled with the game, repeatedly jerking the ball upward and failing to catch it. "Ain't working."

"That's because you're applying too much centripetal force to the ball. At that rate of velocity, the force of gravity isn't strong enough to—" Tom stopped as he looked into the boy's blank face. "What I mean is, swing it more gently." He closed his hand around the boy's, to show him. Together they swung the ball upward. At the peak of its slow curved ascent, the ball seemed to hover in midair, then dropped perfectly into the cup.

Bazzle let out a little crow of delight.

Cassandra reached the pair and crouched down beside them. "Hello, Bazzle," she said, smiling. "Do you remember me?"

He nodded, seeming dumbstruck by the sight of her.

A regular supply of healthy meals, sufficient rest, and good hygiene had wrought an astonishing transformation since she'd last seen Bazzle. He had filled out, his limbs now sturdy instead of breakably thin, his cheeks rounded. The dark eyes were clear and bright, set in a fine-grained complexion warmed with a healthy glow. His teeth were white and scrupulously clean, and his hair was scissored into cropped, gleaming layers. A fine-looking boy, on his way to being handsome.

"Did Mr. Severin tell you I'm going to live here?" she asked.

Bazzle nodded. "Yer 'is missus now," he said shyly. "I am."

"I likes that pig song you sang to me," he ventured.

Cassandra laughed. "I'll sing it for you later. But first I have a confession to make." She crooked her finger for him to come closer, and he obeyed cautiously. "I'm a little nervous, moving into a new house," she whispered. "I don't know where anything is."

"It's awful big," he told her emphatically.

"It is," she agreed. "Will you take me around and show it to me?"

He nodded, a grin spreading across his face.

Tom stood and reached for Cassandra, bringing her up with him. He looked down at her with a faint frown. "Sweet, you would do better to have me show you the house. Or Mrs. Dankworth, if you like. You're not going to receive a comprehensive tour from a nine- or ten year-old boy."

"You show it to me later," she whispered, and stood on her toes to kiss his chin. "At the moment, I'm not trying to learn about the house, but about Bazzle."

He gave her a baffled glance. "What is there to learn?"

CASSANDRA REACHED DOWN for Bazzle's hand, which he gave willingly, and he towed her through the house, starting with the bottom floor. They went to the kitchen, where he showed her the dumbwaiter closet that a tier of shelves connected by a frame could be lifted from the kitchen to the dining room. "They puts the food in there," Bazzle explained, "and pulls this rope to make it go up. But people can't go in there, even if their legs is tired." He shrugged. "Too bad."

Next, he showed her the combination pantry and larder. "They locks it every night," he warned her. "So eats yer victuals at dinner, even the beets, 'cause ye can't eat noffing after." He paused before whispering conspiratorially, "But Cook allus leaves a snack for me in the bread box. I'll share, if yer 'ungry."

They visited the scullery and servants' hall, but cut a wide swath around the housekeeper's room, from which Mrs. Dankworth apparently liked to leap out and make you go wash your hands and neck in the scullery.

They reached the boot room, which contained shelves and rows of hat hooks, an umbrella stand, and a table of equipment for cleaning and polishing footwear. The air was scented of leather wax and boot blacking. A small casement window near the ceiling admitted light from outside. "This is my room," Bazzle said proudly.

"What do you do here?" Cassandra asked.

"Every night I washes the mud from the shoes and boots, and makes 'em shiny, and then I'm orf to bed."

"And where is your bedroom?"

"Bed's right 'ere," Bazzle said brightly, and opened

a wooden cupboard. It was a box bed, built into a re-
cessed space in the wall, and fitted with a mattress and
bedclothes.

Cassandra stared at it without blinking. "You sleep
in the boot room, dear?" she asked very softly.

"A good little bed," he said cheerfully, reaching
over to pat the mattress. "Never 'ad one before."

Cassandra reached down and slowly drew him
closer, smoothing the shiny ruffled locks of his hair.
"You're about to outgrow it," she murmured, her
thoughts swarming, her throat tight with indignation.
"I'll make sure your next one is bigger. And nicer."

Bazzle leaned his head against her tentatively, and
let out a deep, happy sigh. "You smells like flowers."

"No, I DIDN'T know it was the boot room," Tom said
irritably, when Cassandra confronted him in an upstairs bedroom. He had been taken aback and disgruntled when she'd approached him with tight-lipped
displeasure, all vestiges of their honeymoon bliss
completely gone. "Mrs. Dankworth told me it was a
room close to hers, so she could help him if he needed
something during the night."

"He would never go to her for help. He's convinced
she would only try to wash him." Cassandra paced
back and forth across the elegant bedroom, her arms
folded tightly across her chest. "He's sleeping in a
cupboard, Tom!"

"In a nice, clean bed," he countered. "It's better
than the rat-infested slum he was living in before."

She gave him a withering glance. "He can't go through the rest of his life being grateful for the bare minimum and saying 'Well, it's better than a rat-infested slum.'"

"What do you want for him?" Tom asked with forced patience, leaning his shoulder against one of the solid rosewood bed posters. "To have his own room on the third floor with the other servants? Done. Now, may we focus on something other than Bazzle?"

"He's not a servant. He's a little boy, living among adults, working as an adult . . . being robbed of his last chance at childhood."

"Some of us aren't allowed childhoods," Tom said curtly.

"He doesn't belong anywhere, to anyone. He can't live between worlds, neither fish nor fowl, never knowing what his place is."

"Damn it, Cassandra—"

"And what will happen when you and I have children? He'll have to grow up near a family, watching from the outside, never being invited in. It's not fair to him, Tom."

"It was bloody good enough for me!" he snapped, with the force of a rifle shot.

Cassandra blinked, some of her anger clearing away. She turned to look at him as silence weighted the room. Her husband's face was averted, but she saw that his color had heightened. He was tense in every muscle, struggling to contain his emotions.

When he could bring himself to speak, his voice was cool and measured. "When the Paxtons took me in, I had the option of sharing a footman's room or sleeping on a pallet in the kitchen, near the stove. The footman's room was too small as it was. I chose the pallet. I slept on it every night for years, and folded it up every morning, and I was grateful. Sometimes I ate with the family, but most often I ate alone in the kitchen. I never thought of asking Mr. Paxton for more. It was enough to sleep somewhere safe and clean, and not go hungry. More than enough."

*No, it wasn't,* Cassandra thought, her heart wrenching.

"Eventually I was able to afford a room at a lodging house," Tom continued. "I continued to work for Mr. Paxton, but I started to manage projects and solve engineering problems for other companies. I began to earn money. The Paxtons invited me to dinner now and then." A short, humorless laugh escaped him. "The strange part was, I never felt comfortable at their dinner table. I felt as if I should eat in the kitchen."

He was quiet for a long time then, staring distantly at the wall as if memories were playing across it. Although his body appeared to have relaxed, his hand had clenched around the bedpost until the tips of his fingers were white.

"What caused your falling-out?" Cassandra dared to ask, her gaze locked on him.

"I felt . . . something . . . for one of Paxton's daughters. She was a pretty sort, a bit of a flirt. I wanted . . . I thought . . ."

"You asked if you could court her?"

A single nod.

"And Mr. Paxton refused?" she pressed.

"He exploded," Tom said, the corner of his mouth quirking with dark amusement. His grip on the bedpost tightened. "I'd never expected quite so much outrage. That I would dare approach one of his daughters . . . Mrs. Paxton literally needed smelling salts. It made me realize how differently they saw me from how I saw myself. I didn't know who was in the wrong."

"Oh, Tom . . ." She came up behind him and slid her arms around him, and laid her cheek on his back. A tear tracked down the side of her face and was instantly absorbed by his shirt. "*They* were in the wrong. You know they were. But now . . . *you* are." She felt him stiffen, but she hung on doggedly. "You've created a situation in which Bazzle's going to experience exactly what you did—a boy who has no one, growing up in a house with a family he can never be part of. Close enough to love them, without being loved in return."

"I didn't love them," he growled.

"You did. That's why it hurt. Why it still hurts. And now you're following in Mr. Paxton's footsteps. You're doing it to Bazzle." She paused to swallow back her tears. "Tom, you've taken this boy in because you saw many worthy qualities in him. You've let yourself care about him, just a little. Now I'm asking you to care more. Let him be part of the family, and treat him with the affection and respect he deserves."

"What makes you think he deserves it?" Tom asked curtly.

"Because you did," she said quietly, letting go of him. "Every child does."

And she went from the room quietly, leaving him to face his demons.

CASSANDRA KNEW IT would take some time for Tom to come to terms with his past and the feelings he'd kept bottled up for so long. He might deny everything she'd said, or refuse to talk about it at all. She would have to be patient and understanding, and hope he would gradually come to acknowledge she had been right.

In the meantime, she would settle into her new home and start to build a life.

With her lady's maid's help, she spent the rest of the afternoon putting away her clothes, accessories, shoes, and the thousands of items necessary for a lady to be turned out properly. There was no sound from Tom's connecting bedroom and sitting room. When Cassandra risked taking a peek, she discovered the bedroom was empty.

Perhaps he'd gone to his club, she thought with a touch of gloom, or a tavern, or some other place men went to avoid their wives. She hoped he would return for dinner. He wouldn't be so inconsiderate as to miss dinner without telling her in advance, would he? Hadn't there been something about that in the contract? Yes, she was positive there had been. If it turned out he'd violated their contract after one week of marriage, she was going to do something drastic. Crumple it up in front of him. No—she would set fire to it. Or maybe—

Her thoughts were interrupted by a gentle knock on the doorjamb. She glanced at the doorway, and her heart gave a few extra thumps as she saw her husband standing there, big and dark, with his hair slightly disheveled. "May I come in?" he asked quietly.

"Oh, yes," Cassandra said, flustered. "You needn't ask, just . . ." She turned to her lady's maid. "Meg, if you wouldn't mind."

"Yes, my lady." The lady's maid moved a fabric-covered box of stockings from the bed to the dresser. As she passed Cassandra, her eyes glinted with mischief, and she said beneath her breath, "That dog's going for a trot again."

Cassandra frowned, and ushered her from the room.

Tom came in, bringing the scent of winter air and dry leaves with him. He leaned back against the dresser and slid his hands in his pockets, his expression unfathomable.

"You went for a walk?" Cassandra asked.

"I did."

"I hope it was pleasant."

"Not especially." He took a long breath and blew it out slowly.

"Tom," she said uneasily, "what I said before—"

"Feelings are inconvenient," Tom said. "It's why I decided to limit mine to five. For most of my adult life, it's been easy to keep to that. Then I met you. Now my feelings have multiplied like rabbits, and I seem to have nearly as many as normal people do. Which is too many. However . . . if a man with the average brain can manage all these feelings well enough to function efficiently, I, with my powerful and superior brain, can as well."

Cassandra nodded encouragingly, although she wasn't quite sure what he was saying.

"Bazzle no longer has to be a hall boy," he said. "He can sleep in a room on this floor of the house, and eat at our table. We'll educate him as you see fit. I'll raise him as . . . as mine."

She heard him with a sense of wonder, having expected a long siege and instead been met with un-anticipated surrender. For him to set aside his pride like this was not something to take lightly. Understanding the difficulty of the concession, and the changes he was going through, Cassandra went eagerly to press herself against his motionless form. "Thank you," she said. His head eased down to her shoulder, and his arms stole around her.

"I didn't make this decision to humor you," Tom muttered. "You made some logical points I happened to agree with."

Her fingers combed slowly through the fluid black layers of his hair. "And you care about him."

"I wouldn't necessarily put it that way. I just want him to be safe and comfortable and happy, and for no one to harm him."

"That's caring."

Tom didn't reply, but his arms tightened. After a long moment, he asked against her shoulder, "Are you going to reward me?"

Cassandra chuckled. "My body isn't a prize for doing the right thing."

"But it makes doing the right thing so much easier."

"In that case . . ." Her hand caught one of his, and she pulled him toward the bed.

# *Chapter* 26

*I*MMEDIATELY UPON THEIR RETURN from Jersey Island, Cassandra was beset by a torrent of calls, which she was then obligated to return. Tom was bemused by the complexity of the social rules his wife navigated so adeptly. She knew exactly when and how to call on people, and who received visits on which days. She knew which invitations could be refused, and which ones had to be accepted unless one was at death's door. A bewildering variety of cards was required for this business of paying and receiving visits . . . individual cards for Tom and herself, a slightly larger card with both their names engraved on it, cards printed with their address and preferred receiving days, cards to be left after a chance visit, and cards to be left when no visit had been intended.

"Why would you go to someone's house if you don't want to see them?" Tom had asked.

"When you owe a friend a visit, but have no time to spend with her, you leave a card on the hall table to let her know you were there."

"More precisely, you were there but didn't want to see her."

"Exactly."

Tom didn't bother trying to make sense of that, having accepted long ago that a small group of elevated individuals had decided to make human interaction as complicated and unnatural as possible. He didn't mind that nearly as much as he minded the hypocrisy of a society that would condemn someone over a minor transgression, while letting one of its own off the hook for doing far worse.

He'd been disgusted—but hardly surprised—by the upper crust's reaction to the *London Chronicle*'s exposure of the Marquis of Ripon and his son, Lord Lambert, as vicious, lying bastards who'd intentionally tried to ruin Cassandra's reputation. Ripon's friends and associates had hastened to excuse his actions, and cast as much blame as possible on the young woman he had publicly humiliated.

The marquis had made an error in judgment, they had said, while he'd been distraught by the misbehavior of his son. Others had claimed it was a misunderstanding that, while unfortunate, had turned out well enough in the end. The wrongly accused Lady Cassandra had ended up married, they reasoned, so no real harm had been done.

It was generally agreed in elevated social circles that although the marquis's behavior was regrettable, the lapse must be overlooked in a gentleman of such assured rank. Some people pointed out that Ripon had been punished enough by the embarrassment of his son's infamous conduct, as well as the shadow cast over his own reputation. Therefore, the brunt of the blame was heaped on the absent Lord Lambert, who it seemed had decided to resume his grand tour of the continent for an indeterminate length of time. Ripon, for his part, would be welcomed back into the fold when the scandal had faded.

In the meantime, social mavens decided that no harm would come of paying calls to Lady Cassandra and her wealthy husband, and cultivating an advantageous association with them.

Tom would have liked to stick to his original plan of telling them all to go to hell, except that Cassandra seemed pleased by the visits. He would tolerate anything, no matter how galling, if it made her happy.

Since the age of ten, work had been the main part of Tom's life, and home had been the place of brief but necessary intermissions, where he conducted the rituals of sleeping, eating, washing and shaving as efficiently as possible. Now, for the first time, he found himself plowing through his work so he could hurry back home, where all the interesting things seemed to be happening.

In the first fortnight after their honeymoon, Cassandra had taken charge of the house at Hyde Park Square with an impressive attention to detail. Despite all her talk of lingering and being a lady of leisure, she was a whirlwind in disguise. She knew what she wanted, and how to give directions, and how to approach the complex web of responsibilities and relationships that comprised a household.

An assistant had been hired for the elderly cook, and new dishes were already being served at the table. After reviewing the household routines with Mrs. Dankworth, it was agreed that two additional housemaids and an extra footman would be hired to reduce the staff's workload in general. They had too little time off per week, Cassandra had explained to Tom, which was exhausting and dispiriting. She and the housekeeper had also agreed to soften a few rules to make the servants' lives less codified and uncomfortable. For example, the housemaids would no longer be obligated to wear the silly popover shaped caps that served no purpose other than to designate them as housemaids. Such small concessions seemed to have buoyed the general atmosphere of the house noticeably.

The extra parlor Cassandra had commandeered for her private office was filled with sample books of paint, paper, carpeting and fabric, as she had decided to replace portions of interior decorating she considered shabby or outdated. That included the servants' quarters, where worn bed linens, blankets and towels had been replaced, as well as several pieces of rickety or broken furniture. A better quality of soap would be ordered for their personal needs, instead of the coarse soap that made the skin dry and the hair brittle.

It annoyed Tom that there were details about the lives of his household staff he'd never been made aware of, nor had he thought to ask about. "No one ever mentioned that my servants were being given the cheapest possible soap," he had told Cassandra with a scowl. "The devil knows I've never been a miser."

"Of course not," she soothed. "Mrs. Dankworth was only trying to be economical."

"She could have told me."

Diplomatically, Cassandra said, "I'm not sure she felt comfortable talking to you about household soap. You seem to have told her you didn't want to be bothered by the details, and to use her own judgment."

"Clearly my opinion of her judgment was too high," Tom muttered. "I'd rather not have my servants scoured raw with caustic soda and petroleum soap."

In the ferment of activity, Bazzle was hardly forgotten. Cassandra had taken him to a dentist for a professional cleaning, and then to an oculist who administered an eye examination and pronounced his vision excellent. After that, she'd taken him to visit a tailor who had measured him for new clothes. Although Cassandra hadn't yet found a private tutor to bring Bazzle up to the educational level of other children his age, she had undertaken to teach him the alphabet. He'd found it dull and tiresome, until she'd purchased a set of painted alphabet blocks that featured pictures as well as letters. At mealtimes, she labored to teach him basic manners, including how to use his utensils properly.

Although Bazzle adored Cassandra, her relentless attentions were probably a large part of the reason the boy was so insistent about continuing to accompany

Tom to the office in the mornings. Once a tutor was found, however, Bazzle's visits would have to become curtailed.

"Fingers is as good as forks," Bazzle grumbled as he went with Tom to a food stall for lunch one day. "Don't need no utenskils, and no alphabet neither."

"Look at it this way," Tom said reasonably. "If you're eating at a table beside a fellow who knows how to use his fork properly, and you can only eat with your fingers, people will think he's smarter than you."

"Don't care."

"You'll care when they give him a better job."

"Still don't care," came Bazzle's sullen reply. "I likes sweeping."

"What about operating a big excavating machine, and digging up an entire street instead of sweeping it?"

To Tom's amusement, Bazzle's expression lit up with interest.

"Me, dig up a street?"

"Someday, Bazzle, you could be in charge of a fleet of large machines. You could own companies that make new roads and dig tunnels. But those are the jobs that go to men who use forks and know their alphabet."

ON THE DAY Tom brought Cassandra to visit his offices, he hadn't expected that all businesslike decorum would have been so utterly abandoned by everyone from department heads down to the secretaries and accountants. They crowded around her and fawned as if she were visiting royalty. Cassandra was gracious and charming amid the crush, while Bazzle clung to Tom's side and looked up at him with mild alarm. "They all gone orf their chumps," the boy said.

Tom kept a protective arm around him, reached for Cassandra, and managed to usher them both to his private offices on the top floor. As soon as they reached safety, Bazzle looked up at Cassandra with his arms locked around her hips. "I got squashed," he told her.

She smoothed his hair and straightened his cap. Her reply was forestalled as someone approached and stumbled against a chair, nearly tripping.

It was Barnaby, who had just entered the office and caught sight of Cassandra. Tom reached out automatically to steady him.

"Oh no," Bazzle groaned, "not 'im too!"

Barnaby, to his credit, managed to recover his composure, but his face was infused with heightened color that electrified his wild curls until they seemed to radiate out from his head. "My lady," he said, and bowed nervously, with a stack of ledgers and papers clutched in one arm.

"Is this the indispensable Mr. Barnaby?" Cassandra asked with a smile.

"It is," Tom replied for his assistant, who was too befuddled to reply.

Cassandra moved forward, with Bazzle still hanging from her hip, and extended her hand. "How happy I am to make your acquaintance at last. According to my husband, nothing would be accomplished around here if it weren't for you."

"Is that what I said?" Tom asked dryly, while Barnaby took Cassandra's hand as if it were a sacred object. "Barnaby," Tom continued, "what is that stack you're holding?"

Barnaby gave him an owlish glance. "What . . . oh . . . *this* stack." He released Cassandra's hand and hefted the pile of materials to Tom's desk. "Information on the Charterhouse Defense Fund, sir, as well as the local businesses and residents, a summary of the pending report of the Royal Commission on London Traffic, and an analysis of the joint select committee that will vote to authorize your bill."

"What bill?" Cassandra asked.

Tom drew her to a map of London on the wall. With a fingertip, he traced a line that went under Charterhouse Street toward Smithfield. "I've proposed a bill to build a connecting underground railway line to an existing one that currently ends at Farringdon.

"The proposal is currently being examined by a joint select committee of the Lords and Commons. They'll meet next week to pass a bill that will authorize me to proceed with the line. The problem is, some of the local residents and tradesmen are fighting it."

"I'm sure they dread all the inconvenience and construction noise," Cassandra said. "Not to mention the loss of business."

"Yes, but they'll all eventually benefit from having a new station built nearby."

Barnaby cleared his throat delicately from behind them. "Not *all* of them."

Cassandra gave Tom a quizzical glance.

Tom's mouth twisted. Resisting the urge to send Barnaby a lethal glance, he indicated a spot on the map with his fingertip. "This is a remnant of Charterhouse Lane, which was left after most of the thoroughfare was converted to Charterhouse Street. Right here, there are a pair of tenement slums that should have been condemned years ago. Each one was designed to house three dozen families, but they're crammed with at least twice that number of people. There's no light or air, no fire protection, no decent sanitary arrangements . . . it's the closest thing you'll find to hell on earth."

"They're not your slums, I hope?" Cassandra asked apprehensively. "You don't own them?"

The question annoyed him. "No, they're not mine."

Barnaby spoke up helpfully. "Once the bill is passed, however, Mr. Severin will have the power to buy or underpin any property he wants, to make the railway go through. That's why they've organized the Charterhouse Lane Defense Fund, to try and stop him." At Tom's slitted glare, Barnaby added quickly, "I mean, *us*."

"So the slums will become yours," Cassandra said to Tom.

"The residents will have to move," Tom said defensively, "regardless of whether or not the railway line is built. Believe me, it will be a mercy for those people to be forced out of those hellholes."

"But where will they go?" Cassandra asked.

"That's not my business."

"It is if you buy the tenement buildings."

"I'm not going to buy the tenements, I'm going to acquire the land beneath them." Tom's scowling gaze softened slightly as it fell on Bazzle's upturned face. "Why don't you fetch your broom and do some sweeping?" he suggested gently.

The boy, who was bored by the conversation, seized on the suggestion eagerly. "I'll start on the outside steps." He hurried to Cassandra and tugged her by the hand to one of the front windows. "Mama, look down there and watch me sweep!"

Barnaby looked stunned as Bazzle ran from the office. "Did he just call her Mama?" he asked Tom blankly.

"She said I could!" called Bazzle's retreating voice.

Cassandra sent Tom a troubled glance as she remained by the window. "Tom . . . you can't make homeless outcasts of all those people."

"Bloody hell," he muttered.

"Because—in addition to your natural sense of compassion—"

A peculiar snort came from Barnaby's direction.

"—it would be disastrous from the standpoint of public relations," Cassandra continued earnestly, "wouldn't it? You would appear completely heartless, which we know you are not."

"The residents can apply for help from countless charities in London," Tom said.

She gave him a chiding glance. "Most of those charities won't be able to offer *real* help." After a pause, she asked, "You want to be known as a public benefactor, don't you?"

"I'd like to be known as one, but I wasn't necessarily planning to *become* one."

Cassandra turned to face him. "I will, then," she said firmly. "You promised I could start any charity I wanted. I'm going to find or build low-cost housing for the displaced Charterhouse Lane residents."

Tom regarded his wife for a long moment. The flash of newfound assertiveness interested him. Excited him. He approached her slowly. "I suppose you'll want to take advantage of some of the undeveloped lots I own in Clerkenwell or Smithfield," he said.

She lifted her chin slightly. "I might."

"You'll probably rook some of my own people into working for you . . . architects, engineers, contractors . . . all at cut-rate fees."

Her eyes widened. "Could I?"

"I wouldn't even be surprised if you forced Barnaby, who has access to all my connections and resources, to act as your part-time assistant."

As Tom stared into his wife's beautiful face, he heard Barnaby exclaim in a heartfelt voice behind them, "Oh, must I?"

"Do you think I could succeed?" Cassandra whispered.

"Lady Cassandra Severin," Tom said quietly, "that you'll succeed is not even a question." He gave her a wry glance. "The question is, are you going to spend the rest of our marriage trying to make me live up to your standards?"

Her eyes flickered with impish humor. She was about to reply, but she happened to glance outside at the front steps several stories below them, where Bazzle's small figure stood waving up to them.

At that moment, a huge, hulking form ran up to the steps and grabbed the child, lifting him off his feet.

Cassandra let out a cry of panic. *"Tom!"*

He took one glance and bolted through the office as if the devil were at his heels.

BY THE TIME Tom had reached the front steps, the stranger had made it halfway down the block with the wailing child, and had shoved him into a dilapidated hackney cab driven by a skinny, whey-faced young driver.

Tom sprinted to the horse's head and grabbed the bridle. "If you try to drive off with him," he panted to the cabman with a murderous glare, "you won't bloody live to see another day. I swear it." He directed his voice to Bazzle. "Get out of the cab, boy."

"Mr. Severin," Bazzle sobbed. "It's . . . it's Uncle Batty . . ."

"Get out of the cab," Tom repeated patiently.

"The 'igh and mighty Tom Severin," the big, grizzled brute sneered. "Noffing but a common thief! Stealin' away a man's living! This 'ere is *my* pigeon. You wants to make a nancy o' the little sod, you 'as to pay for it."

Bazzle called out tearfully, "I ain't no sod! Leave Mr. Severin alone! 'E ain't done noffing to yer."

"'E robbed me o' yer rightful earnings wot I was due," Uncle Batty retorted. A sneer twisted his face. "No one steals from me. I'm taking back wot's mine." Without looking at Bazzle, he said, "Mind me, boy, or I'll wring this fine feathered toff's neck like a chicken fit for the plucking."

"Don't touch 'im," the boy cried.

"Bazzle," Tom said, "listen to me. Climb out of that damned cab and go back to the office building. Wait for me there."

"But Uncle Batty will—"

"*Bazzle*," Tom said curtly.

To Tom's relief, the boy obeyed, slowly descending from the cab and heading toward the steps. Tom let go of the horse's bridle and moved to the pavement.

"Wot's the brat to yer anyways?" Uncle Batty sneered, circling him. "Bazzle ain't worth the time o' day to yer."

Tom didn't reply, only countered his movements, keeping his gaze fixed on the other man's face.

"Going to lay yer flat, I am," Uncle Batty continued. "Pound ye to a paste. Or . . . if ye cares to toss some blunt me way, I might leave yer be."

"I wouldn't give you a farthing, you gatless arse-wit," Tom said. "It's the surest guarantee you'd come back for more."

"As the gen'leman wishes," the other man growled, and lunged for him. Tom sidestepped, turned swiftly, and was ready with a jab, cross and a hard left hook when he came upright.

Uncle Batty stumbled back and roared with outrage. He plowed forward again, absorbing a blow to his side and another to his stomach before landing an overhand punch that sent Tom reeling back. Pressing forward, Batty pounded him with an uppercut and another right, but Tom sidestepped to deflect the force of the blow. With bullish rage, Batty launched at him, sending them both to the ground. A burst of white sparks went across Tom's vision as his head hit the pavement.

When Tom came to himself, he was rolling across the ground with the massive figure, trading blows, using knees, elbows, fists, any means to gain an advantage. He smashed a fist into the bastard's face, sending a spray of blood over them both. The big body beneath him went still, groaning in defeat. Tom kept pounding, machine-like, the breath sawing from his lungs, his muscles burning in agony.

He felt a multitude of hands grabbing him, pulling him away. Unable to see clearly, he dragged his sleeve across his eyes. In the tumult and fury, he became aware of a small body pressed tightly to him, skinny arms cinched around his waist.

"Sir . . . sir . . ." Bazzle sobbed.

"Bazzle," Tom slurred, his head spinning. "You're my boy. No one takes you away from me. No one."

"Yes, sir."

Sometime later, he heard Cassandra's tense, quiet voice. "Tom. Tom, can you hear me?"

But his vision had gone gray, and he could only mumble a few words that he knew weren't making sense. Feeling her arms around him, he sighed and turned his face against the perfumed softness of her bosom, and let himself drift into the inviting darkness.

"I HAVE NO middle name," Tom said testily, as Garrett Gibson leaned over his bedside and moved her finger across his field of vision.

"Keep following my finger. Who's the queen?"

"Victoria."

Cassandra sat at the foot of the bed and watched the examination. After the previous day's events, her husband's face was a bit worse for wear, but the bruises would heal, and thankfully, he had suffered only a slight concussion.

"What year is it?" Garrett asked.

"Eighteen seventy-seven. You asked me the same questions yesterday."

"And you're just as cantankerous as you were then," Garrett marveled. Sitting up, she spoke to Cassandra. "Since the concussion is minor, and all indications are promising, I'll allow him some limited activity for the next day or two. However, I wouldn't let him overdo. He should rest his mind and body as much as possible to ensure a complete recovery." She wrinkled her nose playfully at Bazzle, who was curled up on the other side of the bed with a ball of red fluff cuddled against his chest. "That means we mustn't let the puppy disturb Mr. Severin's sleep."

The puppy had been a gift from Winterborne and Helen, delivered just that morning. They had received word of a new litter from a friend who bred toy poodle dogs, and at their request had sent the pick of the litter when he was ready to be weaned. Bazzle was enchanted with the little creature, whose presence had already helped him to stop fretting over the fright he'd received.

"There's a dust wad on the bed," had been Tom's comment upon first seeing the puppy. "It has legs."

Now the toy poodle stretched and yawned, and toddled up along Tom's side, staring at him with bright amber eyes.

"Was this thing on our approved list?" Tom asked, reluctantly reaching out to stroke the curly head with two fingers.

"You know quite well it was," Cassandra said, smiling, "and, being a poodle, Bingley will hardly shed at all."

"Bingley?" Tom repeated.

"From *Pride and Prejudice*. Haven't you read that one yet?"

"I don't need to," Tom said. "If it's Austen, I already know the plot: two people who fall in love after they have a terrible misunderstanding and have many long conversations about it. Then they marry. The end."

"Sounds orwful," Bazzle said. "Unless it's the one with the squid."

"No, *that's* an excellent novel," Tom said, "which I will read to you, if you can find it."

"I know where it is," Bazzle said eagerly, and jumped off the bed.

"I'll read it to both of you," Cassandra said, "after I see Dr. Gibson out."

"I'll see myself out," Garrett said firmly. "You stay with the patient, dear, and don't let him overexert himself today." She stood and collected her bag. "Mr. Severin, my husband asked me to convey to you that Uncle Batty will be incarcerated for a good long while. By the time he's released, he'll pose no more problems for you or anyone. In the meantime, I'm treating the boys who were living with him, and endeavoring to find them new situations."

"Thank you," Tom said, seeming disconcerted as Bingley snuggled into the crook of his arm. "You're not supposed to be on the bed," he told the puppy. "It's contractually prohibited."

Bingley didn't seem to care.

Cassandra leaned over Tom. "Does your head hurt?" she asked in concern. "Do you need more medicine?"

"I need more you," he said, and pulled her down beside him. She snuggled against him carefully. "Cassandra," he said huskily.

She turned her face until their noses were nearly touching, and all she could see were the mingled depths of blue and green in his eyes.

"When I woke up this morning," Tom continued, ". . . I realized something."

"What was that, dear love?" she whispered.

"What Phileas Fogg learned after traveling around the world."

"Oh?" She blinked and raised herself up on one elbow to look down at him.

"The money meant nothing to him at the end," Tom said. "Whether he won or lost the bet . . . that also meant nothing. All that mattered was Aouda, the woman he fell in love with along the way and brought back with him. Love is what's important." His gaze locked with hers, a smile deepening at the outer corners of his eyes. "That's the lesson, isn't it?"

Cassandra nodded, wiping at the sudden watery blur of her vision. She tried to smile back, but a wave of pure emotion made her mouth quiver.

One of his hands touched her face reverently. "I love you, Cassandra," came his shaken voice.

"I love you, too," she said, and her breath caught on a little sob. "I know the words aren't easy for you."

"No," Tom murmured, "but I intend to practice. Frequently." His hand slid around her head to pull her down to him, and he kissed her ardently. "I love you." Another longer, slower kiss, seeming to pull her soul from her body. "I love you . . ."

THE SOUND OF shattering glass caused Kathleen to start as she walked through the entrance hall at Eversby Priory. Or waddled, rather, she thought ruefully, one of her hands pressed against the curve of a distinctly rounded tummy. With only two months left to go, she had become heavier and slower, her joints loosening until the gait of impending childbirth was unmistakable. She was grateful to be away from the social whirl of London, back in the comforting surroundings of Eversby Priory. Devon had seemed equally as happy, if not more so, to return to the Hampshire estate, where the winter air was bitten with the savor of wood smoke and ice and evergreen. Even though she was too far along to ride, she could visit her horses in the stables, and take long walks with Devon, and return to snuggle beside a snapping fire in the hearth.

They had just finished afternoon tea, while Kathleen had read aloud from a letter that had arrived that morning. It had been from Cassandra, amusing and chatting and brimming with happiness. There was no doubt she and Tom Severin were good for each other, and their feelings were developing into a deep and enduring bond. They seemed to have found the remarkable affinity that sometimes occurred between people whose differences added spice and excitement to their relationship.

As Kathleen passed the door to the study, she saw her husband's tall, athletic form crouching over a pile of sparkling glass on the floor. "Did something fall?" she asked.

Devon glanced at her and smiled slightly, his eyes glinting in the way that never failed to spur her heartbeat to a faster pace. "Not exactly."

She drew closer and saw the object had been deliberately smashed onto a canvas tarp, which would allow the glass to be picked up and carried away easily. "What is that?" she asked with a bemused laugh.

After pulling something from the tarp, Devon shook away the last few shards of glass and held it before her eyes.

"Oh, that." A smile curved her lips as she saw the trio of little taxidermied birds poised on a branch. "So you finally decided it was time."

"I did," Devon said with satisfaction. He set the display, now divested of its glass dome, back on the shelf. Carefully he drew her away from the heap of glass. One of his arms drew around her, while his free hand slid protectively over her stomach. His powerful chest lifted and fell with a deep, contented sigh.

"How far you've brought us," Kathleen murmured, resting against him, "in such a short time. You've turned us all into a family."

"Don't give me credit for that, love," Devon said, ducking his head to press a crooked grin against the side of her face. "We all did it together."

Kathleen turned in his arms to regard the trio of goldfinches. "I wonder what they'll do," she mused aloud, "now that they're out in the world, in the open air?"

He snuggled her back against him, and nuzzled her cheek. "Whatever they want."

# Epilogue

*Six months later*

"B . . . A . . . S . . . I . . . L," Cassandra said, while the boy laboriously copied the letters in a little blank book.

"Are you certain that's the right way?" he asked.

"Yes, very."

She and Basil sat together on a bench at the docks, beneath the soft blue sky of Amiens. Nearby, spoonbills and raucous oystercatchers waded through the waters of the Somme Bay in search of a last few mollusks before the tide rolled in.

"But why does the *S* make the same sound as a *Z*? I wish each letter had only one sound."

"It's rather annoying, isn't it? The English language has borrowed many words from other languages, and those languages have different spelling rules." She looked up with a smile as she saw Tom walking toward them, relaxed and handsome. The sunny fortnight they'd spent in Calais had tanned his skin, and made his blue and green eyes startlingly bright by contrast. He had brought them here for a day trip that would include a mysterious surprise.

"The surprise is almost ready," he said. "Let's collect our things."

"Papa, does this look right to yer?" Basil asked, showing him the blank book.

Tom scrutinized the page. "It looks perfect. Now let's put it into Mama's tapestry bag, and—Good God, Cassandra, why did you bring that?" He was staring into the contents of the bag as if aghast.

"What?" she asked, bemused. "My extra gloves, a handkerchief, a set of binoculars, a packet of biscuits—"

"That book."

"*Tom Sawyer*'s one of your favorites," she protested. "You said so. Now I'm reading it to Basil."

"I don't dispute that it's one of the best novels ever written, with an excellent lesson for younger readers. However—"

"What would that lesson be?" Cassandra asked suspiciously.

"Papa already told me," Basil volunteered. "'Never do yer own work if you can make someone else do it for yer.'"

"That's not the lesson," Cassandra said, frowning.

"We'll discuss it later," Tom said hastily. "For now, put it at the bottom of the bag, and *do not* let it be seen for the next two hours. Don't mention it, and don't even think about it."

"Why?" Cassandra asked, increasingly curious.

"Because we're going to be in the company of someone who, to put it mildly, is not especially fond of Mark Twain. Now, come with me, you two."

"I'm hungry," Basil said sadly.

Tom grinned and ruffled his hair. "You're always hungry. Fortunately, we're about to have a nice, long afternoon tea with all the pastries you want."

"That's the surprise?" Basil asked. "But we have tea every day."

"Not on a yacht. And not with this person." Tom picked up Cassandra's tapestry bag, latched it firmly closed, and offered his arm to her.

"Who is it?" she asked, amused by the lively excitement in his eyes.

"Come find out."

They proceeded down one of the docks, to a modest but well-kept yacht. A fine old gentleman with a nicely trimmed beard and a shock of silvery hair awaited them.

"No," Cassandra said with a wondering laugh, recognizing the face from photographs and engravings. "Is that really . . ."

"Monsieur Verne," Tom said easily, "here are my wife and son. Lady Cassandra and Basil."

*"Enchanté,"* Jules Verne murmured, his eyes twinkling as he bowed over Cassandra's hand.

"I told Monsieur Verne," Tom said, enjoying Cassandra's dazed expression, "that you gave me the first novel I ever read, *Around the World in Eighty Days*, and for personal reasons, it remains my favorite."

"But what about—" Basil began, and Tom gently placed his hand over the boy's mouth.

"Madame," Jules Verne said in French, "how delighted I am to host you for tea on the *Saint Michel*! I hope you have a sweet tooth, as I do?"

"I certainly do," she answered in kind, "and so does my son."

"Ah, wonderful, come with me, then. If you have questions about my novels, I would be most pleased to answer them."

"I've always longed to find out how you came up with the idea for *Around the World in Eighty Days.*"

"Well, you see, I was reading an American travel brochure . . ."

Just before they boarded the yacht, Cassandra glanced at Tom and reached up to a delicate necklace she'd worn constantly since the day he'd given it to her. She touched the little charm, made in the shape of Euler's infinity symbol, that hung at the hollow of her throat.

And as always, the private signal made him smile.

# *Author's Note*

Dear Friends,

I learned some interesting facts while researching *Chasing Cassandra,* but none that surprised me more than finding out Mark Twain's novel *The Adventures of Tom Sawyer* was first released in Great Britain in June 1876, several months before it was published in the United States! Mr. Twain wanted to secure a British copyright, and was reportedly more highly esteemed in Great Britain. The British first edition featured a red cover, with the title reading simply as *Tom Sawyer.* When it was published in America in December, the cover was brilliant deep blue, with the full gilded title emblazoned across the front.

Also, Mark Twain apparently harbored lifelong hostility against Jules Verne starting in 1868, when Twain was trying to finish writing a balloon story, and Verne beat him to the punch by publishing a story titled *Five Weeks in a Balloon.* (Alas, we writers can be sensitive at times.)

The first mention of the traditional wedding rhyme of "something old, something new, something borrowed and something blue," in its entirety was in October 1876 in a Staffordshire newspaper.

I found a thorough description of the concept of "photographic memory" in an article titled "Natural Daguerreotyping" from *Chambers's Edinburgh Journal* dating from 1843.

Although the oldest versions of *Cinderella* didn't include the pumpkin, Charles Perrault added it in his rewrite in 1697. Apparently, the pumpkin was brought to France from the New World during the Tudor period between 1485 and 1603. Naturally the French knew just what to do with the "pompion," as they called it. Reportedly the first printed recipe for pumpkin pie dates back to 1675.

The British stone equals 14 pounds in weight.

King George V had the first railway train bathtub installed on the Royal Train in 1910. However, I felt certain the innovative and fastidious Tom Severin, as a man ahead of his time, would definitely install one on his private railway carriage. In deference to reality, however, we'll let King George V keep the credit for being the first.

I hope you had fun reading *Chasing Cassandra*, my friends—it's a privilege and a delight to be able to create stories I love and share them with you!

Love always,
*Lisa*

# Lady Cassandra's Afternoon Tea Scones

*I* FOUND THE RECIPE FOR these soft and perfect little scones in several Victorian era cookbooks, and tweaked it just enough to make it work for us. The Victorians often added corn starch or potato starch to baked goods like this, and it makes the scones incredibly light and fluffy. Unfortunately, Greg and the kids and I can't make afternoon tea a daily ritual like the Ravenels do, but when we get a chance, we always include scones. These are easy and delicious!

## Ingredients

1 3/4 cup flour
1/4 cup corn starch
1/2 tsp. salt
3 tsp. baking powder
1 stick butter, cold and chopped into dice sized pieces
3/4 cup whole milk
A little half and half or cream for brushing over the scones

### Directions

Preheat oven to 425.

Mix the dry ingredients with a whisk or fork. Cut in the butter with a pastry blender or a fork, mashing and mixing until it's all crumbs. Pour in the milk and gently mix until it's a big ball.

Sprinkle the dough with flour, sprinkle a rolling pin and cutting board/mat with more flour, and roll to $\frac{1}{2}$ inch thickness. (Tip: The less you touch, mash and fool with the dough, the more tender the scones will be.) Use a small biscuit cutter (mine's about 2 inches) to cut little circles, and put them on a nonstick cookie sheet or pan (I like to cover mine with parchment)

Use a pastry brush to brush half and half over the top of each scone.

Bake for 12 minutes. (This is where you have to use your judgement—if they're not nicely golden brown, keep them in another couple of minutes)

Serve with butter, jam, honey, clotted cream, whatever you want to put on a perfect little scone!

Do you love historical fiction?

Want the chance to hear news about your favourite authors (and the chance to win free books)?

Mary Balogh
Lenora Bell
Charlotte Betts
Jessica Blair
Frances Brody
Grace Burrowes
Gaelen Foley
Pamela Hart
Elizabeth Hoyt
Eloisa James
Lisa Kleypas
Stephanie Laurens
Sarah MacLean
Amanda Quick
Julia Quinn

**Then visit the Piatkus website**
www.piatkusentice.co.uk

**And follow us on Facebook and Twitter**
www.facebook.com/piatkusfiction | @piatkusentice

piatkus